A WOMAN OF ANGKOR

A NOVEL

John Burgess

RIVER
BOOKS

First published and distributed in 2013 by
River Books
396 Maharaj Road, Tatien, Bangkok 10200
Tel. 66 2 622-1900, 224-6686
Fax. 66 2 225-3861
E-mail: order@riverbooksbk.com
www.riverbooksbk.com

Editor: Narisa Chakrabongse
Production supervision: Paisarn Piemmattawat
Cover design and photographs: Paisarn Piemmattawat
Design: Reutairat Nanta

Map: Richard Furno

ISBN 978 616 7339 25 2

Printed and bound in Thailand
by Bangkok Printing Co., Ltd.

To Karen

Mekong R.

SIAMESE
TERRITORIES

THE

Chaiyapoom

KHMER

Sugar Palm House

Mekong River

Angkor

Parasol Village

EMPIRE

Freshwater
Sea

CHAMPA

River rite embankment

Mekong River

miles

100   200   300

Historical Note

The Khmer Empire ruled much of Southeast Asia for six and a half centuries, uniting lands of present-day Cambodia, Thailand, Laos and Vietnam. Its people lived and died in the belief they had a divinely commanded mission: Build heaven on earth. With strength and artistic vision rarely seen in human history, they toiled generation after generation to construct scores of 'mountain-temples' that replicate the Hindu cosmos in stone, sculpture and epic vastness. The focus of this energy was the capital, Angkor, Great Holy City.

Like all civilisations, this one reached its peak, then unravelled. Angkor was largely abandoned to the jungle half a millennium ago, for reasons that remain unclear. But its temples, shrouded in tropical growth, endured, awaiting rediscovery by the outside world. They are today drawing ever-larger numbers of foreign visitors. Awe is never in short supply. Whether the language is French or English, Greek or Japanese, the question is asked over and over: how was it possible to build such things?

The names of Kings and a few court notables have survived. Of the personal histories of millions of people lower down in society, absolutely nothing is known. What follows is a tale of one of the forgotten, a woman whose life coincided with construction of the greatest of the mountain-temples, Angkor Wat. Her story opens in the year Europeans marked as 1110 AD. The heat and privation of dry season have just ended; the rains are falling again, opening a new cycle in the sometimes tempestuous compact between Heaven and humankind.

Characters

Sray, wife of Nol
Nol, husband of Sray
Bopa, their daughter
Sovan, their son

Subhadra, the Brahmin priest
Narin, the priest's scribe

Prince Indra, Nol's master
Princess Benjana, Indra's wife
Aroon, son of Indra and Benjana
Rom, concubine of Indra
Darit, son of Indra and Rom

Heng, Nol's father
Prince Vira, Nol's father's master
Prince Teng, usurper of the estate

Sen, sergeant in the palace guard
Pala, Sray's assistant
Chen, the Chinese merchant
Veng, Nol's senior bearer
Yan, Bopa's maid
Da, Sray's maid
Rit, Prince Indra's military commander
Kiri, keeper of the King's cattle
Ton, Prince Aroon's riding instructor
The Architect, builder of temples
Pin, assistant on the architectural team
Sao, the cart driver
Koy, Sray's first husband
Vin, elder brother at the estate
Grandmother Som, Sray's stand-in mother

Kumari, the holy elephant
Sadong, Kumari's mahout

Part One

Recalled to Service

What if I'd told my husband no, no, we must reject the priest's command, we must take the children and run away. I will do it on my own if you don't agree. To this day I have wondered what our life would have been had I somehow acted in that way. I did voice questions, but my husband pushed them aside as visions of wealth and prominence took hold. Back then, I rarely challenged him. I placed myself under his protection in times of danger and followed his lead, as I had done at the very first moment we met.

I have wondered too which gods and ghosts played a role in the events of that day, though I know a life's course is not set by a single intervention of the divine. Heaven steers us constantly, like an oxcart driver flicking a long-stemmed reed at his animals' rumps to keep to the desired direction. Yet up until the priest's arrival, everything that had happened seemed somehow inconclusive, a preparation about which Heaven might change its mind.

I will begin my story on that day, the day on which I enjoyed my last moments of true peace. Some things that I will tell you I saw with my own eyes. Others I did not and will describe in the way I believe they happened. All of them I will attempt to recount in a spirit of acceptance. Yet I know that when I retire to my mat tonight I will be unable to sleep. Lying in the darkness, I will wish again that a different plan had been devised for me. I will wish that the priest never came, that the King's eye never fell on me, that a rebellion was never mounted in my name. Sleep will come only when I succeed in imagining that I was allowed to live out my life as the village girl I was born.

1: The Brahmin

Brahmin priests chart the turnings of the cosmic engine. They counsel princes and craft judgments of holy law. But concerning simpler things, such as getting where they want to go? They often need some help.

Perhaps that is why I felt no apprehension when I first caught sight of the priest that rainy season afternoon. All I saw was a man who looked to be lost, and my sympathy went to him. With two soldier-guards, he had arrived on foot at the tiny settlement in the Capital's eastern reaches that was home to my family at the time. Then he began a search for someone or something that wasn't being found. He went first down one lane, then retreated from it and tried another, striding past a puddle and scavenging rooster, only to come back out from that one too. Rather, I should say that he and his guards and a small crowd did these things. Word of this visit had spread – could it really be that a man of high holy orders was muddying his toes in our humble quarter? More and more people were finding cause to step out of their homes for a look. A few bold children were following right on the heels of the priest, who did his best to pretend he didn't notice.

He was tall, perhaps in his thirty-fifth year, and of course he was wearing the white silk garment that marks members of his sect. A silver neckpiece hung across his chest. His hair and whiskers were turning colour sooner than his age might suggest, as if they wanted to match that neckpiece.

These details I took in as I stood watching, unnoticed by anyone. It was not for a woman to approach and offer assistance. But neither did I want to be part of making this man an afternoon's entertainment, so I told myself to continue on home.

But before I could, he spoke to one of his soldiers.

'Ask, then.'

The man at arms stamped the base of his spear in the dirt, then called out to no one in particular.

'Where is the house of the man known as Nol One-Ear?'

My husband! The breath went straight out of me.

Recalling that moment still causes me dread. But let me try to put it aside. I could see that people were surprised that a visitor as fancy as this was looking for Nol. In their minds, Nol was just the little man with an ear on one side of his head and none on the other. A man of no consequence, a petty thief, no doubt, who'd been caught and paid the price. And on top of that, a canal dredger. That is how he earned his rice in those days. Day after day he would head for places around the Capital that had need of his labour, the clearing of muck from the bottoms of silted-up moats and canals. He would stand chest-deep in the water, lifting up load after load of the black stuff with arms that had grown thick from years of this repetition. The local men laughed at him, but I think not a few were afraid of him. He never cowered in the way expected of someone who is missing an ear.

To my left were two old bent-backed women, oblivious to me. 'Surely it's not Nol he wants,' said one. 'It's Sray. He's going to call her as a concubine for a prince.'

'Oh! What a pity she'll be taken,' came the reply. And after a moment: 'But strange that it took so long. As the epic says, *"Pure and beautiful, she glows like the moon behind clouds."'*

I tell you this with hesitation. Likening me to the divine Sita, consort of our Lord Rama! There is no resemblance, in appearance or in character.

I found my wits and backed away. Panic was setting in. I raced the short distance to our house by a round-about way. I clambered up the bamboo steps, breathless and tearful. Just then the priest and his soldiers appeared from the side. They had come by the direct way, led by the settlement's headman.

Nol was at home, thank goodness. Alarmed at my state, he dropped the bowl of cold greens and rice he'd half eaten and came quickly to me. There was no time to find the children and run away, no time to explain. All I could do was huddle at his side, for some false feeling of safety. His arm drew me close.

Now the priest was splashing his feet in the earthen pan at the base of our steps. I froze, listening to that sound, which normally was a welcome sign that husband or child had returned at day's end. Now the priest was climbing the steps. The house trembled, as I did. Nol's response was to hold me tighter. Whatever happens, I will take the lead, he was telling me. I will not abandon you.

The day had begun with no sign that something terrible might happen. I rose before dawn and cooked the first rice of the day on my clay brazier. Our boy and girl came to eat. Soon they left the house to wander with others in search of amusement, as children do. Nol went out to look over a potential dredging job and I to engage in my own trade, the selling of duck eggs at the market.

Everything unfolded in its normal, reassuring way. At mid-afternoon, I walked down the eastern trunk road toward the great mountain-temple Pre Rup.

As I drew nearer, the temple showed itself in stages. First the central tower that points the way to Heaven, then the sacred heights of brick and stone, guarded by sculpted lions. And finally, as I passed a stand of gum trees, the walls and gates and moats. The sun was beginning its daily gift to the temple, rays that have softened from their midday prime and in the hour before dusk will dress each of the bricks in a scarlet glow.

The ground beneath me was becoming more holy with each step. I paused to put hands together to show respect to the temple. But of course I was not going there. Like all of the mountain-temples, it was a place for priests and nobles, not a woman who sells eggs at the market. Rather, my feet were taking me to my usual destination, the shrine that stands just outside the moats, perhaps a hundred paces from the temple's eastern gate.

The shrine is quite elaborate now, but in those days it was small and simple, barely taller than I. Just a weathered wooden box on four posts, a bit of thatch on top to ward off the rain. How old? From well before my birth in this life, certainly. Perhaps it was built by humans, perhaps by the god who lived inside. His name was Bronze Uncle. At least, that is what we called him, inspired by the kindly metal visage that was his greeting to worshippers.

I knelt and lit a stick of incense, then placed a lotus blossom at his feet. I had picked it not a quarter hour earlier; the god smiled down upon its freshness. I said a prayer. Then I took in hand an old reed broom that lay waiting and swept the area in front. There wasn't really anything to sweep up, but I wished to show the god that his servant was making herself useful. After that, I sat down to the side to see if anyone else would come and need a lotus as an offering. Such things are usually sold but I always gave them away for nothing. I don't say that as a boast. It was simply that it was my privilege to attend this god. He had done too many things to count for me and my family.

No other worshipper came that afternoon. I savoured a breeze and the faint clink of bells on an oxcart that passed unseen behind me on the trunk road. It came time to leave. I rose, placed a silver pebble and the rest of the blossoms before the deity and began the walk home. The sun was hiding for a bit now. The sky had reached that pregnant stage of late day in the monsoon season, clouds gathering purposefully, about to bless the earth with another shower. I looked up. I remember thinking how lovely the first drops would feel on my skin.

Our settlement lay to the west of the temple, on a rise just high enough to keep from flooding in the rainy season. You turned off the trunk road, followed a trail through forest for a minute or two and there it was, a clutch of thatch-and-bamboo houses with banana trees spread among them. By now you would catch the scent of charcoal cooking fires and the calls of playing children. No different, really, from a hundred other quarters in the Capital city that we call Angkor. On this day, this walk too proceeded by the routine, until I neared the houses and saw the Brahmin.

And now he was standing in our doorway, a large, foreboding outline, lit from behind like some avenging deity. I went straight to the floor, pressing my face hard against the bamboo slats. Nol did the same, though not as quickly as I. He insisted on keeping an eye in the direction of the man, though of course he did not look straight at him.

The priest stood motionless for a moment more. 'I won't be invited in?'

That was not what I was expecting to hear, of course. My husband and I murmured assent, keeping our faces down. The priest stooped to pass through the door, then, getting no guidance from me, he lowered himself slowly onto the house's main mat. I remember he let off a barely discernible groan from some ache of midlife.

Another troubling silence followed. I stole a glance out the doorway. Not twenty paces from the house stood one of those sturdy-shouldered soldiers, clutching his spear. I resigned myself. It would not be possible to run and in any case we could not abandon our son and daughter. Where were they? They must not come back right now, I thought – may Heaven keep them away!

The silence continued. Then, from his place on the mat, the Brahmin said: 'You won't offer me something to drink?'

I shuffled on my knees to the wooden box where I kept the only thing of value that we had in those days, a Chinese tea set of blue and white porcelain. It was the kind you might see in the house of a rich merchant, arrayed on an elegant teak tray. The pot and cups are so smooth, so shiny, that you think they will improve the taste of the tea they hold. I filled a cup. With trembling hands – I worried the priest would take the shaking as a sign of disrespect – I placed the cup on the mat in front of him. That done, I moved back to my place beside Nol, feeling some tiny portion of safety there.

The priest looked down at the tea and, after a moment's consideration, decided it was fit to drink and brought cup to lips. His eyes moved around the room with silent disapproval, taking in mats, brazier, and the upended bowl that Nol had dropped. I only noticed the bowl now. As quietly as I could, I reached out a hand and set it right.

The priest's eyes came back to us.

'I am sent by command of Prince Indra, Whose Arrows Darken the Sky, Holder of the Third Rank, Trusted of the Gods.'

The words were recited with a certain weariness. But my husband and I pressed our faces to the floor again before even the first title was out. Our voices returned. 'May we be worthy to gaze upon the dust of his feet,' we responded, in a murmur lest we sound too eager to do even that.

I waited for the next words from the priest. But it was my husband who spoke up, in a voice whose steadfastness seemed at odds with our precarious situation. 'Sir, it should be known from the start that whatever was done was by my hand alone, and that this woman my wife had no role whatsoever.'

'That isn't true!' The words flew out of my mouth like a startled bird.

'You must pay her no mind, sir,' Nol said, refusing to look my way. 'She is a woman who tells lies by second nature, even before an image at a shrine.'

'Husband! How can you say such a thing?'

'You must ignore anything that she may try to...'

'WILL YOU BOTH BE QUIET!'

The priest spoke sternly, yet I could sense that such a tone did not come naturally. I felt less threatened.

'That's better,' he said. 'Now, then. I need some information. Are you the man known as Nol One-Ear?'

'Of course,' Nol replied, because this was self-evident. 'I don't deny it.' He turned his head to demonstrate; the Brahmin frowned.

I looked to my husband. I was stunned. I only now grasped that he had been speaking the language of the palace, fluently. Like many people, I could make out the basics but I never dared try to speak it.

The Brahmin continued. 'Are you the son of the late Heng, who was parasol master to the late Prince Vira?'

Now this question startled Nol, and there was a long pause. Then he answered, with dignity: 'Sir, I am.'

'Were you raised at the Chaiyapoom estate of the late Prince Vira in the Upper Empire?'

'I was.'

'And your father died at the time of Prince Vira's own passing, is that right?'

'Yes, that is correct.'

'And Prince Vira's successor decided that responsibility for his parasols would pass to another family, is that right?'

'It could be said that way, sir.'

'How many years ago was that?'

'Twelve, sir.'

'So you were too young to have learned your father's craft.'

Nol hesitated. 'Sir, I was in fact young at the time, but what you said about my training is not entirely factual.'

I had never heard any of this. Not a word in twelve years with this man. I was listening now as closely, I think, as the Brahmin.

'What are you saying, then?'

'I am saying, sir, that I did an apprenticeship under my father. At the time of my father's passing, I had completed it.'

'Now be careful that you tell the truth. Heaven is listening, and so am I and this woman, your wife.' I was uncertain how to feel about the priest placing me in opposition to my husband. 'You're saying you know how to maintain the parasols in question? All kinds of them?'

'Yes, sir. All kinds.'

'With silk and peacock feathers?'

'Yes.'

'With lotus ornaments at the peak?'

'Yes.'

'With silver-plated handles?'

'Yes.'

'Well, by now the artisans who made these things for your father, the ones who did the actual work, will have died or scattered.'

'It is not like that, sir. They live at a parasol-making village six hours' walk from here. I saw them shortly after my father's death. They were devoted to my family and promised always to be ready to serve, if ever they were called on again. I know they would be ready, sir. Ready...like I have remained ready.'

I was still frightened, but my husband seemed no longer to be. There was in his voice a tone approaching full confidence, as if it was he who was in control of this encounter.

The Brahmin turned aside to chew over what he'd been told, like unpleasant food that must be swallowed. Then he let out a sigh and spoke.

'Well, then. I have come to inform you, Nol One-Ear, that you are called to be Parasol Master at the palace of the lord Prince Indra. You will move to quarters there with your family. You will oversee the production of parasols, fans and fly whisks bearing emblems of the Third Order. You will be responsible for the recruitment, training, feeding and housing of young men to bear these implements, to keep sun rays and insects off the blessed form of the prince. You will keep track of our master's schedule and you will be sure that the necessary equipment and men are ready whenever he goes into public or holds court.

'You will receive a salary in silver, rice and fish and rights to collect payment from young men whom you train, up to when they complete their training, or reach age sixteen, whichever comes first. You will feed and house them until that point; after that, the men will receive wages and rations from the palace. You will have the right to train your own son to succeed you, if you have a son. The prince will provide protection against arrest or harassment by any other princely authority, and will expect you to show full loyalty and to obey only him among princes, and to obey him in all ways, without hesitation or question. And of course you will feel the full force of his justice if you fail in any of these assignments.'

Nol pressed his face to the floor. His eyes were running with tears of the most abject gratitude. It was just one more surprise that day – I had never seen such an outpouring from him.

The priest gave him a moment to recover, then said: 'Now His Highness will leave tomorrow morning for the Chaiyapoom estate and...'

'*What?* His Highness lives there?'

'Now, you will come with your family to his palace an hour after dawn tomorrow to pay your respects, then you will go to your artisan village to obtain the necessary equipment and recruit parasol bearers. From there you will go directly to Chaiyapoom so as to escort His Highness on his return journey to Angkor. These are the prince's instructions. Do you understand them?'

'I do, sir.'

'Now in your behaviour, you must conduct yourself from this moment as if you are living inside the prince's walls already.' He looked around in a way that said that in such a house and such a neighbourhood that would be difficult.

The Brahmin was finished and made to get to his feet but Nol stopped him, by speaking.

'Sir, I have no right to ask by what generosity the prince has chosen to call me this way. But I request, sir, that my deepest gratitude be conveyed to the prince, may I be worthy to gaze on the dust of his feet. His orders will be carried out without fail, whatever the cost or hardship. His Highness will have the finest parasols in the Empire!'

'That is certainly what he wants,' the Brahmin replied. 'Now do your best to make good on it.'

That was all. The priest pulled himself to his feet and, stooping at the door, he passed out of the house. How I wish he had passed out of our lives as well.

2: The ghost's demand

Perhaps you think my terror that day grew from the bent-backed woman's speculation that I would be taken as a concubine. Fear of that would have been to my credit, a woman distressed at the prospect of carnal relations with an unknown nobleman, of forced separation from husband and children. But let me confess it now. The cause was different altogether. Nol and I had something terrible to hide, an event in a far-away forest clearing twelve years earlier. Nol had alluded to it, however inaccurately, in his first words to the Brahmin. 'Whatever was done was by my hand alone.'

So long was it all held as secret that even today I can scarcely form the words. Please, give me time before I describe what happened that day. But for now you will appreciate how blasphemous were those words likening me to the divine Sita.

After this event in the forest, Nol and I ran away to Angkor and found refuge in the hidden quarter near the mountain-temple. No soldier or magistrate followed us, but a certain ghost did. It established itself high in the boughs of a tree that stood over the little bamboo house we built. On many days I could feel its eyes upon me as I went about my business in the neighbourhood. Sometimes it appeared to me when I slept, hovering, watching, eyes wide and face specked with blood, drawing nearer until I awoke with a fearsome start. 'Turn yourself in to the magistrates for judgment,' the spirit was saying. 'If you don't, I will alert the soldiers and they will take you and your husband away as criminals, hands bound behind your backs.' Sometimes it underlined this message by creating some simple misfortune. One day, for instance, as I descended from our house's door, a bamboo step gave way, though Nol had replaced it just the week before. I tumbled to the ground. Soon after, I was laid low by stomach fever, though I had eaten nothing spoiled.

Nol did not share my concerns over these events. He was constantly on the look-out for any *person* who might do me harm, but as for the ghost, I am not sure he believed it even existed. He was that way throughout his life, really, more concerned with the world of humankind than the world of spirits. He never conceded, in fact, that we had done anything wrong in that forest clearing. By his logic, that meant that no ghost would have the power to come here and haunt us – other spirits would prevent it. 'Please, wife, you must stop your worries.' He would scold me like that. 'I must have failed to fasten that step properly. You must have eaten a piece of fish that had gone bad. Let me buy you an herb from the doctor in the market and your stomach will be better.' But I knew differently. After a while I stopped sharing my concerns with him. Having to carry this burden alone made it all the more heavy.

Each morning I woke up thinking I must present myself to princely authority for punishment. The ghost was only demanding what I knew in my heart to be right. But each day, I lacked the courage and went instead to the little shrine down the road. There I knelt and gave offerings and prayers of atonement. I dared not address the ghost itself, but perhaps the god Bronze Uncle would agree to act on my behalf.

He was at first unreceptive. How undeserving I must have seemed, whispering claims of deepest remorse, and yet still cooking rice every day, drawing water at the canal, lying down to sleep at night as if nothing had happened. The god wanted proof of sincerity. I think I provided it not by some single act or prayer, but by the force of daily repetition. I wore the god's resistance down. I came every day to his presence, each time with lotus blossoms, and never tried to make a profit selling them to others. On each visit I left silver as an offering. The little shrine was not well kept up, so I cleaned, I swept, I dusted. On festival days, I sewed a garland with my bone needle and placed it around Bronze Uncle's neck. I polished his metallic form until he glowed. And perhaps the god could sense, observing me as I went about this work, that though I did lie down each night, my sleep was troubled; that though I cooked rice in my earthenware vessel each day, I could never find pleasure in this simple act of a woman's existence.

Gradually I began to feel as I knelt in prayer that communication was flowing in two directions. Bronze Uncle was whispering that he would help. It is impossible for us to know what goes on between two spirits, but I can say that as time progressed, I no longer felt the eyes of the ghost upon me. There was an end to the strange mishaps. My heart was lightened of some of its burden. Bronze Uncle had frightened the ghost away, or more likely he had convinced it that however terrible the thing I had done, it was past. This woman my servant, he was saying, is showing proper penitence. Please direct your attentions elsewhere.

Bronze Uncle went on to show remarkable benevolence in many other ways. Under his patronage, Nol and I were able to enter into an existence that now seems idyllic. We were poor, yes, but we had work, we had rice to eat, garments to wear, a bit of silver with which to shop in the market. We had a bamboo house adequate to our needs, with jars for rain water and a pen for ducks. And by the god's grace I gave birth to a son and a daughter who were growing up healthy and free of evil influences.

So you will understand why the arrival of the priest set off panic in me. On seeing him I had the terrible thought that the ghost had only pretended to go away, and had finally found the means to betray our presence to human authorities. Yet now the priest was making his way down our steps. We were not to be taken away, hands bound.

I held position, face to the floor, eyes closed, until his footsteps faded. Then I let out a very deep breath, and, trembling, turned to seek my husband's embrace again. His arm brought me close and I wept, my cheek against his shoulder. Then we broke apart, because just then we each had separate concerns and priorities, as we did so often in our life together.

I stood up, intending to go straight to Bronze Uncle to give thanks. My husband stood up too. I saw on his face yet one more expression that I had never seen before. His eyes were clouded, his mouth slightly open. He was unaware of me; he was off in his past, or his future, someplace, but not here and not now. He was standing straighter than I could ever remember. It was like his soul had flown clean out of him.

I had to speak.

'My husband, trained in the bearing of a prince's parasols? And fluent in the language of the palace? You never told me any of this.'

His trance broke. 'It was a long time ago – you heard me just now.'

'I'm surprised nonetheless. I've told you everything of my life before we met...'

'It was safer if you didn't know.'

'Why do you say safer? Is there some danger other than what you and I shared?'

He frowned. 'Please, please, wife, don't ask so many questions. But you don't believe I know the craft? Well, look at this!'

He began to walk up and down in the room, chin tilted up, hands out, gripping the shaft of an imaginary parasol, and I must say that he did look like the men who walked at the sides of nobles processing down the Capital's avenues, always attentive, holding aloft beautiful, delicate things that provided shade and colour and signalled to one and all that the master was a person on whom Heaven smiled. But still, this was my husband, who was a small man and a canal dredger at that. For a few beats of the heart a look of amusement came to my face.

He saw it, and I felt sudden shame for such unkindness.

'You still don't believe it?' I nodded that indeed I did believe, but he kept up. 'Well, you will when you see the grand house you're going to have at the palace, the maid who will sweep your floors. The garments you will wear will be made of silk, not this cheap cotton. It will be embroidered. One tatter and you'll throw it away! We're going to be important people – can't you see? We won't be sparrows any more, we'll be swans!'

He turned his back, following his thoughts, and I knew to leave him to himself. After a moment, he asked, without looking at me: 'How much silver do we have?'

'None, husband.'

'But I saw some yesterday in the market bag...'

'I ordered a week's supply of eggs from one of the wholesalers, to supplement the ones our own ducks produce.' As I have told you, that was my occupation at the time, the vending of duck eggs in the morning market.

A husband and wife always have secrets from one another, and each knows it. The real secret, I suppose, is how big the secrets are. My husband had kept a very large one from me; now I was keeping a small one from him. You see, I left unsaid that I had given a quarter of that silver at that shrine down the road. My husband would not approve. He believed, dare I say it, that silver put before a god was silver thrown away, that the priests who eventually collected it took their vows to avoid honest labour and faked their spiritual revelations.

'We'll need to raise some money,' he said.

That didn't sound like being rich.

'Now then – please, don't make such a face,' he told me. 'But you heard what the Brahmin said. I should begin on my own to obtain the necessary things. It will be like your duck-egg business, though you'll have to close that down, of course. We can't have ducks quacking around in a prince's compound. We'll spend money getting started, but we'll make it back when the prince gives me a salary. And once we get established in the palace, people who want to serve as bearers, or come inside the palace and petition the prince will have to pay a fee to me.'

He cast his eye around for things to sell, and everything he saw seemed to inspire in him the same disapproval the Brahmin had shown. Everything except the Chinese tea set. The Brahmin's cup remained on the mat; Nol's eyes lingered on it.

'Husband, we can't sell that. Please.'

I had acquired it perhaps five years earlier, as payment for a debt by a market woman with whom I did business. I hadn't wanted to take it, feeling it was too fancy for a family of our standing, but over the years it had grown on me, and now it came out on those few occasions for which the coconut shells and clay cups from which we normally drank seemed unfit. Sometimes, when I was alone in the house, I sat and took cups and pot in hand, just to experience their smoothness again. I had no idea of the meaning of the strange patterns – blue and white lines and curves – nor the writing, nor how the lithe people pictured on the pot could bear to wear clothing that covered their entire bodies, even their breasts and shoulders and feet. My husband's eyes left the cup. 'In any case, we'll need much more than what we'll get for the set.'

'The house....'

'Perhaps the house, Sray.' Now there came from him a sympathetic tone. You know, for all his shortcomings in sensing a woman's feelings, my husband could always see when I was truly upset. He put an arm around me. 'Don't be sad! Please! But the fact is it's all we have, don't you see? We could lease it to someone. Or we could go to the men in the market who lend. They would give us something with the house as security.'

Raindrops were pattering on the thatch over our heads. That normally comforting sound seemed now to signal impending dark events. We would arrive at the palace gate, belongings packed in old baskets, and be turned away and have no place to return to. Or we would be let inside, only to be scorned by people who lived there, who would laugh at my unschooled way of speaking.

Shouts carried in from outside. Was there more? I stole to the hole in the wall to look. My son and daughter were approaching the house, surrounded by neighbours who were peppering them with questions. How remiss it was of me to have forgotten the children.

My girl was in those days in her ninth year. A small, delicate beauty, blessed of Heaven. All mothers think that of their daughters, of course, but I do feel it was true. Her brother was two years older. Thankfully, he continued to mind his sister at a later age than most boys do. He had followed her that afternoon as she went to play in some alleyway and now people had spotted the two of them and demanded to know why the Brahmin had come. It was that kind of neighbourhood – your long-ago past was your own, with no one daring to pry. Nol had never been asked how he lost the ear. But things that happened a few minutes ago? That was everyone's business. My boy was leading his sister by the hand, shaking his head politely to the questions. He had maturity beyond his years, even then. A man stepped in my children's path, seizing my girl's arm. He seemed to say: Stop this insulting behaviour! You must answer the questions! I sprang up to go help, but when I got to the door I saw my son dealing with the problem himself. He had pulled his sister free of the man's grip, and was hurrying her toward the house.

When they reached the door, I put a mother's hand to both,

then directed them to the mat. 'Sit down, children. Your father has important news to tell you.' They looked to me, uncertain. News from their father was often something unwelcome. But this news was too large, too complex for me to give them any idea in advance. So I merely mouthed a blessing and motioned that they take their places, remain quiet and listen.

'Children, don't look so worried!' Nol began. 'A fabulous thing has happened. We have become rich!'

'Give thanks to Heaven, children,' I added. They were finding Nol's expansive mood unsettling, and so was I. I wished that I could sit between them to give reassurance, but for now my husband would not like that. The children put hands together as directed and murmured thanks. Their father smiled, told them how it passed that we would be rich, then looked to them, inviting reaction. But they said nothing. How could a child be anything but confused?

Nol chided them: 'What, Sovan – you want a life of canal dredging, then? I've been teaching you how to shovel silt, but now you'll become my apprentice in the craft of the parasol and fan. You'll work alongside me in the prince's parasol pavilion.'

'Yes, father. I'm very glad.'

That was not the enthusiasm Nol was after, so he turned to our daughter. 'And Bopa – You will wear your hair in a bun, like palace girls do. You will paint your palms and the bottoms of your feet with red dye.'

My girl's face lit up at these practical examples. She touched her hair and then turned a palm up, looking to see if the dye was somehow already there. My husband beamed too. Finally someone was showing the right attitude.

He announced that to mark the occasion, we would drink tea from the Chinese set. I didn't like the idea, thinking it might be the last time, but Bopa and I dutifully laid out pot and cups. We drank and Nol talked more about the future, this time the obligations.

'We must all work hard. We must stand straight, and use only the politest of language. We must make the prince proud we are in his service. We must remember that from here on, everything we do reflects not only on us, but on him and his palace.'

Nol stood up again and resumed that private reverie. I wondered how the children would take it.

By now it was dark, too late to rouse Bronze Uncle from his sleep for a prayer. We in our family went about our evening household routines, as if nothing had happened. Sovan went below to bring up charcoal. Bopa and I cooked rice and strips of catfish.

Nol ate, never leaving his reverie, then left the house. He was carrying a straw bag. I tried not to think what must be in it. Instead, I got the children settled on their sleeping mats, in the light of a single lamp's flame. Bopa refused to close her eyes. She lay back, whispering question after question. That red dye in particular – would she wear it every day? I answered as best I could, trying not to betray my own apprehensions. Sovan lay silent, looking to the thatch of the roof. He had always been a boy who thought more things than he said.

It took time, but Bopa's questions died out. I sat over the children until the deep breath of sleep took over. Then I turned to our household shrine affixed high on the wall, a tiny box with a flower for an offering. I said a silent prayer, asking that Sovan would continue to watch over his sister in this new life, whatever form it might take.

Then – I could not help myself – I rose quietly and went to the wooden box. The tea set was gone. I shut my eyes, frowning. Put aside those feelings! It was only a thing.

I went slowly down the steps, careful not to disturb the children, and bathed in the darkness at a jar below the house. Back inside, I knelt at the shrine again and whispered another prayer, then blew out the lamp.

The shrill song of a mosquito sounded near my ear. I wondered, had it been sent to mock me?

My husband returned two hours later, as I lay on our mat, unable to sleep. Even in the darkness, I could see that he did not have the bag.

Presently he took his place next to me.

'Husband,' I whispered after a moment, rolling to face him. 'You have always protected me when danger came, putting yourself at risk for me. I thank you for what you did today, before we knew the reason the Brahmin had come. I don't deserve a husband who is so brave.'

He said nothing, but I knew he was smiling with pride in the darkness.

'But,' I said, and for a moment I felt I should abandon the thought, 'I wonder, perhaps these sparrows should not try to be swans. We have been very lucky, living here so long with no one coming to trouble us. Wouldn't it be wiser just to move away? There are other cities. They all have markets and I could set up an egg stall in one and we would...'

'Please, please!' He let out a deep breath. 'Find some calmness in yourself. If this is all you can say, please go back to sleep.'

'I wasn't asleep, husband. How could I sleep now, with so much to think about? You've always said we mustn't call attention to ourselves. Going to live at a palace would be doing exactly that.'

'The thing that happened, well, it happened a long time ago and we can stop worrying about it now. It won't matter if people notice us. We have the prince's protection. And we'll be prominent in our own right. People will come to us asking for things, seeking favours, not trying to arrest us. And, dear wife, I will have silver to buy you lots of nice things.'

In the years we had been together, Nol had never stopped trying to prove his devotion through gifts, through things, because I had failed to make him understand that he had proven himself for all time in the very first minutes we had come together. No, my husband was always trying to follow up. His work earned him very little, of course, but sometimes he managed what in his mind were important achievements in his effort, bringing home a ring with silver plating that tarnished in a week or a length of gaudy fabric. They were always presented to me with touching earnestness, and I accepted them quietly, all the time wishing he would recognize that I already had what I wanted. If I lived with a man who was less than perfect in body, and inept at those times when husband and wife draw together at night, it was a small price to pay for the many other things with which I was blessed. Really, the only thing that I wanted was for our existence in this little settlement to go on, for Nol to find contentment in it. But he never had. I had sensed from the beginning that an indefinable anger resided in him. It was rarely openly expressed, to me, at least, but it collared his view of life. Many times I had prayed for it to depart but without effect. I had given up trying to understand it, taking to skirting it like I would a scorpion on a forest path. But now the Brahmin had provided insight. My husband had lost a place in a palace and become a canal dredger.

In the darkness, I looked to the ceiling, conscious he was awaiting my response to his pledge of wealth. Suddenly I had a thought: If we did come by some real money, I could increase my offerings to Bronze Uncle. And I could not just clean his shrine, I could have it repaired. The first job would be to replace its four foundation posts, which had begun to rot and split as termites made their homes inside. Any day, the posts might give way, spilling everything to the ground, god included. New posts, then, and perhaps new roofing as well. I could go to the market and make arrangements with the thatchers there to...

Then I put a stop to those thoughts. I was spending money that was not in hand and likely never would be.

So I said: 'A lot of silver? Husband, please don't talk that way. We can't see the future. Only Heaven can. We must expect nothing.'

'For a woman who spends so much time in prayer, you seem tonight to have very little faith.'

'This does not concern faith in Heaven, husband, but faith in people, who like you and I are prone to deception.'

'But this is a prince.'

I let that thought sink in, and presently I began to find some comfort in it. It is taught that Heaven is just with its rewards, that the wealth and power that princes possess flow from lives past and present lived in virtue. Most princes, at least.

I said nothing more. Nol lay still and I could sense that I had slipped from his thoughts; his mind, I guessed, was churning through some list of preparation tasks. Then he put that aside too. My husband had a way of finding sleep instantly. Presently he was puffing out heavy breaths. I lay back, relieved he had not chosen this night to put hands to me.

I remembered again just then that I had failed to go give thanks to Bronze Uncle.

The little shrine presented itself again in my mind's eye. Perhaps, perhaps, Heaven would forgive my vanity if for just a few more moments I contemplated how I might repair it. Posts and thatch – I had no idea of the cost, but I knew that craftsmen in the market would charge less than if the materials were for a house, because this would be Heaven's work and bring merit for the next life. And perhaps I would see also to a wet-season garment for the god. Yes, of course – the rains had begun, and Bronze Uncle might be feeling chills.

He would be cold no more. I knew a place that stitched such things.

3: The princely compound

I had intended to go straight to Bronze Uncle the following morning, but my husband did not allow it. There was no time, he told me as we both rose well ahead of the sun. 'You heard the priest. We are to go to our master's palace, and from there Sovan and I will depart for the parasol village.'

Whatever things I did not know about serving a prince, I did know how to prepare food for the road. I fanned my brazier's slumbering coals back to life. I grilled strips of catfish. These I placed with rice in banana leaf wrappings, and this leaf bundle I placed in a krama cloth, folding its lengths to fashion a bag that Nol would carry over his shoulder. By now the children were up too. The splash of bathing carried up from the jars beneath the house. The food prepared, I went through our family's garments by lamplight and brought out those that were in best repair. We all dressed, me fussing over the two children. Nol was the first to be ready.

Our sudden rise in society seemed somehow to be known now by everyone in the neighbourhood. When we left the house just before sunrise, a small crowd had gathered. Some people stood silently, palms together, as if they hoped that they would absorb some of our good fortune merely by being close. Some called out blessings, some whispered hopes that day work might be sent their way, it didn't have to be anything much. Some of these people my husband ignored, others he greeted in a way that suggested they might in fact be remembered. He was more than comfortable with this attention. I was not.

On the road we turned west, toward the royal sector. Nol led; I was just behind with a hand to the shoulder of each child. You know, with my daughter I think my purpose was to hold her back – she was already excited about this new life, and kept trying to rush ahead in a way that made me uneasy. With my boy, my hand was meant to urge him on, to do his duty toward his father. Even at his young age, Sovan had the same misgivings as I.

We passed the market where on normal days I sold eggs. I imagined myself stopping to buy fish, then heading home. Why did I torment myself that way? Presently we crossed the stone bridge that spans the Capital's main river and I sent a silent prayer in the direction of the seven-headed Naga serpent that guarded it. Then, before I knew it, Nol was leading us off to the right down a side lane that ended at a door in a tall bamboo wall. A soldier-guard there called out to us to stop, but Nol answered confidently, not even breaking his stride, that we were on the business of Prince Indra, holder of the Third Rank. That silenced the guard. He opened the door and all four of us passed through, just like that.

I later found out that this was an entrance for retainers to the royal sector. But inside there was no gleam of gold or precious stones, just a path leading through some woods. It soon brought us to a road, alive with people who looked to be those retainers. We were directed first this way, then that, along walls and canals and over footbridges. We walked quite a distance. Finally we came to a wooden gate. It was stout and solid, but not particularly adorned, a bit rough-hewn, in fact, still bearing the scent that saw and chisel draw from fresh wood. Nol looked to us significantly to convey that this was the main entrance to our master's compound. It was not for us to use, of course. We made our way around to a rear wall and stepped through a small door there. Inside I expected to finally behold the glitter of gold. But instead we found ourselves among a collection of wooden houses. I was surprised that they were small, and not built on tall stilts, as was ours back in the settlement, but stood just thigh-high on bamboo supports. They looked new, yet not of good construction, as if thrown together in a hurry by workmen seeking quick wages. Thatch was missing from some of the roofs; here and there, rainwater had already stained sideboards.

Nol kept us moving, past men and women who variously ignored us or eyed us silently. We came to a grand wooden building. Now this was more my idea of princely glory. Its walls were made of finely carved teak, its roof of red tile bright as fire. Enclosing it was a gravel path marked every few paces by a shrub with blossoms brought out by the recent rains.

Just ahead was a courtyard. There the traveling party had

assembled to await the prince. My eye was drawn to the glint of the palanquin he would ride. It was for now resting on the ground, but nearby stood six slaves who would carry it. Retainers were milling about: team foreman, gong player, cook. There were also two parasol bearers, hired by the day from the market, I later learned, because my husband had yet to begin his service. There was an oxcart for baggage, and a driver. And a comely young woman who looked to be a concubine. She was holding out her right hand, to which a maid was applying red powder. Little Bopa's eyes went to that.

The Brahmin was present too, standing by a mare. He caught sight of us and motioned that we should come forward. At least that's what I thought he meant. I took a few steps, and then he was mouthing the word 'no,' to me. Only the males of the family were required. I blanched. Already in this place I had committed a breach of etiquette.

Nol and Sovan stepped forward to the priest, who positioned them by the palanquin.

I expected a lengthy wait, because for what do retainers exist if not to wait? But before I knew it, the thud of firm footsteps came from inside the palace. This prince of ours was bounding down wooden steps I could not see. Then he came into view, striding away from us toward the palanquin. The traveling party, Nol and my boy, Bopa and I, we all went to a crouch. The priest did not, of course.

One is meant to keep eyes to the ground in the presence of nobility, yet I found myself stealing a look. Because I was to the rear, I had no view of our new master's face. But what I could see suggested a man of near perfect construction. He had broad shoulders, well-muscled arms and the tautest of calves. His hair was pulled back in the style of royalty; the lobes of his ears hung low from the weight of jewelled insets. He wore a heavy silver neckpiece, armlets, a silver diadem and around his waist an embroidered blue sampot garment. It was quite a load of jewellery but none of it had a chance of distracting from the body it adorned.

I cast my eyes toward my husband. I will admit it – my mind entertained an unkind comparison. But I quickly put it aside. This was Nol's moment, and I did feel pride for him. He touched his forehead to the dust three times at the prince's feet. My boy Sovan did his best to imitate. The Brahmin gave an introduction that did not carry to my ears. Nol raised his head just slightly and voiced what was no doubt a declaration of loyalty. The prince barked a word or two in response. Then Nol and Sovan withdrew, walking backwards in a crouch.

That was it. The prince bounded onto his palanquin. From this first sight of him, I learned that he never simply moved, he bounded.

The foreman voiced an order to the slaves, who hefted palanquin and prince smartly to their shoulders. The bearers stepped to the side of the conveyance, holding twin parasols overhead. The priest climbed atop his mare. A gong sounded once, twice, three times, and to its rhythm the journey began.

Soon the procession had passed out the gate. I relaxed a tiny bit.

Nol approached. 'It's quite a prince we serve, don't you think?'

I said yes, ours was quite a prince.

Nol looked about, still savouring the moment. 'Well, then! It's time for me and our son to take our leave as well.'

That was the cue for my boy to present himself. I gave him a tearful embrace. 'You must be careful in this new life,' I whispered as we held close. 'You must listen to your father, and remember that everything you have, no matter how much or how little, is a gift from Heaven.'

How I wished the boy could remain with me. I knew I would want his comfort in the days ahead. He had been a child who remained in his mother's lap long after the age at which most get to their feet and amble away.

My good-bye to my husband was more formal. I put hands together in farewell, and he did the same, quickly. I could sense that, though he was loath to express it, he felt, right there, a new surge of devotion to me. If only all women could have as faithful a man as I did.

So, off went my husband and son. I stood watching, wondering how I would make my way alone in this place.

Then a young, slightly built man came up to me, squinting.

'Mrs Sray, my name is Narin. I am scribe to our master's Brahmin. May I welcome you to the prince's household? You will find this place to be a good home.'

A hint of kindness in this place, at last. I began an elaborate expression of thanks. The young man heard me out, then said: 'Come – I'll show you and your daughter the place where you will live.'

From behind, Bopa giggled in delight.

Mr Narin walked us back toward the retainers' houses. I grew bold to ask a question, then another. Could he please tell us where we would draw water? How far away was a market? He listened attentively, treating each question as just what he would have wanted to know. He seemed not to notice a fray on my sampot's hem or my stumbling use of palace terms.

Bopa, always impatient, ran ahead of us.

'A delightful, beautiful girl,' remarked Mr Narin. 'Surely I'm not the first to notice that she looks remarkably like her mother.'

'You are kind. But if she does, it is no great asset.'

I felt eyes on me from windows and doors as we passed houses. But each time I tried to turn and give greeting, those eyes disengaged.

The house at which we soon stopped was as small as any here. I said a quick prayer to its resident spirit, then followed Mr Narin up the steps. I was met inside by the smell of spilled wine. The floor was warped and littered with rice husks and the skins of fruit, as if its previous occupants had been itinerant men living on their own. Soldiers, perhaps. Even the house's own shrine looked untended.

I walked about, trying to look pleased. Mr Narin stood to the side, squinting again – it was a good thing he couldn't see me well, as my act was transparent. I wondered if he could see the litter on the floor.

After a bit, I said: 'We are blessed to have such a fine place. We thank you for bringing us to see it.'

He smiled. 'We'll send some slaves to your old house to move your things. Would tomorrow morning be a good time?'

I imagined the fuss that would occur if a line of men came

walking into the other neighbourhood, and how we had so few possessions that most would have nothing to carry.

'It's all right, really. You're kind, but we'll manage on our own.'

When Mr Narin had excused himself, Bopa spoke up in a small voice. 'Mother, it's so small. And so dirty!'

I put a hand to her, feeling sympathy in light of the promises her father had made. 'It is, dear. The previous occupants showed no respect to the resident spirit. But we won't be like that. We will honour the spirit and keep the house clean.'

Bopa put her head out the door, crinkling her nose at the smell of standing water beneath the house. She asked: 'Can't we just let the slaves help us? Father said we're not poor any more. If we carry our own things here, won't people laugh?'

She thinks like her father, I reflected, picking up a reed-handled broom that lay in a corner.

We began to clean and straighten up as best we could. We showed ourselves at door and window, but still no neighbour came to greet us.

4: Portal to the absolute

It was early afternoon when we left the new house. I hurried Bopa along until we passed out of the royal sector. Then we slowed a bit. We did not go straight home – Bronze Uncle would finally receive his thanks. Near our quarter I bought two garlands from a woman by the road.

We knelt before the god. It was my intention to lead my daughter in a lengthy prayer. But before I knew it, she was whispering a few words on her own. She got to her feet, placed a garland around the holy neck, then hurried off toward the house. She had forgotten her disappointments, it seemed. I hoped that Bronze Uncle would excuse this behaviour.

I lingered, my own garland still in hand.

I have told you of the comfort I always felt in this god's presence. Large images intimidate me; this one was of a small, intimate size, not even as tall as my forearm. He sat hands in his lap, in the pose of meditation. His lips bore that hint of a smile, just enough to convey assurance that anything voiced before him would be considered with sympathy. His eyes were closed. This of course helped him meditate during those hours when he was alone, but I believe that it could also help him listen more intently to prayers.

Many of the gods whom humble folk kneel before are claimed to have powers to communicate with the religious realm of Kings. But we can sense that some gods, like some people, don't live up to what is said of them. It was not so with Bronze Uncle. Let anyone who doubts explain those twelve years of protection that he afforded my family. Early in my time in Angkor, an acolyte who came to collect the silver left at the shrine had told me the source of these powers: Bronze Uncle had the ear of a favoured attendant of our Lord Shiva, ruler of all realities, destroyer of all illusions, whose true nature is proclaimed without words. He had the ear because in a previous cycle of creation he had faced down a demon rather than let it advance upon Lord Shiva, and in recognition of this service Lord Shiva had instructed his attendant to be forever open to prayers conveyed by Bronze

Uncle. And that the god's earthly abode would be forever nearby. So it was in this way that the little shrine came to stand outside the east gate of the Pre Rup mountain-temple.

My prayers, then, if deemed worthy, might pass inside the walls of that great holy edifice, though of course I myself could not. Only Kings and noblewomen and priests of high holy orders could cross the moonstone which lay at the gate's threshold. Still, there were times when I found courage to turn and gaze on the mountain-temple from the little shrine's embrace. Heaven on earth! Enclosing the great citadel was a moat, dappled with lotus pads and blossoms – the Sea of Creation. Beyond it were those walls that glowed red in the late day sun, marking off the holy precinct. And rising beyond these walls, a sculpted mountain of stone and bricks, topped by five towers. They were the five peaks of Mount Meru, abode of the gods, kernel of the universe. Sometimes I would look and dare wonder, what would it be to put a foot to the great eastern staircase, its steepness akin to the difficulty of ascending to Heaven? How would it feel to pass between the stone lions standing guard on either side to repel any demon that attempted to rise so high?

I will admit that on these occasions my thoughts could become collared with vanity. The silver that I left at the little shrine passed inside the temple along with (or so I could hope) my prayers. So if I saw a white-garbed priest walking its heights, I sometimes allowed myself to think: this man, though he lives more in Heaven than on earth, must nonetheless eat, and the rice and fish that he partook this morning might well have been bought with silver that this very women left as alms, having earned it in the marketplace selling duck eggs.

This was the temple of the Ninth Reign, now a century and a half past, the time of our lord King Rajendravarman, quick to drive his sword into the bellies of enemies but possessed of an ocean of compassion for the meek and loyal. Here before me was his personal portal to the absolute. I am told that before his passage to the next life the King came here frequently in procession, to climb those steps in the way that I only imagined, and to enter the torch-lit chamber of the central tower. There

Shiva's linga shaft stood – and still stands – in silence, pregnant with cosmic force collected from the four cardinal directions. Kneeling, the King anointed the linga with lustral water. With this act, Heaven and earth were kept in harmony. Our Lord Shiva received a new demonstration of the devotion of the Khmer race; in response he allowed rains to fall, seedlings to sprout, life to continue in its many forms.

On days of those royal visits, common folk from all over the Capital thronged to this area to the temple's east, getting as close as the palace guardsmen would allow, hoping to bask in the primal energy that the temple radiated during the King's presence. But this is not to say that the grounds were deserted on ordinary days. Bronze Uncle had much company all the time. Pilgrims from around the Empire stopped here year round. They knelt, they prayed, they chanted. But they also had to sleep, so rest houses were built for them. They had to eat and sometimes they wanted to drink a bit of wine after a long journey and buy a holy amulet or two, so vendors laid out their mats. If the visitors were blind or lame or suffering from a cough that would not go away, healers were on hand.

All this bustle ceased with the end of the Ninth Reign. That was no surprise. We are taught that what is busy today will become serene tomorrow, that what was built will one day erode, that youth will be transformed into doddering age, strength into weakness. By my time, only the tiny weather-beaten shrine remained on the eastern grounds. This decline mirrored changes in the great temple itself. Though tall and imposing as ever it was, it had fallen into obscurity and even disrepair. Flakes of gilding peeled off the spires, mould discoloured the breasts of stone goddesses, weeds took root between bricks beyond the reach of attending acolytes. This sad deterioration I could see even from my place far down on the ground.

Where had the people gone? Most people hold that prayers and sacred labour are best focused on a new temple. The succeeding King breaks ground for his own edifice, larger than the last King's, and people direct their attention there. But the monarch reigning in the time when Nol was recalled to service was a man

38

who had come to the throne late in life and loved orchids above all else. He had taken no steps to begin a new temple. Would he ever? No one could say.

Now, Angkor has many holy reservoirs that, like the moats of Pre Rup, are the Sea of Creation on earth. The two largest are almost mirror images of each other. One occupies much of the eastern part of the Capital (our house lay quite near it, in fact), while the other does the same in the west. Each has a temple on an island at its precise centre. During my time, the temple of the western reservoir was being enlarged. This was the primary building project underway in the Capital, so people naturally directed their attention there.

One day I went to look. Thousands of pilgrims from the provinces were staging day-long circumambulations around the western reservoir, finishing weary but fulfilled at the mid- point of its eastern bank. There they knelt at a shrine, home to another god for ordinary folk who was said to have powers to send their pleas and aspirations wafting across the waters to the spires that glinted gold. The rest houses, the markets, the noise and spiritual exhilaration – they had all been transplanted to this place on the great reservoir's banks. Priests circulated among the people collecting donations. If no new temple was to be built, at least this one could be made more glorious. But it was not only stonework going on. There was a major restoration underway of a huge bronze image of our Lord Vishnu, reclining, his navel emitting the jet of water from which Brahma is born to begin a new cycle of creation. A lucky few among the pilgrim-supplicants were chosen to ride boats to the island temple to offer their own toil to Heaven's purpose.

But as I said, I went only to look. I never thought of shifting my loyalties. I found it difficult to pray amidst the noise and commotion. And whatever people said, how could it be that the god on the bank could listen to a thousand prayers at once? Surely mine would be lost amidst ones that were louder or more deserving. And could it truly be that Heaven, with its teachings of devotion and service, could countenance the abandonment of a god who had brought spiritual sustenance to so many people? I could not accept that. I remained loyal to Bronze Uncle.

With my daughter gone, I placed my garland gently around the god's neck. I knelt again, head bowed, palms together.

'Deity, I come today to honour you who have been so kind to your servant. So much have we received from you that we do not deserve. And, I apologize, but I ask your leave that I might not come to you as often as I have. Many demands are being made upon me now. As you know – for you know everything – I am moving with my family to a new place. There will be new gods there who will expect my tending. I will come often to you, but please forgive me if sometimes I miss a day.'

I looked up. I could sense that my words had passed beyond the gently closed eyes.

'I know that in this world truth is hidden,' I continued, 'like a seed in a fruit hanging high in a forest tree. Without your help I can never hope to find it. Guide me toward this truth.' These were verses I had learned as a girl. Then I added words that came to me on the spot. 'Please! I am not done with my requests. As my fate unfolds, make me deserving of what has been given for reasons that you understand but I cannot. Let me follow without question or complaint the husband to whom this calling has come. Let my children find some measure of happiness in this new place, let the people there be not cruel, let the dogs not bite. And please, forgive even one more selfish request from this woman before you: let my tea set return one day.'

Feeling better, I walked toward my house. I now had courage to face the fact that soon it would not be mine.

5: The holy elephant

Bronze Uncle had sent courage, but before I had taken twenty steps from the shrine, I saw that he had sent something else as well, the elephant Kumari. The great animal was plodding toward me. Atop her neck sat her mahout, the gap-toothed man Sadong.

'Mrs Sray!' He called cheerfully from his perch, a smile displaying the gap. 'Your friend the holy beast has things to tell you! And she is hungry, hungry even in this great city that has so much food.'

I put palms together, to him, but also to the elephant. Her large eyes inspected me; she fluttered her ears, fan-like. Her trunk rose. I took its tip in my hand for a moment. Kumari was offering a blessing. I reached out to stroke the rough skin of the beast's right shoulder.

Sadong let himself nimbly down, and with strokes of a cleaver began cutting a stick of sugar cane into finger-long sections. He presented the food to me with some formality. I thanked him and gave a silver pebble in exchange.

In an opened palm, I presented a piece of the cane, its dripping sweet juices kissing my skin. Kumari's trunk rose again, took the offering in the most delicate way, and after a moment's pause to show thanks, hoisted it to the mouth hidden behind the trunk.

'Eat and let the gods relieve your hunger, Blessed Kumari,' I whispered. 'You will always have friends here.'

A priest finds spiritual realization readily, but throughout my life this has shown itself to me only an instant at a time, like a fish jumping out of water, coming and going so quickly that it's hard to grasp if it was there at all. But some of those instants have come when I peer into the eyes of this elephant.

Many things have been said about Kumari. That a sliver of her tusk had the power to cure blindness, that powder made from the thick hairs that grew from her forehead could enable a woman to give birth to ten children one after the other, with not a single miscarriage. Some people say she was not born but brought to earth whole. I was not there at the time, of course, but I believe that Heaven chose to establish her on this earth in the same way as it does other elephants. I say this because I came to know this man Sadong quite well, and he recounted her story to me. He was too pure a soul to invent such things.

She was captured in the forest as a year-old calf, by men from his village who with torches and gongs drove her and her mother into a hidden enclosure built of stout bamboo. The two were taken to the village corral for initial training, and when the young elephant was old enough to leave her mother's milk, she was presented to Sadong, who in human terms was as young as she. She became his property, though like anyone in his calling, he felt that he as much belonged to her. He was acting as helper and guide for an animal that had condescended to devote her strength to ease the burdens of life for humans. From the start, Sadong knew that Kumari was unusual: On her front feet were five toenails, rather than the usual four, and between her eyes the skin bore the shape of a diamond. Sadong took that as explanation for her uniquely gentle disposition and her ability to quickly learn human words. After a month or two she knew more than fifty. Kneel, push with your forehead, lay down, trumpet. The standard repertoire of the working elephant, but quite a bit more.

Calf and boy grew up together, and when both were old enough, they were sent to work a riverbed quarry. This was a place where, in dry season, the water dropped low enough to expose sandstone that Heaven had placed in great quantity along the river's path. Masons used hammer and chisel to fashion rectangular blocks, each about as long as a man's arm. It was the task of Sadong and Kumari to drag the blocks up and away from their points of birth and place them at the bank's top. Then the masons went to work on stone newly exposed below. As blocks were removed row by row, level by level, the river bank came to resemble a giant's staircase.

When the rains returned, the river rose and covered those steps. The men went now into the forest to cut stalks of thick bamboo. These the elephants dragged in huge bundles back to the water, where they were lashed together as rafts. One after the other, the blocks were pushed aboard these rafts and sent on their way down-river, toward a site where a provincial temple was taking shape.

In evenings, Kumari browsed untethered in the forest beyond the light of the cooking fire where Sadong and the other handlers sat eating dinners of rice and fish paste or sipping cheap palm wine from coconut cups. Sometimes the masons joined them. In this isolation, the usual barriers against men of different trades mingling quietly fell away. Home was far off for everyone.

One day, following two weeks of rains that fell longer and heavier than usual, a man fell sick with mosquito fever. Then another and another, and then Sadong, until almost every one of the hundred labourers and masons was stricken. What spirit have we angered? the men wondered. How did we do it? Prayers were said in the greatest number. Someone broke bark off a neem tree and boiled it in water to make a draught. Everyone drank, but neither the draught nor the prayers had effect. One man died, then another. The few who remained healthy ran away in fear, leaving the afflicted to face the disease alone. But in fact they were not alone. Kumari was there. Late one morning, she went to her master, who lay on a mat in the open, and lingered over him, then to the other stricken men, and she seemed to contemplate and feel pity. She walked to the river and drew water into her trunk. She sprayed it over Sadong and men who lay near him. Those who received the water recovered; those who did not, died.

Word spread. A priest came to investigate, and declared that Kumari was a vessel of divine assistance. The extra nails on her feet, the diamond-shaped patch of skin – these were signs. Sadong, it seems, was made to feel dull for having failed to recognize these things earlier. Kumari could no longer work as a draft elephant, the holy man declared. Her gifts must be shared. So she and Sadong set out for the Capital, and there she quickly achieved celebrity. Physicians brought to her their most gravely ill patients to receive the spray of reviving water from her trunk. Newlywed couples engaged her to wet down the steps of their first homes. Her dung was collected by children to be spread in gardens for special fertility. There was interest too from Chinese merchants – water from Kumari's trunk blessed shipments of porcelain and silk that had arrived safely by ship in ports on the Freshwater Sea.

Sadong had come to the city a man who knew only the honest life of work in a quarry. As the elephant's fame grew, he became more and more interested, as anyone would, in the silver that people put in the bowl that he set out before Kumari's huge five-nailed feet. He began to feel that most everything was an occasion for palm wine; sometimes the first cup was poured in the morning. He spent less time with the elephant, leaving her alone in a rented corral, sometimes neglecting to walk her to the canal at day's end for a bath. He took up with a string of young women he met in various drinking houses. He bought them silk sampots and bronze armlets; he began to wear jewellery around his own neck and arms. The silver began to run short, so he wondered how to bring in more.

One night, as he sat with a new lady friend in a drinking stall, worried that he could not match the gift that she had received from her previous man, it suddenly came to him: Kumari could earn more by telling fortunes. The next morning, he paid a priest to write a series of proverbs on votive sticks. It took only a few days for the elephant to learn a new skill and for it to catch on with the city's people. The sticks were spread on the grass in front of the beast. The client paid a fee, posed a question to Sadong, who then whispered it into the elephant's ear. After a moment's contemplation, she picked up a stick with her trunk and presented it to Sadong. He could not read but he memorized the words based on the script's appearance, and the customer always listened with gratitude as he voiced the elephant's advice.

What a time that was. Everyone was talking about the elephant. It seemed that every question, large or small, that arose in the Capital was put to Kumari, to the point that the elephant seemed to tire and disapprove of the attention. Still, merchants and labourers, soldiers and princes sought her out, day and night. Even the aged King, the orchid lover, took notice. One day, his procession was moving past the main market when it came upon Kumari telling fortunes. The royal locomotion stopped, and the King watched for a long while from atop his palanquin.

We are taught that everything that rises high must fall. About two years after they arrived in the city, Kumari and Sadong experienced their fall. It began with a summons from one of the Capital's wealthiest families. Sadong led the beast into the family's compound, passing through a gate to a small garden with a lotus pond. There, the family's patriarch was waiting, wearing a costly embroidered sampot and ruby-studded armlets. He was a large and impatient man, and he spoke sharply to a guard who did not close the gate quickly enough. Sadong was paid his fee in advance, getting hardly a glance. Then the man posed his question. But he didn't give it to Sadong for conveying to the elephant, as was the normal practice. He stepped forward and whispered it into the elephant's ear himself. Servants would later relate that the beast seemed indignant about this man and his question. She huffed, flapped her ears, and passed the tip of her trunk back and forth across the sticks, huffing again, refusing to pick one up. Finally she went still. It was clear she was refusing to make a divination, but the man would not accept that and chose to take her answer as the stick that lay closest to her unmoving trunk. He picked it up. It read: 'One dove, then two, take shelter in a bamboo thicket during afternoon showers.' The man pondered that, and then smiled slyly. It came out later that his question was: what will happen to the value of silver in the next six months? He took the verse to mean it would double during the rainy season. Kumari and Sadong were sent on their way, and in following weeks, the family converted all its wealth to silver. It borrowed quite a bit more on the strength of the blessed elephant's supposed answer. But in fact, silver's value fell by half during the rains, because new mines to the far north turned out to be more productive than predicted and ten Chinese ships arrived unannounced in the Freshwater Sea to purchase, with silver bars, as much rice as could be found, to take back to a famine zone. The rich family was ruined. Creditors descended on its house, escorted by magistrates and guards. On one of those visits, there was shouting and foul language, and a son stabbed a guard. He was arrested. Magistrates seized and sold the house, and everything in it. The family took refuge in a monastery, living on alms. The wife accepted this life as the will of Heaven; the husband did not and told anyone who'd listen that it was the fault of the elephant Kumari. He asked: had she really saved anyone at the quarry camp? Who could attest to actually seeing this happen? And here in the city did any good really come from water sprayed from that trunk? Stories began to circulate that to increase business Sadong had paid people to fake recovery from disease, and that the diamond between Kumari's eyes had been placed there not by the gods but by Sadong, using paint and brush at night.

That was all it took. People turned their attention elsewhere and soon Kumari and Sadong were almost as poor as the fallen family. They walked Angkor's streets largely ignored. I can only imagine the shame that Sadong felt. Children shouted after him as a charlatan! They made fun of the gap in his teeth. But there was a change for the better in him. He faced up to this challenge bravely. He stopped drinking; he faithfully bathed the elephant each evening, going into the water with her, whispering endearments, rubbing down her rough skin with an old krama. I am sure there was no shame felt by Kumari. She knew she had done nothing wrong. She was happy to be spared all the attention. She seemed contented again.

There was a small group of people who never lost faith in her. Some said that the verse had in fact signalled what would happen to silver – each bird represented the Empire's supply of the metal, not the price. When the supply doubled, the value fell by half. In his greed, the merchant had taken it as the answer he wanted to hear. He had triggered the next cycle of existence – where there had been wealth, now there would be poverty, for family and elephant alike. In any case, the arrest of the man's son was not a bad thing. Everyone knew he had committed murder twice, avoiding punishment because of his father's payment of bribes.

During Kumari's days of fame, I had many times watched the elephant pass by, and could always sense the divine presence. I could rarely afford to pose a question, because the price was so high. But now it was low, just a few lengths of sugar cane, bought from Sadong for some small amount more than its worth, and so I began to consult each time I encountered the elephant. Such were her powers that I always came across her when something was weighing on my mind. And no one can say that she didn't answer wisely each time. The mysterious pain in Bopa's shoulder? It will go away. The best place to sell duck eggs in the market? Move to the north side and business will improve.

Now I had again encountered Kumari, and at a very important point in my family's life.

As I stood before her, she took the other bits of cane one by one from my hand, in a patient, grateful way that prolonged the satisfaction I felt in watching the great animal feed. When the cane was done, the trunk rose again and the large, pacific eyes turned my way. A trumpet of thanks sounded.

Sadong spoke. 'And now, Mrs Sray, it is our turn to serve you. What question would you like to pose?' He was laying a cloth on the road and arranging on it the votive sticks bearing the texts. He also set out a bowl and filled it with water from a clay jug that was wrapped in a krama.

I sank to my haunches before the sticks and elephant. 'Ask the Blessed Kumari, please, is it possible for a simple family to find contentment in a new and strange station, one that is not simple?'

Kumari took her time swinging the tip of her trunk across the sticks, expelling blasts of hot breath that knocked some of the sticks awry like straws in a monsoon wind. And then she stopped, considered something, and picked up one with the same gentle grace she had always shown me.

Sadong voiced the text: 'Given a boon, one person makes something foolish with it, a second makes something on which Heaven smiles, even though that which is given both people is the same.'

There was hope, then.

'And now,' said Sadong, standing up, 'your holy water.'

'But I haven't paid for that...'

'A boon, Mrs Sray. A small one, but Kumari's gift to you.'

The elephant dipped her trunk into the bowl at her feet. A torrent of bubbles broke the surface of the water – it was as if it was boiling on a fire. Then the level sank rapidly and silently and the trunk withdrew. It was time to close my eyes. There followed the most pleasing spray on my face, shoulders and breasts. I savoured the holy coolness.

But when I opened my eyes, I saw something disturbing, a lesion on the elephant's neck.

'Oh! You have an injury, Kumari?'

Sadong replied sheepishly for the beast: 'It's been like that for two days, I'm afraid. She scraped against a tree. But we don't have...'

I handed him more silver. 'For the man in the market who sells balms. He'll have one for that.'

Sadong thanked me profusely, hands together.

But on the contrary, on this day it was I who owed thanks, to the elephant, for putting things in perspective. I placed one more piece of silver in Sadong's hand. 'For sugar cane. But not now. Later. Give it to her after her evening bath in the river.'

The elephant's eyes met mine again, calmly. For just an instant, I experienced that immeasurable something.

6: An honourable occupation

I returned to our house determined to take Kumari's answer to heart. Through the afternoon, I busied myself sorting possessions and placing them in baskets. Bopa was bright-eyed. We'll live only a little while in that dirty little house, she declared. Our prince will come and order some men to knock it down and build a big new one, with tiles on the roof and polished wooden floors. Mother, the floors will be so smooth we'll slip and slide! There will be fruit and palm sugar every day, and ivory combs, not wooden ones. My little girl, prancing about, chattering like this – always so optimistic, she was. For a time I was buoyed by her example, but then, as evening neared, my spirits sagged again. The tea set kept presenting itself in my thoughts. By now, I concluded, it must be in the home of some other family. The pot was being filled by some other wife, the cup being raised by some other husband. By nightfall, I wanted it back desperately, though I knew that it could now bring only disappointment. If it somehow returned, it would simply open the way for another craving, desire for the resumption of the old life altogether. The set would be a reminder of the bygone existence, all that I had lost, causing dolour each time I touched it.

I slept badly that night. Before sunrise, I rose and left for the central market. This is what I had done every day, but this time I was going to close the egg business I had run for a decade. The ducks in the pen beneath my house I would give away to neighbours.

I arrived at the market. How foolish I was! I had thought I could merely say I was moving back to the countryside. But of course the news had reached here too. People with whom I had worked for years had already become strangers, variously distant or overly friendly. When I sold the lease to my space on the market's ground, where early every morning I had spread a mat and arranged eggs atop it, the buyer gave me quite a good price, but there was some unspoken suggestion that I would later steer some business her way from the prince's pantry. As I stood talking with her, my every move was watched, just as it was in the neighbourhood. I finished as quickly as I could. On the way out I shopped for fish. The price asked was absurdly high. This time I was viewed as a wealthy woman who'd be too proud to bargain.

I returned to the house at mid-morning, climbed the steps and found Bopa gone and a pair of strange men inside. I was already dispossessed, it seemed. One of the intruders I recognized as a man who had a stall outside the market. His business was the sale of houses. Nol must have made arrangements with him to find a buyer. The second man wore bronze jewellery that signalled no particular occupation, just possession of money. They turned my way when I appeared at the door and the man in bronze gave a leer, in that way that certain men do, but to all women.

I retreated down the steps – my own steps! In a few minutes, the men followed. 'You could get rid of these things in the space below the house,' the agent was saying, 'and put the looms right here. Four or five of them would fit, I would think.'

My heart was breaking. Everything around me would be lost – the jars at which I had bathed on a thousand evenings, pouring water gently over my skin, then, as I dried myself, listening for the voice of Heaven in the chirping of crickets and the stirrings of the breeze in the palm trees' fronds. The pen from which I had released my ducks each morning to forage for rice crabs in the nearby paddies would be broken up for kindling. The house where my children were born, where my husband and I had found sanctuary and a measure of quiet happiness – this house would become a place where hired women wove fabric.

The following morning, two slaves from the palace showed up unrequested, sent by Mr Narin. There was no more putting it off. Bopa and I said prayers before our household shrine, the men waiting silently below. They draped our baskets' handles over either ends of bamboo poles, then lifted with their shoulders, balancing the load. With me in the lead, walking slower than I might have, we set off for the prince's compound. The new neighbours watched our arrival with the same noncommittal eyes. When the job was done, I gave the slaves rice and vegetables and they bowed and thanked me elaborately.

Alone now, Bopa and I knelt at our new household shrine.

'Spirit of the House,' I murmured. 'Accept us as your new occupants and know that we will always honour you.'

At mid-afternoon, we gathered the day's washing and passed through the door in the compound wall, headed to the canal that Mr Narin had told us of the first day. It had only one small bamboo dock and four women were squatting on it, chatting and laughing together as they scrubbed garments. We stood waiting to be noticed and invited to join. But not one of the four looked up and their washing seemed to take a very long time. So we turned back toward our house, in silence.

As we neared our steps, a girl approached. Bopa stopped and stood, with a tiny smile that said, please look to me, I am ready to be your friend. But the girl averted her eyes and hurried past. As she did, her lips mimed two words: *canal dredger*.

In the house, I gathered my daughter in my arms. 'My girl, your father's occupation is an honourable one,' I whispered. I could not bring myself to say former occupation. 'If the canals were not kept deep, how would boats pass through to carry our food? How would the waters of the sacred reservoirs and moats be clear and please the gods? Each person has his work in this world and your father's has built him merit to advance to a holier plane in the next life. But we are still in this life, and now Heaven has chosen to raise his station. We cannot know why, only that now his place, and our place, is here, serving the prince. The people here will come to accept us and you will have friends. Maybe that same girl whom we passed just now.'

I gave a squeeze but it seemed to have no effect. Bopa sat morose with misty eyes. What more to say to convince her? But then, a welcome distraction – Mr Narin calling from outside the door. We got quickly to our feet to welcome him. How was the first day going? he asked. Did we need anything in particular? I brought tea. I told him that all was working out well. His visit, I reflected as I put a cup before him, made that partly true.

After he left, Bopa and I went to the dock again and this time no one was there. We did our wash. The coolness of the water, the busy cooperation, put us both in a better mood. Then we stood and unknotted the garments we wore. We bathed. We returned to the house feeling fresh, but we slept fitfully that night, circled by mosquitoes that came up through cracks in the floor. I would have to deal with that standing water.

Sometime before sunrise I was awakened by voices outside. I got up to look and saw that the compound was alive with people, despite the hour. Women stood in groups outside houses, holding small children close, trading words I could not discern. Something told me to dress and go see what it was.

'There's been trouble at the estate where our prince went,' a woman explained anxiously. 'The prince has been killed, the other prince, I mean. They say that the King and his priests are very angry and that our prince did the killing and they're going to take away his title.'

My hand went to my heart. I resolved on the spot to take Bopa from this place. We would find Nol and Sovan and move to another city. We would live as fugitives again. I awoke my daughter, then quickly gathered up a basket of things – an iron cooking bowl, the previous day's rice, a comb, a single change of garments. I led my sleepy girl down the steps of the house and toward the gate – I was pulling her, really. But then I saw something truly frightening: A line of soldiers was blocking the gate, holding shields that bore the symbol of the King's guard.

One of them yelled in our direction: 'Go back! Nobody leaves!'

I blanched. I knew now that I had been right. The ghost had only pretended to go away. Now it had succeeded in corralling me and Bopa in this awful place. But we would try to escape. I hurried Bopa to the compound's front gate. But there were soldiers there too.

We retreated to the house. Inside, we sat huddled together. I was completely at a loss. I wished I could ask the elephant Kumari. I wished I could pray before Bronze Uncle.

In half an hour, rough male voices carried in from outside. I looked from a window and saw soldiers moving among the houses. Then three were striding right up our own steps, right through our own door, asking no permission. Just like that! I put arms around my daughter and determined to offer myself in exchange if the girl was threatened. Don't close your eyes,

I told myself. You must see whatever they plan to do. But the men merely leered at me. 'So this place does have something worth finding!' laughed one of them. Then more shouts came from outside, and they left quickly. I peered after them. In front of the next house they joined other soldiers who were forcing a man to the ground for binding.

I understood now. They were looking for any of the prince's men who hadn't gone to the provinces with him. In the meantime, they would keep the families penned up in the compound.

We remained inside the rest of the day. I wished I had brought more food from the old house. We had at most a two-day supply. When night fell, we did not light our lamp, lest it attract soldiers.

Early the next morning, we heard distressed voices again. Outside, two women were carrying the bloodied body of a boy. An arm dangled. I watched, horrified. The boy was hardly older than my own Sovan. Soon we learned that the boy had climbed the compound wall during the night in hopes of being a hero, of getting rice for his family from an uncle outside. Two hours later, soldiers dropped his body inside the gate. He was dead, a spear wound in his side.

I filled a bowl with uncooked rice and hurried to the boy's house. But at the door I was stopped by harsh words from a woman inside: 'Stay away from here, stay away! We had no trouble before you and your canal dredger came into service. You have brought some wicked spirit to this place.'

I accepted the rebuke silently, feeling I had done exactly that.

I put the bowl down at the door and stole away. That night, as I lay close to Bopa, trying to sleep amidst the mosquitoes' song, it came to me that with talk like that, the neighbours might be as much a danger as the soldiers. Mr Narin – he would stand up for us. But I had not seen him. He could only have been bound and taken away with the other men.

7: The prince's aspiration

We are taught that everything in this world is transient, and that we must accept the inevitable changes. It is easy, I think, to live by that creed concerning some things, such as age. Yes, all women grow old and feeble, but the change comes so gradually that we hardly notice, we adapt to each little step. It is another thing altogether when a change, a big one, comes in an instant, as it did with the soldiers that day. One moment we could come and go as we pleased; the next we were no freer than captured thieves in cages by the market.

Far away, out of my sight, beyond my knowledge, events had begun that would have deep bearing upon me and my family. Some had occurred just in previous days; others had been building for months or even years, each unimportant in itself, but compounding themselves. It was like with a trickle of water flowing at a paddy field's side. You pay it no attention. But that trickle combines with others from other fields to become streams, then rivers, the waters flowing great distances to join with those of yet more rivers. Those tiny trickles, each nothing in itself, come together to be a calamitous flood.

Many people played a role in the prince's visit to the Chaiyapoom estate, and often with the best of intentions. Let me tell you about one of the most important, the Brahmin.

His name was Subhadra. We imagine that priests of this rank are guided by Heaven's law in every thought and action. But I gradually came to know that he was a man like any other in many ways, that though he had taken holy vows, he passed through life making compromises, sometimes obeying commands with which he did not agree, sometimes pretending he had not heard them. I think that, like me, Subhadra would have preferred to have lived out his years in obscurity.

At the time he appeared at our house, he was still new to the Capital. He was a country man, with the accent to prove it (though I was too anxious that first day to notice it). In the western part of the Empire, there is a small hermitage, one of those isolated places where for many generations a single family of Brahmins has been in charge. It was here that Subhadra was born, raised and initiated into the priesthood. I think he had no ambitions, if that is the right word, beyond remaining in prayer and service at this place. In time, he would become abbot. But then one day Prince Indra's father came calling. He had raised the prince in the same kind of rural seclusion, in an estate two hours' journey from the hermitage. My son insists on moving to the Capital, he told the priest. He is a grand nephew of the King, you know, and he thinks this means his future is there, in the great city. I can't talk him out of it and now he's been granted a palace.

At first it seemed as if the father had come to seek advice but then, as the third cup of tea was sipped, the real purpose was revealed: Would you, Brahmin, consider going along as adviser and tutor? Just for a while, until he finds his place. He needs a steadying hand.

I came to know Subhadra well and can say that he was a man with a genuine vocation to help. But at this moment it was not only a question of help. In theory, it was Subhadra who was the superior in this talk over tea, this blessed man, learned of the sacred texts. But he knew very well that his family's hermitage, indeed, an entire way of life, existed at the pleasure of the visitor, a benevolent man who was the current head of a land-owning family that for generations had donated rice, cooking oil and white sampots, enough to support forty people in prayer. What would become of all that spiritual toil, all those efforts to touch the rays of Heaven, if support fell victim to a wealthy man going away disappointed?

Subhadra said yes, and who can say how much considerations such as that cooking oil weighed on him. He said yes even before hearing a promise that if Indra became successfully established in the Capital, there would be a special grant to the hermitage. Land would be set aside at the donor's estate, its production reserved entirely for the priestly family.

Now Prince Indra was away on a hunting trip when the request was made, so it was decided that Subhadra would not wait to meet his charge, but would leave right away for the Capital to begin arrangements. Ten days later he stood in front of what had been described to him as Indra's palace. The priest once told me that it was when he peered in from the front gate that he got his first inkling of just how hard this job was going to be. The gate's doors were rotten, barely hanging on their hinges. The palace was in fact a set of old military outbuildings that had lain empty and mouldering for a decade. Stray dogs and lunatics slept in them; much of the timber had been stripped as firewood. And whether this place was truly in the royal sector at all was not clear. That was how far from the King's compound it was.

But Subhadra was the kind of man who would say to himself, never mind, it must always be this way for a newcomer prince starting out. He began organizing to make the place liveable. He brought in priests who specialized in blessing domestic spaces. For hours they chanted, they splashed holy water, they ran holy twine from post to post and generally made peace with the spirits, friendly and otherwise, who were about to be displaced. After that, a team of carpenters, thatchers, mat makers and wood carvers got to work. The bills were steep and the craftsmen not always the most honest or skilled – you will recall how poorly built the houses seemed to me and Bopa on our first visit to the compound. I take that now as another sign of the priest's inherent decency, that he was trusting, that he lacked the city wiles to avoid being cheated. In any case, the prince's father sent payment in silver without complaint.

For a long time there was no fit place in the compound for a Brahmin to sleep, so Subhadra lodged at a temple nearby. One evening, as he sat outside its wooden guesthouse, taking in the air after the last rice of the day, he got the full grasp of his job's challenge. It happened because two priests were taking their own meal by lamplight inside. Subhadra heard his name and turned to respond, then realized he was not being greeted, but talked about. One of the priests was saying what sympathy he felt for the country Brahmin. It seemed that for two years, court officials who oversaw palace assignments had been refusing to designate anything for this Prince Indra at all. When finally they gave in, they chose something so run-down that they hoped he would never come. The reason, this priest continued, was that, sight-unseen, the prince had a reputation in the Capital. He was believed to be a rather impetuous young man, forever at odds with his elders. He drank, he chased after village girls, he spent his father's silver. He had his own ideas about everything, it seemed. Even his spiritual life was suspect – he had consulted with a blind jungle mystic in secret. And it was better not to be around him when he was armed. There was at least one prince of the realm who had scars on his face from an altercation with this Prince Indra.

Subhadra stood up and stole away, reluctant to hear more. I can picture him – perhaps he got as far as the temple's pond, and there he stood, gazing on placid water topped by lily pads. I wonder if this was one of those rare times when he had an uncharitable thought. Certainly I would have. Namely, was it by chance that Indra's father had come asking for help at a time when his son was away hunting and not available to meet? Perhaps he smiled at his own naiveté. How was it that over all the years the patron had been coming to the hermitage, all the priest had learned, through overheard remarks by the man's retainers, was that the prince was very spirited and had been somewhat difficult to raise?

I have no doubt that Subhadra gave not a thought to backing out. He had made a promise, and in any case he was a man who believed deeply in the reforming powers of prayer and education. So, in the following days he began forming in his mind a program to mould the character of his charge. After Indra took up residence, he was told in no uncertain terms that the first task of a young prince come to the Capital is to show the royal court that his life is founded on respect and religious orthodoxy, that he aspires to be as cultured, as charitable, as anyone there. He cannot expect instant acceptance. He must build up a record over time that will make sceptics wonder why they ever doubted. So, on the priest's instruction, regular donations of silver flowed from Indra's treasury to a fund for construction of a new hospital in the city, where Brahmin physicians would treat patients free of charge. Any beggar who appeared at Indra's gate was fed. If the prince suggested going outside the city for martial sport,

Subhadra proposed instead going to a temple with offerings of rice and fruit and passing the night there in vigil. Certainly no drinking in market stalls was allowed. And no ostentation. That new palace gate installed under Subhadra's supervision was plain compared to others in the royal sector. It had no gilding, lest other nobles passing by think that Indra believed himself to be already their peers. Likewise, the equipment of office that was acquired was meant to convey earnest humility. The palanquin on which slaves carried the young prince in procession was not new but the refurbished cast-off of another princely family.

And of course there was extensive instruction in the texts. Each afternoon, the prince sat, sometimes restless, on the mats of the tiny chapel that the carpenters had built in his palace. With the scent of incense inspiring pious thoughts, the priest led him line by line through the Hindu classics. Subhadra put particular stock in one passage, found in Lord Krishna's sermon to the warrior King Arjuna on the eve of battle.

Greedy desire and wrath born of passion,
These are the great evil, the sum of destruction.
They are the enemy of the soul.
All is clouded by desire, as fire by smoke,
As a mirror by dust, as an unborn babe in its covering.

They are favourite words of mine as well – though I have always wondered how the covering of an unborn babe can be likened to greedy desire.

8: The toy battle club

When instructing Indra, Subhadra often spoke as if the King, Lord of the Seventeenth Reign, was paying personal attention to the young prince's progress. In fact the King had far too many grandnephews to keep them straight. And in any case, he was oblivious to the most basic of things that occurred outside the palace walls. By all accounts, our sovereign of those times was content to pass his days behind closed, guarded gates. He was the orchid-loving King. He spent most of each morning tending the plants outside his sleeping chamber, pruning, watering, addressing them as living beings. Afternoons he spent at the palace dance pavilion, watching rehearsals, sometimes making suggestions about staging, before returning for more time with his beloved plants. His life had always been like that; he had done nothing to make himself King. It simply happened, six years earlier, by virtue of being brother to the previous monarch, whose heart stopped beating one afternoon as he lay with a concubine fifty years his junior. By the time word reached potential pretenders, the palace priests had designated and blessed the orchid lover, in the belief that he would be steered by their constant advice. When he was moved to the palace, he showed right away that he would. His only initiative was to ask if carpenters might build a covered nursery outside the window of his sleeping chamber, and when that was done he resumed his life precisely as before.

Still, how people loved this King! They loved him because they sensed that from behind the palace walls he loved them back. At festival times, he offered large gifts to the Capital's common folk – rice, palm oil, straw bags for market shopping, all placed in stacks just outside the royal quarter. If the gifts were all taken before evening, then more were put in their place. But love, of course, cannot be bought with material things. People felt as they did because everyone, even a slave in the market who heard only stories passed from person to person to person, could sense that the King took to heart the lessons of Heaven that the Empire was a family in which he was benevolent father. Those orchids? They embodied the pureness of the royal heart. That submission to the palace Brahmins? It was not that but submission to Heaven's will. On a simpler level, no tales ever made their way from the palace of the King growing angry, beating a retainer, or deciding on a petition in a way that enriched a relative. In those rare times when he moved in procession through the city, he looked out from atop his elephant with a gentle smile that could only be born of compassion.

But those same people who gave their love also thought it no surprise that the reign of a King who had never held a battle sword, only a pruning knife, had brought trying times for our race. We Khmers have of course been blessed from the time the first of us was born from the union of a Brahmin from India and a maiden daughter of the Naga King. We have multiplied, inhabiting as we do a realm so fertile that a plant placed in the soil simply grows on its own. But in the days of which I speak we had come under pressure from beyond our borders. It was said that the peoples there lived in league with demons. In the far northwest, at the edge of the Upper Empire, were the Siamese, who claimed knowledge of a way to break the cycle of reincarnation. Each year, they sent tribute to our Capital, but every so often there filtered out reports of rebellious stirrings in their territories. To the east, on land that abutted the great Saltwater Sea, lived the Chams. Do you know, they claim to worship our gods, but they speak a strange language, wear strange caps and garments and eat even stranger food. The Chams had grown bold to build forts closer to our frontier, and to tax and sometimes seize the Chinese vessels that passed through their waters enroute to our ports. We began to experience shortages in the market.

People should stand together in trying times, but the fact is that not all of us did. Bandits plagued our roads. Here in the Capital it was not unknown that neighbour killed neighbour and paid no price for it, like the son of the rich man who had summoned Kumari. Even some of the Empire's own princes, lords of estates in outer districts, were behaving in shameful ways. They began to short-change the royal storehouses of rice they owed. They dared to bestow rank on their own, without a word of permission from the Capital.

So there was much talk in those days of how those peoples beyond our borders could be held at bay and the criminals within brought to heel. Might some mighty commander emerge who, misty-eyed with loyalty, would bow at the King's feet, receive one of those blessed orchids, then lead our armies to victory? These yearnings came to figure in Subhadra's plans for how to rehabilitate his prince. No, he never saw Indra as that great commander. He merely formed the idea that a modest role could be won for him in restoring security and imperial cohesiveness. In view of his notable martial skills, the prince might be dispatched to some distant frontier district to command a military unit there. With that, the Brahmin would return home to the family hermitage, his task completed, his obligation cleared.

But such an appointment could be sought only after the prince had put an end to his bad reputation and shown that his true character was imbued with obedience and humility.

One day, Indra presented the priest with a way to do that. During a session with the texts, Indra declared: I have wronged a prince, a prince named Teng. I must perform a pilgrimage to his estate and make amends.

You recall that I mentioned a prince of the realm with a scar on his face? That was this Teng. He had come to have the mark because one evening, when Indra was just eight years old and Teng perhaps twice that age, Indra approached him at a temple festival and with no preliminaries delivered some insult. Teng turned toward him, prepared to laugh it off, I'm sure, and instead he got a blow to the face with a toy battle club. This from a boy half his size! Such was the fighting spirit our prince possessed, even long before he became an adult. The blow landed hard enough to open a cut on Teng's jaw. Indra's father was on the scene instantly, aghast, and delivered all manner of apologies and a formal offer of compensation. I suppose that Teng was too proud to accept the payment. What man would want to admit being bested by a child? Teng simply walked away. But later, the wound grew infected, and when it finally healed, it left a small scar on his jaw. No one ever mentioned this to his face, of course, but when people met Teng, they could not help but notice the scar. So it was that almost everyone knew the story of how an eight-year-old boy had placed it there.

What was the reason behind the fight? I will tell you. You will see that it shows that our prince already had concerns that normally wait until later years. He insulted Teng because there was a rivalry between the two princes' families over property, including rights to the Chaiyapoom Estate, in the Upper Empire, the place where my husband grew up. Men of Indra's bloodline had been its lords in previous generations. It was now the realm of Teng, who had seized it years earlier citing lineage flowing back to a previous King. If the Brahmin knew more than this about the dispute, I would be surprised. He would not have cared about details or legalistic questions of right and wrong, only that as a boy Indra had allowed hatred to defile his heart.

You can imagine how warmed was the Brahmin on hearing the prince suggest this pilgrimage. An expression of irreproachable virtue, flowing unsolicited from his charge's mouth! In subsequent days, priest and prince discussed it many times. Of course the priest had some specifics to suggest. The journey must be performed with a heart full of piety, with prayers said at shrines along the road. A gift must be presented to mark the end of the feud. It should be a beautiful silver bowl. The Brahmin went himself to a smith in the market to commission its production, and composed a verse of reconciliation that was inscribed on its side. He also set the prince on a series of preparatory vigils in the Capital, and made sure that fellow Brahmins, and through them princes, were informed of the journey's purpose. Indra would return to the Capital a peace maker. He would have shed his reputation.

Do you understand, then? This was the pilgrimage that the prince began that morning in his palace compound, Nol and Sovan kneeling before him, me watching silently from behind.

9: Fateful journey

The pilgrimage to Chaiyapoom of course became known to every soul in the Capital later on. Retainers, slaves, virtually everyone connected to it – they all talked. Some became renowned purely on the basis of having been there. You will hear even today many versions of precisely what happened. I will tell you here what I believe to be true.

None of what I know, however, came from the Brahmin. All through the rest of his life, he said not a word to anyone. We all have a decision that we regret more than any other, don't we? Even priests. This was his, the decision to facilitate the visit to Chaiyapoom.

I believe that he began to feel misgivings at the very beginning of the journey. His first concern was the size of the procession that departed the Capital. You see, people in the prince's retinue were always trying to undermine the priest's edicts against ostentation. Why had they come to serve a prince if not to bask in the rays of his glory? So they polished up the palanquin in hopes of obscuring its hand-me-down origins. They added bodyguards and a gong player to the travel group and soon a baggage cart was needed.

Off they all processed that morning, off to play their role in events that Heaven had determined in time immemorial.

In the streets, whoever heard the gong stepped aside to clear a path, knelt and put hands together. I don't think many were fooled by the palanquin. But on it was a sight to behold – a prince with a body like a god's, well-muscled in arms and legs, strong in the skills of war but putting them aside to make peace with an enemy.

Eventually, with parasols floating overhead, the procession passed through the stone gate at the Capital's north edge and took to a trunk road that traversed the open paddy land beyond. Planting was underway. You know that time of year, that sight – a sea of the brightest green seedlings, newly planted, motionless save for waves that a breeze stirs here and there. The potential for life, the start of a new cycle of renewal, villagers shouting to each other cheerfully across the fields, the sky clear, the sun shining down strong. And on that day, all this was at odds with the fate carried forward by the prince's procession.

The slaves made good time with their load. But by early afternoon, the job was taking its toll and they were relieved to see a small way station ahead, the first planned stop. The prince hopped from the palanquin and strode up the station's steps. The concubine – her name was Rom – hurried right behind, startling the Brahmin. He went inside too, then in a minute or two, he emerged, looking troubled. The Prince and Rom were alone inside. It seemed that the Brahmin had been dismissed.

It is a sin to judge others, but I must tell you that in the case of this Rom, everyone committed this sin, myself included.

Our prince's household might have been short of many things at this time, but not of concubines. He had four already, quite a number for a noble of his age and rank. Rom had arrived only a few days before, a large-eyed girl of stunning beauty, the physical kind, at least – skin like polished stone, perfect breasts. She had been summoned from a village to the south by the prince himself, though no one could say how he had come to know of her. Already she had established herself as senior of the concubines, cowing the others through words alone. Everyone in the prince's household, in fact, was afraid of her, except the Brahmin, who, standing outside the inn, was only just now learning why perhaps he should be.

After a while, the prince stepped out of the station, followed by the concubine. The palanquin slaves, resting on their hunkers in the shade of a gum tree, looked discreetly to her garment and hair. Each of them, no doubt, imagined having time on a mat with Rom. Such was her power over men, to make them do foolish, dangerous things. The slaves exchanged silent leers; Subhadra put a stop to that with a glower. Then he stepped to Rom, who was standing hands out, so that her maid could apply new colour to her palms.

'You should not have rushed into the dining area that way,' he told her. 'You should wait for instructions.'

'I heard no objection from His Highness. He seemed to want me there.'

She did not even do him the courtesy of looking down when she spoke! Everyone noticed. He tried again. 'You can be sure that he dislikes that kind of behaviour. You would do better to follow the rules.'

She shrugged, in a way that suggested the Brahmin should not be so sure he knew the prince's thoughts better than she. She looked back to her hands. The maid, pretending she had heard none of this, applied more colour.

Subhadra walked away, fuming again.

A stallion had been brought to the station in advance, and the prince mounted it. The slaves lifted the empty palanquin, now so light that they smiled in unison, feeling they were carrying nothing at all.

Late on the third day, the road began to climb and cut back on itself. The attendants whispered among themselves that it was a fine view they were getting from up here – the bend of a distant river, a provincial temple's spire, more paddies full of those young green seedlings, and everything alight in the brilliant hues that the sun offers as a gift as it departs. The prince, atop his horse, seemed not to notice. Nor did Rom, dozing in space she'd demanded be cleared for her in the baggage cart.

Soon there appeared ahead a long and tall ridgeline, broken by a pass, entryway to the Upper Empire. On its right was an old brick temple, surrounded by miniature wooden houses on stands, placed there as resting places for spirits that moved through the pass on their own travels between lands high and low. The party broke travel. Prince and Brahmin were shown to the head priest's house for the night; everyone else laid out mats on grass by a stream. The travellers' cook borrowed an ember from the temple's fire to get a brazier going. Acolytes wandered out to sit with the travellers in air that was now charcoal-scented. Chaiyapoom? You're a bit less than half way there, the group was told. Night fell, stars began to show themselves.

In subsequent days, the party passed through landscapes that were strangely different from the flat, cultivated expanses of the Capital's region. This place had hills with gentle contours, covered with waist-high grass, rivers that followed winding courses between those hills and sometimes flowed fast and noisily. Local people grew rice in flooded paddies near the rivers' banks; in places, their fields extended up the slopes of hills, nurtured only by what water Heaven chose to provide as rain. The travellers wondered what kinds of spirits lived in these places. No chances were taken. Each time Indra paused at a roadside shrine to say the prayers of repentance required by Subhadra, one of the retainers made sure to leave offerings of rice and fruit on behalf of the group's lower ranks as well.

After five days, with monsoon clouds gathering overhead, a stone boundary marker bearing the Chaiyapoom name was spotted beside the road. The prince switched from horse to palanquin and continued the journey in that more dignified fashion. Everything from this point had been arranged in detail by a messenger who had gone ahead. The travellers passed through a small market town. Then, in a forest beyond, they rounded a curve and another procession came into view. This one was far larger, with perhaps one hundred attendants and guards. Four red parasols shaded its prince. Prince Teng!

Indra got down and walked slowly forward, crouching just discernibly. He knelt and put palms together before the other prince, who sat on a very large palanquin and gave an offhand greeting in response. Subhadra watched silently from the rear, looking pleased, as if thinking that every so often his prince could do things correctly. But the sight made other members of Indra's party feel suddenly unsure of their own standing. Their prince's conveyance now looked small and battered, his parasols cheap and poorly sewn. And even from this distance, they could see that the other prince was a portly, diffident man and it pained them that their master, so strong and determined, so skilled with weapons, was the one who had to crouch.

The formalities completed, the princes began talking in a more casual way. Water was brought in silver bowls and they drank. The portly prince mimed the shooting of an arrow. After a short while, Indra returned to his own palanquin, and the journey resumed, the host's party in the lead.

An hour later, with a shower wetting their hair and shoulders, the slaves were pleased to see they were approaching a wooden lodge, built at the edge of marshland. Just as they reached it, the rain let up. Sunbeams shone through dispersing clouds overhead, transforming the area with dazzling greens and yellows. It was so stunning a sight that Indra's slaves couldn't stop looking and almost lost their footing as they lowered the conveyance by the lodge. The princes got down and stood admiring the scene, the host pointing out from between a pair of bodyguards something out across the reeds and mist-caressed water. Then the princes went behind the lodge in turn to bathe with water scooped from a large earthen jar; Indra's retainers were shown to a set of small bamboo pavilions that had been specially built for them. After dark, the princes ate and drank together in the lodge's eating hall, a bodyguard from Prince Teng's detachment watching from each of the room's four corners. The gong musicians performed. Most everyone who passed close enough to hear the conversation felt that the guards were unnecessary. The princes were taking a liking to each other.

The next morning the two walked together into the marshland with their hunting bows and a detail of the host's guards. Boys who had been sent out into the reeds flushed out wild water fowl and released a few more that they had captured for the hunt. The princes sent arrows aloft. Indra's palanquin bearers were surprised that their master's missed so often. They decided this was another courtesy to Prince Teng, who by even his own slaves' accounts was no great shot. There was some small comfort for Indra's men in knowing that up close, a scar would be visible on Teng's face.

In early afternoon, the princes left by palanquin for the estate's palace. They arrived just after sunset, as two retainers stood at the gate with torches. From beyond the outlines of trees came the whisper of rushing water – a waterfall's greeting. Indra's slaves, exhausted, squinted in the darkness to see how grand a thing this country palace was. Soaring eaves, large windows and inlaid glass reflecting the torchlight suggested it was quite a place despite its isolation. The princes bathed, then, dressed in fresh sampots, they walked the short distance to a stone temple that was the estate's principal place of worship. Carved gods gazed down on them from niches beneath a pyramidal peak. Inside the sanctuary, the princes gave thanks at Shiva's linga for the safe journey and the hunting. Afterward, each member of Prince Indra's party, slaves excepted, was given a chance to say devotions too, closer or farther from the sanctuary according to rank. Rom, however, announced that she had a headache and would say her prayers later. She instructed one of the portly prince's servants to show her and her maid to their quarters immediately so that she could lie down. Subhadra overheard. He winced at such forwardness.

The princes sat down in the audience hall for evening rice. There were no guards this time. Subhadra looked in briefly; trust and maybe even the glimmerings of friendship seemed in evidence. The silver bowl, the gift of reconciliation, was at Indra's side in its wrappings, and would be presented when the princes finished their banquet. Servants laid out bowls of food and drink in the lamplight and Prince Teng launched into an explanation of repairs he planned to make to the estate's irrigation canals, how much he'd have to pay hydraulic engineers to come up from the Capital, how his villagers were already trying out tricks to avoid the extra rice tax that would underwrite the work.

What happened next was witnessed only because an attendant forgot to remove an empty water bowl and re-entered the hall to get it.

It is painful for me to describe. Prince Indra reached under the mat on which he sat and took out something small. He leaned close to Teng as if to whisper to him, still drawing him in with pleasantries, and with a quick stroke, he slashed him across the belly with the thing in his hand! The man's entrails suddenly burst out. It was shocking, the attendant said later – like startled snakes fleeing a hiding place! Prince Teng shrieked, and Indra then drove the thing in his hand, it seemed to be an arrowhead, into the prince's eyes, first the left, then the right. Then across the throat. How can a man be so cruel? The victim somehow got to his feet, splashing blood, pressing at his escaping innards with his fingers. He stumbled a few steps, crashed into a post, then fell in a heap. Indra's attention, however, was elsewhere – he was reaching behind a drape, and from it he took a bow, his war bow. Gandiva was its name. Two guards came racing in with spears ready. Indra sent arrows streaking the length of the hall, felling the men one, two. There was a pause, then the thump of many feet outside; the attendant who witnessed this had fallen to the floor now, immobilized by fear, but the prince ignored him. Because perhaps twenty armed men pushed into the hall, breathing hard, ready to fight. Indra simply stared them down along the shaft of another arrow.

'The usurper is dead!' he declared, kicking at the body, which now lay still. 'The temple, the paddies, the palace, the people of Chaiyapoom – by the authority of the Lord Shiva, I take possession of them all. My family's rights, blessed by Heaven, are restored!'

The men looked to each other. It took just an instant, I think – then they threw down their spears and pressed their faces to the floor.

Roused by the noise, Subhadra hurried to the hall. Perhaps he was fearful his master had been attacked. But, seeing the body and the bow, he grasped what had happened. He froze. One can imagine his inner tumult. Those months of teachings, those long hours over the holy texts, the vigils – all to no effect!

Rom stole in from behind and went straight to the motionless Prince Teng, whose torso was emitting a red pool onto the matting. She gazed down with ghoulish interest. Then, for just an instant, her eyes left the corpse and met Subhadra's, and suddenly he understood who had placed the weapons in the room, and what she and the prince had been discussing in the way station that first day of the journey. She made an expression of mock surprise that he hadn't known what was planned.

He left the hall.

Soon came another surprise: two large shapes emerging from the darkness beyond the estate's gate, smaller ones alongside them. Grunts and voices and the clank of martial equipment. It was the forty members of Indra's personal guard, with a pair of elephants forced to act as engines of war.

Subhadra wandered the compound all night, it seems, looking more and more disquieted. He entered the estate's armoury, and there spoke with Indra's military commander, a man covered with war tattoos, by the name of Rit. This Rit seemed to know his way around; he did not hesitate at all in the way of someone new to a place. He was inspecting armour that hung on hooks on the pillars, putting hands to it, as if he recognized it. There were some words between priest and soldier, on the face of it fully civil and respectful, and after that Subhadra walked out, almost staggering, people said. And then the concubine Rom, seeming still to take pleasure in the priest's distress, approached him. She said just a few words. But enough, it seems, to make the Brahmin realize that she too was not a stranger to this place.

My husband, of course, was also from Chaiyapoom. So, have I made it clear? Indra had in secret begun to reassemble the court of his late kinsman Prince Vira, who years earlier had been dispossessed of Chaiyapoom by Teng. Not the original people, because they were dead, but whichever of their children could be found to be still living. My husband, the concubine, the commander.

This had all come about because six months earlier, Indra had had a dream. He had dreamt that he was standing in an audience room, and somehow he knew it was the Chaiyapoom estate's audience room, and yet there was no one present. So he stepped outside and there he saw men and women going about the usual tasks of estate life. He felt he knew each of them, and yet he could not summon a single name. He was just stepping toward the first of them when he awoke. It was such a powerful dream that he consulted with a seer, the blind shaman Vibol.

Have you heard of this Vibol? He passed most of his life as an ascetic in a straw hut on a hillside not far from Chaiyapoom. Every so often, he came to the Capital to consult with nobles for high fees, generally in secret because no one was willing to admit contact with the man. I can recall passing him once on the street. Due to his sightlessness, a boy led him by the arm. I have no doubt that he had true mystical powers, that he could contact the supernatural. I would guess that he was in league with some powerful, discontented deity, one that dwells in those Chaiyapoom hills.

Vibol told the prince that the dream foresaw that he would take possession of Chaiyapoom. Those people whom the prince could not name in his dream were the children of the former household, placed in the dream in their dead parents' positions. Those children must now be found and brought to your service, the shaman said, or the repossession of the estate could never take place. Vibol undertook to find these people, for an additional fee of silver, I'm sure. How he accomplished it I don't know. Perhaps it was by dispatching agents, perhaps it was by supernatural means. In any case, Vibol later told the prince where Nol could be found, and the same for Rom and the commander. And each time the Brahmin was sent in ignorance to recruit these people. Vibol promised that their presence would please local spirits, who would then help in the seizure of the estate by such means as causing guards to fall asleep and dogs to fail to bark. All those things did happen that night.

People saw the Brahmin standing alone at the estate that night, for a long period, in the dark, beneath a tree. Then he called to a servant to bring his mare. To me there is no doubt he had decided to go back to the Capital and take responsibility for what had happened. Such was his devotion to honour. And what a risk he would have been taking. The easy response to this crime would have been a spear point through the heart of the priest, who had been heard to say in the Capital that the prince took no decision without his approval.

But instead of the mare coming, the prince came. Then another surprise: the prince dropped to his knees before the Brahmin, palms together.

I need your guidance, I need your wisdom, he was heard to say. I am young. I have avenged a grave crime against my family, my bloodline, for that I can have no remorse. But from here on I am at a loss as to what to do. I ask, I beg that you stay. He said all that, almost weeping as he did. Then he pressed his face to the dust and held it there.

All who witnessed this were deeply moved. A prince of such

martial strength was reaching out for guidance. He recognized his shortcomings, he hungered for teaching. In the face of such a plea, what could a teacher do but acquiesce?

So right there, in the darkness, with the prince remaining on his knees, the priest began to deliver moral instruction. What had happened this night was a grave sin, the Brahmin declared, regardless of questions of rights and bloodline. An estate is not a prize to be jostled over. An estate does not exist to glorify its prince, but to provide food and assistance to the holy men of its temple so that behind the walls they might perform rites that keep the cosmos in balance. A prince is only a tool of this transcendent purpose, organizer of earthly activity, preserver of social order so that Heaven might be petitioned and continued life made possible.

I believe that the priest that night suddenly saw the glimmerings of greatness in Indra, but a greatness that, left to itself, might turn against Heaven's design. There could only have descended over Subhadra's heart a conviction that it was his responsibility to assure that such a corruption did not occur.

10: Siege

I have told you these details of the Chaiyapoom killing, but we knew none of them at the time we were prisoners in the compound. All we knew was that the estate's prince was dead and soldiers from the palace guard were eying us through the gates.

We lived in the most abject kind of fear, wondering if the soldiers would tire of merely watching and come through those gates to kill us. People said many prayers, extra prayers, some to prepare for death, some to try to persuade Heaven to put it off.

My little girl and I stayed in the house, somehow feeling safer behind the flimsy walls, but after a few days, we grew restless and ventured out. It was more out of hunger than anything else. We had run out of food. Perhaps someone had some to sell? But everyone we approached shook their heads.

On the morning of the fifth day we went out, to try again, and found ourselves drawn toward the gate. There were quite a few people there. I saw then that the gate was open. It was possible to go right up to it, as many people were doing, and look out, though not to go even one step further. There were still soldiers just outside. Gradually, I summoned up the courage to try myself.

From the gate I noticed two things. First, that the soldiers in the lane outside were different ones, with different emblems on their sampots. And the young wife Mrs Pala! Outside, selling coconuts to the soldiers.

I felt remiss for not guessing that she would find a way to reach us. She was my most important friend from the old neighbourhood, my only one, really. She had been born there before we arrived, but lost her parents to mosquito fever before she reached her sixth year. Another household took her in, but it fell to me to give her an occupation. She became my apprentice at the market. My own daughter was too young at the time and in any case, to be frank, was short on the necessary aptitude. But how quickly Pala learned the skills of a duck egg vendor! How to raise your own birds and keep them healthy, how to supplement their production by arriving at the wholesalers' carts before sunrise for the good pick, how the market men would try to be familiar with you, but would generally accept that you'd keep some distance, as long as you were cordial about it. I taught her how to pile the eggs in a pyramid at the stall, to sprinkle them with water to make them look extra fresh and to spot the shoppers who, if you gave them the chance by looking the other way, would slip one or two into their market bags and make off. I was sad when the time came that she married and started her own stall on the other side of the market, in coconuts, actually – there were too many sellers of duck eggs. But, do you know what happened late each morning? A boy would show up at my stall carrying a gift, an opened coconut, its sweet milk ready to drink.

How I remembered those coconuts, and how I could almost taste the ones that Pala was, right now, selling to the soldiers. She was down the alley, on her haunches at a spot where the soldiers slept and ate their rice. She was in her element – cleaver in one hand, coconut in the other, expectant customers looking on. With a deft whack of the blade, she opened a shell and passed it to a young soldier.

When she turned my way, I dared make a little wave. There was nothing in return, and I worried she hadn't seen me. But in a few minutes, Pala was on her feet, a bag over her shoulder, drifting toward the gate. She stopped to ask something of a soldier, then waited to the side while he consulted with another of the men. I think it was now that I remembered something. Her husband was a member of the guard of some minor prince. She knew these men, perhaps. At the least, she knew how to talk to them.

Then she was standing in front of me. We quickly embraced, across the threshold.

'Oh, Mrs Sray!' she whispered. 'You're all right! I'm sorry it took so long to come.'

'It seems like right away, Pala. And you're the first person to make it in. I'm so happy to see you.'

'See now, we must be quick. I have some things for you. Coconuts and some food.' Pala put down her bag, as if she were just resting a moment and was going to pick it up again. My eyes were misting now. 'I prayed,' I said, 'and now Heaven has sent you. And thank goodness – we've run out of everything. My girl is going hungry.'

Pala shared what news she had. The King's soldiers were out and around the city. Some had begun the march to the estate where the killing had taken place. At first everyone thought they were going to capture and punish our prince. But now a new story was circulating – he might be forgiven. The soldiers from the Capital might join forces with him. Why? Who could say? It was hard to know what to believe. Today it was that the palace priests were arguing among themselves. It all created a feeling that no one was in charge.

'So,' said Pala, 'when the soldiers get an order, they delay carrying it out, because they wonder if it's going to be reversed the next day.'

'Time's up.' It was one of the sentries.

'I'll come again tomorrow,' Pala whispered. 'Same time. Meet me here.'

She left. I tarried a moment, then picked up the bag. The sentry saw, I'm sure, but did nothing to stop me. I hurried back to the house and with Bopa looking on impatiently, opened the bag. The most wonderful aromas rose from it. Inside were boiled rice, chicken, water spinach, lotus seeds, fish and peanut paste, all wrapped in leaves, ready to eat. At the bottom were four coconuts, each in perfect ripeness.

Bopa reached for the chicken, poor girl, but I knew we had to do something else first. We knelt at the household shrine, placed rice offerings on it and prayed. Then we ate very quickly – like ravenous animals, I imagine. It would have been easy to finish it all, right there, but half way through, I called a stop. 'We have to give some to the neighbours. To the woman who lost her son.'

The next morning, Pala was at the gate as promised, with another bag. I took it gratefully but then I shared an idea that had come to me overnight. Perhaps if the people inside made a gesture to help the soldiers, to make them more comfortable, they'd allow Pala to bring in supplies for everyone. Pala said she'd try, but first she'd have to talk to the sergeant in charge.

Soon the soldier was approaching. It seemed he wanted to

talk to the lady inside. Me! He was rather powerfully built, with a small tuft of hair in the middle of his chest. A dagger was tucked at his waist. I regretted having called attention to myself.

'Good morning, sir,' I said, trying for a courteous voice.

'Good morning, ma'am.' It surprised me that he replied at all, and that he followed with a morose smile.

'We'd like to tell you,' I said, feeling for the words, 'how grateful we here are for the protection you and your men are giving us.'

He shrugged, as if sorry I should have to say such a thing.

I continued. 'I can see that this is unpleasant duty. Inside, we get to sit in our houses or in the shade but you soldiers have to stand in the sun all day. You know, you and your men might be here for quite a while. It would be much more comfortable, don't you think, if someone came and built a small pavilion as a place for you and your men to rest, to get out of the sun.'

One of the sentries was listening, and I was happy for that. Word would spread and it wouldn't be a decision for the sergeant alone to make.

'That would be pleasant, yes,' he replied. 'But unfortunately, we have no money for such a thing.'

'Sir, what I meant is that we in the compound would like to help with that.'

'That's very kind.' He was playing along, this man. How fortunate I was; he seemed a decent type.

'A small thing. But Mrs Pala here could see about getting a thatch pavilion built. She knows people who do that kind of work.' The sergeant nodded and signalled that I could continue. 'And maybe next time she comes to sell to your men she could sell a few things to us inside as well. We're running short; the children are complaining that they don't have anything sweet and it's a bit heart-breaking.'

He made a show of thinking it over. 'All right, she can sell to all of you. But I'm afraid it will have to be with the understanding that she does it here at the gate and that no one comes out.'

'Of course. No one will leave.'

'Good. That way, we can continue to protect you.' He gave me a small, ironic smile, and turned to leave.

'Sir, there's one more thing...' He turned back, as if he'd known there would be. 'There's a body inside here, sir. The body of a boy. Cremation needs to be arranged or his soul will become confused, and wander aimlessly. I hope it wouldn't be too much to ask that his mother be allowed to take the body out to a temple and see to the service.'

'You said a boy...?' He had turned serious. 'No one told us about that.'

'Eleven years old, sir. He was killed with a spear outside the wall. It must have been an accident.'

The sergeant's face clouded. Then he told me that, yes, the mother could take the body out.

I hurried in to tell the mother, and then went house to house to explain my idea. People were willing to speak with me now – perhaps they knew that my daughter and I had shared from our first bag of food. I explained the deal I'd made. Some people predicted the soldiers wouldn't keep their side of it but I said that the sergeant seemed like he could be trusted. In the end, most people put in some silver to see what would happen. By the time I arrived at the gate the next morning, I had a sufficient sum in a pouch. Pala met me, the money changed hands, and that afternoon workmen arrived with thatch and bamboo and began putting up the shelter. And Pala came with two very large baskets of food and drink, suspended from a rod across her shoulders. She could barely walk, it was so heavy! First she sold to the soldiers, then she moved the baskets to the gate. Women lined up at the inside and bought her out.

Later, a priest with two assistants entered the compound. In half an hour they emerged, the assistants carrying the small body shrouded on a board. The mother trailed behind. The soldier on guard at the door looked under the cloth and made a face of pity.

The sergeant waved the man off, then stepped to me. 'I'm sorry, ma'am. The body should not have been disturbed. But the man thought he was required to do that.'

Life was easier after that. Pala came every day, and people had enough to eat. I was able to persuade the sergeant that women should be allowed to go to the canal in the afternoon to wash clothing, with a soldier in escort, of course. The day after that, I pointed out that the skies had remained clear for a few days and that the houses' jars were running out of the water they collected as run-off from roofs. He said all right, and they found a pushcart and took several jars to the canal to fill. Several of the soldiers put down their spears and helped.

But one morning, the sergeant came into the compound with four of his men, without warning. People turned out to watch as the group moved from house to house, entering each to look around inside.

A woman strolled up to me. 'It's very important that they don't come inside my house,' she whispered. 'The one by the wall. Over there. Can you help?'

I did not ask why. But I went and found the sergeant. 'Sir, the previous group of soldiers did this already. They searched the whole place. Is there really anything here worth looking for now?'

'Oh, just bear with us a while,' he replied pleasantly. 'Some new orders have come down, and we can't just ignore them.'

We stood together, watching the men check the house next to the one by the wall.

'You know, sergeant, I've been thinking. The mats your men sleep on seem awfully thin and ragged. The women who went out to wash clothes were telling me just last night. I know a shop in the market where they could get new ones. And no, no – I wouldn't need to go there myself.'

'Mrs Pala could take care of it.'

'Sir, you read my mind.'

'Now, I suppose that the best way to get those mats would be to end the search right now.'

I'm sure I was smiling nervously now. 'Why do you say that? We just want to help.'

'That I know. We've really been made quite comfortable here. It's going to be a shame to have to go back to our barracks.'

'Is that a possibility?'

He shrugged. 'Perhaps, before long, and after that all of you people will be free to go where you please. There will be no need to protect you anymore. In any case, don't worry about getting the mats. We're comfortable enough.'

But what was he communicating? The four soldiers were walking toward the house by the wall now.

Then I did something I should not have. I blurted: 'Please, sergeant! There's no need to look in that one.'

I closed my eyes, appalled. I'd given away the secret.

But just then the sergeant called out to his men: 'That's enough then, come on back.' With his usual courtesy, he said his good-byes to me and led his men out the gate.

My heart was beating so fast. I let it calm down, then wandered in what I hoped was an inconspicuous way to the house by the wall. Its woman came to the door, whispered her thanks, then brought me inside. A man was sitting on the floor.

'Mr Narin! You've been here all this time?'

'Yes!' Our good friend and helpmate smiled wearily. 'Since the first day. The soldiers were taking away all the men at Prince Indra's palace. This lady is my cousin. She took me in.'

The woman explained that there'd been a close call that first day. The soldiers came to the house, but Mr Narin had hidden in a big water jar. 'He may have to do it again,' she laughed. 'He'll be safe, though. Those soldiers are just stupid country boys.'

I wanted to speak up for the sergeant, but thought this was not the time.

Two days later, word spread that the soldiers outside were packing up. I went to look. There was already a crowd at the gate. It was true – the sentries were gone, the sleeping pavilion was being dismantled. One by one, people began stepping out of the gate, to see what would happen, and nothing happened. I joined the flow, feeling a thrill at passing through.

I saw the sergeant consulting with one of his men. Something made me turn away, then I wondered if I should go and thank him. But there was no need to decide; he was walking toward me.

'We're leaving, ma'am. Back to the barracks.'

'Oh!'

'Your Prince Indra has become quite a hero. He's securing the Upper Empire against the Siamese.'

I found my wits now. 'Before you go, sir, I want to tell you that I appreciate all that you have allowed us here.'

'Oh, it should have been much more. Holding women and children prisoner isn't my idea of proper duty. And we got something out of it too, don't forget. Probably more than we should have. So here's a bit of it back.' He held out a handful of silver nuggets. 'We sold the materials in the pavilion to a scrap man. Here's the money, with a little extra. The men all contributed.'

I took it. 'Sir, you and your men are very kind. May Heaven bless you all.'

'I suspect that it blesses you more.'

Perhaps my face showed a bit of colour when he said that. 'Well, good-bye, then. But – sir, may I know your name?'

'I am Sergeant Sen of the King's compound guard, second squad.'

'I will convey word about the kind things that you did for us here, sir. And...my name is Sray. Mrs Sray.'

'Yes, I've been told. You are wife of Prince Indra's parasol master.'

I went back inside and found Bopa. Together we walked to Bronze Uncle to give thanks. He was not cross with us, I'm sure, for staying away so long. We had reason. That day in my prayer I did not include anything about the ghost. I knew that the god knew what happened and would take steps to protect us.

Then our feet took us to the central market. We bought rice and fish and fruit and coconuts, as much as we could carry, but sat down to eat right there. I looked to my daughter, who was sipping from her second coconut, and I felt overcome with affection. I reflected what a gift from Heaven was this girl. The danger had passed, but I found myself wondering again if we should run away from this new life, which had come close to killing us. So I decided we would ask Kumari.

But when we went looking for the elephant, she wasn't in any of her usual places around the market. I asked the man who from a mat at the market gate collected rents from the vendors.

'You didn't hear, Mrs Sray? She has entered the royal stables, by the King's order.'

I did know that in the period when Kumari still had a broad following, His Majesty was passing in procession one day and stopped to watch as she told fortunes. Now I learned that while we were imprisoned in the compound, our King had formally declared that she was in fact possessed of special powers, regardless of her decline in public regard, and had brought her into the palace.

So – another shock, another friend lost. But then I found myself with a comforting thought. In the King's stables, the elephant would be given leaves and stalks in abundance, and balms for any problems with her hide. And His Majesty, I knew, would never attempt to abuse her powers. He would put to her only questions that Heaven intended she answer. Perhaps some small aspect of this event was a signal, dare I think it, from the elephant to me. I have entered service of royalty, Kumari was saying; so have you. Life behind the royal walls will seem strange, but in time we will both make good of it. Don't you recall the fortune I selected for you that day by the shrine?

I had one more question for the rent collector. 'And Sadong, the elephant's keeper. Where is he?'

'In the palace too. He is to continue in his role.'

That seemed like another sign. So I embraced my daughter, who didn't quite understand why, and together we walked back toward the prince's compound, slowly because we were carrying that big load of food.

When we reached our house, we saw that three small banana leaf bundles had been left on the steps. Bopa always liked a surprise, so she ran forward and opened one. It contained sweet meats. She smiled, bringing a sample to her lips. I picked up the other two bundles. I was feeling a bit embarrassed. Why should there be gifts?

Then I turned and saw in the window of the neighbouring house a woman, who put hands together to greet me.

11: The novice parasol bearers

So after that, Bopa and I were safe. We had plenty to eat. And we were no longer shunned. But we did not become normal members of the prince's household, far from it. Women invited us to walk with them to the canal for clothes washing, but there they tried to take our dirty garments from us and scrub them themselves, saying, please, let us help, you take a rest. Others came to the house to inquire after us, but they also brought more gifts of food – catfish, rice cakes, water spinach, sugar cane. I had no idea how to respond. I wanted only to be no different than they.

Each morning I awoke and wondered if this would be the day when my husband would return and show me the way to live in this strange place. And my boy – he would come too. This new life would not be so bad if I could see my boy.

But each evening, the lamp extinguished, my daughter and I lay down to sleep having seen neither of them.

It was not that we had no news. It was that it was always unreliable, never the same day to day. We might hear one morning that our prince had become established at the Chaiyapoom Estate. But an hour later, it would be said that he was on the march to some other estate. My husband and son were at his side. No, don't believe that – they were not, they had remained behind at Chaiyapoom.

Then late one morning, as I sat on my haunches in the rear of the house, cleaning ash from the brazier, Bopa called to say there was a young man in front asking for me.

I went to the door. My goodness, how respectful this young man was – like the compound women, in fact. He was kneeling at the foot of the steps, hands together, looking to the ground, as if I were some kind of royalty.

I descended, rather too quickly, and stood facing him.

He spoke up, in a rather timid voice. 'I bring a message to Mrs Sray, wife of Nol the parasol master. The message is from Nol the parasol master.'

I think I began to tremble. 'Well, please, go ahead and tell me it.'

He closed his eyes to recite. 'Dear wife, your son and your husband are in good health. We are at the prince's side daily. We hope to see you soon.'

'That's all?'

That brought a grimace – he took it as his own fault. 'I am sorry, wife of the parasol master. There is no more.'

I had prayed so hard for any real news at all, but now I felt disappointed, even cheated, that what came was so little.

'Well, then, young man. Come inside and drink some water.'

'You are very kind.' He stood up and now I noticed that behind him lay a bundle wrapped in cotton fabric, a long one. Of course! A closed parasol. He picked it up, and brought it up with him into the house. It was an awkward fit inside – he was afraid he would bump something with it. He apologized more than once, but you can imagine that he had the strictest orders never to let it out of his sight. He laid it down along a wall.

I poured him a bowl of water from our stoneware jar.

'And what is your name then, please, young man?'

'Ma'am, I am Veng.'

'And who are you, Veng?' He had the weathered skin of a boy raised in the sun that shines hard on rice fields. His skin would change, surely, in his new calling.

'I am a parasol bearer, ma'am. A member of your husband's team.'

He made a smile of the most genuine pride, and I was warmed as well. Perhaps my husband's new occupation was for the good, bringing such feelings to a farm boy.

He finished his water quickly, not wishing to inconvenience me, and made to leave. But I gave him more water, then spoke to him softly, doing my best to put him at ease, and presently he began to tell me a little bit, glancing from time to time at his bundle, even inside here, to assure it was safe. This Veng was quite a sharp young man, it turned out. Within an hour, I had the first reliable picture of what had happened to my husband and son in the many weeks they had been gone.

Veng had grown up in Kralann village. Do you remember? That was the one that had made the parasols. One day a runner arrived from the city with a piece of slate, the one my husband sent shortly after the Brahmin called at our house. The slate was placed in the hand of the headman, and of course everyone crowded around to hear the headman read it aloud – it wasn't every day that a runner came to this place. The message announced a return to service and it placed an order for four parasols. People were variously elated, or dumbfounded, or disbelieving. After all these years? Are we too being recalled? Could it be some joke that a city person is playing on us country folk? The headman examined the writing and the choice of words. On the spot he announced he believed it was in fact the hand of Nol, son of Heng the late parasol master of the Chaiyapoom Estate. There was no questioning after that. Everyone got to work.

Three days later, my husband and son arrived, on foot, walking along a paddy dike.

The entire population of the village, fifty or sixty people, turned out in welcome. All were on their knees, with the grey-haired headman in front.

'Mr Nol, sir, it's really you! You've come back to us, as you said you would!'

I tell you, this Veng's face lit up all over again recalling this moment. His new life had begun with my husband's arrival.

The headman explained to Nol at some length that the village had never forgotten the skills of fashioning the blessed implements. The skills had been kept in reserve for such a revival. Parasols for a prince! A prince of the Third Rank!

The headman led the way for an inspection, amid a general scurrying about of adults and children. Nol and my boy were taken to a pile of thick green bamboo, newly cut and neatly stacked. I would come to know this process quite well, and I can picture how it was presented that day.

The basic framing material, located by the village's own men in the forests, was taken only from groves that get just the right amount of water and light, where the soil is friendly. It was not bought from merchants. Step one in the fabrication process: a man taking up a saw and with quick, strong strokes cutting a section lengthwise, a bit longer than an arm, then standing it upright. Then out comes a heavy iron knife. Its blade is placed on the fresh cross-section, then forced quickly downward. The bamboo splits smartly along the grain – this is the most pleasing thing to watch. This the man does over and over, creating strips. These are taken to the next artisan, who sits on a low wooden platform. She is a women – this next step is too delicate for a man. She has a knife too, but a smaller one whose long handle she braces between elbow and torso. Its blade dances about, guided by some friendly spirit or else it would cut her. It creates smaller, more delicate strips, each notched in just such a way, with identical curving contours. The pieces are taken and assembled by other workers into a parasol frame. Ribs radiate from a hub, everything held together by white string that runs a complex course through tiny holes and notches.

My husband and son were also shown a woman who painted tiny lotus blossoms on stretched silk, a man who applied silver paint to handles. Each parasol would come with three of these handles – short for use when the prince was walking, mid-length for when he rode a horse or palanquin, long for when he sat atop an elephant. Finally, the visitors inspected a pair of women who sewed the silver-trimmed sampots that bearers would wear when on duty.

My husband told the headman: 'Very good job! No one here has lost the skills. Our prince will be pleased.'

He went on to say that the prince's household would also need four palm-leaf fans with silver shafts and four fly whisks, for keeping winged insects clear of the royal form. These were to be delivered to the Capital in two weeks' time. It would be good if the artisans also began working on spares for these.

The headman of course wanted some news of this prince, and everyone around him did too. 'Your message said he was going to Chaiyapoom, sir. Has he now returned to the Capital?'

Nol answered that for now he was at the estate. 'But it is not important where the prince is,' he said grandly. 'What matters is that, wherever he comes and goes, he continues to rise in the esteem of King and Heaven.'

The foreman glanced toward the gathering visitors, as if to

say, hear this wisdom, let it improve you. Veng would not have dreamed of telling me, but I can guess that the headman was also saying, pay no attention to the fact that our patron has only one ear. How he must have wanted to ask how that came to pass.

Veng would have talked on and on about my husband, but I steered him to tell me something about my boy. Oh yes! he said. Our master Nol put a hand to his son's shoulder when the two of them arrived. 'This is my son, Sovan. He will train as a parasol master, like his father, and one day will take his place.' The villagers all turned Sovan's way and raised hands in greeting, some of them going back to their knees. I can imagine that my boy looked to the ground, uneasy. He was always that way, preferring to watch, rather than be watched.

That night, the visitors lay down to sleep in the headman's house; outside, people were still hurrying about, attending in lamplight to final preparations. By morning, the parasols were closed up and wrapped for transport. The headman brought four young men he had chosen to be bearers – Veng was one of them, of course.

Mothers packed clothing and food into kramas for the journey. At their request, the four formal sampots were brought out of their coverings and displayed, to general delight. Then good-byes were said and the four young men fell into line. I am sure they felt a bit apprehensive about what life would be under the stern little man who was now their master. Final prayers were said, and the headman stepped to Nol with last-minute directions on how to cross the paddy land and reach the north trunk road by nightfall. Nol made a show of listening, but he wouldn't have needed need the directions. He knew these paths from childhood.

They walked all day. Late in the afternoon, monsoon showers wet them down, but the oiled coverings protected the parasols. Nol checked them several times. Toward dusk the skies cleared and the village men, tiring from the pace and the weight of their burden, were hoping for a break. They whispered to Sovan. No doubt they had begun to see him as their interlocutor, and he tried gently to persuade his father. But Nol wouldn't listen – they would keep up until they came to the north trunk road.

Finally, under the light of a gibbous moon, they reached it. There was no village here, just more rice paddies. But in one of the fields they could make out an old thatched shelter in which farmers slept at harvest time. Nol gave instructions that they would bed down there for the night. On its floor of split bamboo, the bearers-to-be ate rice their mothers had sent with them, then lay down gratefully, ready to sleep amidst the warmth of their friends' bodies, trying to ignore the mosquitoes that quickly found them. But Nol wasn't done – those poor boys, they hadn't yet learned what kind of man they were now serving.

He made his new charges sit up and watch lesson number one: Their master walking up and down outside the shelter, in the light of the moon, holding a length of cast-off bamboo as the staff of a parasol.

'The goal is that the parasol seems to float on its own. Do you see what I mean? It has life and grace in itself. You the bearer just happen to be walking beneath it.'

Veng saw that, even in the dark and with imaginary parasol, things really did look that way. It was as if the bamboo staff would have continued on its own had my husband let go.

'Soon,' said Nol, 'you'll all be able to do this. Or you'll be sent back to the village. There will be no appeal.'

They got back on the move at dawn. Nol bought morning rice for the group in the first village they reached, and stood over them, watching them eat, before he took some himself. When it was time to leave, he commandeered a passing oxcart, citing the needs of the prince's business.

He rode, so as to devote all his energy and concentration to lesson number two, which he delivered sitting on the back, legs dangling, facing the trainees following just behind on foot.

'The bearer must always know instinctively where the sun is in relation to the royal personage. The bearer must anticipate turns that the procession will make and position himself accordingly, so that the sun's rays never strike the royal skin. This helps assure that the royal personage's skin remains pale and beautiful, like a god's, as Heaven intended the skin of its earthly representatives to be, not baked brown like a farmer's. It is of course not possible to completely shield that skin in every conceivable motion and eventuality, but that is the ideal and it can be achieved in all but the most exceptional circumstances.

'When operating a palm fan that is mounted on a pole, the bearer must be aware of the state of the air. When it is still, strong, firm strokes of the fan are warranted, to give maximum cooling effect to the personage. When the air is moving, the fan plays a complementary role, not fighting the air's flow but filling in, bringing coolness to the side of the royal body that the flow neglects.

'In all of this, there is one sin that can never be committed. At no time can the implements come into contact with the royal personage's body. Leg, arm, chest, hand – any part of that body. And, Heaven save you, not the head. Can you imagine what would be the penalty should a fan or a parasol touch this holiest of things? You would not dare touch the head of a beggar by the roadside; imagine what would happen were you to touch the head of a prince!'

The party spent the night at a country shrine that took in travellers. The next morning, with his men bathed and ready to go, Nol announced that today the training would be different. The men would move as a mock procession. He formed them up two-by-two and told each to hold his folded parasol up, as if it were open – it could not, of course, be opened, given the absence of a royal personage. He played the role of a prince, walking in the middle, and on his cue they advanced as a group. With a strip of bamboo, he smacked the shoulders of any man who fell out of step or let his staff waver.

'The bearer is constantly at close quarters with the royal personage and sometimes overhears private words. Under no circumstance can the bearer appear to comprehend – indeed, in your case, that will generally not be a problem, because among themselves Their Highnesses often speak a language that village men cannot understand, the language of the palace and Heaven. But it is possible that as time passes you will come to know certain words and phrases. You must give no sign of this. And anything learned in this way must be treated in the strictest confidence, never repeated to anyone. *Anyone*. It is the moral thing to do, of course, and also the safe thing. The penalty for revealing the private words of your royal masters can be – well, the same as it can be for touching the head.'

On until evening, it was like this – Nol dispensing knowledge, the four young men listening closely, fearful they'd miss something and displease the master. I am sure that Sovan struggled too.

After five days, the team arrived at a small crossroads settlement, a collection of huts and market stalls, the last before Chaiyapoom. Nol sat the four men and my boy down in an eating stall and ordered rice soup all around. Then he walked knowingly to the old woman who was stooping by the fire.

She looked up. Her hand flew to her mouth. 'My goodness, it's the little parasol bearer!' It was like she'd seen a ghost. 'And now a man! We all thought your soul had passed long ago...'

Nol beamed. 'It hasn't yet, as you can see. I've come back. And I'm a full parasol master now. For Prince Indra. Perhaps you've heard the name.'

'Of course I've heard the name!'

'Well, you might spread the word here that I am in his service and if anyone from Prince Teng's household brings trouble to me, he'll have to answer to Prince Indra.'

'Oh, no need to worry about that! Teng's people are all swearing allegiance to Prince Indra or running for their lives.'

'I don't understand...' That just slipped out, I'm sure. My husband tried always to hide that he might be ignorant of something.

'You don't know? Prince Teng is dead, thank goodness! Prince Indra killed him and is master of the estate.'

Can you appreciate what those few words meant to Nol? Not a hint of the happenings at Chaiyapoom had reached him. Yet he could now imagine a life of serving his prince in the very audience hall where his father served his. The children and I would live in the house in which he was raised. Sovan would be parasol master of Chaiyapoom, the bloodline would be restored!

'From what we hear,' the woman was saying, 'the new prince is quite deserving and blessed by the gods. And very fine looking too! The old one? Selfish. And fat.' She put hands out before her belly. 'He never even paid his bills in the market here! And he was getting way too friendly with the Siamese.'

'The Siamese?' There was no end to surprises that day.

'Yes, them. They sent a high-ranking man to the estate to talk last month. He came at night and left at night. But before he did, his servants came here to buy food and to drink with the girls.'

'You're sure they were Siamese?'

'Oh, yes. One of them spoke our language, a bit. He had a drink or two – in that stall right over there – and made a point of saying how big the city back in their territory was and how important his master was in the Siamese chieftain's army. Everyone in the market heard it. You can ask.'

When my husband had gotten all he could from this woman, he strode about the market, questioning other people. Then he returned to the bearers and told them to put aside their food – it was time to go. They set off down the road, Nol striding so quickly that Veng and the others had trouble keeping up.

The party followed the road up a hill, past an outcrop of rocks, and – there it was, across an expanse of open land below. The Chaiyapoom Estate. Nol stopped and turned away from the others, I imagine because tears had stolen shamefully into his eyes. Perhaps he had expected the palace would be changed, but it was not. The dark polished teak of its walls reflected the sun like a sheet of water. Large windows gulped in the breeze. On the eaves of its soaring red-tiled roof a hundred minor deities stood guard as before, repaying the favour of depiction by protecting against fire and enemies. Red standards that fluttered from bamboo poles signalled that the lord of the estate was in residence. That would be the new lord. His lord.

The palace stood in the embrace of a loop that the district's primary river traced out here – there was water on all sides except the one that faced the arriving travellers. To the left, the old stone temple, built near a small waterfall, showed itself above the trees, its pyramid spire reaching a respectable height for a country place of worship. To the right were the blacksmith shed, the rice stores, pens for pigs and poultry, houses of senior retainers. His house among them – he could see its roof and its private jetty on the river, even from here.

Sovan looked too. I think perhaps now he was sharing some of his father's excitement. Veng and the other bearers eyed the sight with less complicated emotions. This was simply the first country palace – perhaps the first palace of any kind – that they had ever seen. They began whispering, until Veng signalled for quiet, concerned that their talk would disturb the master. Perhaps it was at this point that Veng first realized he had become the team foreman.

Nol snapped out of his reverie. 'Form up!' he ordered. 'Two-by-two. Sovan, I will lead, and you will fall in behind me. We will proceed to the palace. We will bathe in the river to wash off the dust of the journey and then we will begin our service to our prince.'

The waterfall's gentle call reached the men as they passed through the front gate. Ahead they saw the Brahmin Subhadra and Commander Rit. A welcoming party, no doubt. But then my husband's triumph ended abruptly. The two men turned their backs on him. They were in the grip of a very emotional argument.

12: Nol's entreaty

'The order is clear, commander,' the priest was saying. 'It's from the prince himself, and it won't be reversed. You and your men have one hour to prepare.'

'I don't believe it,' the soldier responded. 'Our prince would never order us home this way, heads down, no weapons. The order's from you! Only a Brahmin would tell military men to disarm. Leave it to Heaven, never mind that people will come cut our throats!' He turned to an aide. 'Tell the men to stay where they are.'

'You will do no such thing,' Subhadra countered. 'I forbid it.'

The commander's hand was on his knife. Subhadra steeled himself: 'Commander, I will not be intimidated. But if you don't accept my word, hear it from the prince himself. Come see us right here in half an hour.'

The man spat on the ground.

Subhadra watched him leave, then turned to my husband. 'So you've arrived, Nol One-Ear,' he said wearily. 'I'm afraid it turns out there's no need for you. We're cutting back the prince's household staff by half. That includes you and your men. Drink some water, collect some rice from the kitchen, then head back to the Capital.'

'But we, we can't!' Poor Nol would have been practically stammering. 'We've come so far – and we have four parasols.'

'Princes of the Third Rank get two.'

'I know, sir. But now he is Lord of Chaiyapoom, and that makes him...'

'He is still a Prince of the Third Rank, and he is not Lord of Chaiyapoom. Now, leave without delay. Send your men back to their village and go wait in your house to hear from us. And pray that it's us you hear from and not the King's guard.' Then he called to a passing servant. 'Take the red standards down. The lord of the estate is not in residence. He is in Heaven, taken there by the fumes of his funeral pyre.'

So you see what had happened. The priest was taking very seriously the prince's plea for direction that first night at the estate. The direction he was receiving was to disperse his men and make gestures of atonement to the Capital in hope of somehow winning forgiveness.

The Brahmin went off to tend to some other matter. Nol gestured that the bearers and Sovan follow him to the river. There he told them to bathe. He joined them in the water, hurrying them along. Then when they stood on the bank, drying themselves, unsure what to do, Nol gave another order.

He pointed to Veng and another bearer. 'You two – put on your ceremonial garments. Take two parasols and come with me.'

This did not sound like what the Brahmin had ordered, of course, but no one challenged it. Nol led the way to the hut where the estate's parasols were stored. There he found two young bearers lounging about, the ones who'd been engaged in the Capital for this journey. With a few sharp words, he dismissed them.

He turned to his own two men. 'Our prince will not be served by market hirelings, but by people who serve by loyalty to the bloodline.' He looked them hard in the eye – you will not fail me, he was saying. 'Now bring your parasols. Prepare for your first duty!'

He led them to the palace door, and positioned one on either side. Then he paced up and down, waiting.

Then there he was, striding out the door – Prince Indra. And again, what a prince he was! Nol, Veng, the other boy, none could keep his eyes down as protocol required. They saw arms that were thick and able to swing the heaviest sword, jewels in the neckpiece catching the light. But the face? The face did not fit. It bore a doleful look.

Nol recovered himself and signalled to the two bearers. They did not disappoint – they snapped open their parasols smartly, then fell in on either side, as they had learned on the road. They moved with the prince toward the centre of the courtyard, followed by the Brahmin, who seemed not to notice that they were not the hired bearers. Ahead was Commander Rit, hand to his heart in a salute, dropping to his knees.

The prince spoke, but hardly in a booming voice. 'Commander, I have decided to return our forces to the Capital. It is a...temporary redeployment. We have seen with our own eyes our men's bravery and skill with weapons. That will always be remembered. But by Heaven's will there are times when...when the proper use of martial power is to choose not to use it. This we learn from the verses of the Mahabharata, may its texts be blessed.'

The Brahmin gave an approving nod. Nol grasped the obvious, that the priest had composed words that the prince was now reciting. What argument had the Brahmin made to him privately? An elaborate spiritual one, no doubt, with citations from scripture. Rank is a prize awarded by Heaven. It reflects virtue and it cannot be seized. But likely the priest added some real-world facts as well: The palace will not tolerate this, the other princes will not tolerate this. The people in the market will not support you. You are unknown to them. It is only a matter of time before an army marches on this estate to take you back to the Capital in a bamboo cage for a long and painful execution. Your only hope is to do no more wrong and plead for mercy.

'Highness,' said the commander, still on his knees. 'I ask you to reconsider. For my men it would be as if they'd been defeated, going home without their weapons, in small groups. Surely military men should remain together as a single force. There are a hundred different campaigns that show that.'

The prince seemed at a loss to answer; Subhadra took over. 'As the prince has shown us, there is no need to worry. Heaven smiles on a gesture of conciliation. And it provides one in return. Our King is a learned, pious man, imbued with holy virtues. He is forgiving and merciful. After our men arrive in the Capital, after he has received a letter of verse that His Highness Prince Indra will compose explaining what happened here, he will look on our prince and his soldiers with a similar conciliatory frame of mind.'

Tears were glistening in the commander's eyes, but he did not argue further. It was the soldier's way. He too had made a pact that the prince would be obeyed no matter how hard the order.

It might have all ended right there – the prince's career, my family's elevation, even the future course of the Empire. But then my husband spoke up.

How could he, why did he? It's true that in his lectures to his young charges, Nol had stressed a need to be servile, even deaf and blind in the presence of royalty. What he really meant is that that is the rule for the craft's foot soldiers, the men who clutch the staffs of the parasols and worry only that the shade will fall in the right direction. A parasol master is something more. He has sufficient rank in a court that physical proximity can breed familiarity and trust. Indeed, I am told that in our race's history not a few parasol masters have acquired power that rivalled that of the royalty they served. Normally, of course, that power is built up over the course of many years of service. A parasol master cannot be seen to be grabbing for it. But, as I said, the entire new life was at this moment hanging in the balance. Nol realized that he had what the prince's commander lacked, the wherewithal to undo the priest's order. He sensed too that whatever the prince might be saying, he was also yearning for a reversal.

'Highness.'

My husband's word was barely audible. The Brahmin glowered. He only now noticed Nol's presence. The prince frowned too at the intrusion. But Nol kept going.

'Highness. I beg permission to speak.'

The prince was squinting his way. The disfigurement was being examined, in the way that many men had done over the years and which in Nol only created determination.

'You are the new parasol master.'

'I am, Highness.'

The prince signalled he should proceed. It was because Nol had provided a distraction, I think, from a very painful encounter.

'I believe, Highness, that perhaps there is no need for your soldiers to turn in their weapons.'

'Be quiet, parasol master!' It was the Brahmin, indignant. 'You have no place to say such a thing. Highness, the audience is over and we...'

But just those few words from my husband had deprived the priest of control of the audience. Nol had restored a glimmer of hope in the prince. 'No, go on, parasol master. Why is there perhaps no need?'

'Because when news of what happened here reaches the Capital, the people will celebrate. The people hate the Siamese. And Siamese treachery has been defeated at this place.'

The prince turned to face Nol head-on. 'How is that?'

'The late Prince Teng was conspiring with the Siamese, Highness. He was about to become their vassal. His death has saved an entire province from being carved away and given to the Siamese enemy. He was conspiring with them to declare independence from the Empire.'

'Oh?'

'Yes, Highness. A senior Siamese man visited this place one month ago. The late Prince Teng received him in his audience hall. They carried out their plotting there.'

Subhadra tried again, stepping between the prince and my husband. 'I don't believe that such a person came here, Highness. And if he did, he was no doubt coming to negotiate terms of tribute that his Siamese master would pay to the Empire.'

But my husband had one more fact in him. 'It was a military man, Highness. A high-ranking one. Visit the market down the road and you will be told by everyone that this man's subordinates were not afraid to walk up and down there, fully armed, and to say who they and their master were. They seemed to feel this territory was theirs already. Now Prince Teng is dead. He was guilty of treason. All over the Empire people will learn about it and they will know that Your Highness has saved the Khmer race from catastrophe.'

Prince Indra pondered this for just a moment. Then he spoke. The loud, booming voice of a prince had returned. 'Commander, recall the soldiers!'

'Highness, you must not!' The blood had left Subhadra's face.

'The orders are cancelled, commander. Give the men back their weapons and then meet me in the armaments pavilion.'

'Yes, Highness!'

The prince gave a nod in Nol's direction, then strode back into the palace. Subhadra went hurrying after him, but it was clear to everyone, even to this young man Veng, that there would be no reversal of this decision.

And Nol? He was on his knees, eyes closed, whispering thanks. At times like this, he did see Heaven's hand in earthly events. Then he rose and went off to find his other bearers. Prince Indra is Lord of Chaiyapoom, he told his team. 'From this point on, our prince will have four parasols over him.'

13: The precocious young retainer

Perhaps you wonder how my husband came to have such determination. I will tell you now. Nol withheld the story from me for many years, and when he finally revealed it, it caused me both pity and deep disquiet. What kind of life did Nol live in the past to earn the one in which I knew him? It is not for me to know.

He was born at the Chaiyapoom Estate, as I have told you. But his birth is not where the story begins. We need to look back quite a few years earlier than that.

In those old days, everyone at the estate knew the woes of Nol's father Heng – how he had waited patiently for the birth of a boy, waited as baby girl after baby girl, eight in all, were presented to him by the estate's midwife. How his father took two minor wives, only to obtain more daughters. And how Nol finally appeared one morning sixteen years into the effort, after fully half of his family's wealth had been paid in silver to a jungle-dwelling shaman – this same Vibol – who specialized in commissions to steer the future. His father picked up the new-born and through tears of ebullience made an announcement to the people who had wandered over to see if this time the man's fortunes had changed.

'From the day this boy takes his first step,' he declared, 'he will begin his training.'

There was a practical reason for starting so quickly. Nol's father had married late, and now there loomed the danger that he would die before he could convey the skills of his craft. His master, Prince Vira, had begun to hint that as much as he disliked the idea, the post of parasol master in this provincial court might have to pass out of Heng's family, where it had resided for six generations. There was a logical replacement, everyone knew, the newly married second son of the master on the estate whose land began two hours' travel up the river.

So training did begin the day that Nol's first step occurred. His father was summoned home and, taking the tiny boy's hands in his, he walked him over to the parasol pavilion. That place became his nursery, and the men and women there his adoptive family.

Surely he would have been a different man had he had more time in his mother's lap. But those sweet times were not to be for him. He had to absorb the craft. In the pavilion, whatever the work at hand, there was always this boy in the midst, looking on, and, as he grew older, applying his own hands to the tasks. Quite a precocious boy, I'm sure. He was never allowed to wander out of sight, never even to join the children who gathered in the late afternoon for play at that waterfall near the palace. They would be a distraction from his training, and who could say but that on one of these occasions that second son up the river might pay a visit with a knife and a plan for securing his own future.

Over time, some of the estate's children came to treat the boy as already an adult and steered clear of him. Others made fun of him. Some did it right to his face – children can be cruel in that way. There was one little girl who, though she was much younger than he, delighted in trying to unsettle him by making demon faces in his direction when he stood in procession.

'Don't be so proud, Nol,' she whispered to him one morning as he waited with a parasol team for the lord Prince Vira to appear. 'You're only a boy.'

'Don't talk to me like that!' It would have been said in his best imperious voice. 'You have no right. You're the daughter of a concubine.'

'Be careful what you say! My mother is closer to our prince than your father, don't you think? I can make trouble for you.'

'You wouldn't dare.'

He turned his back on her and walked away. Supposedly, he had only just then thought of something that needed tending to before the procession. But I think that in fact he felt shame that this girl was not frightened of him.

By the time he was twelve, Nol knew as much as his father about how to distinguish good silk from bad, how to replace a fly whisk's missing strands, how to keep mildew from forming on palm-leaf fans during rainy-season storage. He had learned the calling's human side as well, which in some ways is as important as questions of craft. He could pick the right team for a particular audience, matching experience with the visitor's rank and business. He knew to get men into place without taking them past the estate's kitchen house, where at least one would otherwise stop to flirt with a maid. Inside the audience hall, he could recognize the subtle motions of the prince's hand that signalled how many petitioners gathered outside should be admitted to the hall. That is my husband, then – very sensitive to subtle things if they concern work, less sensitive if they concern life at home.

Nol travelled with his father, visiting twice a year the village near the Capital that made the estate's fans and parasols, the village Kralann. They went to the Capital itself for annual meetings of the guild of parasol masters. Twice they went along on military campaigns against the Chams, at the side of Prince Vira, who led a militia unit contributed by the estate.

And when he was thirteen, his father included him in an embassy that Prince Vira led all the way to the Siamese territory. There he sat nearby as the prince negotiated terms of the tribute the Siamese would send to the Capital. Nol learned customs of the Siamese, their language, their very way of thinking. What an honour it was for a boy that age, and how it must have affected his own assessment of himself.

When the embassy returned to Chaiyapoom, Nol's admirers were even more impressed with the boy and they began to show it. Probably it was at this time that he began to feel accustomed to being addressed with honorifics normally reserved for grown men. The estate's silversmith gave him armlets of a kind that normally would have come only after his training was complete. His father took pride in this treatment, as any father would. Probably he had come to feel by now that Nol would achieve more as a parasol master than he had. Yet there was no sign of when the boy might inherit the post. The father, people said, had stopped aging the day Nol was born.

Let us move forward now, to Nol's fifteenth year. One day, his father returned from Prince Vira's audience hall. He called his son, told him to sit, and then informed him that the prince had received an invitation to visit the estate up the river.

I've told you now perceptive my husband was, even as a boy. So you can understand that he grasped right away that this was significant. The estates' two princes had not met in years. I must tell you – this other prince was Prince Teng. He had become a chronic and delinquent debtor to Prince Vira and therefore avoided him. Year after year, the yields of Teng's paddyland had been falling. The local spirits had been courted with offerings and Teng's engineers had secretly built dikes to divert some of the water that by rights and tradition fed the fields of Prince Vira. But nothing worked. Each year, Teng sent an apologetic steward down the river to negotiate loans of rice and other staples from Vira's surplus. It was always depicted as a temporary advance against production that was sure to improve the following harvest. His steward never offered even a hint of acknowledgment that things could not go on in this way. So Vira and his courtiers made a decision. This year, when the man stepped up from the boat at the dock by the palace, he was welcomed, given cool water to drink, then politely informed that Vira's surplus had shrunk so small that sadly no additional loans could be made.

My future husband's first question to his father was: 'Did the invitation from Prince Teng include any word on what he plans to do concerning his debt?'

This was the question to ask, of course, and you can imagine that Heng smiled in pride. 'Yes. It expresses hope that he and Prince Vira can discuss the future ownership of paddy land that begins at the second village on the river.'

'Shouldn't Prince Teng come here instead?'

'The message suggests that our prince will want to inspect the land and therefore he is invited to go there, and that Teng wants to entertain him.'

Nol had seen the land in question from a distance, during one of Vira's tours of the outer sectors of his own estate. 'I would think, father, that it's just his opening offer – that land's not very good. Only a bit of it gets water.'

'You're right, it's not the best. But keep in mind that this is the first time we've had any kind of overture at all from Teng's side. Our prince is quite happy over the news. He believes, and so do I, that what's most important is that the prince there recognizes that things have to change.'

Nol was troubled, but he merely answered: 'Yes, father.'

I am finding I have difficulty continuing with the story. If only Heaven had seen fit that my husband, this boy, press his case more strongly that debtor should come to creditor! Or if only Heaven had sent a thunderstorm the next day, putting off the departure.

At that moment a servant brought bowls of water to drink.

'You know, Nol,' said Heng after a moment's reflection, 'in the old days, this kind of thing would have been settled by the magistrate in the provincial town across the hill. Our master would have sent a man there with the loan records. Someone from the other estate would have been called to answer for it. A decision would have been made. But the magistrate seems afraid now. He has no soldiers to back up his decisions. None of the noble families around here seem to care what he does now.' His father smiled grimly. 'But what can we expect when in the Capital we have a King who worries mostly about orchids?'

After morning rice the following day, the prince emerged from his palace and walked to the estate's dock. Waiting there was a long wooden boat with four parasol bearers, eight rowers and a helmsman wearing a bright blue sampot. Heng and Nol stood to the side and bowed as their lord passed, then followed him onto the vessel and sat down in the rear. Out on the water another boat was waiting, carrying bodyguards, the chief of the estate's grain stores and a scribe.

Rowers pulled at the water and the boats proceeded gently upriver. After a bit, Heng and Nol were called forward to join the prince. He sat cross-legged on a dais lined with silk, shaded by his four parasols. A tray with water and rice sweets had been set before him, but these he ignored. What always drew the prince's attention on a trip like this were sights of nature. As the boat advanced against a lazy current, he took pleasure in pointing them out to Nol and Heng – a gibbon peering out from a treetop, a pair of crocodiles sunning themselves on a sandy bank, an eddy covered with lily pads. I can see Nol smiling as he was expected to, trying to show interest, though for his whole life sights like these made him uneasy. He preferred the man-made order of a city or an estate's grounds.

After a while, Prince Vira turned to the business at hand. 'So, Heng, were you able to find those figures?'

'Yes, Highness. I spoke with the chief of the grain stores and he estimated that the land Prince Teng's people are offering would produce about six hundred weight of rice per year.'

'And what have they been borrowing from us?'

'About sixty-four hundred weight last year, Highness.'

'Ahh – so they're offering land that would take more than ten years to produce what they borrowed in just one year.'

'That's correct, Highness.'

'So what is your view?'

'My view, Highness, is to treat it as a given that you will get that piece of land, but that it will be just the appetizer to the meal.'

The prince smiled. 'And the main courses?'

'I spoke with a farmer who used to live on that estate. To the east of its principal settlement is a large block of paddies. They are old and fertile and on the far side there's a stream that flows into Your Highness's land. It's the one from which they've been diverting water. Those paddies would be a very good addition to your holdings and getting control of that stream would also end the problem of diversion.'

The prince mulled that, and then turned to Nol.

'And what does the boy think? I wonder if he's got some idea that wants to come bursting out.' You see, it was not only the retainers who took a special interest in Nol. 'Now come on, boy, don't be afraid to speak up.'

Nol was not afraid, of course. He was only pretending to be.

'My idea is the same as my father's, Highness.'

'But...'

'But perhaps Your Highness should add some type of security for the existing loans?'

'What kind? I'll bet you've thought it out.'

'Silver from Prince Teng's own body, Highness.'

Vira's eyes went wide at this suggestion. He was enjoying himself. 'Now why do that, boy?'

'Because every day he should be reminded that he owes a debt to Your Highness, that something important is missing from his own personal wealth. He won't like to give land, of course, but once you have taken it, he will forget it. He'll never visit it. But if each morning, after his wardrobe servants have applied his jewellery, he looks down and sees that a pendant is gone, he'll be reminded again who is the real lord of this region and what he must do if he is ever to get the pendant back.'

'So you know all about jewellery – no doubt from wearing some yourself, boy.' Prince Vira gave an approving tap to Nol's armlets. 'Now, it won't just make him angry?'

'There will be some anger, yes, Highness. But he will recognize that he has to put it aside. His estate is small compared to yours, his militia is smaller, and he will know that he must keep things peaceful.'

The prince turned to Nol's father. 'This is quite a strategist you've produced.' Then he looked back to the boy. 'It's an interesting idea, but I worry that it would get things off with the wrong tone. I would like to keep things friendly when we talk this time. It's been quite a few years, but I'd like to give Prince Teng a good-faith chance to set things straight, with his honour intact.'

'Yes, Highness.'

'Still, a very interesting idea, that one. Keep thinking them up.' Then the prince stirred: 'Now look there, Nol – a wild boar, a big one!'

Two hours later, the boat passed a stone marker on the shore that marked the start of Prince Teng's holdings. Nol looked up the river and saw the spire of a distant shrine. A sign of civilization. It was a welcome sight after this passage through the wild.

An hour later, the boats came upon a tangle of lily pads that covered much of the river. The prince's helmsman stood up to look for a way through, then called out a turn to the right, where there was a clear channel close to the bank. The boat entered it, with the second one close behind.

It was then that the wickedness began. There first came a whistle and a dull thud, nothing very loud. But the sounds were sufficiently odd that Nol glanced about seeking their source, curious. He looked to his master. A shaft of wood extended from the prince's upper chest. His jaw was slack; he was trying to raise his hands, but they wouldn't come. A storm of these whistle-thuds sounded and Nol realized that arrows were striking the boat.

He grabbed the tray that had held the prince's water and food and held it up as a shield, for him and for the prince. But it did no good. One arrow cut right through the tray, coming to rest half way along its shaft, another pierced the prince's neck.

Shouts of panic came from the rowers; some of them had been hit too. Prince Vira began to sink to the mat on his dais, bleeding. Nol used his free hand to try to hold him up, but the weight was too much.

Suddenly, noise that seemed a mix of human shouts and animal snarls was coming from below. There were men in the water, concealed in the mass of lily pads, and they were thrusting knives and spear points over the edge of the boat. More shouts were heard, this time from the boat of bodyguards behind. It was capsizing.

Men in Nol's boat began swinging their paddles at the men in the water, but to pathetic effect. More arrows streaked in from the bank. One grazed Nol's upper arm. The prince was lying face down now, blood pooling around his face. Nol could not help. It was now that he remembered his father. He dropped the tray and turned to look for him, but he was gone. A struggle was underway in the water over the side, and Nol saw men setting like wild dogs on a bleeding form clad in the same colour fabric that his father had been wearing. The prince was in even more trouble now. A dripping man in a loincloth was squatting over him, thrusting a small knife into his body again and again.

Another hand with another knife lunged up from the water. Nol dodged it, and I think that now, for the first time, he became terrified for himself. He turned and launched himself head-first high over the side of the boat. He passed over writhing forms, then hit the water, or rather a wet tangle of leaves and stems. He struggled to stay beneath the surface, to move away as fast as he could. He came up for a breath, pushing off a stout root that seemed to grab his ankle, and then he went down again. He had one objective, to fight his way clear of the vegetation. In open water he might find a friendly current that would carry him downstream, away from the mayhem. He bumped against human forms, some dead, some alive. Wicked hands reached for him, but found nothing to hang on to. Surfacing for a second time, he heard noise only from behind. He was free of the vegetation now. He caught a glimpse of the far bank – it seemed to be moving, but then he realized it was he who was moving. He was in the current's grip. He went down again and kicked hard to help it move him along. Then he felt terror as he met something long and abrasive, first on his face, then the length of his body. He realized it must be a net, strung across the river by Teng's men to prevent their victims from escaping. The current was now his enemy, pressing him against the net, holding him under. His breath was giving out, but something told him not to try for the surface, but to go further down. He did, feeling with his hands, the water becoming a deeper brown, then a terrifying black as he descended. Then he felt the sand of the river's bed. Here the net was not taut. He lifted it. The current, now helping him again, propelled him through. On the other side, he broke to the surface, gasping. The shouts and the clank of metal on metal were receding now.

The current kept him moving, but soon it was all he could do to stay afloat. His armlets were heavy, and so he pulled them off and let them sink into the darkness below. After a while he grew fatigued again and felt himself sinking and only then did he make for the bank. His feet found bottom. He stumbled ashore and collapsed on a bar of sand. He lay panting, but when his breathing calmed he felt exposed, and forced himself to crawl up the bank and hide behind a gum tree.

What a shock it all was. He was only fifteen and had never been in personal danger.

He took stock. The cut the arrow had made on his arm was small and no longer bleeding. He had no other real injuries. But he was sure he was still on land owned by Prince Teng. He had nothing, save the sampot that clung to his waist and silver bangles around his wrists. He began to consider how to get home. Perhaps he could float the rest of the way once he'd rested. He looked back to the river – but no, the current was quite slow from here on. And with a start, he remembered the crocodiles. He would have to go on foot and steal past villagers and guards. He would wait for darkness.

He lay down and began to shiver, though he was not cold. Scenes from the slaughter replayed themselves in his mind; he was horrified at how loud and messy the process of killing was. He searched his memory for clues as to what had happened to his father, but he had only that single image of a bleeding form in the water. Perhaps Heng was already dead even then.

When the sun was low, he saw something long and large approaching in the river. At first he took it for a crocodile, but then he saw it was a body, lashed to a log! Behind it, as if in procession, were half a dozen more. Prince Teng's men had removed the net, it seemed, and were sending the dead downstream as a taunt. Can you imagine such cruelty?

As night fell, Nol sat with knees pressed to his chest, casting glances into the foliage overhead. He had become convinced that there was a menacing spirit in the leaves, one that had been feeding off the floating bodies and had now alighted here in hopes of getting live flesh. He crawled away from the tree and waited some more, and when full darkness arrived and the night insects began their chorus, he took a deep breath and marched himself into the jungle. Immediately, rocks were biting at his feet, vines and low-hanging branches at his face and shoulders. Each step seemed to disturb some creature that fled unseen with a terrifying rustle. He soon realized it is not possible to move in pitch black through jungle. There wasn't even starlight to help. He made his way back to the riverbank and found another tree, this one seeming more receptive to his presence. He pressed his head to the dirt to ask its spirit's protection. Then he sat himself down, back to the bark, to wait out the night.

He'd chosen the tree well, because its spirit let him sleep and kept animals and all but a few insects away. When dawn began, he got to his feet, then set off again through the jungle. But before he'd moved even a short distance, the foliage gave way to paddy land. Not so far across it were perhaps twenty farmers, Teng's farmers, weeding. Beyond them was their village. Nol could see no way around. The river now seemed more appealing as a route home.

Find a log, he told himself, and float with it downstream. Any of Teng's people who see it will think you're just another of the dead. And perhaps, perhaps any crocodile that sees you will no longer be hungry. He began searching and not ten paces from his friendly tree he found a log – a freshly fallen one, with some wilted foliage on it. He turned to the tree and its empathetic spirit, put hands together to express thanks, then dragged the log to the water. He grabbed hold of a branch, and kept all but his head submerged.

After perhaps half an hour, he saw the stone that marked the border of Prince Teng's estate. A bit beyond was another horrifying sight. Caught in an eddy was one of the waterborne corpses, still in a blue sampot. It seemed to be the helmsman.

Several hours later came the tree where the prince, the late prince, had pointed out the gibbon. Not much further down, on the left bank, would be the retainers' houses, his own family's among them, the first sign of the Chaiyapoom Estate's main settlement. Then the river would curve sharply right and back to the left to trace its arc around the estate house. Nol mouthed a prayer of thanks to the log, and said good-bye to it.

He came ashore near the houses, hiding himself among brush. Things were strangely silent. The scent of smoke hung in the air, stronger than what cooking fires make. From the top of the bank, he saw another terrible sight: two of the houses were smouldering ashes. All others that he could see, including his own, seemed deserted. But soldiers with spears were standing by his very own house, conferring about something. They wore helmets of a kind he didn't know. Then one of them moved and Nol saw behind him a corpse, its sampot stained in red. *Who?* It seemed to be one of his sisters!

I half imagine that when he came ashore he was still a boy, but when he saw this, he became a man.

He crept back down to the river, swam out to the middle, then let the current carry him around the great bend. Just above the waterfall, he emerged again, this time on the right bank, where a thicket grew. He hid among its friendly leaves. From here he had a partial view of the estate palace and temple. Again – bodies sprawled in shocking poses on the ground. And armed men standing around everywhere, seemingly bored by the sights around them. A few had straw bags over their shoulders, others had jewellery draped over their arms.

Then the men came suddenly to order. A horse with rider appeared, with an escort of guards and four parasol bearers. It was Prince Teng, inspecting his conquest. He got down from the horse, then entered the palace. It was his now.

As dusk approached, Nol lay hidden, nibbling nervously at the leaves of strange plants, spitting them out. He decided he must get away from this place. He had no idea where to go, but somewhere Prince Vira's people would be coming together, gathering weapons, preparing to retake to estate. He would find them.

He began to walk, hoping that maybe just in the next grove was such a gathering. But there was no one. He pressed on. One moment he was hurrying along a trail through tall grass, the next there was a woman right there on the ground in front of him, lying still. It was the wife of Prince Vira's militia commander.

He went to his knees by her and her eyes opened.

'Nol – you, at least!'

Her eyes closed and she let out a long breath and said it again: 'You, at least.' There was blood on her calf; her garment was stained.

Then she asked: 'Do you have any water?' He answered no, ashamed that he could not meet even this simple request.

She lay back, panting. 'Where is the prince? And the guardsmen?'

Nol could only say: 'Not with me.'

'But they'll come soon?'

'I'm sure.'

'They have to, they have to. The whole estate is filled with these men....They came at midday. I don't know how it happened – but they got past the guards at the gate. It was awful. I hid, for the whole afternoon, I hid in a rice bin and I heard a man say,

say, that the prince's staff and all their families must be caught and killed.'

'Did you see my mother, my sisters?'

She did not answer.

'They got my husband. Oh, I saw that. They got one of my two boys. And they got me as well, but in a different way. But...then I went into the water and swam.'

Nol looked down at her. All he could hope to do was comfort her with his presence.

'You! Hold it there!'

Two soldiers had come into sight down the trail.

'Let's run!' Nol cried. But she seemed not to hear. He tried to pull her to her feet. But she merely stared blankly, unable to move, and then collapsed to the ground again. And so Nol ran away on his own.

When he stopped, exhausted, deep in the forest, he could hear no steps behind him. Darkness had fallen. He stepped off the trail and lay down.

Early the next afternoon, he sat in a food stall in the market of a small town, gobbling down noodles bought with silver from selling the two bangles, the only jewellery he had not abandoned to the river. A magistrate's assistant arrived with two guards. The man announced to the market goers that members of a terrible criminal gang were on the loose, having murdered their own prince and master, the beloved Prince Vira, even their own parents. There would be a reward of fifty silver ingots for anyone turning members of the gang over to Prince Teng, who was safeguarding the late prince's property as he worked to avenge this crime. Then came the names of the fugitives: Nol, son of the late parasol master; Rom, daughter of the late chief concubine; Rit, son of the late militia commander. Nol looked the assistant's way, because that seemed the inconspicuous thing to do, and kept eating.

From that market, he set out for the village that produced the parasols. He arrived at night, four days later. He was hungry, dirty, exhausted. The headman gasped on seeing this and took him directly into his house. But really what could this man do? He kept Nol in hiding a few days, sent word to a relative in the Capital who of course lacked power to help. Prince Teng's account of events had been accepted in the palace, where he had powerful family members. The Chaiyapoom Estate was indeed now his.

After a few days, it was decided that for the safety of everyone, Nol would go to stay with a cousin of the headman far to the south, near the Salt Water Sea.

'I will come back here one day,' said Nol, as he took his leave. 'And this village will make parasols again for the lord of Chaiyapoom.'

'I know it will happen, master Nol,' said the headman. 'When you are ready, we'll be here.'

So Nol departed. But he never made it to that cousin's village.

After a day on the road, he stopped at a travellers' hostel and lay down to sleep on a mat. He awoke to find that four young men had come in during the night. He began talking with the one who seemed to be in charge.

They were dredgers, headed for a job three districts away at a reservoir that had silted up.

'We're short a man,' said the head, a jovial type who found nothing suspicious in Nol's accent. 'Do you want to come? One silver pebble a day, plus food and a place to sleep. And lots of pretty girls in the market. The job will run about two weeks. What do you think?'

My future husband said yes.

There it is, then. He began his life in privilege. His entire family was murdered, and he was reduced to being a canal dredger. When I learned this story many years later, I finally understood the anger that I had always sensed within him.

14: The palace pantry

I have told you that on the day when peace returned to the prince's compound in the Capital, I had hoped that the people there would accept Bopa and me as no different from them. But special treatment continued, in ways larger than being offered little gifts.

One day, Mr Narin called at the house with news that Bopa and I would move. He described the new place, and I knew it immediately. It was the largest retainer house in the compound, with a new tile roof and a carved doorframe. I was quite sure that two families, maybe three, had been living there, sharing it. I asked him.

'Oh yes, that's right,' replied Mr Narin. 'Three families. But now they've moved back to their home villages, on business of the prince. They will have large houses there. And since their former place is sitting vacant, going to waste, I thought...'

I protested that he must reconsider. But the next morning, six slaves showed up with empty baskets. Other women from the compound – they had been told what was happening – came and helped us pack our things. And when the baskets were filled and lined up at the foot our steps, as if awaiting a journey across the Empire, I went back into the house for a last time and knelt at its shrine. I gave thanks to the household spirit for the shelter and protection it had accorded Bopa and me, and asked please that it would recognize that we'd rather have stayed put, but that people more powerful than we had arranged this move.

There are times when kneeling at an image that I say things that are less than true, that I make excuses for my own behaviour, but this was not one of them. Mr Narin was a kind man, he had gone out of his way for us more than once. And he was our guide and protector here, with my husband still away. So I resigned myself, saying nothing when the day after we moved into the new house I discovered that the former occupants were in fact still in the compound, now sharing a smaller house.

But I was finally driven to action a few days later when a girl of maybe twelve years appeared at our steps and announced that she had been sent as a maid.

I went right away to see Mr Narin. I found him at work in his pavilion, palm-leaf ledgers spread out before him. He was at a low teak table that had a flawless finish and, like so much else around the prince's compound in those days, looked brand new.

Mr Narin rose with the genuine courtesy he always extended. He invited me to sit. A servant I hadn't seen before brought tea.

'Sir,' I said after some small talk, 'Sir...' And then it began. 'You have given us too much, sir. We don't need such a big house. We don't need a maid. There is only myself and my daughter. And women in the compound are always leaving gifts at the door. The gods will think I want too much, that I'm greedy and I....'

'Please, please,' he replied softly, seeming to have known what I would say. 'Don't you see that everyone in the prince's service is coming to live better? It's quite natural you should have some comforts. Our master is rising in stature and he is sending silver and valuables from the campaign in the Upper Empire.'

'But sir, we don't need anything more than we already have.' I was already losing control of the conversation.

'Perhaps you don't need it, Mrs Sray. But you deserve it. Especially you. You are the wife of a man who is fast at His Highness's side, who is loyal through and through. And your husband's rank can only rise further. As you know better than I, Mrs Sray, the priests teach that certain rewards are enjoyed by those people who serve well on this earth, who assist Heaven in bringing order and prosperity to society. Your husband does that, and you do it too. Don't you think it would be unfair if the other women were not allowed to show respect to you and your family with gifts from time to time, for the help you gave during the siege here, the food you shared, for the risks you took to safeguard us all? I am among those who are in your debt.'

I frowned. For an instant, my mind pictured a jungle clearing, in which a man lay dying, his skull crushed from the blow of a shovel.

Please! I will tell you about that in time. But for now, take it as enough to know that I was not at all deserving of this kind of praise.

So, I began to cry, right there, with Mr Narin sitting across the table. His face fell and he hurried around to my side and knelt. But he did not know what to do. Oh, what I put the poor man through.

'Mr Narin!' I said presently, wiping back a tear. 'Sometimes I wish I could go back to my old house. The one back in the little quarter behind the mountain-temple Pre Rup. Our life was so much simpler there. The children played outside, there weren't so many temptations, there was no problem with soldiers. I had something to keep me busy, I had a life in the market. I sold ducks eggs, did you know? I did it every day, for twelve years.'

'Please, Mrs Sray,' he said, finding his voice. 'Give it a while longer. You'll come to feel comfortable here, maybe sooner than you think.'

I thanked him and walked back to the house. I arrived there to find Bopa sitting alone in the front room, playing at a dice game. Where had it come from? I had no idea – probably another gift. The little maid was in the back, trying to manoeuvre a broom that was too large for her. Sweeping was supposed to be Bopa's job. I felt exasperated all over again.

The next day, a slave from the palace kitchen came and announced that the presence of Mrs Sray was requested.

I followed him. Why wouldn't I? My life was no longer my own. We walked silently past a pond, then a stable, to a part of the compound I had never visited. In it stood a long wooden house that announced its function with the scent of charcoal and sizzling greens and spices. Inside, a large man turned from a collection of braziers, wiped his hands on a dirty cloth tucked into his waist, and put them together to greet me.

'I'm told, Mrs Sray,' he said cheerfully, 'that you might be able to help solve a problem.'

'What problem?'

'This!' He reached into a basket and held up a mango.

I could see that it had been picked too early; the colour hadn't come in properly. He passed it to me and I confirmed with my fingers. Its flesh lacked the requisite bit of give.

'And this.' He gestured toward a bucket. There were live prawns in it, in water. 'Too small,' he said, stating the obvious.

'And tasteless. Not even fit for slaves! We have young girls without a trace of sense in their heads going to the market for us in the morning. And they're supposed to find the good stuff? They hardly even know how to count. You give them silver and they come back with no idea or how much they've spent and for what.' He grimaced. 'And I'm supposed to make food fit for serving in a palace.'

'That can't be easy...'

'Yes, yes. Now, don't you see, Mrs Sray, that if these girls had some direction, from someone who knew the market, and all the tricks people play there, our life would be much easier? We'd get the respect we deserve from the vendor women. We'd get good produce and good fish and meat. And save money, even.'

I asked: 'What time do they go?'

'An hour after dawn, usually.'

'That's too late. The good things are all gone.'

'Of course they are! But do they listen to me?' He laughed. He was enjoying talking market. And so was I.

'Perhaps I will speak with them.'

'Yes, yes! And go with them too, maybe? Just one day? I will send them to you. At the right hour.'

He told me their names. Then he made a bow and a grunt and turned back to his pots and fire. He tossed a handful of greens into an iron pan and a cloud of spiced smoke billowed into the air. I walked out smiling, for the first time in weeks.

The next morning, before sunrise, I found the girls gathered outside my house. (Bopa was still sleeping, having pled that this trip was starting too early.) They sweetly put hands together in lamplight when I came down the steps. There was no mischief here, I could see, just inexperience. I led them forth as the first hints of daylight coloured clouds in the east.

The market had the pleasant bustle of its first hour. We walked a circuit of its many aisles, not buying anything yet, just taking in what was on offer in lamplight, which stall had what fish from the Freshwater Sea, which had the sweetest rambutans. The girls seemed to like being under my wing. It was rather like in the old days, when the young Pala came with me. Baskets over their arms, they listened as I showed them how to tell real dew from water splashed on fruit for appearance of freshness, how to spot a crooked scale when silver was weighed.

Then we bought. The final stop was the stall of the grown-up Pala, where we purchased sixty coconuts – it felt good to give her so much business – and hired four boys to carry them back to the palace kitchen. Then we all sat down on Mrs Pala's mat and drank some of the sweet milk themselves.

When I arrived back at the house, there was another surprise waiting – a novice priest.

He bowed, and, eyes on the ground, announced: 'I have been sent so that the woman called Mrs Sray may have the ability to read the holy scriptures.'

I took a moment to compose myself. Please don't smile, but I had always believed that ability to read came from revelation of a secret that priests and nobles guarded closely. There would be a rite in a dim chamber, the smell of incense and mildew on stone. An aged abbot would chant for an hour or more, then whisper a single magic word that would infuse meaning into the symbols I had seen etched on palm leaves and festival banners.

So now I asked the novice to which shrine we would go for this rite. The question seemed to confuse him; he responded by asking if the house had a place where we could sit down. I directed him to the front veranda, where passers-by could see us, because it would of course not do for a woman and a young priest-to-be to be alone in a private place. We sat, rather far apart, and on the mat he unfolded a piece of slate on which he had drawn a chart with chalk. Five lines from side to side and five up and down formed boxes on the sheet, each with a symbol written inside it.

He pointed to the first one. 'Kah.'

'Young novice, what is this 'kah"?

'It is the name of this letter, ma'am. The first letter in the alphabet.'

An hour later, he departed, leaving the slate with me. I peered down at it and struggled to recall the names of the first ten letters.

My life began to change for the better from that day. Each morning I went with the girls to the market. Soon, Mr Narin was asking if I might help out with buying drapes and porcelain and other things for the prince's household. I did, visiting the stalls and Chinese shops where such things were sold. After a while, it began to be quite a bit to handle myself, so Mrs Pala entered the prince's service as well, as my assistant.

We were very busy, going to this market, then that one, then to this warehouse, then to that farm where pigs lived behind bamboo fencing, their little ones scurrying around in the mud. How much we bought! The prince's household had begun at perhaps twenty people, now it was four hundred. I must say that with all this coming and going to places of commerce, I began to buy things for my own home, and then, then to trade on my own account. Just a little bit, then a bit more. It was a kind of game of chance that I enjoyed. One day I bought a dozen vats of honey though the prince's household needed only six. I stored the extra six under our house on a hunch that their value would rise. Why did I think it would? Because I had heard talk in the market of a new water route opening to the Cham lands (we were at peace with the Chams at that time) and it was said that people there loved honey but had little of it. Later I sold those six jars to a wholesaler at a mark-up. I swear to you that I never cheated anyone at this, that profits I made were only reasonable. But they were large enough to allow me to hire men to make repairs to the big house that we now occupied. It seemed wrong to let the roof leak water onto the lacquered floors. And I bought some things for Bopa. Shiny things made her happy and she deserved some happiness. Still, was I wrong to profit this way? Though I tried to avoid it, I know that I was sometimes offered a better price when I sold things because people imagined that they would get some benefit next time, when I was buying for the prince's household.

But I am getting ahead of myself. There is one other thing I must tell you of that time, back before I was trading in honey, repairing my roof. Too many days passed before I thought to remember the person who was the reason why my life and my daughter's life were getting better. I knew I must give thanks. So shortly afterward a hired boy appeared at his house, carrying a gift of ten duck eggs in a basket decorated with pink lotus blossoms. With them was a note. I had spent a long time thinking out what it would say.

Dear Mr Narin,

Through the help of the novice priest, I have written those first three words. The rest is written by a man in the market who earns his rice doing such things. My brain is weak, my concentration short, I am unable to finish it myself. But because you have shown faith in me, I will continue the lessons and I hope that one day I may write a complete note of thanks in my own hand. Toward that time, please accept these eggs, as a token of my gratitude to a man whom Heaven has sent to show the path to happiness in this new life.

May the spirits protect you and your family and bring health and prosperity always.

With deepest respect and gratitude, this comes from

Sray, the market woman

15: A clearing in a forest

It is time. I am ready to tell you.

But, but...let me begin at the proper place. The story has its origins at a temple that took in girls who had no parents. That is where I grew up. I was not born there, of course, but it is there that my recalled life begins. My very first memory? The scent of the cheap matting that was my bedding. Each morning, I would emerge from my dreams with its scent in my nose. Like many of the girls, I also awoke with its mark on my cheek, the kiss of its rough reed, on which my head had lain all night.

We were always roused by the voice of the old priest who ran the place. Holding an oil lamp, he would poke his head into our sleeping pavilion before sunrise and with sympathy that somehow never flagged call out that it was time for his group of very fine ladies to get up. We would stir, scratching at bites the mosquitoes had left. There was no netting. It's too expensive for a humble place like this, the priest told any girl who asked, and he would point to the red spots on his own arm. In any case, he would say, a bite or two from these little creatures that are Heaven's creation just like you will help build character that you're going to need for the life ahead. Now hurry along, please! Our friends the ducks are awake already. Don't you hear them quacking? They're already out there foraging and you girls haven't even sat up yet.

The orphanage existed because three reigns earlier, after another of the wars with the Chams, the King of the time was inspecting this province. His procession passed a child begging at roadside in front of a temple. He stopped, took pity and ordered the creation of an orphanage in this very place. Normally, of course, other families in a village take in children if their parents die. But war produces orphans so fast and in such numbers that in that year the traditional way was not sufficient.

There were about forty girls in residence in my day, and each morning after the priest's call we lined up and went to a pond to bathe. Back in the pavilion, we rolled up the mats and stored them to the side. Then we were led in chanted prayer by the priest or the designated Leader Girl. Afterward, we gathered in a dirt courtyard and waited, the day's first tentative rays of sunlight peeking through a palm grove. It was never clear how long the wait would last, only that it would end when a village woman retained by the priest emerged from the kitchen hut in the back, pushing a cart bearing a large pot of rice soup. With a coconut ladle she scooped the breakfast into our bowls, paying little attention to who got how much. That is another very early memory for me, joining the line behind whichever of the older girls was being kind to me at the time. Often I would offer a silent prayer that this morning there might be a bit of fish or meat for me. I would glance from time to time toward the reassuring sight of the old priest, who stood to the side, bantering with his girls, and keeping order if there was a need, which sometimes there was.

Later in the morning, we all did cleaning jobs. My favourite was sweeping the leaves and footprints from the dust in the courtyard. I liked the patterns I could make in the dust, and if there weren't too many leaves or grass fronds to sweep, I did the job two or three times over, because it was fun and because it was always said at the home that an idle girl was a girl unloved of Heaven or humankind. Some mornings the work was followed by a bit of formal learning in the pavilion. We memorized fragments of verse from the hymns and epics, or we heard a sermon from a visiting priest, a long one full of big words. This was rather unusual, of course – normally girls of our birth would grow up knowing only of village spirits, or perhaps the deity who inhabited a small roadside shrine. But here we got a small view into the realm of the royal gods, through the whiskered mouth of this visiting priest. Still, much of what was said in those sermons and those prayers I couldn't understand. When I could, the message often seemed to be that we girls should avoid the kind of lives our parents had lived, because if those lives had been upstanding, we would not have met the tragedy that brought us here.

There was another meal, a small one, past midday, with any leftovers from the morning thrown into the pot. In the afternoon, we worked with our hands, back in the pavilion, piecing together cheap charms and trinkets. These were taken away by cart once a week, for distribution to vendors who sold them at the gates of far-away temples.

The day's only real freedom came after the evening meal, when for an hour each girl could go her own way. Sometimes the priest came from his quarters to pass time in the cool air with whichever girls chose to join him. I was always one of those, and I would sit close and try for his attention. If he didn't appear, I followed other girls to the open area beyond the walls, where we played. Often the ducks were there. I would bring whatever scraps of food I could find. They waddled up and ate from my hand.

At planting time, the routine changed. We girls were hired out as day labourers to farmers in the area. The work was hard and hot, but we all welcomed it as a break in our routine. We lined up, we waded our way across a flooded paddy, pressing the delicate roots of seedlings into soft submerged soil. It was fun making a row all your own, a row as straight as you could manage. As I grew older, I became aware that sometimes more flirting than planting went on – village boys always managed to assign themselves to jobs alongside us girls. Sometimes the local mothers were mean, keeping a close eye, accusing us of having designs on their sons, though I thought that with some of these boys, at least, we were their only hopes of marriage. At other times, the women showed the deepest kindness. Once a young wife whom Heaven had given no children of her own took me into her house, babied me for a whole afternoon, and gave me sweet things to eat. At day's end, I was sent on my way with a final snack. As I walked off, my eyes were misting at the impossible thought of staying the night, of having this would-be mother and her love all to myself. But once I caught up with the priest and the other girls, who were making their way by moonlight along paddy dikes back toward the home, I cheered up. The priest was in the middle of a story that had everyone giggling, but he stopped and smiled in relief on seeing that I'd re-appeared. We all walked on, beneath the bowl of the firmament, the priest going on with his rather long and amusing story, the distant lamplight of the home coming into view. I felt entirely contented when we passed through the gate. I settled in for sleep at the pavilion's south edge. From the darkness outside came soft quacks of the ducks. This was my place.

Once a year, we girls washed our sampots with extra care and give the entire home a thorough going-over with rags and reed brooms. Then we took places just inside the gate, the priest displaying some uncharacteristic abruptness if our lines were not exactly straight. On his signal, we knelt and the gate opened, and a man in costly silk sampot and silver armlets walked in. He was known to us girls simply as the rich man. Following behind him were a half dozen servants and a cart loaded with sacks of rice and bolts of the sturdy cloth of which our garments were made. Later he presented a sampling of these things in the chapel, and the priest gave a blessing that seemed to all of us waiting in the sun outside to be the longest we had ever heard. Then the rich man was shown to a wooden dais that had been polished and placed in our pavilion. For an hour, girls sang and danced and recited from the texts for him. I was sometimes one of them, dancing with three other girls. He watched, a look of approval on his face, and I felt, despite the vanity of the thought, that he was watching me in particular.

By my thirteenth year, I had left behind the body of a girl, and become the official Leader Girl. I welcomed the new arrivals, played mother as best I could and led the chanting of prayers and the settling of disputes. Smaller girls wanted me to move my sleeping place, to take the one of honour at the east end of pavilion. But I always pretended to forget to move. My place was by the south edge, where I could hear the ducks as they settled down for the night. I was in charge of them now too, gathering their eggs every day. They all had names, my private names, and I could sense the spirits that lived within them. When their time in this life was up, I prayed over them and saw to a clean and dignified butchering that turned them into a meal for the health of us all.

One afternoon – it was shortly after I turned fifteen – I was told to go see the priest. This was very unusual. I found him on a mat at the foot of his temple's steps, waiting. He wore a long face. With some apprehension, I knelt, hands together, but he motioned that this time I should not bother.

'I'm afraid the day has come, Sray. Our patron has called for you...'

Some girls became maids in the towns and cities. Some went into nunneries – there was one a half day's walk away that seemed to regard the home as a recruiting station. Some were married off to those local farm boys, and some became minor wives to prominent men. The rich man had always seemed good-hearted, sitting on that dais as we girls performed, never letting his attention wander. But the thought of him with his garment off...

'But please!' said the priest. 'Don't look so sad. It's not what you think.'

'Sir?'

'He has called for you as wife for a young man on his estate. His name is Koy. That's a very nice-sounding name, don't you think? He is eighteen. He's an apprentice blacksmith. I've made some inquiries about him. There's a priest at the temple down the road who knows him – this Koy was a novice there for close to a year. He is strong, his health is good and he's never been married. Everyone says he's a very fine young man. You are to be married two weeks from now and our patron will provide a house as a wedding gift.'

'Oh.'

'Sray – you should be happy! Most of my girls don't do nearly as well.'

'I will try, sir.' What else could I say? 'But I will miss you...and the other girls.'

'As all of us will miss you, Sray. To be truthful, I'm having trouble feeling good about this too.' He paused. 'But, let's keep our spirits up! In each life, nothing is permanent. Change begins setting in from the moment that something is created and there's nothing we can do to stop it. But you'll come and see us sometimes? You won't be so far away.'

'I'll come often, sir,' I replied, though something told me I would not. 'But, sir...I'd much rather remain...'

'My dear Sray...'

I was crying now and had he not been a priest who had taken

vows never to touch a woman, he would have placed an arm on my shoulder for comfort.

'I'll be all right, sir,' I said after a bit, still sniffling. 'I've known for a long time that one day I would leave here, but now that I have to...'

'You'll be fine, Sray. You are a beautiful young woman, whose real life can now begin. When you were born, I'm sure that your parents said the traditional prayer – may you have a hundred, a thousand husbands. Now you will have one, which is really all that any woman needs. You have graced this place for fifteen years, and that's all that Heaven will allow. It knows you deserve something better. You'll have a husband, children, your own house – you'll forget this place.'

'I won't forget it, sir.'

'I hope not, I hope not.' He cleared his throat. 'Now, Sray, there is a practice here, that when a girl leaves, we tell her how it happened that she came to live with us, if she came here too young to remember.'

'Yes?'

'You were brought to us when you were not more than a few months old. There was a war at the time. Many villages in the frontier districts were razed, many people were killed. Your parents and all your brothers and sisters – I don't know how many there were – died in one of those raids. It was a terrible thing. But you were the one whom Heaven chose to preserve. The soldiers who found you said it was a miracle that you survived. Everywhere were bodies and smouldering debris, but then they heard a baby's cry from the ruins of a house and they began to dig, and they discovered you there, under the house's mother beam, unhurt. The house's spirit, or perhaps some larger god, had created a space in which to save you.'

'Sir, I don't know that I deserved to be saved, when my mother, my father...'

'You did deserve it – otherwise Heaven would not have arranged it. Now, you were brought here. We had no idea what name your parents had given you. So – and it was I who chose – you became Sray. There are fancier names, of course, with all

124

sorts of meaning about flowers and jewels and beams of light. Sometimes I feel that these names are given in desperation that they will somehow make the child measure up to such things. But with you, even as a baby, I could see that you would have no need of such help. Sray. One might think it's too simple a name – it just means girl, after all. But how can it be simple when it sums up the essence of all things female and feminine. Softness, strength, renewal and birth, whether here on earth or in Heaven.

'Sray, you have always had the character of one blessed. For a long time I believed that you would take vows in the holy orders. But as you have grown, I have seen that it is instead your place to move in the secular world, to carry with you the grace of one so favoured, and to share it with people, not by instruction, perhaps, but by example.'

'Sir,' and now I wanted to cry again, 'I am nothing like what you describe. You frighten me.'

'That is not my intention. My intention is only to send you on your way with encouragement to accept the path that Heaven has set for you. I know you will. You will be kind to those whom you encounter, whether they are sick or hungry or unstable of mind. You will go to the shrine and burn incense and give offerings. When it is necessary, I think, you will stand up against injustice and violence. You will find that in this life men too often act under self-delusion. They tell themselves they are following Heaven's will, but in fact they are following their own. Your family died in such a war, Sray. Whatever we are told, what happened is that the King of the time began the war saying that our Lord Shiva desired an expansion of the Empire's borders; in fact, it is said by people who know that our monarch had heard that the enemy King had a boar-hunting ground like no other and he wanted it. Can you imagine? For that, ten thousand people died. And in the end, our King did not even get the hunting ground. The enemy was too strong that time.'

I thought for a moment, then asked, 'Sir, how could I...?'

'Have an effect on something like that? I don't know, but who can say? As your life unfolds, you will be surprised at the places where fate places you, at the people with whom it brings you together. When the time comes, you will know what is required.'

'I hope so, sir.'

'Well! I had not meant to make you cry, Sray.' In fact, it was now he who was misty-eyed. 'This is a day for celebration. You are going to married, and to a very fine young man!'

Two days later, I stood at the gate, my possessions packed in a single straw basket. With me was every girl of the home and, of course, the priest, but still I felt alone. An oxcart had arrived, driven by a man in his middle years. He was given water to drink, my basket was placed in the back. There was no way to delay now; I got aboard. Then the priest pulled himself together and gave a blessing. The cart rolled off, the new Leader Girl leading a chant of farewell. The words carried to me even as I passed far across the rice land. I could not bear to look back.

The driver saw my tears, and looked away, finding no words. But when we came to a small market at a crossroads, he stopped the cart. He jumped down and returned with a coconut, freshly opened. 'Drink this down, young lady,' he said. 'You'll feel better.'

His name was Mr Sao. He made conversation the rest of the way. Partly it seemed intended to calm my sorrows, partly to satisfy curiosity about this new member of the estate. He shared things too. 'Our master is only two generations removed from the King and he owns a dozen villages...He's a good master and makes many donations to many places of the spirit. You'll be surprised when you see how much he gives on holy days. And he never plays favourites with his people, no, not at all....He's a widower. The estate's lady, as fine a soul as he, died in childbirth, may she be blessed. She left two sons, both of them strong and determined. A handful, those two. But it's good when boys are that way. They'll both accomplish great things...And did I tell you that the master is a scholar? He's got a room full of holy texts on leaves, old leaves, old enough that I'd think ten generations have read them by now. Some of them are crumbling, and the master is going to have them recopied – a scribe came to the estate to show how he would do it. You should have seen! He gave us all a demonstration. First he took a sharp little thing – a stylus, he called it – and traced out each letter of each word as a groove, then he went back and filled the grooves with ink. Quite a long time it will take when that job gets started...Our master, he's a devout man, yes, always helping out with religious matters. He's going to renovate the old shrine by the road too. Right up ahead now, you'll see it, and just before is the turn into our estate. It's really not the biggest place, you'll see, but did I tell you our master's family has rights to another estate? A large one, several days' travel from here. But the noble family there now won't give it up. Who knows, maybe you'll see the day when we get it. Our master's not the kind of man to take up arms for it, though. But look – there's the shrine's spire, just like I said.'

I did look, and a smile came to my face. I imagined myself visiting it, alone, to give thanks for my wedding.

Mr Sao called out greetings to a pair of farmers who were walking the track, kramas wrapped around their brows, and to children wading in a stream. I felt embarrassed because each person looked me over, though in a welcoming way. Soon the estate house came into view across a stretch of paddy land. The tile roof was brilliant red, the wooden walls solid and elaborately carved. To either side was a pond and a dozen or so small houses for retainers. But what really defined the scene were rows of towering sugar palms to either side of the house.

Mr Sao stopped the cart. 'There it is,' he said proudly. 'The noble people have a fancy royal language name for the estate that means Community of Great Dazzling Prosperity. To the rest of us it's just Sugar Palm House.'

When the cart passed inside the gate, the rich man came quickly out to receive us, a small boy and a nursemaid in tow.

'Welcome, welcome, Miss Sray,' he called, even before I could kneel and put hands together. His voice was kind and reassuring, as it always had been in the hall when we girls performed. 'You'll find it a bit quiet here after where you've come from, but we do like our little community.' The cart driver beamed, happy that his words about the master's kindness were confirmed so quickly in person.

The boy tugged at his father's garment. 'Lift me up, father! Now!'

The nursemaid let off a twitter of laughter that the young master was so assertive. His father laughed too and lifted him to his shoulders, though he was a bit big for that. There the little boy perched, shoulders quite broad for his age. I smiled up to him. In return, I got an imperious gaze, conveying a determination I had never seen in a boy so young.

'This is my second son, Lon,' said the rich man, drawing a bit nearer. 'Lon, say hello to the new girl who has come to live on our estate.'

I bowed and put hands together, smiling again, but the boy said nothing. Suddenly he reached out and with thumb and forefinger pinched my cheek.

It hurt! I sprang back.

'Lon! Lon!' laughed the master, looking up at the boy. 'That's not how we greet a newcomer!' He turned back to me. I was blushing, ashamed. 'I'm sorry, young lady. He does get carried away sometimes.'

The boy kept his gaze on me even as he was lowered from his father's shoulders and hustled off by the maid.

'Come on now,' said the master. 'We'll take you to where you'll be staying.'

He led me along a path that wound past a pond to the retainers' area. We stopped at a house where an old woman sat in the door.

'This is Grandmother Som,' the master said in his jovial way. 'You'll be staying with her, for now. Now Grandmother, you understand, don't you, that everything that this young lady wants should be provided? Just send word to me and along it will come.'

Through a toothless smile, the old woman whispered that she would.

The master left and I was shown inside, where my host sat me down and gave me water in a clay cup. Then she sat down too and regarded me in an amiable way. 'Poor girl – you're wondering, if I'm a grandmother, where are the grandchildren? The master just calls me that to be kind, actually. I was married, but no children ever arrived. Now my husband's passed, and hopes for those children have too. But I'd have been pleased to have a daughter as fine as you, and for a little while, at least, I will.'

I smiled at the woman, who said nothing more and seemed content just to be near someone young.

After a bit, I rose and made myself useful. I swept the floor and renewed the charcoal in the fire. Through until late afternoon, people kept finding reasons to stop by the house and chat with the old woman, looking me over as they did, but again the attention was all friendly and I began to grow accustomed to it.

That evening, there was yet another visitor, a small boy carrying a large basket. He called up from the house's steps. I turned to go down to see to him, but the old women stopped me. 'I'll do it.'

She hobbled down the steps. 'Now what's all this?' she asked in a voice meant to carry. She was rummaging in the boy's basket. 'Two fresh coconuts, an ivory comb, a bronze neckpiece – quite a nice one, too.' She held it up for me to admire. Then she addressed the boy. 'Now who's this from?'

'From Koy the apprentice blacksmith.'

Grandmother Som beamed at me. 'Why, it seems this man is courting you! You're lucky. He's got to be the very best-looking at Sugar Palm House and all the villages around it. If I weren't so old, I'd have scooped him up myself long ago!'

That night, the old woman presented me with a mosquito net. A gift from the master, she explained. I lay down inside the net. It was a strange feeling, like being confined, and I was unsure I could sleep. But I was happy to be alone for a while. Then Grandmother Som blew out the lamp and for few minutes I shed tears, missing the touch of my old mat, the whisperings of other girls nearby, the quacks of the ducks outside.

The next morning I heard the sound of hammering as I prepared rice. 'My goodness,' said Grandmother Som, looking out the window. 'The estate carpenters are building a new house. Who can it be for?' Later, we went and looked, and it was a large, solid thing going up, with plank floors and thatch roof.

That afternoon, Grandmother Som placed the gift jewellery around my neck. Then the two of us processed solemnly to the house of the apprentice blacksmith's family. It was as if all the fields were deserted right now; every man, woman and child had found duties in the settlement and all paused to watch. The young man Koy stood waiting in front of his house, flanked by his parents. He was exactly as promised, of stout physique and handsome face and thick hair, with a kind and quiet disposition that communicated its presence without words.

He put hands together, daring to smile at me. I presented him with a lotus blossom.

From there the old woman took me to see the estate's garment maker, who took measurements for a wedding sampot and as she worked said under her breath, as if no one could hear, that it had been a long time, quite a long time indeed, since she'd made a nuptial garment for anyone quite so lovely. How people can stretch the truth! I blushed, as I did a few hours later when the priest who would perform the wedding rites gazed on me with such approval that I looked away.

I fell asleep that night imagining the touch of my husband-to-be.

The next morning, I awoke with a start, feeling eyes on me, from very close up, right at the door. The house shuddered as someone jumped down the steps. A male laugh broke through from somewhere below. My face burned with mortification. I wondered, was this some strange custom that people at this estate might practice? I turned to Grandmother Som.

'The master's eldest son,' the woman said, in a voice that tried to hide concern. 'Back from a trip somewhere. His name is Vin. We'll do our best to keep away from him. It will be all right once you're married.'

Later that morning, when I went to the pond to draw water, this Vin was waiting by the path, leaning against the trunk of a palm. He was a larger version of his little brother – same well-formed shoulders and imperious gaze, eyes that held on me without shame. He smirked as I approached. I hurried past, saying nothing. I looked back and shuddered. He had not followed, but he was still at the tree, watching.

Word of this attention got around. No one could directly protect me, but everyone became even more solicitous. Young men called greetings from the tops of sugar palms which they climbed to hang cups that collected sap drippings. On the ground, their wives and daughters invited me to join in boiling and stirring the sap in an iron vat, and pouring the resulting yellow-orange syrup into moulds to make candy. I was given the first piece to sample – the women burst into delighted laughter when my face lit up at the sweetness. There had been nothing at all like that at the orphanage. Grandmother Som took me walking in the afternoon sun through paddies where farmers tended rice stalks half grown. Mr Sao the driver happened along with his cart, and he insisted that he give the two of us a ride back to the settlement, though it was just a few minutes' walk. I helped Grandmother Som aboard. But then – Vin was there, watching from a spot at a bamboo fence some distance away. The estate, which had seemed so large when I arrived, was now too small to avoid him.

On my third day, when I went again to draw water, he sprang out from behind a tree and grabbed for my arm. I was quick enough to get away.

'Doesn't his father know what he does?' I asked Grandmother Som later.

'We've tried to tell him. You're not the first to get this treatment, you see. But his sons are his pride, and who can blame him? For a while it was said that Vin would become lord of an estate to the north of here, but that talk has ended and now Vin has no place. He's angry and often his anger is directed at us. He'll straighten out, I'm sure, once some other place is found for him. But in the meantime the master doesn't want to hear. He's deaf to any talk of fault in his sons, I'm afraid.'

The wedding was just three days away, and in fact it arrived with no more trouble from Vin. With Grandmother Som presiding, retainer women of the estate gave me a ritual bath beneath her house, dried me and sprinkled my body with a mist of holy water. I put on the wedding sampot and armlets and headdress that the priest provided. My wrists and neck and breasts were dabbed with scent. Then I was walked in procession to the house of Koy's parents. There my first act was to look to see if Vin was present. He was not.

On a stand set up at the foot of the house's steps, I knelt next to Koy. The priest begged our indulgence, then cut locks of hair from our heads. He circled us seven times carrying a burning candle of beeswax. As the final step, he tied our wrists together with string he had blessed. I closed my eyes. What a moment it was! I felt such enormous hope for what our life would be.

We spent our first night in a nuptial house outside the settlement. By the light of single lamp, I stepped from my garment and I stood before this young man my husband, presenting myself, trembling with an excitement that I did not know I contained. Koy took my hand, then pressed it to his chest and held it gently there. Together we sank to the mat, and there he made of me a woman whom Heaven might allow to have children.

Just before dawn, with Koy lying asleep next to me, warming my thigh and arm, I awoke to a faint rustling in the forest outside. It was likely some small animal, but I could not shake the sense that it was Vin, watching again. I closed my eyes, and pulled closer to my husband. When he awoke, I said nothing.

Two days later, we moved back to the compound, to the house the carpenters had built. The master was there with greetings. He announced that credit had been arranged in the market in the nearby market town, so that I could select clothing, jars and other essentials for the new household. It was our first day of normal life together. Koy squeezed my hand and left for the blacksmith forge. I walked to the town, chose our things, and set out toward home, a heavy basket over my arm.

Half way back, I saw Vin ahead, standing in his loutish way at a bridge that spanned an irrigation ditch.

There was no way around. I would have to bluster my way through. I quickened my pace, and as I passed, he grabbed me hard by the arm.

'What's this, don't want to talk to me?'

I tried to shake free, but he tightened his grip. It frightened me how strong it was.

'Let go! I'm a married woman.'

'Oh, brave enough to talk now?'

'It doesn't frighten me to talk.'

'Good. I like it when you do.'

I tried again to shake free.

'Look,' he said, holding me fast. 'Don't be so prissy. We all know what kind of girls come out of the place where you lived. There's one in the town you just went to. She's a maid – they say. But it seems her work takes place entirely at night!'

What vulgarity! No one had ever spoken to me like that. I stamped a heel on his instep. Where I'd learned to do that, I don't know. He gasped, astonished, and lost his grip. I ran as fast as I could, all the way back to the estate. At the door of my house I stopped and calmed myself. I cooked the evening rice for my husband. I said nothing about Vin.

In the next weeks, I took care never to be alone on the road or in any secluded spot around the estate grounds. Eight days went by without Vin showing himself. I began to hope he'd lost interest.

The news came late one afternoon, as I was at Grandmother Som's house, getting ready to go to the pond with her to wash clothing. A boy arrived at her house in a run, breathless.

'Mr Koy – he's hurt, very badly, out on the road! I saw blood.'

I raced off with the boy, the old woman following as quickly as she could.

Oh, how hard it is to recount what I saw. If only someone had got there before me and held me back. Koy was lying still, dead already. Blood soaked the dust on the road, there was a horrible gash across his belly. Flies were all around, buzzing. I saw it all. I fainted. They told me later that I fell right onto my husband's body.

The next day, a magistrate came and took statements. No one had had much to offer, except for Vin, who presented himself and related that he'd been walking along a road a few days earlier when he saw, hiding in the trees, a strange man with a knife tucked in his sampot. He seemed to be waiting for someone to rob, but Vin hadn't had any trouble. Probably the man was too smart to attack a fit young nobleman, remarked the magistrate.

At the cremation rites, people stood close to me to lend support. The master honoured Koy by helping carry the washed corpse on its bier, and then lighting the pyre of aromatic wood with his own hand. He stepped over to give words of sympathy to me, now a young widow. I had no strength to carry the burden of grief. Koy had been a fine man, but Heaven had taken him and I saw no reason why it would send another man who would make me happy in the same way.

When the rite was over, I closed my eyes and wished with all my might that I had never been brought here.

I thanked everyone, then went back to my house, insisting on being alone, and there I lay down. But I could not rest. Presently I rose, with an idea, to walk to the shrine by the road, the one I'd seen that first day, while riding the cart from the home for parentless girls. There I would pray, and seek a signal from Heaven as to whether I should stay in this place.

I was drawing near the shrine when I became aware of feet treading on leaves behind me. I knew instantly who. I ran, but after just a few steps, as I entered a small clearing, I was tackled full-force from behind. What a shock – I came down on my belly, he on top, pinning my arms, pressing his cheek to mine.

'Not married any more, are you?'

I twisted my head to the left and bit his lip! I was like an animal. He let out a howl, but kept me beneath him. He freed up a hand and wiped away some blood. 'Oh, it's fun when they fight. Come on, try again.'

I lay still, breathing hard.

'Not willing? Well, how about if I do *this*?'

He rolled me over and his free hand went down and tugged at my sampot. I struggled, screaming, and tried to bang my head against his, but it wouldn't reach.

'Keep it up!' he laughed. 'You're putting up as much of a fight as he did. I'll have to fight back.' With that, he struck me hard across the mouth. Then his hand went down again and there was a ripping sound. The sampot tore away. He pressed his weight down on me, forcing my legs apart.

'Are you ready, then?'

'You will not treat her that way.'

The words came from above. I will always remember how calmly they were voiced. Vin went still, then craned his neck to look. Standing over us was a man, rather young. A stranger. Short and wearing a coarse sampot, his hair cropped close in a labourer's cut. He held a shovel and the straw bag of a traveller.

'Get away – don't interfere,' Vin growled.

The little man did not move. 'No, you will get off her.'

Vin exhaled heavily and rolled himself over, slowly, as if to declare it was by his own choice. He stood full up. From somewhere, he had pulled out a small knife.

'I'm off her now, for the moment,' he said. He flicked the point of the knife toward the man. 'Now are you glad I am?' He flicked the knife again. 'Maybe not. Maybe, filthy runt, you're wondering what you've gotten yourself into.'

The man said nothing. He didn't move, or display any fear and this seemed to anger Vin. The young prince began dancing around him, the point of the knife striking out again and again.

'You don't talk much, do you? Just like her.'

The knife shot closer in, this time etching a small line of blood on a shoulder.

The man looked to me and with a flick of his head, said, run! I watched. I was unable to get up.

Vin continued the dance and opened more of these minor cuts. Then he stepped back and seemed to consider something. He raised the knife high, held it there an instant, then brought it down lightning-fast on the left side of the man's head.

'Got it!' he shouted.

Then the little man came alive, and his shovel moved in an arc. Vin sprang back, but not soon enough. The shovel's blade caught him full on the side of the head, digging deeply in. He went down heavy as a sack of rice.

I was on my feet now, telling myself to run. But then I saw the little man sink to his knees, clutching the side of his head.

I asked: 'What can I do?'

He did not respond, but closed his eyes, and I saw blood running through his fingers, down his neck.

My sampot lay a few steps away, tangled in some brush. I went to it and tore a piece off.

'Here. Use this.'

He took it without a word, and pressed it to his head and looked away. I stepped back and, feeling shame, put on what was left of my garment.

I asked: 'Who are you?'

'My name is Nol. I was passing by on the road and I heard you. Are you all right, then? Your mouth...'

'I'm not all right. But neither are you.'

'Nor him,' he said. Vin lay still. 'I guess I hit him with the sharp side, not the flat one.' He turned away, remorseless. 'Come on, I'll take you back to your house.'

I couldn't go there. 'No, no, I need to go somewhere else, not around here, back to my real place.'

I turned and began walking quickly. The main district road was just ahead; I would follow in reverse the route by which the cart had brought me here. I was pretty sure I could remember the way. I reached the road and began to hurry down it, then realized I should not be in the open. I'd be seen. I turned down a small path that cut through forest land. But in a few minutes, I felt afraid to be alone with the creatures and spirits of the wood, and perhaps the ghost of the dead son, flying through the thick foliage in pursuit. My mouth, I noticed now, was strangely warm and wet, with a taste in it. I stopped. I heard footsteps, but this time they were comforting.

I waited for this man Nol to catch up. He said: 'Wherever it is you want to go, I'll take you.' He was still holding the cloth to his head.

'It's a long way.'

'That's all right – I can go. Wait – you're bleeding too. We have to find a place for you to wash.'

I looked down. My breasts were streaked with something red. My hand went to my mouth and I realized there was a strange taste there, a wetness of blood. My fingers found a gap. Vin's blow had knocked out a tooth, one in the back.

'I'll be all right,' I said, turning from him. I felt ashamed again.

We walked, the little man now in the lead, his shovel in his hand. He seemed to have an instinct for avoiding people. We circled a settlement unseen; just beyond it, he signalled me to step off the path. We crouched in the vegetation, ants labouring silently around us, while a pair of farmers passed. Then we rose, and he led me further. When we came to a pond, we waded in to wash, I turning my back to him, then stealing looks to make sure he had not abandoned me. When I was clean, I made him lift the rag away from his head, and I winced when I saw there was no ear. It had been cut clean away.

'I brought it with us. Your tooth too.'

'What?' I was horrified again. He motioned to his waist, where he had stuck a folded rag.

Six hours later, with a three-quarter moon overhead, we approached the home for parentless girls. Faint voices carried out from over the wall. So carefree, they were – it was almost sleeping time in the pavilion. They would be unrolling their mats now.

I told this man Nol that we would wait until everyone had settled down, then I would go inside. I sat down by a ditch; he joined me, keeping a proper distance.

I asked: 'Do you suppose he got up after we left?' I would have been both relieved and terrified if he had.

'I don't think so.'

'They'll come after us, won't they?'

'Yes. But that doesn't mean they'll catch us.'

I wondered how he could be so calm. Even if there were not magistrates coming after us, there was still the ghost, whose presence I could feel nearby. I shuddered.

Later I entered the gate and crept to the priest's quarters. I called to him softly through the door. He lit a lamp and came outside, and gasped when he saw me – my mouth was blue and swollen. He went for a cloth and dabbed my lips, putting aside for the moment his vows of never touching a woman. Then I sat before him and told the story. He listened solemnly. And when I told him that this man Nol who had rescued me was outside, he insisted that we go to him.

'It's a brave thing you've done,' the priest told him.

'Thank you, sir.'

'You saved the girl who's the most decent, the most innocent and faultless in the whole Empire. Now, your name is Nol?'

'It is, sir.'

'What is your occupation?'

'I am a clearer of silt from canals, sir.'

'Are you married, Nol?'

'No, sir.'

'Do you have a family that relies on you?'

'No, sir. I am alone.'

'Where are you from?'

'Nowhere, sir. I travel. I was walking through the district, on my way to a job on the southern coast.'

The priest looked at him hard in the dark. 'Well then, Nol, you must forget about that job and do something more important. You must take this girl to the Capital, without anyone taking notice, and you must protect her and find a place for her to live. You must behave honourably toward her; you will be all she has.'

'No!' I cried. 'I have to go back and tell the rich man what happened.'

'You can't do that,' replied the priest. 'A member of a noble family has been killed. He was a corrupt one, a criminal, it is clear, but if you go back you will never get a chance to explain. I will say prayers to try to assuage the man's ghost. I will give you some rice and silver, and an introduction to a cousin I have in the Capital. He is a priest, and he will do what he can for you. And when some time has passed, I will go to the patron and talk to him privately, and tell him what happened. Maybe he will be ready to hear it then, from me. He is a good man.'

He went back to his cell. Presently he returned with a note to that cousin, and with food and things in a bag and a cloth wet with cream to prevent infection. He took the rag which contained the ear and tooth and promised to deal with them with fire, as should happen with any fleshly loss.

Then the priest gave a whispered blessing, and ordered us to go.

Six days later, we reached the Capital, having encountered no real trouble on the way. Still bearing the dust of the road, I knelt at the first shrine for humble folk that we came to. It was in front of the mountain-temple Pre Rup. Thus did Bronze Uncle hear my first prayer. Nol did not pray; he stood back and kept watch. We found the cousin and on his advice we built a house in the out-of-the-way neighbourhood behind the temple. After some time, Nol resumed work as a clearer of silt. I began selling duck eggs in the market, but I gave most of my earnings as offerings at the shrine. Each day I prayed to Bronze Uncle, seeking forgiveness and intercession for my role in the young prince's death. I knew, of course, that he was probably my husband's murderer, yet this second killing would not have followed had a foolish girl not offered temptation by walking in the forest alone.

It was my hope, of course, that this stay in the Capital would be of limited length. After some time we would receive word from the old priest that he had gone to the estate and convinced the patron that we deserved forgiveness, or at least some lesser punishment. But then, several weeks after we arrived, there came quite different news. The cousin sought us out to tell us that the priest had suddenly died. How I wept that night, for the soul of this remarkable man, but, I will confess it, for my own sake as well. Clearly he had not yet gone to the estate – he would have sent word right away. This life as a fugitive was to be my life forever.

Now, it was safer if people thought that Nol and I were a married couple, so in public we behaved as one. But in private, no. Nol could have imposed himself on me – I had nothing of my own, no money, no place to go. But he always behaved with the utmost honour, as if the old priest's commission outside the temple that night remained ever in his mind. Other women might have begun to wonder if he really was a canal dredger by birth, but I did not. I merely saw him as a man who was devoted to me, devoted far more than I deserved. In the house at night, he always turned his back when I removed my garment to prepare for sleep. He unrolled his mat well apart from mine. I would blow out the lamp, and sometimes fall asleep right away. Other times we would talk for a while, in whispers, in the darkness. It was always according to my whim; he never insisted on anything.

One day he came home with something white and delicate in straw wrappings. A mosquito net. It was for me alone, of course.

He had saved his silver, in secret, putting aside bits of it for months, and he bought the net, even though when at night we strung it up with yarn and I went inside it, he would feel the barrier between us to be all the greater.

This situation continued for perhaps six months, maybe a year. I have no clear memory. What changed? I cannot say exactly. Perhaps it is that Heaven does not intend that a young man and woman live in proximity this way indefinitely. Either the two must grow apart, becoming impatient and cross with each other, or they must come closer together. All I know is that one morning, as I folded the net to put it away, I decided that this life would not go on. I went to Bronze Uncle. I placed my bit of silver in the tray, I lit a stick of incense and I said one more prayer seeking peace with the dead prince's ghost. And then I said another, for dispatch to the soul of my late husband. I said to him, silently, my love, please grant forgiveness for what I am soon to do. I don't mean to abandon you, but since you have gone ahead and I remain behind in this life until such time that Heaven decides differently, I must move on to the next phase of it, to be united with another man, to have children. I do believe that my words reached his soul, and that he gave approval.

That night, I bathed at our rainwater jar for an extra-long time, I put on scent I had bought in the market. In the house, after darkness fell, I put up the net as usual and went inside it. I did nothing to signal to Nol that tonight would be different. I was having second thoughts. But then Nol unrolled his mat across the room, as he always did, and I had before me proof again of what an honourable man he was, living at close quarters yet never taking advantage. So...I came out of the net, bringing my mat. I rolled it out alongside his. How shocked he was! There was no talk between us, just awkward silence. For a long time we lay there in the darkness, on our backs, our upper arms touching. He was trembling. It was going to be up to me. And so I rolled over, and I pressed myself to him, and we proceeded from there. Even in the darkness, I could see his deformity, but it seemed not repulsive but yet more proof of his courage and devotion to me, a sign again that Heaven intended that we should now live in this intimate way.

I believe I was the first for him, though a wife can never ask her husband such a thing.

Let me finish the story now – it is almost done. Not long after that first night, Nol and I were formally united in a rite conducted by the priest cousin. No one else was present. Just before the start of the rains the following year, I gave birth to a baby girl. But she was sickly, unable to feed from my breast. Her spirit departed after only eight days. I was grief-stricken. The following year, Heaven smiled on us. We welcomed another child, a strong one, a boy. We called him Sovan.

16: Freedom

Let my story return now to the prince's compound in the Capital. I was becoming a trader and learning how to read. My girl had found a few friends. Life was stable. But there was still no sign of my husband and son. And even if I had come to learn that they were in no danger, it is Heaven's design, is it not, that a family will be together, a wife at her husband's side.

So I formed the notion that Bopa and I should go to the Upper Empire and find Nol and my boy.

Probably four weeks passed between that thought and the day that Bopa and I put spare garments, a brush and a few other essential items in shoulder bags. Early the next morning, we walked to the compound's gate. Mrs Pala would see to the business of supplying the prince's household while I was gone. I felt a bit guilty. We were in essence sneaking away. I had not told Mr Narin of my plan – I knew he would be concerned, and see it as his own fault in some way, and try to talk us out of it.

But what a sense of liberation I felt as we passed through the gate and walked on, moving fast in case someone came after us. We were on our own! Perhaps you have guessed, but this was another big part of the reason why I wanted to make this journey.

In my life, to travel had always meant to walk, but this trip's distance was going to be so long that I knew our feet would not be up to it. Certainly my daughter's would not. So we went to the north gate of the city, and there, in exchange for a few silver pebbles, we got our first ride, on a farmer's oxcart returning empty to an estate a day's journey up the trunk road. At a crossroads, we picked up another cart, going toward the mountain pass, and after that another. Most of the drivers were pleasant, helpful men, who welcomed the company on the long journey, but a few looked on us in the wrong way, especially when we were passing through strange forest land. In those cases, I made a point of working into the conversation a mention that my daughter and I were of Prince Indra's household. That never failed to correct any troublesome behaviour.

What a long trip it was – I had no real idea of the size of our great realm – and there were times my girl pled that we turn around. But after twelve days we reached the estate where the last report had placed the prince and his entourage. There was no sign of an army, though. I should not have hoped for that. We could not expect to find Nol and Sovan in the first place we looked. But at least it was true that the prince and his people had been there, until about ten days earlier.

We heard all about it as we sat eating and drinking that evening in the estate's guest pavilion. Servants, retainers, farmers crowded around to hear our story and to tell theirs. Happily the estate's lord was away.

From their accounts, it seemed that across the Upper Empire, Indra's army on the march had become a familiar sight. He was on a mission to secure this entire part of the realm and root out any other traitorous lords who had secret dealings with the Siamese. People at the estate talked about the visit as if it had happened just an hour before. First came the scouts, restless young men on snorting mounts. Next a dozen fighting elephants, plumes on their heads, red silk drapes flapping from their sides, followed by the prince himself, in jewelled armlets, atop an elephant, with four parasols aloft. Then chariots, cavalry, archers, great ranks of spearmen. Finally, an extended tail of camp followers – wives, children, cooks, prostitutes, baggage wagons, scruffy brown dogs quick to fight over anything edible that the column cast off.

It seemed that when the prince's throng entered your district, the only sensible response was to put face to dirt and submit. That was what had happened here. There was no fighting, no resistance of any kind. Farmers presented rice, fish and fruit in baskets to soldiers and found places for them to sleep, often in houses made empty for that purpose. The estate's lord came to the prince with a higher grade of gifts: heirloom swords, silver boxes, samples of the district's specialty honey wine, a jar of ritual bath water that signified the lord was no more than a body servant to the prince. The lord also brought a daughter, wearing her finest sampot, as a candidate concubine. Bopa perked up on hearing this; I wished that that particular detail had been withheld.

And, I asked, what of the parasol master and his son? Oh yes!

they replied. The parasol master was always at the prince's side, walking by the elephant, so attentive to every detail in the fans, the fly whisks, the other beautiful and delicate accoutrements that he oversaw. The boy? The same – scrambling to serve the prince, to serve his father. In Sovan's case, at least, I felt that our hosts were saying what they assumed we wanted to hear. Never mind. They had seen the both of them alive and well.

Now, as we sat eating that night, there was one man, the estate's granary manager, who said nothing for the longest time, but then he spoke up to observe that theft and drunkenness on the part of the prince's men had been something of a problem. The estate's rice stocks were now well down and there was no divine explanation he could think of. There was also the issue, he said, of soldiers paying attention to females who weren't on offer. That was as far as he got – other retainers him cut off and said no, it wasn't like that at all. Eyes began darting to me. Clearly people worried I would report these remarks as disloyal. I felt the best I could do was change the subject. I did, but not before the granary man got one more point in. 'If we had to grovel, at least we grovelled at the feet of a prince who looks chosen by Heaven.' That brought nods all around.

I asked, so where had Indra's army gone? Everyone knew the answer. The prince was eager for a real fight. No Siamese were to be found around here, so he had set out for their districts to the north.

'Your husband,' said one of the retainers, 'helped persuade the prince to take that step.'

'What? That cannot be.'

The man seemed at a loss – he'd thought I'd be delighted. 'It was that way, Lady. Your husband is a very influential man. He was always with the prince, even when there was no need of parasols or other ceremonial implements. Sometimes they conferred in the prince's own pavilion. We all were aware of it.'

You can imagine my feelings – joy turned to dismay. My husband and son gone off to a real war, my husband encouraging fighting and the violent release of souls from bodies. This was so different from what my daughter and I had come expecting.

17: The Siamese territories

Was I remiss in doing what I did next? Everyone said the prince and his men could not yet have reached the Siamese territories, but must be just in the next village to the north. Hardly an hour away. So the following morning, I led Bopa north for a look. Despite what I'd heard about an impending campaign, it was my hope that we would meet the army marching toward us, coming home, my husband and son among the ranks. We would all return to the Capital and be a family again.

We walked, then, bags over our shoulders. There was no doubt we were going in the right direction – there were so many footprints in the mud, left by men, by horses, oxen and elephants. And long snake-like marks of the twin wheels of carts. We came to the village. Prince and men were not there, but they had been. Try the next village, people said. So we went on. This one was somewhat further. We reached it in late afternoon. Again, there was no army. The headman took us in for the night.

The next morning we took to the trail again. It narrowed and entered a forest. We passed through places where the foliage grew so thick that the sun was blotted out. I began to feel uneasy. If we see anything unusual, I told myself, we will turn back. But we kept moving deeper and deeper into this woodland, as if it were drawing us in. I began to sense emanations from the vines overhead, from holes in the earth that looked like the dens of animals. Were we welcome in this place? I could not tell. Then came a terrifying thought: what if the dead prince's ghost had followed us here? Don't believe that, I told myself – all chances are that we are being watched only by this forest's resident spirits. They will let us pass. We have done them no harm. I took Bopa's hand and we hurried on. I felt some comfort in continuing to see footprints. Many, many people have been right here, I told myself. Soon we will be with them.

Then we rounded a bend. A bamboo fence showed itself, the first sign of a village. But as we drew near, we saw that this place only *had been* a village. The houses, perhaps they had numbered a dozen, it was hard to tell, had all burned, leaving just their stilts, standing but charred. Shards of broken water pots lay scattered. There was no sign of farm animals. And, of course, no people.

'We turn back now, daughter,' I announced, suddenly feeling reckless for having come so far, and with my girl in tow. 'There may be Siamese here.'

She, however, wanted to go on. She cocked her ear and claimed to hear the army, just ahead.

It is rare that I become angry with Bopa, but now I did. I took her hard by the arm to cut off any protests. But just as suddenly I went still. We both saw that a column of soldiers, two officers on horseback in the lead, was approaching from down the trail. Who were they? It was too late to hide. I stood facing them, afraid, hoping to protect my daughter with a show of stern dignity.

One of the officers jumped down from his mount.

'Khmer women in the Siamese territories!' he declared. 'How did this happen?'

He spoke in our native tongue. We were safe.

I of course had no idea that we had left the Empire's soil. I explained who we were and who our prince was, which brought on the usual eagerness to assist. Why, the army is just an hour's walk ahead, the officer said. We will take you to it. There is an equipment cart at the rear of the column – please, please, you will ride. Orders went out that room be created. So from there on we did ride, foot-sore, while bundled arrows and sacks of rice that had been in our place were born on the backs of walking soldiers.

But it turned out that, again, the army was not the promised short distance ahead. We went on for many hours, the officers saying again and again that surely it was just over the next ridge, or just across the little stream ahead. They were cheerful, almost too much so. I suspect they were trying in part to distract us from the sights that the trail had begun offering up. Awful things. There was another burned village, then a dead water buffalo, bloated. And then – two human bodies, men by the look of them, the blood all bled out of them, lying beneath a gum tree. I shielded Bopa's eyes, and again reproached myself for bringing her here.

Dusk came. The soldiers made camp, setting up a portable pavilion for Bopa and me. Cooking fires were fanned to life. An orderly brought us a lamp and some cooked rice and fish. Don't be afraid, he told us. You are surrounded by the Empire's bravest fighting men. We slept only fitfully that night.

In the late morning of the following day, we finally did arrive. Emerging from leafy forest cover, we found ourselves at the top of a large hill of grass that spilled down toward a stream. The entire area was filled with Khmer soldiers! Thousands of them, camped out, having flattened the grass in many places. It was a city transplanted to the countryside. Some of the men were drawing water from the stream, others were lying on mats beneath shelters, or tending horses and elephants, or carrying out tasks of military life that I couldn't understand. I was wondering how we were going to find two people in this multitude.

But then – I think the officers had sent someone ahead – there he was. My husband.

What pride he showed! Smiling broadly, he approached with a confident stride I had never seen. He wore a fine blue sampot; jewellery I didn't know hung around his neck. He stood before me and I felt a surge of pride as well. My own husband, so happy, so accomplished. The morose airs with which he and I had lived for so many years – gone! I began to raise my hands in greeting but, what was this? He stepped close and embraced me, right there in public! I must admit I was so joyful that I submitted, not caring that men were looking on. You must understand that never had he and I been apart for more than a day or two.

He broke away, looked to me, and said: 'And now, with you and our girl, I have everything.'

Then, behind him, running as if he were afraid he would miss us, was my boy. And so much bigger! But when he drew near, he stopped. Rather than jumping into my arms, he put hands together.

My husband turned to the soldiers and announced in a rather grand voice: 'My wife Mrs Sray, together with my daughter Young Mistress Bopa.'

The men – these strong soldiers – went to their knees, hands together.

My husband led us down the hillside. How quickly emotions can change. As I walked with him, already I was wondering whether, now that the initial excitement of reunion was over, he could really welcome us in this place, this man's place.

He brought us to a pavilion, in an area that seemed set aside for the prince's senior retainers. It was much better than the rude shelters in which the soldiers were sleeping. 'You will want to rest, I'm sure,' he said, motioning us to enter. An orderly appeared with our bags, another brought bowls of water, and we drank together. My husband watched, proud again. My boy sat alongside me.

Just then a messenger came running up and announced that my husband's presence was required at the prince's pavilion. Nol jumped to his feet, squeezed my hand and went off. We had been together not ten minutes.

Another women might have made a trip like this out of fear that her husband, away for so long, would take a minor wife, a young thing of such allure that she would displace the first wife in his affections and refuse to submit to her authority. I had no such concern. Nol had been loyal from the moment we met, and, unlike so many men, he never saw rise in wealth and influence as an opportunity to bring a new female into the household. To say it directly, he was awkward with other women, barely looking at them. But, as I sat in that pavilion that day, separated again from him, I grasped that another kind of newcomer wife had moved in, rolled out her mat and lit the coals of her stove. This wife? Her name was duty.

Bopa lay down on a mat and dozed. Poor thing – the journey had exhausted her.

Sovan and I were left together.

'Just look at my boy,' I said. 'So much taller than when he left his mother.'

He smiled in the sheepish way that had always touched me. 'I am so happy that you came, mother.'

Another shock – the voice of a man! My eyes teared up again and I moved to put an arm around him, to draw him to my lap. He was of course too big now for that. But he submitted to this motherly gesture.

After a while, he tactfully removed my arm and shifted slightly away. He took my hand and looked into my eye. 'It must be like this now, mother.'

We both laughed.

'I had known this day was coming, Sovan. I had always hoped to put it off.'

'Don't worry. Everything else will remain the same.'

Do you see what a jewel this boy was? Having sympathy for his mother, not just respect. But I cannot say this was a surprise. I have told you how as a small child he stayed in my lap beyond the usual years. And when I got up, he followed. If I moved to the water jar beneath the house, he went there too and sat near, watching me fill a jug, holding it for me when he became big enough for that. If I beat the dust out of our sleeping mats, he was just behind me, adding a stroke or two of his own with a twig he'd picked up. He came to the market with me many mornings, ready to run whatever errands I had for him. Later, when he became old enough to help in his father's work, I had to give him up, but I would always see him off in the morning. He and his father would be gone for long hours. But if he had a concern, it was me who heard it first, not his father. If I worried over my boy, it was that he was too content to be alone, too enamoured with private thoughts. I was never aware that he had real friends among the boys in our old quarter. And now I wondered how happy he would be in this camp. He would not complain about the hardships of life on the march. Yet I had no reason to think he would be drawn to this world of soldiers and war elephants. As a boy, he had never played with make-believe spears and armour.

So I asked. 'You are happy here, Sovan?'

'Yes, mother.'

'You have things to do?'

'Many things.'

'You have friends?' I was hoping now...

He thought a moment, then said: 'Let me show you, mother.'

We walked a few steps to another, larger pavilion. Inside it, laid on the floor in straight lines, were four folded parasols.

He took up one, very carefully. Then he pushed on something with one hand, and the holy implement opened.

What a thing of beauty! Bright red silk, alive with white lotus flowers. Surely our lords in Heaven had no parasol finer than this one. I approached it; Sovan stood proudly, holding it upright for me. With an index finger I dared touch the fabric, silk made taut from application of oils. The edges were trimmed in silver, with tassels hanging down. At the crown was another lotus, a large one, formed of silver-dyed cloth. Underneath, bamboo ribs radiated from a carved wooden hub in the most astonishing way, like rays of sunlight. To this hub was attached a sturdy bamboo shaft, with silver rings tight around it top to bottom, each spaced the length of an open hand, as if it were a divine species of bamboo. Perhaps it was.

I put a finger to one of those silver rings. It was faintly wet. A hint of varnish came off on my fingertip.

'A repair, mother. It's not yet quite dry. If I'd known you were coming, I'd have made sure it was done.'

'You fixed it yourself?'

'Yes. I spend a lot of time here. Father has taught me.' He gestured to the parasols. '*These* are my friends.'

18: The girl in the hidden teak house

You know, I had recognized this quality too in my boy some years earlier. He appreciated beauty. How old was he that first time I took notice? Maybe seven. Early one morning, I came upon him standing in the door of the old house, looking out. He was so still that I thought something must be wrong. But when I asked what, he just looked at me and said that it was nothing. I persisted. Finally, he explained. 'I am watching the sunrise. Look there. It was dark purple a few minutes ago, now it's almost pink. Heaven puts on a show for us every day.' This at age seven.

I took note again when he was older and going out with his father to help with canal-dredging jobs. One day they were called to work inside the walls of one of the older mountain-temples southeast of the Capital. It was the first time they'd been accorded such a privilege. They came home that night with Nol in a bad mood. The boy wouldn't work, wouldn't work, all day long, he said. All he wanted to do was look up at the temple, never the water, though that's where the work was. Later, I sat with Sovan and he told me, yes, his father was right. He couldn't stop looking. He whispered to me: 'A mountain temple is not one piece of stone. It's tens of thousands of small ones. Each one fits together perfectly with those around it like they're one. How can that be possible?'

That day at the camp, Sovan took some time putting the parasols away.

Afterwards, I said to him: 'The parasols are fine friends, son of mine, but do you have any friends of the human kind? Other boys, perhaps?'

'Yes, there are other boys here, but...I don't see much of them.'

'I'm sorry.'

'Don't be, mother. I am happy enough.'

'Perhaps there are girls, then?'

What spirit made me ask this? There were clearly no girls here. But it was the right question. My boy went red, right there before me. I was not prepared for so many changes in him!

Of course on something like this, he was not willing to come out with it all immediately. But, as his mother, I had to know.

So as the afternoon wore on (Bopa slept most of it away), I got the story.

It had happened back at one of the estates through which the army had passed. The supply of varnish for the parasols and other implements was running low, so Sovan had walked, by himself, to a nearby market town, to see if any could be found.

He was happy to be alone. He was getting away, for a while, from the hubbub of processions and princely audiences. So when he reached the market, he took his time buying varnish and brushes. When finally he felt he must return, he picked up some dried banana sweets for Veng and the other bearers, who always expected that a trip like this would produce something good to eat for them.

As he neared the estate, he turned and set off down a side track. On a whim, he told me, but I think it was to further put off the return to the estate.

Rounding a bend in the track, he saw a house ahead. At first he thought it was some hermit's dwelling, but as he drew closer he saw it was large and built of fine teak, its eaves carved with images of gods. In the back was a lotus pond. Probably it was the forest retreat of a local noble. He walked closer, drawn by the beauty of the house and its grounds. No one seemed to be home. At the front gate, he took a breath, muttered a prayer of apology to the household spirit, and passed through. No one came out to challenge, so he moved down the entrance path, passing manicured shrubs. The eaves seemed almost to float above walls and windows. He circled around the house and arrived at the pond. How peaceful it was – a long rectangle, edged with stone, the water half obscured by floating lily pads. With straight lines and a surface undisturbed, the pond defined an enclave of calm and order, keeping out the chaos of the jungle beyond.

'*Go away!* There's nothing to steal here!'

He spun around. Behind him stood a grey-haired woman, an angry one, a lady's maid by the look of her. Yet, a lady's maid holding a rather stout stick over her head.

'I'm not here to steal,' sputtered Sovan. 'I'm sorry – I'll leave.'

'Go, go, then! Now!' cried the woman, stepping closer and swinging the stick. Sovan hopped back to avoid it.

'Nang! Please, it's all right. He doesn't look like a thief.'

On the terrace above him stood not a lady but a girl. Sovan described her to me as a bit younger than he, a year or two shy of the age at which she could bear children. The sun shone full on her. Her face and hands bore the rouge of aristocracy; her hair, pulled back, was secured by a bronze clasp.

'Thank you!' called my son. 'I'm sorry – I thought no one was here. I just thought I'd sit for a bit by the water.'

'You can if you want to.'

He didn't feel like sitting now. Especially with the maid still eyeing him suspiciously.

The girl came down steps from the terrace.

'You're from Prince Indra's army?'

'No, I'm not! I'm not a soldier.'

'See, Nang? No need to be worried. And look – he doesn't even have a knife.'

The maid lowered the stick. 'Still,' she said, keeping her eyes on Sovan, 'we should be getting home now. I told you we shouldn't have come.'

'Just a few more minutes. Please...?'

The maid gave in – Sovan sensed that she often did for this girl – and left to fetch cups of drinking water. The girl turned to Sovan, who was now very nervous, never mind about the issue of trespassing. He had never in his life spoken with a girl of her sort, certainly not when we lived in the old neighbourhood. He wondered if he should be kneeling, looking down to avoid her eyes, summoning up that special palace language to keep her from laughing at him. But before he could do any of that, she began to speak, the sun again full on her face.

'I couldn't bear to go home now. My elder sisters and I have been cooped up for days, ever since the prince's army arrived in the district. All anyone's talking about is getting outside again.'

'But staying inside is not such a bad idea for now,' ventured Sovan.

'No, it's terrible!' She had opinions, this girl. Then she took on a confidential tone. 'But do you know, this afternoon I found Nang in the cooking shed and talked her into taking me out on a walk, just a short one. But once we were beyond the gate I, well, managed to stretch it into a long one. She kept whispering the whole way that we had to get back!' She made a mischievous face. 'But never mind. Now we have you for protection!'

The maid brought water in porcelain cups, and my boy remembered what was in his bag. He asked the girl: 'Would you like some banana sweets?'

'Oh, yes! My favourite.' She put up both hands, enthusiastically, and Sovan took note how smooth and delicate they were.

After that, they sat up on the terrace, with Nang hovering near, still not trusting my boy. They drank the water and ate their way through the banana sweets. The girl asked where he'd got them, and when he told her the market, she wanted to know whether he'd seen any girls of the district there. No, he replied, but maybe they were they all being kept in their homes too. Did he have any idea when the prince's men would be moving on? Sovan told her probably in a few days.

'That's wonderful!' she said, eyes flashing. 'I'll tell my sisters at the house. They'll be jealous when they find out how I know.'

Sovan wondered if that meant getting out or meeting him. But before he could think further of it, she stood up and took his hand, pulling him to his feet. 'Come on! Let me show you something fun. Down at the end of the pond.'

She led him to a spot where water fed in from a creek that coursed unseen through the jungle beyond the grounds. There were cracks in the channel's stone lining, and in these spaces she pointed out four frogs hiding. Sovan was past the age when boys care about frogs, but now he found new interest. He thought the girl would sit and wait for one to jump. Instead she picked up a reed and tickled the back of one of the little creatures. It duly sprang fast and far, making her jump back in shocked delight. They laughed together. Then they sat in silence for a while, the girl stirring the water with the reed, humming some local melody to herself.

Later, Nang came out with more cups of water, but this time she was not so accommodating on the question of remaining. The girl agreed reluctantly to go. But my boy was not ready to give her up just yet. 'Let me walk with you back to your estate. You might need protection.' She seemed to like the idea. And it was a fact that his face was known among the soldiers. If any were encountered, they would behave.

They walked down the track, passing in and out of sun rays that found their way through the foliage. The girl chattered some more, in the same carefree way. Their house, she said, was bigger than the one they'd just left. That one wasn't really a house, just a place where her father went sometimes when he wanted peace and quiet for his official duties. Their real house was much bigger, but much noisier because there were all sorts of people around, but even when she wasn't locked up, she liked to go to the little place in the forest.

Too soon, the estate house came into view. It was in fact quite a bit larger than the one they'd left, yet it had the same crafted beauty.

Nang made Sovan say good-bye here. It wouldn't do to arrive back with some strange boy in tow, she observed, in a voice she didn't bother to lower.

The girl said: 'But he can come and see us later, surely that's all right?' Nang replied yes, maybe they could figure out a way.

'I know where to find you,' volunteered my boy. 'But you never told me your name.'

'Come see us and I'll tell you then!'

She laughed again and scurried off toward the house. Sovan watched, smiling, until the pair passed through its gate.

An hour later, he arrived back at the occupied estate. The four bearers looked to him, hoping for something from his bag, and he had to invent an excuse about having had no money left once the varnish and brushes were bought. His full stomach protested the lie.

Later, he found his father at the bathing jars. Nol showed no curiosity about why his trip had taken so long. Rather, he announced that they were leaving first thing in the morning. The prince would go with his private guard and entourage to take a first look at the Siamese frontier. The main army would follow.

You can imagine what dismay Sovan felt.

Now, was this girl really so charming, so playful, so beautiful? I remember feeling unsure as my boy recounted all this. I half wondered if his enthusiasm reflected mainly that his hour with her was the only time that year that he got a hint of the old life – no soldiers, no processions and gongs, just the simple pleasures of eating banana sweets and watching a frog leap into a pond.

19: Martial might

My husband did not return to me that afternoon, nor that evening. I began to wonder when I would see him again. Bopa and I were in my son's hands, it seemed. Sovan found some lamps and sleeping mats and helped us prepare the pavilion for passing the night.

The next morning, we awoke to great urgency around us. To our left, to our right, soldiers with spears and shields were running down the hill, as if late for something. At some distant location a drum began to beat.

Sovan came with news. 'I'm afraid, mother, that the attack is about to begin.'

I could only say: 'Attack?'

'Yes, mother. Against the Siamese fort. That is why the soldiers are here.'

He gestured. There it was, far away up the other side of the valley, a kind of large wooden structure, situated at a pass between two hilltops.

So my children and I did what we were told. We joined other camp followers to climb to a lookout spot atop a hill on our side of the valley.

I didn't want to watch, but something about the strength, the organization, the frenetic motion of the massed men insisted on my eyes' attention. Ranks of soldiers were moving up the hill toward the Siamese fort, bringing with them ladders and spears and torches and strange rolling engines of war. What things men do in the cause of violence! I had never witnessed a battle before.

Off to the left, a great war chariot appeared, drawn by four white horses. Next to its driver stood a warrior, taller by a head. Even at this distance, I knew it must be Prince Indra. His chest was encased in silver armour that gave off a gleam like a daytime star. An escort of soldiers trotted to either side.

The prince raised his sword in some kind of martial greeting, and cheers arose from the ranks. There was a pause, then an officer's shouted order. The attack was starting, and so quickly! A giant, flaming arrow took flight. It seemed to hang for a moment in the heavens, before heading down, gaining speed, then disappearing behind the wooden walls of the Siamese fort. More cheers rose from our men, then a brace of smaller flaming arrows shot up from a row of archers.

Then the chariot darted ahead, those four horses at full gallop, leaving the men of its escort behind. What a sight it was – I would not have been surprised if the vehicle had taken flight across the sky.

Soldiers raced forward to try to catch the prince. Arrows were streaking the attackers' way. One caught a charging soldier right in the belly. I winced, but was not able to look away. Some of the men made now for a smouldering part of the fort's walls and stood ladders up against it. Another group took shelter behind large shields arranged in a row, making ready for an assault of their own, I think.

Indra's chariot raced up and down the length of the wall, he unleashing arrows as it went. All the time he was within range of the defenders' bows. Not a few enemy arrows were protruding now from the chariot's sides. It was a fearless performance.

Now the prince raced toward one of the erect ladders. Two men were climbing it, slowly, timidly, crouching behind shields. Even from here, I sensed their fear at being in the very front. The prince gestured abruptly to them, and they jumped down. Then he took their place! You recall how I felt when I first saw the prince that morning in the compound, that he never walked, he bounded? What he did next was like that again. He ascended that ladder as if with a single jump, sword in hand. And with no shield! More arrows came his way, but none struck him. At the top, he swung his sword at some unseen defender and then disappeared from sight.

Watching him, I will tell you, created a sort of spell in me. But then it broke and I turned away and mouthed a prayer.

Spirits of this isolated place, may all men find protection through you.

'Come now, children, let's not look at this anymore.' I turned my back on the battle and led them away. We found a grassy place and sat down.

When the din had died out, we looked again. The fort was now a smoking ruin. Men were carrying various things from it.

Sovan gestured to the left. 'Look!'

Climbing the hill across the valley was a team of parasol bearers. Nol was in the lead. His small stature told us it was him. In the way he carried himself I could see he was feeling proud all over again.

The team reached the fort's entrance. Prince Indra stood waiting there, his silver armour still marking him. A dais had been set up. The prince took his place on it; at my husband's order, four parasols snapped quickly into place over his head. It was a makeshift princely court, bringing order to the mayhem of a battlefield.

Now two soldiers bundled a captive toward the prince. They pressed the poor man to the ground; he crouched, hands bound behind him. People around me were saying that this must be the Siamese commander, captured rather than killed.

The prince sprang to his feet and went to this man. He circled him, prodding at him with a foot! I pursed my lips – was such humiliation necessary? And there was Nol, right at the prince's side. He was addressing the prince. It was not a long conversation, but it seemed intense, as if there was some disagreement. It was true then, as people had said. My husband was already an intimate of our master, so confident that he dared challenge his word.

Here is what happened next: The soldiers rolled the captive onto his back and unbound his hands. He began to struggle, but they held him down, extending his left arm outward. The prince raised his sword and without an instant's hesitation, brought it down, hard, on the man's arm! He cut it clean off. Even at this distance, I could see the blood spurt forth.

I was appalled. I took Bopa and Sovan by the hand and hurried them away.

Later, I sat in the pavilion and wondered, why had I come here? Why was our family serving this prince? We did not belong in this world.

Perhaps an hour later, Nol appeared.

'I am back, wife. My work is complete for now.'

I said nothing. Anger, or maybe it was disappointment, was welling inside me.

'What is wrong?' he asked, stepping closer.

'What is wrong? What is *wrong*?' I found my tongue. 'What is wrong is that I have a husband who is involved in cruelty of the worst kind. I watched! I saw that man be deprived of his arm! How can you live with such a sin? You were right at the scene. Did you do nothing to stop it?'

'I did not, in fact...'

'Very well! I will leave. Right now. With our daughter.'

'Please...'

He put a hand to my shoulder, but I shook it off. 'Say nothing more!' I cried. 'Look at this, you were so close that there are spatters of that poor man's blood on your sampot!'

'Please. I will tell you what it was that happened there.'

I looked to him and for a moment, the self-important Nol had departed and the old one who cared for me, who protected me, was in his place, hoping for a favourable answer.

'Tell me, then.' I crossed my arms across my breasts.

'The prince was prepared to carry out a killing. It is that way in war – the losing commander forfeits his life. But I persuaded him to instead let the man go, alive. The lost arm was the price of release. It is a small price compared to a lost life.'

I looked to him, and could see he was telling the truth. That is another problem I never had with my husband. He never lied to me.

'That was all, husband? The prince decided to show mercy?'

He smiled wearily. 'Dear wife, I have always known you are wise. Yes, things were not as simple as that. I pointed out to His Highness that this man, if returned to his own lord in a less than intact physical state, would be a much more powerful message than merely the news that he had perished. Our prince saw the logic of that, and agreed to spare the man's life, in this way.'

It seemed heartless and calculating, but at least I could take comfort in knowing my husband had not been party to murder.

'This is a different world we inhabit now, husband, you and I.'

'It is.'

He reached for my hand, and I let him take it. What a look of love and gratitude came to his face! And of course he assumed that now everything was now fine.

'So!' he cried, looking on me again. 'Let me bathe and we will have dinner. And then I will present you to our prince.'

That I did not want, and as it turned out, we did not meet the prince that night. Within a few minutes of our sitting down to rice, word came that torches had been sighted just beyond the fort. It seemed as if another Siamese unit had formed up. Our prince, we were told, had immediately mounted his horse and, against the advice of his officers, gone riding off with a detachment to investigate. And shortly, before my husband had even finished his meal, came word that his presence was needed. 'One can never tell when a court session must be held, or a procession staged,' he explained as he stood up. And so off he went, again, in company of that new wife of his. Bopa and I remained behind, again, with Sovan.

We passed the night in worry, but in the morning came word that there were in fact no Siamese beyond the fort but that the prince's detachment, and my husband, were pressing on further. They had sent back for supplies and more soldiers and would be gone two weeks at the least.

Bopa and I stayed two more days, then said goodbye to Sovan and left for the Capital. We walked not a single step on that journey. We rode an oxcart, alongside silver bowls, inlaid trays and various other plunder from the Siamese fort. In the Capital we were deposited right at the door of our house.

Inside, Bopa and I knelt to say a prayer of thanks to the domestic spirit. We had found Sovan and Nol; their lives were no longer a mystery. Perhaps soon this campaign would end and they would return home. And yet, as I mouthed those words I found myself picturing not them, but the prince, bounding up that ladder.

20: The world his to take

For Bopa and me, the following year went smoothly. We continued to live in the big house in the compound. We prayed as often as we could at the shrine of Bronze Uncle. Like Sovan, my girl began to blossom into physical adulthood. My work for the prince's household expanded, as did my private trading. We were on the road to becoming rich, I must admit. There were evenings when Mrs Pala and I added up the accounts, and we could not believe the sums. Some of the wealth I gave as anonymous gifts to temples, but some I put aside for later use.

Almost every week we heard claims of the progress of the campaign in the Siamese territories. The prince has captured a great riverside city, he has taken four quarries, two ruby mines and a forest with the finest teak. He has seized riceland sufficient for a hundred thousand Khmer settlers. How much was true we couldn't know, but what was undeniable was that every week more cartloads of plunder arrived at the Capital. People gathered to watch them roll in. The prince was on everyone's mind, and not just at that gate. Story tellers entertained crowds at festivals with the exploits of the war bow Gandiva. At temples, worshippers chanted prayers seeking protection for him. There was at least one shrine that was claimed to have power to grant young men similar appearance and martial ability.

Inside our compound and out, people began saying that it was time for the prince to come back to the Capital and receive an honour from the King. Yet month after month passed with no word that such an honour would be bestowed. The Council of Brahmins was consulting to discern Heaven's intention, it was said. No doubt they were. But Brahmins are men like any others, vows notwithstanding, and later I learned that in the council there was a point of view that whatever honour was bestowed would best be posthumous, that if the council waited long enough the campaign against the Siamese would open the way to Prince Indra's next life. Each time a field dispatch described him as completing a battle blood-splattered, these priests wondered whose blood it was and if the next dispatch would recount fever, infection and final breath.

But that news never arrived. So it was that the council finally deemed that Indra would be honoured. But behind the walls of the prince's palace, many people were offended by the terms: He would be promoted to the Second Rank, not the First. He would enter the city with just a small escort. The famous war bow would have to remain behind – he could bring only ceremonial weapons. There would be no victory parade. His schedule would be set entirely by the Brahmins and at the end he would leave the Capital and return to his army in the north.

You see again how the priests were entirely in charge. They got no direction from the King. When the decision to award the honours was announced to him, in fact, his only comment was 'Indra... Now, which one is he?'

The following day, proclamations were read out to the Capital's people. I was in the central market when a crier arrived there and the news of the honours caused general elation. But the details that followed did not: All residents wishing to greet the prince must wait until after he paid respects to His Majesty the King. They must gather only at approved places where the prince would make brief appearances – the main market, the West Gate, a field by a particular temple in the southern quadrant. They must not commit public offense by becoming loud or disorderly or intoxicated. Many people muttered complaints, some of them right in front of the crier.

But in subsequent days, it became clear that whatever power the priests had inside the palace, it did not extend to the streets. There was simply too much ferment. Travellers arriving from the north reported that Indra had reached such and such temple in his journey to the Capital, crossed such and such river. The beast the prince rode, it was said, was surely Airavata, sacred mount of the god Indra, possessed of three heads but choosing on this particular journey to display only one. Entire villages were turning out in greeting. At one monastery, sixty acolytes emerged from their cells to join the prince's procession. Word spread that he would enter the city by the North Gate. So people thronged out of it and marched north to greet him on the road. Spirits were so high that hardly anyone remembered that this was in violation of the palace proclamation.

Bopa and I left the house early on that day and walked toward the North Gate. But there were such crowds that we could not get anywhere near it. So we claimed for ourselves a tiny patch of trampled grass well back from the street and began a wait.

We waited, we waited, people crowding us all sides. We grew thirsty. Voices would shout that he was coming, he was just minutes away, but then – nothing. Finally, at almost midday, the prince passed through the gate atop his elephant. Rather, I should say that four parasols passed through the gate, floating over the crowd – Bopa and I could see nothing more than that. But what a tumult! People jostled wildly, kicking up dust. They cheered themselves hoarse, they held small children overhead.

Surely Nol and Sovan were somewhere near us, walking alongside His Highness's elephant. But hope that we would spot them faded. The procession moved slowly along the avenue that led to the royal palace, stopping again and again when people broke though the lines of soldiers who were supposed to be keeping order. I held Bopa back, fearful for her safety. When the crowds cleared, she and I went home by a back way, resigned to waiting until our two men presented themselves.

Nol was in fact at the elephant's side , and later he recounted the rest of the day. With enormous pride, of course. It was almost as big a triumph for him as for the prince. You see, at his headquarters in the Upper Empire, the prince had turned furious on first hearing of the palace's conditions. No victory parade! But Nol calmed him, counselling that it was the people who would decide whether there was such a parade. And everyone could see now how they had decided.

It took more than two hours for the prince and his elephant to reach the stone bridge that marked the start of the royal sector. There, on the long terrace at the palace's front wall, the King stood waiting in the heat, fifteen parasols overhead, the flame of royal authority flickering in a cauldron at his side. Fifty priests and twenty concubines attended, as did close to one hundred bodyguards. As the sound of the prince's gong began to carry in, their attention drifted away from the monarch and toward the visitor.

Indra's elephant reached the terrace, and there it knelt. The prince sprang down, all eyes on him, and walked to the base of steps that led up to the royal presence. Between a pair of stone guardian lions, he performed a full crouch of submission.

This was Nol's first look at the King. He later told me that what he saw was a stooped man with pale withered legs, who seemed just to want to last out the ceremony. I winced at such talk, but he went on, hardly noticing: His Majesty wore a tall gold headdress and armlets that enclosed sagging flesh; at his waist was the golden sword of authority, but all these things seemed too heavy for him to bear. To Nol, it was if the people around the King, pressing as close as protocol allowed, were all that kept him on his feet. In my husband's view, even the royal flame burned feebly.

Indra climbed the steps toward the aged monarch, who tensed discernibly at his approach. His bodyguards did too, tightening fingers around sharpened weapons. But there was no need. Well back from the King, the prince knelt again and touched his forehead three times to a mat that had been blessed by priests and laid on the terrace stones.

The prince got to his feet, one of his retainers following, carrying on a red silk pillow something that resembled a large dried fruit.

'Blessed Sovereign,' announced the prince, 'I present to you the head of the commander of the Siamese army.'

Clutching stringy black hair, the prince raised the prize in the air. It is no surprise that the King frowned and took a half step back. But from around him came a collective gasp, and not a few people forgot themselves and moved forward the better to see. Beaming, the prince kept this cruel trophy high, turning it left, then right.

'There are many thousands more like this,' he declared, addressing not the King but the people around him. 'Most of them we left for the birds and animals. But I bring this one to the Capital to show that never again will the Siamese threaten our borders, never again will we live in fear of the heretics.'

There was a pause while this was absorbed. Then a priest

shuffled to the King's side and whispered to him. The King summoned energy to speak.

'Indra, thunder-armed warrior,' he said, his voice barely carrying. 'Sword of Heaven and Empire, protector who sweeps far districts of enemies and expands the Empire's frontiers.' He paused and looked back to the priest, who nodded to him to continue. 'We welcome you, Indra, as a future grandson. We welcome you as the future husband of the Princess Benjana, first daughter of the Crown Prince.'

This caused an enormous collective gasp. People said later it could only have been a last-minute decision by the Brahmins. Having seen the intense public outpouring for the prince, they had decided that a promotion alone would not be sufficient.

Everyone, my husband included, was looking to Prince Indra. He was taking stock. Then the prince recovered and fell to another full crouch. His face remained hidden for what seemed a very long time, then he sat up and put his right hand to his heart. 'Your Majesty honours me in ways that I do not deserve,' he declared.

The King looked to his advisers, inquiring if anything more was needed of him. One of them motioned that he was done. Then, on cue, a royal retainer stepped forward and presented Indra with a single flower, a blue-purple orchid laid on a pillow.

'A gift,' announced the man, 'grown by the royal hand in the palace garden, a symbol of royal love for the subject Prince Indra, soon to be Prince Indra of the Second Rank, Prince Indra beloved radiant son-in-law.'

Now twelve priests stepped forward with bowls of holy water. As the prince knelt motionless, they circled him, splashing water on his head and shoulders and chanting.

Even before that was done, the King began to leave, and Nol took note that his walk was weak – it was a shuffle. The concubines were going too, following their lord through the stone gate into the palace compound. Many found ways to stop and look back toward the prince.

Indra was escorted off to review a regiment of the King's guard. Nol was led to a parade ground nearby, where a collection of pavilions, decorated with flowers and silk hangings, had been erected to house the visitor's entourage. One was marked with the parasol master's name, and inside, Sovan was waiting. Bowls of water and rice snacks had been laid out for them. Father and son ate together. Nol was actually trembling – can you imagine how exuberant he was? He was now serving a man who might become King.

Presently he rose, because he had heard from a distance some kind of commotion in a rank of soldiers. A lone woman's voice carried through. Nol went nearer, feeling he might be needed. But things were under control. The concubine Rom had arrived with a maid, demanding to be taken to her pavilion, and a captain of the prince's guard had explained that there was no such pavilion. He had a list of the prince's official entourage and her name was not on it. She argued some more, then turned spitefully and left.

The following day, the prince went by palanquin through thronged streets to a temple on the south side of the city for purification rites. He was shown through the gates and in the torch-lit chamber inside the great tower was wet down with water made pure by contact with the linga of the Lord Shiva. He passed the night there, meditating, or so it was said. The next morning, priests chanted a long holy program that elevated him to the Second Rank. When he emerged from the temple gate, the crowd erupted in cheers all over again. The prince sprang onto his elephant, in a way that people said suggested he had the power to fly. There began yet another raucous procession. Soldiers of the King's guard, smiling proudly, marched in the lead, and no one made any attempt to keep the crowds back. On street after street, food stalls emptied, masons abandoned tools and novice priests put aside texts, all to go for a look. Venders of coconut milk and cut fruit did a record trade. I would guess that thieves had a record yield in that crowd – that was how distracted people were.

Bopa and I had grown tired of waiting, so we went out of the house again to look. Late in the afternoon, as the procession moved up and down avenues in the vicinity of the central market, I stood before it with four vendor women who had left their wares untended. Bopa ran off somewhere – she had more energy than I to press her way through crowds. The women and I were going to hold firm where we stood in hopes the procession would come to us instead. My eyes were scanning the throngs for husband and son. I prayed for a glimpse of them. And, I will not deny it. I hoped that I might also get a closer glimpse of this prince we served.

Marching soldiers came into sight far down the south avenue, then elephant with prince atop it, shaded by the four parasols.

'A man crafted by Heaven!' declared one of the market women, though we could hardly see him.

As he drew closer, I looked. A red parasol was obscuring the prince's face. Muscled chest and arms were what I saw, adorned by gold jewellery and two white sashes that crossed at the breastbone. How can I explain the shameful thing that my mind now did? Like it had that very first time I saw him, in that first morning in the palace compound, it compared this torso to that of the man with whom I had passed countless nights, to whom I was committed by vows and by common decency to love and stand by loyally.

But then the parasol moved so that the prince's face came into view, and what I saw made my knees give way. I dropped in shock to the ground behind the market women, thankful I was hidden by their sampots. My movement was so abrupt that one of the women forgot the prince and leaned down to me, concerned I had become ill. I waved off the attention, hid my face in my hands and mouthed a prayer. I held like that, crouching, panicked, until the prince's elephant passed. Then I got to my feet and I ran.

The face of the prince was the face I'd seen when I first arrived at the gate of Sugar Palm House twelve years earlier, the face of the boy Lon, who, perched on the shoulders of his father the estate lord, reached out and pinched my cheek. Prince Indra was that boy, grown up, still thinking that the world was his to take.

21: Anxious reunion

Could there be a secret that a wife would more want to share with her husband?

I lay awake that night, thinking, thinking. How could I have missed this connection? There had been hints. I remembered now that the cart driver Sao had told me that first day, during the trip from the orphanage, that there was a question of rights to an estate up north, that the master's family had been awarded it but another had refused to give it up. Why, that estate was Chaiyapoom! The little boy had grown up and taken what was to have been his elder brother's realm. Then there was the prince's father, whose benevolence was so often remarked upon, and the rich man who had endowed the orphanage and welcomed me so kindly at the estate. One and the same! Oh, how like a criminal's mind did mine work that night. I began to think how fortunate I was that I had not been found out already, but how that might change. What would happen if the father came to the Capital to visit his son the prince, and happened upon me in the compound? I am not one who could improvise in such a situation. I would panic, and end up bound and bloodied in a prison cage.

So how, how I wanted to pour all of this out to Nol. He would know what to do, he would comfort and protect me. Yet the knowledge would poison his new life. It would go from ideal to charade. Every moment he would be thinking he was serving a man whose brother we had killed. Every interaction with the prince would be corrupted, every word he uttered might be a slip-up that would give away the secret.

Nol had sacrificed so much for me in the former days. Now it was for me to be strong and repay the favour. Lying there inside my mosquito net, perspiring, I resolved that this would be my secret alone.

Did I sleep at all that night? I'm not sure. I only know that I was on my feet with the first hint of light on the eastern horizon. At a basin, I splashed my face. I knew that I must put on a convincing act for my husband when he finally appeared at the house. All these months, I had been hoping he would come. Now I only wished he would stay away.

And only two hours after dawn on that very day, the maid came to say that the master was approaching.

I gathered my thoughts as best I could, then went to the door to greet him. I wore a simple sampot, an ivory clasp holding back my hair – right now it seemed appropriate that I did not wear jewellery, things that would imply purity of soul.

Nol was about ten paces from the base of the steps. He had stopped and now he was gazing upon me. That old devotion showed through on that face! May Heaven forgive me, I always wished I could love him even half as much as he loved me. It is vain, but I had always sensed an imbalance. I always knew that my presence, the presence of this simple woman born in a village could disarm him, disarm this man who could stand up to a prince.

'We have returned,' he said proudly. 'Your husband and your son.' Sovan was standing behind him. Taller even again.

'You have, husband,' I replied, palms together, for I could think of nothing else to say. 'Heaven has seen to it.'

Sovan stepped toward me. How I wished he were again that boy who would race into my arms. But I accepted. We exchanged greetings.

'We're so happy you had time to come,' I said, looking to Nol, my fingers wiping back a tear. 'There has been so much excitement on the streets. Bopa and I knew you would be busy.'

'Yes, very busy,' Nol replied. We had found a subject. 'We're with the prince almost every hour we're awake.'

'I went out to the street for the elevation parade, but I couldn't see you. Well, come inside and have some refreshment.' I noticed now that some servants had come with him too. I turned to them. 'Sit down in the shade, if you like. We'll get something for you too.'

I climbed the steps to the house, Nol and Sovan following, and called out the news of the arrival. Bopa appeared from a side room, flushed. Nol was caught short – his daughter had become a young woman, and a very fashionable one. Her hair was up in the style of the palace, bound with a filigreed bronze clasp. She wore a crisp silk sampot embroidered with silver thread at the lower edge and flaring panels at either side. She smiled broadly to her father, unafraid, and knelt. The palms of the hands she put together in greeting were red with powder.

At the household shrine, I lit incense. 'Come on, then. Everyone. We will give thanks for the safe return.' We said prayers.

The maid entered and from a tray laid out four silver cups of water before us. Nol silently inspected the cups – they were part of a set he had sent from the provinces. I was glad the maid had chosen them. Now his eyes were wandering, performing a silent inventory. The house was built of teak. The floors were freshly polished, carved Heavenly figures peered out from beams overhead. The windows were hung with red sashes, the mats were new and of a particularly thick weave and there was a collection of varnished fittings – a chest, a low table for eating and the shrine, whose mother-of-pearl inlays registered with Nol's eye.

Presently he turned back to us. 'So Bopa is a woman now.'

'Very much so, as you can see,' I said. 'And young men are starting to show up at the door making excuses to talk to her.'

Bopa beamed. I continued: 'I'm glad she'll have her brother around. She might need some protection.'

'Why would I need protection, mother? If that's danger, then I like it! Anyway, what kind of protection is this brother of mine going to give? Look, he's gone more than two years, traveling in the party of Prince Indra, and still he's so quiet, he hardly says a thing! The boys wouldn't be afraid of him.' She looked his way, challenging him to respond.

'Sister, when I'm around you, there's the talk of two from just one. So why should I say anything?'

Bopa laughed, and I did too, just a bit.

The maid returned with cut mango. The girl took a piece, then stood up quickly. 'Come on, then, brother – I'll show you the new things we have. And after that the market.'

Nol watched them leave, then asked: 'So there really are young men coming around to see Bopa? What kind of men?'

'Young ones, not much older than she is, really. I was joking about needing protection. They are nice boys, sons of retainers, like us, for the most part. But also the son of a blacksmith, from our old neighbourhood. He knew her there. A nice boy. He talked his way through the gate and presented himself one morning with a gift of five rambutans. But don't worry. She hasn't settled on anyone, really.'

'Good. Please keep them away.'

'Well, husband – having respectable young men pay court is no bad thing. It keeps her occupied and away from the temptations here.'

'Perhaps you worry too much?' He gave me a gentle pat to the hand. 'Just like you always did.' He wiped his mouth. 'But here now – I've brought you a gift.'

From a bag, he brought out a silver neckpiece.

'My goodness!' I took it in hand carefully, afraid to touch something so costly and delicate.

'Please,' he said. 'Try it on.'

I hesitated, then fastened it around my neck. I rose, pleased, and went to a table where a polished-metal mirror lay. This piece was in fact a beautiful thing, and for the first time I began to feel calm. I looked at myself silently. Nol followed and knelt behind me, drawing close. He peered over my shoulder at my reflected face.

'It's beautiful, husband,' I said. 'Too beautiful for a woman like me, really.'

'Nothing is too beautiful for you, my dear wife. If anything, you are too beautiful for it. When it's around your neck, no one will notice it. The artisan who made it would be disappointed.'

There were times when Nol could say the right thing. He placed his arms around me and I leaned back into his embrace.

'Husband, you are good to me.'

'If I'm good, it's because you bring it out in me.'

'You flatter me. It is not that way. But how long, how long will you stay with us?'

'Not long, I'm afraid. After the royal wedding, the prince will return to his army. Sovan and I will go with him. But before long, the campaign will be over. The prince will return to the Capital to live and we'll be here again too.'

The maid returned to clear the cups. Nol and I pulled away from each other.

The sight of the silver around my neck brought a stunned smile to the girl's face.

'It's quite special, isn't it?' I said to her. 'It must have been very costly....'

Nol shrugged.

It took just an instant for my smile, my peace of mind, to fade. My eyes met his and I could see that he hadn't paid a thing for it, that it was the rightful property of some woman in the north. More plunder.

I removed it. I spent a moment securing it in a box, then turned back to him. 'Well, then! I must hear about what has happened with you all of these months.'

He told the story, at some length, though I think leaving out things that would upset me, elaborating on ones I would like, such as the prince's donation of forty sampots and a month's supply of firewood to a colony of hermits.

I listened, trying to seem interested, but in fact I could not be.

When he finished, I paused a moment, then said: 'And our prince...where is his home estate?'

'It is to the east. It is called the Community of Great Dazzling Prosperity....'

My eyes closed. I took a breath. I suppose that until this point I had held up hope that I had been mistaken.

'Are you all right?'

'Yes, yes, I'm fine. Now, this estate, did the campaign take you there?'

'No. It's many days' travel in the other direction from where we've been.'

At least there was comfort in that. I began telling Nol what had happened with me and Bopa in the past two years, how the siege had frightened everyone and made life hard but that when it was over things became better. And how one day the palace cook asked for my help in acquiring basics for the kitchen.

Nol cut in: 'He wanted you to go to market and shop for him?'

'No, husband,' I said, though that was of course what I had done at first. 'To supervise the girls who do the shopping.'

Bopa and Sovan returned just then, each carrying cut

173

pineapple on a stick. 'Mother does a lot more than that now, father,' she offered.

I said: 'Bopa....'

The girl launched into a description of how busy I was on any given day. It was all laid out for Nol right there. I oversaw the purchase of just about everything the prince's household requires – food, linens, mats, stable straw, spices, cooking pots, chinaware, incense. I had close to fifty people working for me, in stockrooms, in the market. People used to come around the house all the time, with questions, but a month ago the carpenters had built a special pavilion for me and now I sat there mornings with my account slates to plan and answer questions and settle disputes among the employees. Mrs Pala, the coconut woman from the old neighbourhood, was my assistant now and next week...

Nol broke in. 'I don't see why any of this is necessary. You're the wife of the parasol master. It is enough to see to your own household.'

'It's my way of serving our prince, husband.'

Bopa said: 'And she's done some trading for us too!'

I think that Nol now saw the shrine and the other fine things in the room in a different light. He ground his teeth. 'I'm going to see to it that one day you'll remember this house and wonder how you ever lived in such a tiny place, and how you got by with just one servant.'

'Husband, please accept that I want no greater wealth than what we have now. It's already too much; wanting things brings no peace to the soul. Whatever it is that makes you unsatisfied with this house, please, can't you put it aside? This place has become home for Bopa and me and I hope that when the prince returns to the Capital it will be home for you and Sovan as well, that its spirit will welcome you, and that we will make a quiet life here together.'

Nol took a breath, then put his hand to mine. 'I'm afraid the quiet life is behind us.'

That evening, the children left the house to visit another market. Nol and I bathed at the jars behind the house, then I led him to my sleeping room. I blew out the lamp that flickered on a stand in the corner, and entered the mosquito net that the maid had set up. Nol joined me. I lay still on the mat inside, eyes closed. Presently Nol stroked the curve of my neck where it met the shoulders. He looked down on my face and skin, which glowed from moonlight that Heaven sent through a window, and I could see that old devotion on his face. His hands began to move over more of my body. I did not resist, but neither did I help.

And I committed a deep sin. For just a moment, I allowed myself to imagine that it was the prince leaning over me in the moonlight.

The next morning, the maid put rice, catfish and water spinach before the family in the main room. I asked that Sovan might stay the day, but my husband answered that the boy was needed to help with preparations for the wedding. So, the two of them said their good-byes in front of the house and departed, as ignorant of my secret as I had intended they be. At least I had accomplished that.

So many things had happened in the last two days. Yet the events of one that would soon follow would make them all seem insignificant.

22: The bird-god Garuda

I left the house shortly after my husband and son, thinking I must not stay in and dwell on my concerns. I went about my day's work in the compound, planning for orders of fish from the Freshwater Sea. But each person with whom I dealt wanted not to discuss the business at hand but to ask a question: When will the nuptial rites take place? Word had spread that Nol had been home for the night; I had never thought to ask.

Normally, of course, preparations for a wedding take quite a long time, whether for a village couple or a pair of royal betrothed. There is a need for consultations, astrological calculations and extended prayer, not to mention the organizing of feasts and processions. But the Brahmins were anxious to complete this particular rite and get the prince back out of Angkor, even though he was to be placed in line to the throne. Such was their jealousy, fear, resentment – call it what you will.

In the end, it took them only three days to get things ready.

On the appointed morning, the Capital erupted in another giant celebration as word flew about that the rites had begun inside the palace walls: Now Prince Indra is standing next to his bride, now the King's chief priest is chanting the wedding verse, now the blessing string is being tied around their wrists. Now they are married! Across the city, gongs rang, drums sounded and countless earthen cups of rice wine were upended. People got to their feet to dance. In half a dozen shrines, young couples took their own hastily scheduled wedding vows, hoping for luck through association with what was happening behind those walls, out of sight.

Plans called for a celebration parade in the afternoon. His Majesty would lead atop an elephant, Prince Indra following on the beast he had ridden into the city.

Shortly after the midday meal, the men of the royal wardrobe gathered the garments and jewellery that the King would wear for the parade. They came to his pavilion and, after murmuring apologies for touching the royal body, they applied sampot, golden ear ornaments and pendants, headdress and scent, one after the other. Then they put the golden sword in his hands. They would recall later that their lord looked wearily at it, and then to the grand chamberlain.

'It is time to begin, then?'

'Yes, Majesty.'

'Well, some water first, please.'

He was passed a bowl, and drank, making a child's slurping noise – he was quite advanced in age, after all. Then, on the chamberlain's signal, a pair of servants came close, and after uttering more apologies, put hands to their lord's elbows and guided him toward the door. At the threshold he paused to sniff at a bouquet.

Outside was a set of portable wooden steps, by which knelt an elephant, a gilded platform on its back, red silk vestments hanging from its sides.

'It's Kumari, I hope?' the King asked, squinting. His eyes were no good at this distance.

'Yes, Majesty,' whispered the servant on his right. 'As you requested.'

It seems that one of the few decisions the King made for himself was which elephant he would ride. For today's occasion, the palace staff would have preferred one of the more fearsome beasts of the stable, veterans of war, but Kumari had for months been the only elephant the King would select. I imagine that he was frightened of most of the animals, but with this calm and intelligent one he had established a rapport, even as I had in the old days, and sometimes he whispered to her questions about his next life.

At the steps, the servants put hands to him once more to guide him upward, but he shook his head. He looked to a young man who wore the neckpiece of a royal mahout. 'First, how about something for my big girl?'

'Yes, Majesty!' replied the mahout.

It was Sadong, the man with whom I had been friends for so long. Now he fetched a basket of cut sugar cane. The King stepped in front of the elephant, and held a piece up, looking into the animal's eyes, and then to the diamond of pale-pink skin on the

177

forehead. The trunk rose to signal thanks, then its tip came down and in a delicate motion took the piece from the royal fingers.

'There, there, Kumari, you like it so much! Haven't they been giving you any at the stable?'

Sadong cringed at that remark, and the King, sensing his unease, turned to him: 'Just a joke, young man. I know you take very good care of her. Well, I suppose we have to get going now. We've got to do a little work.'

With the servants' help, the King ascended the steps and sat down on the gilded platform atop the animal's back. Sadong took his own place astraddle the neck. In his hand was a brass goad for guiding, but it was only ceremonial. Kumari was attuned to the lightest touch of the toes at a spot behind a leathery ear. Now Sadong touched that spot and the beast lumbered forward. The King held on tight, because even with Kumari he was frightened at being so high off the ground.

Twelve parasol bearers joined the King and his mount, six to a side, each holding a long shaft atop which fluttered gold and red silk. Ahead, junior Brahmins lifted an ark in which the royal fire burned. Then, to the beat of drum and cymbals, the priests led the way out the north gate of the palace compound. In the open area outside, yet more members of the procession, one hundred twenty soldiers of the royal guard, stood in formation. And behind the men Prince Indra, atop his own elephant.

Kumari turned to follow the fire bearers; I would guess that the King's eyes were not strong enough to see even that Indra was there. Probably no one had told him he would be.

Orders were shouted down the line, and the soldiers raised spears in unison and began marching behind the royal mount. The procession made its way along the compound's north wall, then at the corner turned to the right, to proceed toward the royal reviewing terrace. Her Majesty the Queen, as old and honourable as her husband, sat on a dais at its precise centre, presiding over close to a hundred nobles and retainers seated on mats to either side. Martial games were taking place before them, in which several members of Indra's guard were vying against the King's men in a contest of blunt-tipped knives and spears.

When the procession appeared, eyes turned as one toward it. Whispers arose – see the sun glinting so nicely off the gilding! See the vestments of the King's elephant, the flame of the royal fire! And so many parasols!

Nol was on that terrace, and he had other concerns. I would guess that he found himself whispering now, into the stones, a rare prayer, a request for steadiness and courage. At certain times, he could be quite a religious man.

What I am about to do, lords of Heaven, must be done for the safety of the Empire.

Perhaps those were his words.

The King's elephant was approaching the centre of the terrace, where steps lead down to the grass of the reviewing field. As if as one, spectators placed their heads down in reverence. And then, from the top of the steps, came some kind of commotion. Everyone remembered this: a woman's shout, words of protest. All around, heads came up from the floor to look. 'The prince's concubine,' someone muttered. 'She's got in again – she's demanding a place at the centre. At a time as late as this.' Guards at the base of the steps raced up them to deal with her, and Nol would have understood that at this moment, at least, she was a confederate.

So he hurried down the steps and out across the grass as if to meet the King's elephant. Voices shouted from behind him. 'You!' 'Stop right there!' 'Come back!' He kept going. As the fire bearers and the elephant drew near, he fell to the grass and did a full prostration.

'Get out of here!' A breathless soldier had caught up with him. 'You can't offer a petition this way.'

A spear tip pricked his shoulder, but only pricked it, I think because the soldier had suddenly recognized who he was. Nol bore the pain without response.

Eyes closed, Nol would have sensed the fire bearers passing, then the footfalls of the King's elephant Kumari, with the lighter, faster feet of the parasol men to the side. An instant after that would have come the sound of quick, strong, firm human steps, then a terrible, crushing blow at the centre of his back. My husband's chest collapsed flat against the ground!

The blow was delivered by the right foot of Prince Indra, who a few seconds earlier had dropped from atop his elephant and sprinted forward with the force of a charging boar, passing the ranks of marching soldiers. In his hand he held a short-shafted spear. Even today, I find this all hard to imagine, or believe. But Nol had placed his body on the ground as a springboard, giving the prince the boost he needed to bound straight onto the back of Kumari.

How unspeakable, how tragic it was. The last thing that His Majesty saw in this life was Indra, poised over him, the spear raised high. Its point came down hard on the wrinkled skin of our peaceful monarch's shoulder, penetrating straight to the heart. The royal eyes flashed, then rolled, going dim. Indra pulled the spear's point out, took the sword of authority from unresisting fingers, then pushed the body off the gilded platform. Our lord's earthly form careened limp and bleeding toward the grass, landing full and heavy atop one of the parasol men, who collapsed beneath the weight, totally confused. This man's parasol began to fall, slowly, like a tree cut in a forest. The man behind him grabbed for it, but missed, setting off panic among the entire team. Shrieks were heard; the neat formation of red and gold silk overhead dissolved into chaos.

The prince paid no attention to any of that, but stood full up on the elephant's back. He raised the golden sword with both hands, and shouted, to the people on the terrace, to the soldiers, and, it was later said, to the Empire at large: 'I claim the throne, by right of the Lord Shiva, by right of the needs of the Khmer people! The period of decay and corruption is over! The Empire will expand, it will destroy its enemies wherever they are found! The Khmer race will again live in security!'

Thus began the Eighteenth Reign

People on the terrace stared in stunned silence; on the grass below, soldiers looked up in fear, then at each other. They remained in formation behind the elephant, marching, but then one man broke ranks and went to the ground to hail the prince, then another, until finally all of them were down.

But the prince did not want that. 'Soldiers!' he shouted. 'You will continue your escort. Form up again and follow. Fire bearers! Take the flame back to the palace and safeguard it. Parasol bearers! Get away! Go get a team of my own men to accompany me.'

Then he looked to Sadong, 'And you there, keep the elephant going.'

Sadong muttered assent. It was the first sign he was not going to die.

Behind, Nol raised his head from the grass. People said later he made right away to stand, but on this first attempt he failed. I believe he was already being punished by Heaven for his act – his lower back had been injured by the prince's foot. But he chose to ignore the pain. On second try he managed to get to his feet, then strode past the bleeding corpse of the King, now surrounded by the parasol bearers and a pair of priests who had dared run to it. Nol ignored them, continuing on to a gate through which prince and elephant had left the field. He saw them ahead. But something was wrong. The animal had stopped.

Feel pity for Sadong. He was in a panic himself now. He was astride the gentle beast's neck, bouncing, kicking behind the ears, applying that brass goad so hard to the animal he loved that blood was trickling down a great leathery foreleg. But the elephant would not move. The prince stood atop her, shouting in rage. Kumari's response was to snort and flap her ears and swing her trunk left and right. Do you understand? The elephant was committing an act of disobedience. She would not move as long as Prince Indra remained on her back.

Sadong slipped to the ground and stood face to face with Kumari, stroking her trunk and whispering pleadings.

The prince dropped down too, grabbed Sadong by the hair and forced him to his knees in front of the elephant. A knife gleamed. Sadong offered no resistance. That was his way; his fate was in Heaven's hands.

'I will count to five, elephant,' declared the prince. 'Then I will kill this man, your friend, your keeper. Do you understand? Unless you begin to walk. If you don't, he will die. Right here!'

The prince began to count. The elephant trumpeted in distress and stamped a foot.

Then Nol came running up.

'Highness, please...'

The knife turned to Nol and for an instant he wondered if he might die first. But then it was lowered. 'It is challenging me! You can see!' The prince could barely control himself.

'Deal with these two later, not now, Highness,' counselled Nol. 'And not here. If you kill them here, the whole city will find out and be abuzz about it. We want people to talk about other things today. Better to have the animal led off for now. We will say that it went lame due to Prince Indra alighting on its back...*alighting with the force of Garuda the Bird God.*'

My husband had a way, don't you think? First he saved the life of that Siamese commander, then the life of the elephant handler. In both cases, of course, he acted with practical purposes in mind.

Without waiting for a response, Nol called for the elephant that the prince had been riding to be brought forward. It quickly came; its mahout and Sadong then stripped Kumari of her royal vestments and put them on the other animal. On command, it raised its trunk half way and the prince used the footing to spring up onto its back.

Nol moved to Sadong. 'Take your animal back to the stable.'

For the rest of the day, the prince passed up and down the city's avenues, drawing ever bigger crowds as word spread of what had happened. Here and there the procession stopped, and Indra stood atop his mount, holding the golden sword high, and addressed the people. In late afternoon he returned to the palace. There the war games continued. The prince's archers displayed their skills, as did spearmen and charioteers. The sun set, but the prince ordered that oil torches be lit and the competition extended. Later that night, he retired into the palace, and in the royal audience room commanders of major military units presented themselves to crouch and pledge loyalty.

Indra's own Commander Rit was not there, because on the prince's orders he was conducting more acts of wickedness. He was leading a team of soldiers that was hunting down the Crown Prince and other key members of the royal family, three generations in all, as well as servants and teachers – and executing them, right on the spot where they were found. About one hundred forty people died over the course of six hours, starting with the aged Queen, killed with her four attendants on the palace terrace by spears through the chest, within moments of the King's own death. But by strictest instruction, Princess Benjana and her attendants were not touched; she was Indra's wife now, and the claim to the throne would rest in large part on his marriage to her.

After sunset, Rom went to the concubine pavilion with her own squad of soldiers. They burst inside and ordered to the floor the terrified women they found there. Rom went from jewellery box to jewellery box, taking what caught her eye. Then she shouted that all must clear out immediately and never return.

The Brahmin Subhadra was seen by no one in the hours after the assassination, because he was in the torch-lit chamber of the palace shrine, in prayer. I think he settled with himself that the Empire's welfare required that he serve the future monarch and guide him however he could toward policies of benevolence. When finally he emerged, at day's end, he looked tired and older. The first man who approached knelt extra low and addressed him as *Rajaguru* – Kingly Preceptor. So did the next man, and the next after him.

Subhadra's first act in this new role was to order preparations for formal elevation to the throne. He took possession of the royal flame and the state linga, in which resided the divine essence of Kings. He directed that all retainers below a certain rank remain at their posts. He commissioned a coronation verse in both Sanskrit and Khmer, and gave orders that to mark the coming event gifts would go to every temple in the Capital – cloth for priestly garments, silver bowls, jars of musk and camphor, oil of sandalwood, flutes and brass cymbals.

Subhadra convened a team of twelve Brahmins untainted by connections to the expired sovereign to consult on a name for the new one. Within just three hours they grasped Heaven's will: the lord of the Eighteenth Reign would be called Suryavarman, Sun King-Great Protector. The Empire had been ruled by one other King of that name, a century earlier, and he had achieved magnificent things, suppressing a usurper, expanding the borders, constructing the western reservoir. The new King would continue that tradition.

In private, Subhadra presented the name to his prince. It produced a mood, however short, of serenity in the young man, and this the Brahmin used to offer teachings, that the Sovereign of the World must have strong arms and skills of war, but must also know when to display the jewel of mercy. Heaven would expect it, his subjects would expect it, advancement in his next life would depend on it. In that regard, he should begin by ordering that the former palace Brahmins, now held in a stockade, be spared and allowed to cremate the bodies of their deceased lord and his family. The prince raised a hand to signal acceptance. So Subhadra went quickly to the stockade and informed his predecessor of the commutation. He told him that when the cremation was over, he and the others must disperse to hermitages around the Empire and have no contact with one another, on pain of execution. But first put the late King's ashes aside in a safe place, Subhadra advised, to await the day when permission is granted to deposit them in a monument for permanent honour.

The elevation rite took place the following day, overseen by an aged priest who had enthroned the two previous Kings and, by his presence again, signalled that Heaven welcomed this new one. At the close, bells rang and cups of wine were drained all over a city where people were growing addicted to celebratory tumult.

That night, the new King climbed the steep stone steps of the royal compound's gold-spired pyramid, the Palace of the Air. There Rom awaited him, dressed in silk. Her body had become for the night an incarnation of the spirit of the Naga serpent. The Khmer race was about to be reborn, as it had been in the mists of history by the Brahmin who came from India and united with a Naga in woman's form.

Through all of this I stayed in my house; the servants delivered bits and pieces of information, starting with the role that my husband had played in the assassination. I could not accept that I was the wife of this man. I retired to my room.

That night, Nol came again to the family house.

I was still in my room; his steps brought a creak from the teak planks underfoot, but I did not turn to face him.

'Please...' he said, after a moment.

He put a hand to my shoulder. It chilled me; I shook it off.

'Husband! How could you be party to the murder of the King? A peaceful man who cared about his people, who prayed at the temple and grew orchids. I only hope that our son was not drawn into this.'

'He was not, in any way.'

At least that, then.

Nol dared sit down next to me. But I refused to raise my eyes.

'Yes, the King is dead,' he said. 'He was an old man, he was kind to people in this life and he will be rewarded in the next. He went quickly, rather than declining slowly, unable to see, to walk, even to squat at a privy.'

'Of course you view it in that way.'

'Gentle wife, it is not only I, and you, who will advance from this. The past reign brought trouble, decline, corruption, even danger from our enemies beyond the frontiers. Now the Empire will thrive by having a King who can not only love his people but protect them as well. People in the market, they recognize this.' He was quiet a moment, then added: 'What has happened was willed by Heaven.'

'Did Heaven also will the death of tiny grandchildren? Killed on their mats as they slept! I have heard about it. Even his orchids will be uprooted, they say.'

'It is sad, but when a new reign begins there must be a clean break. For the sake of harmony on earth, everyone must know that the old order is finished, gone forever, that no trace remains. Even the King's elephant will die.'

'*Kumari*?'

'I do not know its name. But it is the elephant on which the late King was riding. It could have served the prince, but it refused. Now it is in its stable, waiting to be killed.' He leaned closer, as if to suggest that he found this particular detail hard to accept. But without warning, a grimace cut short this performance.

'You're injured.'

'No, there's nothing wrong.'

'Husband, you are injured and you are in pain. I can see it.'

He denied it again.

'It is from what you did today, isn't it? People say the prince's foot struck your back with the force of a war club.'

Nol denied it once more, and I could tell he was feeling a special kind of misery, from the pain, from his unwillingness to admit it, from my ability to see through his dissembling.

Suddenly, that seemed of no consequence. I was weeping, hands to my face. 'I worry so much, Nol, for what will happen because of this.'

'Darling wife,' he said. 'We are in no danger for what I did. The prince is grateful, and now he is King. What happened today will be recorded in inscriptions.'

It was intolerable to hear this. 'Husband, don't you see?' I could barely get the words out. 'With the prince's support, or without it, we are like anyone else. We can never be sure of what will happen in this life. We can never be sure that we won't fall ill or be bitten by a scorpion or struck by a lightning bolt. Or that powerful people will not find out things we hide and seek retribution. And even if we make it through this life without such misfortunes, what of the next? That is the more important question. Whatever sins remain unaddressed in us will be transformed into a terrible burden that we will carry forward, like a load of stones on our backs, and these can have only the most frightful effect on our next incarnations. Do you want to return as a blind beggar in the marketplace, covered with sores? Do you want to be a rat, stealing its food from the scraps of the poor? My own sins are considerable and I have tried to erase them with deeds on which Heaven will smile. Husband, please tell me you will do the same!'

'What I have done I cannot undo,' he replied. 'I am prepared to accept the consequences.'

I rose and left the room.

I sat on a mat on the veranda which gave on to the house's lotus pond. My lamp burned lower and lower, and then went out, but I did not replace it. My thoughts moved on from my husband. They arrived at the one thing that was not yet done, that I could stop, though doing so would take courage I wasn't sure I had.

Later I left the house in darkness, carrying wrapped in a krama a small but weighty object. I went first to the shrine of Bronze Uncle. It was a long walk, in the darkness, but I could not proceed without first seeking his approval and help. Before the god I knelt and prayed, longer than usual. Then I went to the royal stables. With the god's help, I passed without trouble through the tall bamboo fence. I suppose the sentry was made to think I was a wine-stall woman come to visit a stable keeper.

I found Sadong. He was standing alone, as if paralyzed, and when he saw me, he dropped to his knees and declared his agony over what had been ordered. But I stopped him. I stood him up, placed the wrapped object in his hands and spoke with courage that Bronze Uncle had given me.

'Take the elephant out of Angkor immediately. Tonight. Bribe people if you have to. Take her to a very far village, a place where you and she are not known. Then sell what I have given you here and use the silver to support her. Don't let anyone know of her powers; pretend she's just a common draft animal. Hire her out for labour from time to time to keep up appearances.'

He seemed of two minds about what I was asking him to do. No, not asking. I suppose I was ordering.

'Sadong, there are laws of this world and there are laws of Heaven. We must never forget which have first claim on us. Kumari deserves to live. Your life with her will not be easy, it will require sacrifice. There must be no hesitation, no waste of silver, and certainly no morning cups of rice wine.'

Sadong opened the cloth I had given. Inside was the neckpiece that Nol had brought home. He had acquired it by sinful means; now those sins would be wiped away as the necklace was applied to a virtuous purpose.

Sadong clutched my hand. 'You have been sent by Heaven, Mrs Sray! I can feel it. What you suggest is the right thing and I will do it. Now, please, leave. Someone will see you here.'

But I said no, not yet. I had to say good-bye to Kumari.

In the darkness, the great eyes turned to greet me, catching a glint of light from a torch across the stable. I put out a hand, and Kumari met it with the tip of her trunk and for a moment we held on to each other. I closed my eyes. I was certain that a spiritual essence was flowing between us. Then I looked again and trembled with a sudden realization: *the soul of the departed King resides now in Kumari.*

Some weeks later, Nol came to me. He had noticed that the neckpiece was no longer in its box. Could one of the slaves have taken it? I said no, I had placed it for safekeeping in a locked cell in the palace, a place in which I kept silver for our master's accounts. Nol nodded, though something in his manner made me think he was wondering if that was true. But he never asked again. I have no doubt that he was more concerned that I now communicated with him mainly through the maid, and that I called in a masseuse from the market to knead his back to reduce the pain, rather than doing it myself. And that I always slept away from him, on the veranda.

But then Nol came home one evening and found that my mood had brightened. We ate together by lamplight and then sat on the veranda together. I passed the night with him. The next morning, I heard him asking the maid if anything unusual had happened concerning her mistress the day before. The only thing she could think of was that a messenger had brought me a private communication. Nol asked me about it, and I replied that it was confirmation that a bulk purchase of rice for the royal household had been completed at a particularly favourable price.

How easily that lie flowed from my mouth. But I did not care. The messenger had brought word that the holy elephant was safe.

Part Two
Palace Prominence

We pray with sometimes unseemly insistence for specific things to happen. We give no thought to the myriad ways in which they might come to pass. Do you see? We forget that Heaven has its own designs. It granted my wish that our family would again live together. Nol and Sovan remained in Angkor, to serve the new King. But the resulting existence was not at all what I had yearned for.

For a start, we lived not in the house I had prepared, in which Bopa and I had found some measure of happiness during our lengthy wait. Slaves came with baskets and upended that place, moving our possessions to the newly vacant residence of the Royal Parasol Master near the palace compound. It was a large tile-roofed house with carved gables, pond and gardens and entirely too many rooms to fill. And spirits that seemed not to welcome my presence.

And though I again lived with my husband, I could not but feel he was not the man I had sent off that long-ago morning, carrying fish and rice in a krama. His role in helping that spear point pierce the heart of our former monarch – I could never put that from my mind.

And of course there was the concern that I must never be seen by His Majesty, for who could say but my face might spark a memory across the span of so many years. He was frequently away from Angkor for inspections and new military campaigns, but when he was in residence, I hid behind the walls of our house or left for the provinces to trade or find places where some of the silver I was amassing might go to good works.

What gave me comfort in that period was that I still had my daughter, that sweet, fragile soul in need of guidance in the new life. And I had my son. Each morning, he would come sit with me and take a cup of tea. It was almost as if he sat again like a child on my lap, such was our level of empathy

23: Sergeant of the palace guard

The palace servant who approached that morning was apologetic, as all of them were, even if they had given no conceivable offense.

'Please, Lady, be patient a tiny bit longer,' he said, standing by the covered oxcart in which Bopa and I were waiting for a journey to begin. 'The escort will arrive in just a minute or two, Lady.'

'Oh! I didn't know there would be an escort.'

He had no answer to that, perhaps afraid to acknowledge he knew something I did not. Instead he repeated his message and withdrew.

The words roused Bopa, who had been napping on her side next to me. 'We still haven't started?'

'No, daughter,' I replied, patting my girl's shoulder gently. 'Go back to sleep and next thing you know we'll be on our way.'

I looked back to the holy text that was open before me. I didn't mind the delay, really. I needed to continue with my reading, and that would be hard once the cart began to roll.

Six years had passed since the accession. And almost eight since I began my studies. Please do not take this as a boast, but by this time I had read the entire Baghavad Gita, committed large parts of it to memory, and studied commentaries that were many times longer. Now, with the help of that same young priest who had called at my house that day, I was making my way through the Ramayana. That was my text that day. Lord Rama, traveling toward the holy island Lanka to rescue his beloved Sita, was in alliance with the monkey general Hanuman.

Bopa stirred again, frowning faintly. My girl recognized this trip for what it was, one of her mother's periodic attempts to remind her that outside the palace walls was a quite different world, which the family had once inhabited, however hard that was to believe. In this other place there were no servants to bring rice sweets at any hour, no gong players on hire or silk-edged sampots or silver trays of betel nut. There was peace and fresh air and rights to go about life free from people watching without watching, listening without listening. There was perhaps a better chance to think and act in ways that would purify the soul and build a store of merit toward the next life.

The trick in making these journeys was to get started with minimum fuss and baggage, and certainly with no maids. Take only those things that could be carried, in a straw bag over the shoulder. But a very large collection of people – my husband, the servants, members of the palace staff – looked askance at anything done simply, and conspired to complicate. I would have preferred to travel in a farmer's cart, but the stable master maintained that all that was available was the fancy vehicle in which we now sat, its teak sideboards carved and polished, its hubs painted in silver, its top covered for protection from sun and rain. Inside were finely woven mats and a portable shrine. In its yoke were a pair of well-fed oxen with drapes over their backs and silver caps on the tips of their horns. And now this last-minute assembling of an escort. It was impossible to know who exactly was behind it. My husband was at the parasol-making village today, but perhaps he'd left instructions that soldiers go with me. Though he would often say that the Empire's road were more secure under His Majesty's firm hand than in the old days, he nonetheless worried for my safety. But I think his main worry was that his wife would be seen traveling in the manner of the market women she once was. Or maybe it was just some nameless palace functionary, thinking that an escort was what the Lady Sray wanted but was by the grace of Heaven too modest to request.

This was my life, then. I had a title now. I was Lady Sray. I no longer winced on being addressed with it, but I counted among my accomplishments my success in fending off suggestions that I be awarded another, higher-ranking one.

Another twenty minutes passed. Then, as I was beginning to consider starting off unaccompanied, six spearmen came trotting in formation toward the cart, a sergeant in the lead. They lined up three to each side, and the sergeant spoke.

'Lady Sray, I apologize for the delay. We are at your disposal.'

I tried to hide my surprise. I knew this voice.

'Thank you, sir,' I replied, without looking his way. 'We are ready, and if you and your men are too, why don't we get started?'

'Yes, Lady.'

The tip of the driver's switch touched the oxen and iron-rimmed wheels began to turn. The cart crossed the bridge leading out of the royal sector, then turned to follow the avenue that led toward the city's south gate. I made a show of taking in the sights: the central market, where I could no longer walk without people parting way; a silk merchant's compound, where fan bearers and a tray of rice cakes and imported tea appeared in an instant if I called to ask about samples for the palace; a shrine where a request that a simple prayer be said at festival time caused twenty priests to scramble for the privilege.

But what claimed my mind now was the sergeant, because he was the man who had been at the gate of the retainers' compound during the siege eight year earlier, acting in that strange role of both jailer and protector. I wondered if he recognized me.

Bopa was awake now, examining a painted thumbnail.

'We'll have a good time on this trip,' I said to her. 'You've never seen the Freshwater Sea, have you?'

'No, mother. It will be fun, I'm sure.' Another girl might have said that with some resentment in her voice. My Bopa was not that way. She was doing her best to live up to my hopes.

At the south gate, our party drew a salute from a pair of sentries. Then we entered the forest that began near the city's edge. This was a large, well-travelled road, its spirits known and friendly. A breeze spread a pleasant coolness across my shoulders and cheeks.

From the corner of my eye, I watched the sergeant, who walked to the right of the cart. His hair was thick, like I remembered, cut short in the military way, bound in the back. He had that tiny tuft of hair at the centre of his chest. His arms hung loosely at his side. He was on duty, running a guard detail, and yet he walked like a farmer strolling home from a day in the paddies. I could not imagine him on a battlefield. Nor, really, his men. Normally spearmen were a frightening bunch, but these six seemed to draw from their superior a similar ease with life. I felt no need to shield my daughter from them.

We passed the hillock atop which stands the ancient pyramid

temple that is the grand relic of the Fourth Reign. After a bit, I called to the sergeant.

'Sir, will you keep watch for distance marker number four? I am told there is a small track going off the road on the right just after it, and we're going to turn that way.'

'Yes, Lady.' He gave no hint that he recognized me. But that would be the protocol.

On his instruction, a man strode ahead around a bend, so we'd see it in good time, but a few minutes later he came running back, anxious. The sergeant conferred with him, then turned to me.

'Lady, His Majesty's procession is coming toward us, returning to the city. May I suggest that we stop and bring the cart to the side of the road?'

What was this? My heart began racing. The King was not to return until two days from now. Mr Narin had told me so.

'Yes, of course,' I replied, as if this were just some minor consideration. When the sergeant turned away, I whispered to Bopa. 'We'll stay inside.'

'What...?' Even my little girl could sense that this would not do.

'We'll just say inside. Nobody will know. We'll be quiet.'

'Mother, won't the soldiers know?' Normally, she took my guidance on everything.

She was right. It would be so disrespectful to hide in here that the men would get to talking. So we climbed out of the cart, and got to the ground. I murmured a prayer, and then addressed some words to myself: I will keep my face to the dust. I have done this before on those rare occasions when our paths crossed and it has always been all right. I will steal no curious glance.

I could picture what was happening down the road. The bearer of the royal fire coming into sight, then a retainer holding upright a staff atop which a gilded Shiva rode his mount, the Sacred Bull Nandi. Then men with trumpets and drums, then soldiers with spears, officers on horses and a clutch of whiskered Brahmins. Then a bedecked elephant, a profusion of red and silver parasols overhead. And on a gilded platform atop that elephant, the lord our King.

Massed steps, horse snorts and the clank of soldiers' equipment grew loud in my ears. Then came the scent of raised dust and the footfalls of the elephant. My eyes closed as the animal drew even with where we crouched. Trembling, I counted ten, then ten again, then exhaled in relief. I raised my head.

I cannot say why, but my eyes refused to look to where they should have, to the forest leaves in front of me, or to my daughter at my side. They demanded to see the receding figure of the King, to view his broad shoulders, his bound hair, his jewellery, even if from the back. And so they looked, and what they saw caused a visceral shock: The King had turned full around atop his animal and was looking straight at me. Into those errant eyes of mine, even into my soul.

I could not break it off. What communication passed between us in those few seconds, I do not know, but it left me breathless and afraid.

With great effort, I brought my head back to the dust. I murmured a desperate prayer. When finally I dared look up again, the King was gone but in his place was another unsettling sight: a palanquin, carried by eight slaves, on which reclined a woman, frightfully beautiful, wearing the green sampot of a senior concubine. This creature's eyes found mine too, and held on them in the same possessive, demanding way that the King's had, and across the face there flashed a message: I have seen, I will remember. It was Rom, of course. I remembered her from that first day in the prince's compound.

Finally the procession was gone. I rose and stepped behind the cart to compose myself. The journey resumed. The sergeant and his men displayed no sign that anything unusual had occurred; Bopa chattered a bit about the sights and sounds of the royal party, then began to doze again. In the gentle turning of the cart's wheels, I sought calm for my soul. But how could I achieve such a thing? You recall how a certain ghost took up residence in the boughs above our old little home. I was convinced now that this same spirit was watching again, from the heights of a tree that at just that moment we were passing beneath, and that it was exalting. It had caused the eyes of His Majesty to look in a particular direction, and there to see me. How my mind churned; I barely noticed where we were going. His Majesty's gaze had fallen upon me. But what effect would that have? The King must pass a thousand women a day. I would mean nothing among them. Before today he had seen me only once, when he was a boy, and only for a minute, maybe two. Over the years the memory would have faded, surely. Oh, how I tried to convince myself.

Presently the stone distance marker came into view. A few steps beyond it, just as described by a clerk in the palace land office, a track wound off into the forest to the west. We turned onto it.

Walking to the side, the sergeant asked: 'May I know, Lady, where it is we're going?'

I was happy for the distraction. 'A hamlet called Veya. I was told it's about a half hour down this track. We'll go and have a look.'

'Do the people know you're coming, Lady?'

'Yes, I sent word ahead.'

He seemed to approve of that. A woman of my rank arriving unannounced would throw villagers into panic.

Now, what I wanted to 'have a look at' I in fact owned – well, together with my husband. Ten days earlier, we had gained formal title, etched out on palm leaf. It was part of land vouchsafed to us by the monarch in recognition of Nol's service in the ascent to the throne. About two thousand people lived in Veya hamlet and three adjacent settlements that were part of the grant. About fourteen hundred were of working age.

Rounding a curve, the cart was spotted by a young man who'd been posted to watch. When the village came in sight to us, its people had turned out in full. Bopa and I climbed down and people went to the dirt in a simple country sort of way. It touched me, because it was how I and the girls in the orphanage had once bowed when the rich man arrived.

I voiced thanks. The headman took a timid step forward and showed us to the hamlet's public pavilion, where a lunch of grilled chicken, rice, cucumbers and cool water from a well had been set out in old but carefully polished bowls. We ate, though we were not really hungry, and each time I chewed, the headman watched from the corner of his eye, hoping for a hint that the food pleased me. Then everyone rose, and the headman showed us around the community's grounds, to the bamboo and thatch houses one by one, to a mud oven where charcoal was being made, to the rice-husking place, the fishpond. Then he led us to the edge of the fields.

'Lady Sray,' he began, gesturing toward a far-off grove, 'the fields out there, where the irrigation is not so good, those are ours, as it should be. These that you see right ahead will have the privilege of nurturing your family and the palace's parasol pavilion.'

Certainly the closer fields were well tended, with rice stalks a rich green and standing at half height, the dikes in perfect repair. Of course the contrast with the others was probably not quite so dramatic, but I was not about to go check.

'We have organized two work teams to tend to your paddies,' he explained. 'One, with a foreman and forty-eight labourers, both men and women, will work them during the waxing moon. Another, with forty-six souls, will work the period of the waning moon.'

The last stop of the tour was the village shrine, an old brick structure that stood perhaps as tall as two men. There we heard apologies for its diminutive size and its need of new plaster.

I stepped forward and put a piece of silver in an offering tray. I lit a stick of incense from a glowing coal, and knelt in prayer. It was not the simple pious gesture it might have seemed. My prayer was essentially a long silent petition: By Heaven's grace, may the King not remember who I am.

When I was done, I turned to the sergeant.

'Sir, I invite you and your men to say devotions as well. I will provide the donation.'

While the men knelt, I took the headman aside, thanked him, and told him to have the plaster repaired and send the bill to me. He thanked me with such sincerity that I felt ashamed. Would this man be so deferential, I wondered, if he knew of events in a certain jungle clearing those years ago? As if by a spirit's silent command, perhaps the spirit of the dead man, my tongue touched the gap far back in my mouth, where a tooth was still missing

It was time to go. But at the cart, the headman had a question, which he posed after apologies for taking more of my time. Two days earlier, he said, village women were out gathering firewood to the east, just across the trunk road. They had seen some men working in a field, but they weren't farmers. They were men in city sampots and they had long pieces of cord with wooden stakes at each end. They were planting one stake in the dirt, then stretching out the cord, and planting the other stake, and one of them was writing things down on a slate. It was the strangest thing, he said. The local women were too afraid to ask anything. But would I perhaps know what that was about?

I had seen this happen in the city, and what generally followed was work elephants and masons and coolies. But rather than speculate, because a large temple going up so close at hand would change life in this village forever, I promised to ask and send word.

The cart began rolling back toward the trunk road.

'It was a pleasant village, sergeant,' I said from my perch.

'It was, Lady. The place and the people too. A very fine community.'

'Well, now they can go back to their routines without the disruption of people from the city.'

'I don't think they'll remember it like that, Lady. What they'll remember is that you prayed at their shrine, and for so long. It made them happy. That's what they'll be talking about this afternoon.'

He picked up his pace, to leave me to myself, but I found I didn't want that.

'How would you know, sergeant, what they'll talk about?'

'Experience, Lady,' he said, dropping back to the side of the cart. 'Most city people when they go to a village don't pay them an honour like that.'

'You've done a lot of these trips?'

'Yes, quite a few, Lady.'

'I'm sorry to take you away from more important duty.'

He smiled at that. 'This is my favourite, Lady. It gets me out of the city, to places I've never seen before.'

'But I thought soldiers prefer something more exciting...' I was enjoying this banter; I had forgotten for the moment about the King and questions of his memory.

'I've seen enough of that, Lady. Escort duty will suit me fine for the rest of my days.'

Bopa had begun to take an interest in the conversation, so I broke it off.

The sights of the following hours were ones I remembered from childhood. Dry paddies, with the stubs of harvested rice stalks sticking up; a dog sleeping dead to the world in the middle of the road; a woman selling sweet sticky rice mixed with beans, cooked in sections of bamboo.

Toward late afternoon, a tiny girl walking a flock of ducks toward their home pen forgot herself and drove them right in front of the cart. The fowl scattered beneath the oxen's hooves, quacking up a din. How I recalled that kind of noise! The sergeant called quickly to his men and they all dropped their spears and ran in every direction to round the birds up. The scene turned comic, bringing a smile to my face. I wished I could jump down and take part in the round-up, and feel the soft feathers in my own hands again.

When cart and escort continued on their way, the sergeant stepped over. 'I'm sorry if we startled you there, Lady.'

'That's all right. It was a kind turn. That little girl would have had a lot of explaining to do if you hadn't helped.'

Two hours later, we stopped at an inn for the evening. I gave instructions to the owner to serve dinner to the soldiers and the cart driver. Bopa and I were shown to a separate pavilion. There we took our rice alone.

24: The hilltop monastery

Toward noon the following day, we arrived at a port. It was a collection of weather-worn houses and storage sheds arranged along a causeway that had channels of mud-brown water on either side. At docks by the buildings, water vessels were tied up. There was quite a selection, small sampans of the type found on any village pond but also huge things I had never seen before. Ships. They were great houses on water, really, with poles as tall as tree trunks rising from them. I was disappointed to see no sign of the Freshwater Sea. I sensed that it was somewhere off in the distance, down those channels of muddy water.

In any case, our destination was not the port, but a temple atop a hill that Heaven had placed next to it. Straight on was the head of a trail leading to the top; a novice priest perhaps ten years old was waiting to lead us up.

I turned to the sergeant. 'There's no reason for you and your men to go up, sir. Why don't you all take a break down here? My daughter and I will be back by nightfall.'

He nodded polite assent, but the novice seemed not to like the idea. He whispered something to the sergeant, who turned to me and said: 'The holy boy says the trail is washed out in places, Lady, and he's not sure you could get by on your own. He asks that I might go along to help.' Having taken preliminary vows, the novice could not touch a woman, even if just to offer a hand.

I had tried. 'Of course. If that's what he thinks is required.'

The sergeant asked for Bopa's bag to carry, and she promptly handed it over. He sought mine as well, and it seemed impolite to say no.

The climb commenced. The novice led, then came me, then Bopa and finally the sergeant, who kept his pace slow so as to maintain a proper distance.

What a strange place this hill was. At the base, the trail was of soft, damp dirt, edged by thick greenery. A few steps higher, everything turned to rocks and gravel, with a few lonely shrubs struggling for livelihood. The ascent was steep and not friendly to city feet like ours.

In places, the trail had been washed away by rainstorm run-off, as the novice had said. The sergeant lent a hand first to Bopa, then to me to help us cross. It was strong and confident, and I told myself that so were many men's.

After twenty minutes, we sat down to rest.

'My feet, mother! These stones hurt so much.'

I rubbed them. 'Bopa, these stones may give you discomfort, but try to endure it. They have holy origins.'

She made as if to listen, though I knew her feet were a bigger concern.

'When our lord the monkey general Hanuman was looking for medicine to cure a sickness afflicting the brother of Rama, he overturned entire mountains in his search and left the stones underneath them exposed. So those stones are holy – they have been placed in our sight by Hanuman himself.'

She rubbed her toes. 'How is it possible to overturn an entire mountain?'

'These things a god can do. Otherwise, how would it be possible to see so many stones?'

After forty minutes and two more stops, we reached the top. By a weathered wooden gate, we were greeted by the abbot, an ancient man with a sunken chest. He put hands together: 'It is an honour to receive you, Lady Sray, wife of His Majesty's parasol master.' His speech was unclear; he was missing most of his teeth.

I was winded but did my best to give a gracious reply, ending with an expression of hope that the visit did not inconvenience our host. He replied that there was no such possibility. Then we all walked in silence along the remainder of the trail, which here was mercifully flat. He hobbled, and I understood why he had not come down the hill to greet us. He might never descend from this place again, in fact.

We passed a small wooden shrine, which in former days would have been as close as my daughter and I could have approached. Then ahead, atop a final rise, we caught sight of triple towers, each topped by a large stone lotus. This was our destination, Trinity Temple, its holy grounds marked off by a chest-high wall of laterite.

'It is from the Fourth Reign, Lady,' the abbot said proudly, pausing. 'Our lord the monarch of that time favoured Heaven's wishes and built his holy edifices atop natural hills. This one stands at the very peak of what I believe is the tallest of those hills, so its spires reach closer to Heaven than those of any temple in the Empire. It is small by the standards of Angkor, but that size gives a rather intimate feel to anyone who worships at it. And the style is old, yes, but we like that too. It is somehow more pleasing than the newer ones....'

'I share your opinion, Abbot. It is beautiful, touched by the hand of time.'

We walked closer. 'We do our best on maintenance, of course, but...' Even from here, stones could be seen to have fallen away, weeds to have taken root high in the towers.

The sergeant hung back, no doubt thinking that this was the Lady's time.

The abbot led my daughter and me first to large jars of water, hidden behind a weathered rattan screen near the east gate. He left us. We bathed, emerging fit for the prayers to come.

'Please enter, then, Lady Sray – step over the moonstone and enter holy ground.'

First he led us in a devotional procession around all three towers. Then we knelt at the base of nine weathered steps that led to the chamber of the centre tower, Shiva's abode. I lit incense that had been laid out for us. I did the same at the other two towers, honouring Vishnu at the right hand one and Brahma on the left. Then the abbot showed the way out the compound's west gate.

'Look to your feet, if you would, Lady Sray,' he said. 'The moonstone on this side is the living rock of the hill.'

'It is rock that our lord Hanuman himself has unearthed?'

'It was that way, Lady.'

I looked down at it, but then my eyes rose and I became aware that from this spot I had a clear view outward. For a moment, I do believe my breath came to a stop.

Never in my life had I been so high, and I felt all of a sudden that I knew what it was to be the Bird God Garuda and fly across the sky. Below, the Freshwater Sea showed itself broad and peaceful, taking in the warmth of the midday sun, spanning further than I thought possible, so far that in places the sky came down and caressed its edges. Far off to the right was solid land, some of it covered with jungle, like before the time the gods had placed humans on earth. To the left was land that showed the straight lines and corners of paddy cultivation. Land and water looked entirely different and I knew that there were seasons when they battled each other, water advancing into the land, and then, as now was the case, land into the water. Neither ever overpowers the other. They belong in this conjunction, they depend upon each other.

The old priest was finding pleasure in my silent awe. He had seen it in many visitors, I'm sure.

When I was done and turned back to him, he said: 'You can understand, Lady, why we know this is a holy mount.'

'Yes,' I replied, reflective. 'Heaven's creation, laid out for all to see.'

The priest waited a respectful moment, then said: 'Many people should have the chance to experience this, don't you believe?'

'Why, yes.'

'But we have hardly any sleeping places for pilgrims anymore!' The old man was suddenly animated. 'Look there, if you would.' He gestured toward wooden posts that stood upright in rows, planted in the ground. 'Those once supported guesthouses for pilgrims. Twenty different houses. A storm came three years ago and blew them away. We have only one left, that one down the hill there a bit – can you see it? People hear about this, that there's no place for a group to sleep up here, and they don't come. They hear too that the trail has been washed away and think they'd better not attempt it, it will be too hard, especially for old people, old people who may be near the passage to the next life and need most of all the spiritual comfort of a place like this.'

'It's a pity.'

'Yes. A pity. We have tried to raise money for repairs, but we... we are not clever at such things.'

I could sense his meaning, as I'm sure you can. But I was not offended. I had more than money enough by then.

The abbot took us all to a small pavilion. The novice arrived with a tray from an unseen kitchen and placed rice, fish and greens before us. The sergeant waited outside, hanging back again, but I told him he must come have rice as well.

The abbot watched as we ate – as a man in holy orders, he would take nothing until the evening. After a while, he asked about life beyond his hill. I told him of a new monastery being constructed outside the Capital.

'And the wars? We have heard there is a new war against the Chams.'

The sergeant saw it was his place to reply to this. 'Yes, there is such an action. Three months ago, His Majesty led our armies into two Cham provinces. He destroyed the enemy forces there and brought the provinces into our Empire. Our borders on the cast are now secure.'

'War is always unfortunate,' the abbot observed. 'But...have we, may I ask, taken a lot of prisoners?'

'Quite a few,' the sergeant replied. The old priest seemed to welcome that. Perhaps he wondered if some might be sent here as labourers.

At meal's end, we all rose, then stepped outside for good-byes. But there I was visited with an idea. 'Abbot, my daughter and I are meant to stay in an inn in the port, but how would you feel if we spent the night up here? In that one guesthouse that is still standing.'

Bopa looked a bit askance, and the old priest did too. If we were going to stay, he would have wanted to have time to prepare.

'It's quite primitive, Lady,' he countered. 'You deserve better.'

'If a soul is to obtain any benefit from a night at a place like this, if any merit is to be acquired, the lodging should be primitive. Is it not so?'

He nodded at the logic of that, and told the novice to go find mats and mosquito netting.

The sergeant stepped forward. 'Lady, you're sure you'll be all right up here?'

'Yes, we'll be fine. We remember how to get by in humble circumstances.'

I looked to see if he would find any meaning in that, but he showed no sign.

'Then, with your permission, I'll return to my men, Lady,' he said. 'I'll be back in the morning to see you down.'

I talked on with the abbot and was touched by his devotion to this place, and his hapless inability to organize repairs.

Late in the afternoon, he led me and my daughter to the guesthouse and bid us good night. Inside, mats and nets had been laid out already, as promised, along with an oil lamp, burning, and a jug of drinking water. Bopa laid down immediately; the walk up the hill had left her tired.

'A little adventure for us, daughter, staying in this place,' I said, patting her wrist. She smiled; this was not her choice, but she was willing to give it a try.

I sat for a while, then walked alone back to the old temple's courtyard. I was pleased to find it deserted. I would pray at the tower of Vishnu, that god who shows pity on humankind, coming to earth to rescue us from evil times. I went to my knees and lit incense from a pot of glowing coals. Holding a stick between the fingers of joined hands, I cleared my mind as best I could of all selfish concerns. Then I began.

You are the beginning, the middle, and the end, of all that lives.
With one single fraction of your Being, you pervade and support the universe.
You are unending time.
You are the ordainer who faces all ways,
You are death that destroys,
You are the source of all that is to be.
You are the diceplay of the gamester,
You are victory, you are courage,
You are the goodness of the virtuous.
You are the silence of what is secret,
You are the knowledge of those who know,
You are the seed of all that is born.

The search for the Absolute – how much simpler it had been

when I had just the gleam in an elephant's eye to guide me, the scent of a burning stick of incense. Now I had also the holy texts, such as these words, which of course come from Lord Krishna's battlefield sermon to Prince Arjuna. Have you ever found that on first reading, verse like this can seem as clear as water in a well? But so quickly after that, doubt and uncertainty can come crowding in? My ever-patient instructor novice might offer one view of the meaning, a palm-leaf commentary something else, the Brahmin Subhadra a third approach altogether different. And still another teacher might say that the meaning was not so much in the meaning, but in sounds and cadence. He would counsel that it was necessary only to hear the words again and again to absorb their wisdom. Analysing their meaning could lead down false paths. The words of the texts were not like words that humans use, I was told. Rather, each was a gift from Heaven, perfect in itself, existing to convey a state of mind, if only the mind would be receptive.

I often despaired that the search was beyond my frail spirit's ability. But I continued. I found sometimes that going to new places helped set me on a course, and so I had assigned myself the task of stopping at every place of spiritual discovery that I passed on my travels. There, sometimes, holy words could fuse with setting, time and that sweet scent of incense to move my consciousness toward the sublime.

And this was such a time, kneeling at the stone steps to Vishnu's tower, on a hilltop touched by Hanuman, helpmate of Vishnu's avatar Rama, with words uttered by Krishna.

I rose. My worries about the King had vanished; my presence here, my every breath and footstep, insignificant though they were, seemed in harmony with that point which the great cosmic engine had reached in its eternal motions, its cycles of creation and destruction.

I passed out of the courtyard, crossing the moonstone cut from living rock, and came again into the great open place. A breeze stirred my hair, as if it had been awaiting my arrival. The waning sun was halfway hiding behind hills that ended the marshland to the west. I knelt, oblivious to the advance of time as the sky above the disk turned from yellow brightness to rich reds and oranges, then to brooding greys and finally the full, pure darkness of night.

I picked my way back to the guesthouse.

'Oh mother, this mat is so thin. How am I going to sleep?' Bopa spoke from inside a mosquito net.

'Don't worry, daughter. There are places where it's harder to sleep than this one. But here, take my mat.' There was a pause, then my girl's hand extended from the net.

For myself I spread a krama on the wooden floor. There was another silence, then words from Bopa.

'You're not using your net?'

'No, daughter. I like the open air....And when I was a girl, I was told that a bite or two builds character. I suppose that explanation was in part to make virtue out of necessity, because there wasn't money for nets. In any case, we all did think we'd have very hard lives. That's not been so, has it? But it feels good sometimes to think that maybe I did get a bit of the character for one.'

I awoke before dawn to the sounds of the temple's chimes. I lay still, as traces of light appeared in the patch of sky that showed beyond the door.

My opening thought was: I'll find the money to replace the lost guesthouses, all of them. With Heaven's help, they will be so strong that no storm will ever blow them away again.

25: A proposal of business

After morning rice, Bopa and I knelt before the abbot. He splashed us with holy water, which cooled our heads and shoulders and seemed to carry into our souls the words that he chanted.

May your minds be drawn always and only to merit. May you be pre-eminent in knowledge, virtue and deeds, yet remain without pride.

The sergeant led us down the hill, calling our attention to thorns and loose stones on the trail, taking our hands firmly when the footing was rough.

At the bottom, by the oxcart, two groups were waiting. One was the guard detail, bathed and ready for a new day's duty. The other was a cluster of prosperous-looking men, all facing our way, hands together in greeting.

'Might we have a word with the Lady?' asked one of them in the politest of tones. He wore a sampot, but in most every other way, he was a foreigner: pale skin, body tall and wiry, speech somewhat hard to understand.

'Well, yes, of course. What can I do for you?'

'Might you allow us to show you and your daughter a bit of hospitality? It's not much, but the best our little community can offer.'

I smiled wearily. This was of course a delegation of Chinese merchants from the port. No matter that I'd tried to come here unnoticed; word would have spread overnight that I was passing the night up at the temple.

The man introduced himself as Chen the rice miller. Then he led us down the port's main street, past wooden warehouses, a trader's office, a dock where slaves unloaded straw-wrapped bundles from a boat riding low in the water. The sergeant trailed behind.

We came to something which stood out, a large brick building painted in the brightest red. It had a tile roof with curving eaves. Mr Chen noticed my surprise. 'It was created in the style of houses in our homeland,' he explained. 'We like Khmer houses, but we sometimes get homesick for what we grew up in. It's the office of our Chamber of Commerce.'

We passed through the round entranceway, Mr Chen making a single clap to signal unseen servants. Inside, in a large, airy room, he took some time pointing out to us a polished wooden chest from his country, a celadon jar, a hanging drape that bore large characters of Chinese writing. Then he showed us to a second room, where on a low table servants were setting out a generous selection of pork and chicken, bamboo shoots, peppers, spinach, rice, all cooked in the Chinese style. The other men followed, and together we all sat down. Mr Chen offered another welcome and thanks to Heaven. We began to eat.

After thirty minutes, Mr Chen got to the point. 'We would like to make a proposal, Lady Sray,' he said. 'All of us here, as a group. Word has reached us that you supervise the purchase of various supplies for the palace. And we imagine that you obtain these from the wholesale merchants in the central market. Would that be correct?'

'Why yes, it is.'

'Did you know, Lady Sray,' he said, taking on a confidential tone, 'that before the goods reach the city they pass through the hands of three different sets of distributors, each taking a cut of the final price?'

I of course knew that very well. How else would things get to the Capital?

'Lady Sray, we would like to make a proposal. We can provide quite a selection of goods. Mr Feng here deals in fresh and preserved meats, Mr Cho trades in honey and palm sugar. As I have told you, I myself am engaged in rice milling. The Chinese merchant community has its own boats, which ply the Freshwater Sea and go up and down canals and rivers to reach villages. We buy right at the source, wherever it may be. We also have ships that sail the Great Dual Vector River from the Salt Water Sea to bring in goods from China, a very full selection, whatever might be required. If you buy directly from us you will get a lower price, and the kind of service that comes only from friends. This is something the palace deserves, surely.'

I looked at Mr Chen. A pleasant feeling was coming over me, one I knew from the days when I was just Sray the duck egg vendor.

'What price are you offering on rice today?'

'Forty-four weight of silver per standard basketful.'

I laughed gently. 'I'm a bit surprised, Mr Chen. That's hardly different than what we pay in the Capital. And Heaven has allowed a good harvest this season. There's so much supply.'

He made a pained face. 'Yes, the harvest was good, but there's been a special problem with storage, did you know? Too many beetles and mice. They've eaten about a quarter of the crop.'

'In the Capital we've heard that the priests determined which spirit was causing the problem and said prayers that made it desist. The pests have mostly gone away. What do you think about a price of thirty-six weight?'

He made another face, this one meant to convey both sympathy for my request and its impossibility. 'Lady Sray, may I suggest forty-two?'

I made a show of turning the figure over in my mind. 'That would be the price you'd offer for sales in small quantities, I think. But we would be buying in bulk. The palace has more than four thousand people and each one eats rice every day. You can come down more, I would think. Say, to thirty-eight?'

Mr Chen smiled politely. 'Lady, you're asking me to lose money for the privilege of doing business with you.'

'Mr Chen, a smart merchant like you – I imagine you've never lost money on a deal in your life. Thirty-eight weight of silver. You'll regret it if you say no, I know you will. We pay on time and when word spreads that you've become a palace supplier, all sorts of people will come and want to do business with you.'

Chen surveyed the eyes of the men around him, and then said: 'I suppose we would in fact...regret it.'

I continued: 'Now tell me about honey.'

'Deep-refined, comb-free. Eighteen weight per barrel.'

'What size of barrel?'

'The standard size.'

'And each one *full*?'

By the time we left, I had agreed that the palace pantry would buy quantities of six commodities on a trial basis, starting the following week, and that I would buy some on my own account.

Our usual suppliers would fret and whimper, of course, and maybe work behind my back to try to foil me. I would have to phase in any new arrangements slowly.

I must also say that I was thinking it was time to expand my private trading, and that this Mr Chen struck me as trustworthy, a possible future business partner. I had to expand, or I would have no money to fix the guesthouses up the hill – other projects like it had eaten up most of my previous earnings.

The merchants walked us back to the cart. I climbed on board, then called to Mr Chen.

'There's one more matter, sir. It would be a fine thing for the life of the spirit if someone found a way to repair the trail that runs up the hill. And it would make good business sense, don't you think? Right now it's too rough for anyone but the able-bodied. If it were fixed, more pilgrims would pass through your community here, people would stop into the local restaurants and shops on the way out.'

The sergeant had a faint smile on his face as we moved back toward the city.

'I worry I was too hard on them,' I told him. It was quite easy to talk to this man.

'I think not, Lady Sray. They seemed to enjoy the give and take.'

'They gave a little too easily, actually. I know what these things cost and they'll be selling them at practically no profit at all.'

'Perhaps they want something more from the relationship, Lady.'

'You know something, do you, sergeant?'

'Well, Lady, of course they want entrée to the palace. And also, perhaps help with what the Chinese ships have to pay to ply the Freshwater Sea. Every time they tie up somewhere, an official steps forward. A tax on this, a tax on that, and of course a lot of it is kept by the official himself. The rates have gone up now, what with the war with the Chams to pay for. So, I wonder if the merchants think that you might help them out with that.'

That made sense. But I didn't like the idea of seeking out favours from palace officials.

When the cart entered the city, I asked the driver to go first to the shrine of Bronze Uncle. New wooden posts held his home up straight now; the roof thatch was thick and waterproof. Lamps burned to either side of the god, who gleamed from a daily buffing applied by attending acolytes. I knelt and gave thanks for a journey safely completed.

An hour later, when the cart reached the house in the palace compound, Bopa found energy that had eluded her for much of the trip. She jumped down and ran off, in search of friends and sweets. I was left alone with the sergeant.

'You and your men were a great help to us,' I said, searching for words. 'We appreciate it and will send special food to your barracks.'

'Thank you, Lady. You are kind.'

'But...but what I would really like to say, Sergeant Sen,' and here I paused, because I hadn't meant to show that I remembered his name, 'is...well, that I thank you deeply for what you did in the princely compound those years ago.'

'We were only doing what anyone would have, Lady.'

'Everyone would have, you say, but the other soldiers did not.'

'No, but they weren't offered free food and a pavilion to sleep in, were they?'

He made a deep bow, and moved to form up his men. I watched him go and decided that if I did have to have an escort next time I left the city, I would see that this man was in charge.

26: Unwanted honours

When I entered the house, Nol was eating from plates on a low wicker table, chewing in his quick, impatient way – food was always but fuel to my husband.

'So you're back, my dear wife,' he called cheerfully, getting to his feet. He often proceeded as if there were no tensions between us, as if assuming that manner would make them go away.

Taking my hand, he declared with some formality: 'I have news. I am to receive the Medallion of the Royal Order, First Class, for services during the campaign against the Siamese. His Majesty will personally award it in three days' time at ceremonies to establish a new alms fund.'

'My goodness! What an honour!'

'Yes, I cannot deny it, and it's one I do not deserve.' He beamed again, having gotten out of the way the requisite statement of humility. 'Now, palace seamstresses will come this afternoon to fit us for clothing for the occasion.'

'You said us?'

'Why, yes. We will all be present at the ceremony. It is His Majesty's wish.'

'I wonder if...'

'Don't wonder anything, my dear wife! All will be taken care of.' In his ebullience, he had failed to notice my distress. Then he turned to a maid and ordered that food be laid before me. I was suddenly no longer hungry, but I sat down on the floor at the table, because my husband expected it.

'So!' he said, settling back into his own place. 'Your trip went well?'

'Oh, yes....Bopa and I passed the night...at the Temple of the Trinity on the top of the hill by the port.' My words came out in a halting way because I was thinking about the King.

'And the naval wharf – did you see that? There are three new fighting boats, I've heard. They're being fitted and will enter service next month.' Nol was always proud of inside knowledge.

'Yes, we saw them,' I said, because my husband wanted it that way. 'They, they were very impressive.' *Perhaps the King won't* award the medallion himself; he'll go off and leave it to some priest to do.

'Good! And our village? How was that?'

'It's a pretty place, pleasant and breezy.' *If the King does award it himself, perhaps we of the family will be seated well back from the throne. He won't get a good look at me.*

'I hear you pledged some money to patch up their shrine.'

How would it be taken if we responded that the family would not attend? We could say we weren't with the King during the Siamese campaign, and therefore we didn't deserve to be at the ceremony.

'Dear wife, are you listening?'

'Yes. I'm sorry.'

'I should have known. My wife goes out to the village just once and already they've got her feeling sorry for them.' He laughed. 'What did they do, bring out their cripples?'

'They did nothing like that, husband.' Sticking up for the villagers got me off my worries, partially at least. 'They are hardworking people, and they will give half their labour to us and the palace. The shrine is in very bad condition and fixing it will be a small thing. They will provide the labour, we will provide the materials and artisans.'

The maid put food before me. I ate and answered more of his questions. I said nothing about having promised to rebuild the hilltop guesthouses.

The meal turned out to be the last bit of quiet that I got for many days.

When I stood up, word came that the chief palace seamstress and two assistants were waiting outside to take measurements. Bopa and Sovan were called, and for an hour we all took turns standing motionless while the seamstress ran string measures around hips and waists, from waist to ankles, calling off the numbers to one of her assistants, then consulting on fabric, and later on neckpieces and armlets. You can imagine how delighted Bopa was. Then came the florists, and after that a priest from the palace who coached us on words and gestures of the rite. I could not keep my mind on the responses; I continued to worry over how to avoid going at all.

The next day was taken up with cleaning and purifying the house, and with fittings for silk garments that had been sewn overnight.

On the morning of the ceremony, the servants emerged early from their huts in the back, to help us all get ready. But at the door of the big house, they found a very flustered master Nol, standing alone. He gave them horrible news: the Lady Sray had taken seriously ill. From the door of my room, they peered in, frightened, and saw me lying shivering on my mat, clutching my bed linen to my chest. One of the maids hurried in and fussed over me, putting a folded cloth beneath my head, wetting my brow with water from my night drinking cup. She returned to Nol, and I could hear her whispering that it was all a mystery. The Lady was not warm to the touch. What illness this was only Heaven could say. This made Nol all the more worried, and he sent the girl off to bring a Brahmin physician. Bopa appeared, dressed and powdered and scented, her jewellery shining, and showed some disappointment on hearing about me. Was the ceremony going to be put off? Sovan knelt at my side to offer silent sympathy.

The physician arrived and examined me but he couldn't ascertain the problem either. By now it was nearly time to leave for the palace. Nol pleaded that I try to stand up. Please – His Majesty will be waiting, he whispered. The ceremonial garments, the flowers are ready. Everyone is expecting you. But my response – how shamefully I behaved! – was to babble words that made no sense. Nol blanched, and for the first time he accepted that my presence at the rite was impossible. No doubt he began to feel afraid. Some malevolent spirit might take advantage and put this illness on a fatal course. He turned abruptly to the physician and told him in the firmest of terms that nothing, nothing must be allowed to happen to this woman his dear wife.

The poor physician did his best to reassure, and then, to show that something was being done, he prayed, took out a pestle and ground four kinds of dried twigs into some kind of yellow powder. He mixed it all with water and fed me a few drops at a time. Thirty minutes later, I seemed to be resting calmly. I opened my eyes.

Nol bent close and I whispered that he must go to the palace with the children, that he could not stay back. I nodded. He smiled on me, relieved that my right mind was back.

He returned about four hours later, a new holder of the Medallion of the Royal Order, Second Class. But I had to keep up the game. I said there had been terrible pain in my joints, but now it had let up.

Nol sat on the mat at my side and took my hand. 'We thank Heaven that you are better.'

'I am sorry, husband,' I murmured, weeping. 'I am sorry that I could not be there to share your day of honour.'

I could not simply resume my routine in the house. So I remained on my mat through the afternoon. Nol dismissed the physician, then sat by me and fed me more water with yellow powder, but no food because I told him there was nothing I could bear to eat. This was true, though it was due to the mortification that this deception had brought over me.

Evening set in. Nol remained at my side. I felt that after another hour it would be all right to sit up and ask for a text to read. With it in hand, I would say a full prayer seeking forgiveness.

I dozed, but then I was awakened by voices in the courtyard and the tramping of many feet. Nol rose to go check.

He returned hardly a minute later. 'His Majesty is here!' His face bore a look of sheer bafflement. The King had never come near this house. 'He is concerned about your health.'

I groped for a response. 'Our lord is kind. But there is no need for him to bother himself here. You may tell him that I convey my deepest thanks and hope that he will expend no more time on the health of someone so insignificant.'

Nol hurried out again. His muffled voice carried in; I strained to catch the words. Then he was in the doorway. Yet all I saw was the King, standing behind him, the godly face and shoulders bathed in the soft light of the room's lamp.

I looked away; the breath had gone clean out of me. I rolled onto my side, turning from him, and gathered my arms about my breasts.

Nol spoke. 'His Majesty wishes...' He did not finish, because the King strode past him into the room.

215

There was a long silence, and then I heard the royal voice. 'Your husband has worked so hard to establish and foster the reign. Now his wife has taken ill, so I could only come and express in person my wishes for your recovery.'

His voice was soft. I was left feeling the concern was entirely genuine. How could I have imagined that the first words this man would address to me, this man who had severed the arm of a prisoner, who had ordered the death of the holy elephant, would convey such emotions?

I found a response, which I delivered in a whisper. 'Please, Your Majesty need not concern himself. A physician has come and through prayers and treatment I have recovered.'

'Then why do you turn your back to me?'

A King is allowed to say anything, but this remark astonished me. 'I am ashamed, Majesty. I have recovered, but I am still not in condition to be gazed upon by the royal eyes.'

'Majesty,' interjected Nol, 'my wife, at this moment her senses are not...'

The King seemed not to hear that. 'I have come to your house, Lady Sray. I cannot leave until I have seen with my own eyes that you are well again. Please, I ask you. Show yourself.'

Could he actually be asking, be commanding that? There was nothing I could do but roll onto my back. Eyes shut, I kept my arms across my chest, feeling some security in that. I lay still, and soon sensed the King's breath nearby. He seemed to be kneeling by me. 'If I may...' he said, and then came the shock of his touch. One after the other, my wrists were taken, gently, my arms put to my side. Then the private darkness behind my closed eyes grew bright as he took the lamp in hand and held its flame above my face. It lingered there. My breath quickened. Presently the brightness grew dim; he was moving the lamp slowly down the length of my body. 'Never, never have I...' He was whispering to himself, like that. There was a long pause, and then I believe that his sense of shame caught him short. He put down the lamp and left the room.

27: Flight

In the days when we lived in the settlement behind the Pre Rup mountain-temple, men would sometimes call out to me as I passed by: come, pretty lady, give me a little love, be my sweetheart. For the most part it was harmless, the kind of attention that a certain kind of man, especially with some rice wine in him, pays to, I think, any passing women. It could happen even when I was walking with my husband. The certain kind of man seemed always to think there was nothing to fear from someone who was short and missing an ear. And, oh, Nol did always show him how mistaken that was. When a compliment came wafting my way, I used to try to hurry him along, though I knew it was too late. He would turn and initiate a confrontation, whether with stares, stern words or the occasional use of his fists. The other man always backed down.

So it was no surprise that in the hours after the King left our house, my husband wore the dourest of looks. His sovereign, his lord and patron, the man who had brought him out of rank obscurity – now in the role of a wine stall idler! My poor Nol. Can you imagine any man more unsure as to how to respond? I had no idea either, of course. So what did we do? We both pretended that what had happened was all very routine, a sign of Kingly virtue.

'How blessed we all are,' I told Nol later that night, as we sat together on the veranda, crickets calling to us from the darkness. 'How blessed is the Empire. It has a monarch whose heart contains a sea of compassion, who cannot rest if just one subject falls ill.'

'It is that way,' replied Nol. I do believe he was straining to convince himself of what I had just said. How much easier things would be if it were nothing more than that. 'I see it often in court. Why, only today His Majesty established the alms house fund from his own treasury.'

That night, when we turned in, I made sure that I lay down with him inside his mosquito net. And there I employed all the secret words and touches and bodily alignments that two decades of sleeping mat intimacy had taught me moved him above all others. I was determined to reaffirm to him, to me, to Heaven, that whatever differences he and I might have, our bond of marriage was unbreakable.

I knew when I awoke the following dawn that the question of the King's interest was not resolved, but I was not prepared for it to arise again as quickly as it did.

I was sitting in my room late that morning, going over accounts sent over from a warehouse. My husband was in the courtyard tending to some parasol business that I suspect didn't really warrant tending to, at least not by him – he had announced earlier that he would remain at the house for the day and put off a trip to a shrine across the city where preparations were underway for a royal visit.

A maid entered to announce that a messenger from the palace was at the gate. He was shown in and presented us with a piece of slate, cut in a clean square. It bore words which I could only assume were in His Majesty's own hand.

I beg to express again my relief concerning the recovered health of the Lady Sray and cannot but foresee that there will never be a repeat of the events of a certain visit on a certain evening.

Nol and I looked at each other, stunned all over again. It was an apology, however vaguely worded, an apology from a King. Nol muttered something about His Majesty regretting having broken the protocol of visiting. We'd received no advance notice that he would come to the house, after all. That was a possibility, I suppose, but you can see that my husband was still struggling to keep alive our shared lie. I could read the King's words for what they were. They were an apology for behaving in an inappropriate way toward a married woman.

Then, two days later, we received from the palace a message that the King would come calling. How we scrambled to prepare. His Majesty arrived at the appointed time with only a small entourage. Nol showed him to the veranda. There we had laid out a mat of honour facing the place where Nol would sit. I would sit to the side. But from the start of this visit, the King turned toward me, and it was Nol who was to the side. How awkward it was for him. Was he host or was he a retainer on duty, bound to remain silent?

'The Lady has recovered then? Completely?'

'I have, thank you. Your Majesty need feel no concern.'

'No, I must worry if a subject is ill. It is a King's duty.'

With this kind of talk, I might have thought simply that a third person was joining in the pretending. But through the tone of his voice, his choice of simple words, I was left with the sense that he indeed felt disquiet over my health. How was it possible that a man who had wielded the spear point that pierced the former lord's heart could host this common kind of compassion as well?

I said: 'But a King has so many subjects – he would be worrying all the time.'

'There are many subjects, that is true. But most are far away, beyond sight. The number he can see with his own eyes is limited. In that regard, a King is like any other man.'

What a thing to say! Perhaps it was that the Brahmin's teachings were having their effect. I wished I could look directly at him as he spoke, but of course I could not. Yet from the corner of my eye, I examined him, discerning the stout legs tucked beneath him, sunlight catching him full across the chest. A physically vital man, now at rest.

Just then I realized that in the short span of this conversation, I had completely forgotten that my husband was present. There can be no further delving into the personal, I told myself. So I said:

'The people will praise Your Majesty for the new alms fund.'

'I thank you, Lady Sray. It is a small thing. With so much given to me, there is a need that I act to repay Heaven's favour. I need to do more. But choosing where and to whom to give can be difficult.'

Here was a safe subject, then. I knew exactly what he meant. Many times I had been interrupted by word that at the gate was a woman in need of help for a starving family, but in talking with her she would seem uncertain as to just how many members this starving family had or where it lived. Or a priest had come from a far province professing that his hermitage had burned to the ground, but had forgotten to bring the certificate of loss that he said the local magistrate had issued.

The King said: 'Do I understand correctly that you have philanthropic activities of your own?'

'I give a bit of silver to some people and places.'

'Perhaps more than a bit, from what I am told. Now, may I ask something, how does the Lady decide these matters?'

Again, I sensed sincerity. I thought a moment. 'One gives to places in need, of course, where the silver will ease suffering. One accepts that one cannot know at all times whether claims of need are genuine. Still, one gives freely, with faith that the conditions are as described, and if perchance they aren't, that the good will shown toward the supplicant will result in contrition and a change in character.'

The King thought that over for a moment, and I continued.

'Charity must be given with an open heart, free of any suspicion. It must be given without any expectation that benefit will reflect back to the giver.'

'Do you mean benefit in this life, Lady, or in the next?'

'Both, Majesty. It is best if one gives with the stipulation that any holy merit that the gift will engender will not accrue to oneself, but to a party in greater need. This party should be carefully selected, and formally named when the gift is made – the name can be stated in a stone inscription, perhaps. The purpose of giving can only be to advance Heaven's cause, not one's own.'

The King asked: 'But is not a donor, by stipulating that the merit will go to another party – is not that in itself a selfless act that must by its nature cause at least some merit to accrue to the donor, regardless of the intentions of that donor?'

'I have wondered about that, Majesty. But I have no answer.'

'It is gratifying to learn that I am not alone in having no answer.'

There it was again, the personal finding its way into a subject that should have been safely devoid of it. I glanced toward my husband, who sat glumly. I felt suddenly ashamed at the thought that my comments were at least in part a rebuke of him. Nol, you see, felt that most everyone seeking charity told lies, and that in cases where giving charity could not be avoided, it should at least create some obligation for a favour in return.

Just then there was motion at our house's gate – the Brahmin was stepping into our courtyard. He made his way to the base of our steps. There he stood like a stone image, saying nothing, but all the same, I was sure, conveying disapproval. Presently the King turned and saw him. I believe that whatever pleasure His Majesty was feeling in conversing with me vanished at that point. He had just told me that in some ways a King is like any other man, and here was another example. Priestly chastisement, even unvoiced, had the same effect on him as it would have on a village man who owned no more than a rooster and fish trap.

Within a few minutes, the King rose, gave a polite farewell and withdrew.

My husband and I sat together on the veranda after that, I drawing near to him.

I awoke the next morning concerned the King might call again. But he did not. Instead it was the Brahmin Subhadra who returned, to see Nol. I was not told of the visit but the priest's voice carried to my room and, curious, I stole down the corridor far enough to hear the conversation.

'I have told His Majesty that the idea is an affront to Heaven,' Subhadra was saying.

'So it is,' replied Nol, in the weakest of voices.

'I have told him, Parasol Master, that divine law requires that a King look on another man's wife as a sister or as poison, that he can dally only with women chosen through the laws of Dharma, that the women must be fresh, unencumbered and younger than the monarch.'

Nol replied – it was almost a whimper: 'Yes, yes, that's how it's always been.'

'I can tell you that His Majesty says he wants only to continue the conversation on charity. I asked him outright, was this not really about interest in the Lady Sray entering the concubine pavilion? He denied it wholeheartedly. But...' The Brahmin blew out a breath of exasperation. 'Today he proposed another visit to this house. He asked that it be made to happen when you would not be present, Parasol Master. I, of course, instructed the relevant palace officials to hold off.'

'Yes, yes of course you did that.' Again, a whimper, barely audible, a kind of voice I had never heard from him.

'I then spent two hours with the King, making arguments both direct and indirect and showing him the supporting scriptures. But our lord is an impetuous young man. He does not always see why he must follow custom – never mind that it is Heaven's law. He is King, but in his heart he is still like a virile young man in a village, strolling a new year's festival at the local shrine. There is a side of him that wants to stop and flirt with any woman who meets his fancy.'

'You call my wife any woman?'

The Brahmin stumbled. 'Pardon me, Parasol Master. I used the wrong words. The Lady Sray is not any woman and his interest in her is not to be compared to his interest in some pretty village girl. In fact, I have never seen him like he is when he speaks of the Lady Sray. His voice softens, he uses only the most delicate terms. It's as if for a moment the fierceness is all drained out of him.'

There was silence for a while. Then Nol said. 'What can I do? She is so precious to me. For so long, she was all I had and if I were to lose her....' I began to hear a weeping sound. 'But at least,' he said, recovering, 'there would have to be some compensation. Some land, perhaps.'

Had I heard correctly? I could not bear it. I took a breath and strode into the room.

'It may interest you, husband,' I declared, 'to know that in an hour I am leaving for the provinces. I have work to see to involving the reconstruction of the guesthouses of the Temple of the Trinity.'

Nol came to life. 'You can't! The King has given no permission for you to leave.'

'I am not a prisoner in this house, husband. I will go where I please, where Heaven directs me to go.'

'You cannot speak like that.'

'I will talk however I choose, especially to a husband who is ready to barter me off for some patch of dried-up dirt! And if I have to apologize to you for preserving our marriage, I will take a stick and hit you over the head!'

I turned to Subhadra. 'Sir, if anyone comes here from the palace to request a meeting, that person will be told that I have left and that it is not clear how long I will be away, that my trip is divine duty, set in motion by a dream I had last night, in which our Lord Vishnu appeared to me in the form of a talking deer and declared that I must proceed to the temple without delay and provide the money to begin the rebuilding of the guesthouses and then to stay and oversee the work and say prayers for many days, and that I must in no way be disturbed, because I am doing the bidding of the Lord Vishnu, on consecrated ground.'

The Brahmin saw the potential. 'It's a powerful dream, Lady Sray. I think....I think no one can contest it, not even His Majesty.'

'Very good. And you, Nol, can drag yourself to the palace to apologize for my departure and, if you like, think about the land that you won't be getting.'

In my room, I began gathering up things for the journey, hoping that making my hands busy would calm me. What a jumble of emotions I was feeling, anger for the most part – anger toward my husband, anger toward palace life, anger toward the King for plying me with all those questions about holy giving. And anger toward myself. Each time that I lowered something into my basket, my wrists brushing against its edges, my mind insisted on recalling the touch of His Majesty's hands on that part of me as I lay on my mat that night.

Presently Nol entered the room and hovered behind me, silent. I said nothing either, continuing with my work. After a while, he spoke. 'I want you to know how relieved I am that you're going away. I take back what I said about having no permission. Leaving is the correct thing to do.'

That was all. I took it for what it was, and replied, not looking his way: 'I am relieved too. But I hope that if ever again we are in such a crisis, you will not panic. That first moment we met, Nol, you showed such remarkable courage. You must find it again in your dealings with the King.'

'Please, please understand – His Majesty has given us everything we have.'

'He has given us things and money and rank, but he has not given us life on this earth or our marriage or our children. There are limits to what we owe him.'

I left the house by oxcart, just me and my basket, a driver and a box filled with silver ingots which would finance the work on the guesthouses. At the bridge that led out of the royal sector, there waited the armed escort that Nol had called. I didn't want to think of whether it was out of concern for me or the silver. Sergeant Sen stepped forward and greeted me, showing no sign that it might have been inconvenient to be summoned on such short notice.

28: The bathing concubine

I settled in at the Temple of the Trinity, living alone in that sole guesthouse. I did my best to focus on prayer, on devotion to my far-away husband and to put aside thoughts of His Majesty's touch. One week became two, two became three. I had no idea how long I would remain.

I would only learn of it only later, but back in the Capital things were happening that would have great effect on my family in later years. In some cases it would be a marvellous effect, in others rank trouble.

The things of trouble I will recount first. These involved Bopa, and that was my fault. I had foolishly left her alone in the Capital, rather than insisting that she come with me again to the hilltop retreat. Bopa was a good-hearted soul, you see, but there were times in which she was short on sharpness of mind to sense when people intended harm.

In the previous year, my girl and I had acquired an early-morning routine. I would wake her and bring her with me to bathe in a stone-edged pool for women that lay outside the palace compound. Usually we went before the sun had fully showed itself. This was early, but she always came with me. But after I left for the temple, she began sleeping late, inside the comfort of her mosquito net, sometimes until the sun was well up in the sky.

Thank goodness we had a new maid in the house, the third granddaughter of a man who painted fabric in the parasol-making village. This girl was eager to show she was up to the job. She was not wise in city ways, but she was entirely trustworthy and had a large store of common sense.

One morning, Bopa awoke – rather I think it was this maid, Yan, who woke her, knowing that mischief dogs people who sleep late. Bopa drank down some tea, and then the two of them set out for the bathing pond. They found it deserted save for another maid. This girl was squatting on her haunches, but rose and strode off on seeing the new arrivals.

My daughter took up her bathing bowl, then moved down the stone steps until she was in thigh-deep in water. She began to pour water over herself. At this time of day, the water isn't cold like in the early morning; the sun has warmed it up pleasantly – I suppose I couldn't blame her for preferring to go at this time.

After a while, a young woman in a green silk sampot walked through a gate across the pool. She was someone of unusual rank and beauty – she had large eyes, a confident bearing and not one, but three maids in tow. The woman called out greetings to my daughter and descended the pool's steps, unwrapping her garment in an elegant motion as she immersed herself.

These three maids made their way too down into the pool and got to work on their mistress. You know how novice priests clean a bronze image, with each one worried about offending it by touching it familiarly? One of them wielding a brush, one holding a jar of polish, another a dust cloth? It was like this with the maids. Each seemed in quiet awe of the mistress. One gently sought permission, then poured water from a silver bowl over her shoulders, one applied ash for cleaning, one stood by to dab her dry with a clean krama. The lady's eyes, large and lovely, closed gently as the water passed over her head.

Bopa stopped, looked at this, then looked to Yan. I can imagine that she was thinking it would be nice to be fussed over in such a way.

Yan sensed this. She dried my daughter and helped her into a fresh sampot, doing her country best to match the service that the other woman was receiving.

From across the pool, the woman called: 'That's such pretty material you're wearing. May I know where it came from?'

'From the market, Lady.'

'I don't know why my own people can't find such nice things for me. Please, would you come over here and let me have a look?'

Yan's good sense extended to judging character, and she had already formed a distrust of the woman in the green sampot. Come along, mistress Bopa, the maid whispered. They're waiting for us back at the house – I'll get some nice rice soup for you. Bopa seemed not to hear, though, and Yan did not dare press her.

The elegant woman was gliding up the pool's stone steps now.

One of her maids was holding over her arm another green sampot that had the richest weave and colours.

The woman ran a finger approvingly along the waist of my daughter's garment. 'It's from China, clearly. I'll have to have a word with the head of my wardrobe. She just isn't trying hard enough. Would you consider coming over sometime and letting me show it to my people? This is really just what I want. It's so richly woven, and so stylish.'

'Why yes, of course, I could do that.'

'Wonderful. Perhaps now? Just give me a few minutes to finish here and we'll be off.' She turned to the maids. 'Hurry up, then. Get me dressed.'

'Now, then,' said the woman when the job was done. 'We can go. But first you must tell me your name.'

'I am Bopa, daughter of the royal parasol master.'

'My goodness! They're right. You are quite a beauty.'

My girl surely blushed.

'Oh, I've embarrassed you. Well, Bopa, the first thing a woman of beauty must learn in this life is how to take a compliment.'

This woman spoke from experience, of course. Her eyes were just one part of her beauty. She was, in fact, the closest thing in real life to the *apsara* nymphs who peer out from the stone reliefs at the temples. Her skin was ivory-smooth, her breasts perfect circles, her face and eyes alive with feminine allure.

Bopa ventured: 'And may I know your name, Lady?'

'Certainly. I am Rom.'

Now it was Bopa's turn to be surprised.

'I can tell,' the lady teased, 'that you've heard my name.'

'Of course, Lady. Everyone has.'

'Well, I won't deny that I like knowing that.'

This Rom, she now turned toward the maid Yan and made a gesture with her head that signified that Bopa would come alone. Yan pretended not to see. That was her way – she would not leave her mistress alone.

They walked, the maids trailing behind with the wet clothing and bathing implements.

Bopa said: 'Your maids really know how to do their job.'

'Yes, they're finally learning. These girls come in from the village and you can never be sure what you're going to get. They know rice seedlings, they know sugar palms, but not much else. You know, the other day I caught a couple of them pulling up the flowers outside my pavilion. They thought I'd be happy, that the flowers were weeds!'

'Mine once thought I should eat headache powder right out of the packet,' ventured Bopa. 'She'd never heard of mixing it with tea!'

They laughed together.

Bopa is not cruel by nature, but this was a cruel remark. And with the maid right behind her. But the city, life in court, can work unpleasant things on impressionable minds. My girl was so needful of this woman's approval that she made a joke at the expense of a person who cared deeply for her and always did her best in service.

The women passed through several gates. At each one Rom drew deep bows from sentries and servants.

By the door of a kitchen, they came upon two girls eating cucumbers slices from a tray. When Rom approached, they fell silent, put hands together and lowered their heads.

'Newcomers,' whispered Rom. 'Junior concubines. And just about as ignorant as the maids...' She gave a smile; Bopa felt proud that such a confidence was shared with her.

Rom led the way into a large sleeping pavilion and invited Bopa to sit. Yan sat near her mistress, feeling she needed protection. Tea was brought.

Suddenly there came a squeal from the door, and a tiny boy came toddling in, dressed in just as tiny a sampot with silver brocade. Around his neck was an amulet, a magic one, no doubt, wrapped in cloth so that its identity would remain unknown. A wet nurse trailed behind, and behind her, a man with a knife at his waist. He looked a bit frightening, but none of the concubines paid him any attention.

Rom took the boy on her lap, and there he sat for a while, sometimes studying Bopa and Yan, sometimes thrusting his mouth at his mother's breast, though each time he tried she turned him away from it.

This of course confirmed Yan's feelings about this woman. Wet nursing is a long tradition in the palace, of course, but to see a baby denied his mother's milk, and with no sign of regret from that mother – well, how can one think well of that? Yan shuffled a tiny bit closer to her mistress.

'This is my boy, my son – Darit is his name,' Rom announced. 'He's not even a year and half old yet, but already so strong. But there's an easy enough explanation for that, isn't there? Well, show us, Darit. Show us how you can shoot an arrow.'

The boy struck a pose, miming the drawing of a bow. Everyone laughed in delight, even the man with the knife.

Bopa waited for some other performance by the boy, but Rom simply gave him a hug. It seemed not an embrace of love, though, but of ownership. Then she touched the amulet, mouthed some kind of prayer, and handed him back to the nurse.

'So Bopa,' she said, 'not many girls have a life like yours. Your father is one of the King's closest advisers. Your mother runs the royal stores. Her influence is everywhere, though so few of us ever see her. I don't know that I ever have – maybe just once.'

'Yes, she doesn't go around the palace much. Either she's in the house, or in a warehouse or traveling somewhere.'

'Is she at home now?'

'No, she's gone on a trip. She left yesterday morning.'

'Really? Where did she go?'

'Down to the port at the Freshwater Sea.'

'And what's she doing there?'

'Visiting a temple that's up on a hill there. She's going to give it some silver, I think. I don't know much more, really. I was taking a nap when she came in to tell me she was leaving. I fell back to sleep and when I woke up I hardly remembered talking to her.'

'I'm that same way,' laughed Rom. 'I wake up and I can't remember a thing.' She laughed. 'Well, it was so nice of you to come.'

Yan urged her mistress to her feet. But I think Bopa was sad the visit was ending, just when she was settling in.

They all walked to the gate.

'I hope we'll see each other again soon,' Rom said. 'Perhaps at the bathing pool.'

Bopa and the maid walked home. Yan recalled that the girl was smiling so broadly that people she passed looked a second time.

At the gate, Bopa stopped: 'Wait! We should go back. Rom's garment people didn't get a chance to look at my sampot.'

'On another day, mistress. On another day. But quick – come inside. Don't you smell the rice soup?' It was like Yan was addressing a child, don't you think? Bopa would often respond to that kind of authority, even when she was long past the age. She passed through the gate.

The next morning, without anyone having to rouse her, my girl went to the pool at just the same time. But Rom was not there. Nor was she the following day. Yan said the concubine must have gone out of the Capital. Bopa wouldn't accept that. She insisted that they call at the concubine compound. So they went. The guard at the gate made the two of them wait while word was sent in. Finally, they were admitted and shown to the presence of the concubine, who smiled broadly and declared it was wonderful she'd come to visit.

Yan felt it might be wonderful for the concubine, though she wasn't sure why. She reaffirmed to herself that she would never let her mistress out of her sight during these visits.

29: Sovan's vision

In my absence, there was that trouble for my daughter. But for my son, the seeds of something glorious. I will tell you.

At the start of the Eighteenth Reign, my husband had decreed that our son would no longer maintain or repair the parasols, fans and whisks. I was there the evening when Nol delivered that message. You've learned those skills in full, he said. Quite well, in fact. Now you will supervise. You will serve only the King. You will begin leading a team that attends at court. You will never touch things in the workshop. Sawdust in the hair, gilding on the wrists, the smell and stickiness of lacquer oils on the fingers? Anyone who serves before the King must be perfectly groomed. There cannot be unseemly odours. And there is something else, Nol continued. It was one thing for you as a boy to be seen squatting in the parasol pavilion, sweating over a rip in the silk of a parasol. But if you continue this work now, as you became a man, the artisans will come to see you as no different from themselves. They will take advantage. They will pretend not to hear when you assign them unpleasant tasks. They will connive to borrow money from you or disappear on trips to their home villages. You know the kind of thing I mean, you've heard it. 'Please, I must go be with my grandfather. He is not well. It could be that his time in this life is near its end.' If all these stories were true, it would mean that every grandfather in every province of the Empire was ill all of the time.

I said nothing that evening. These were men's concerns. But I knew very well how my son felt. He told his father that he understood. He told him that, but when Nol was away he continued to go to the pavilion, to squat there contentedly, tools in hand, dealing with those rips in silk and the myriad other things that went wrong with the delicate creations that were stored under the pavilion's roof. One day, when some latest repair had been completed, I saw him take up a slate and sit to the side to sketch patterns for the fabric of a future parasol. Several artisans looked over his shoulder, with interest, with respect, and offered thoughts on this new design. Take advantage? I can assure you they did not.

This state of affairs continued until a rainy afternoon when Nol returned ahead of schedule from a trip, and saw. In the house that night, with our son kneeling before him, he delivered the sternest kind of lecture, and when my boy next stole into the pavilion, during a paternal absence, the chief artisan came near. 'Please, master Sovan,' he whispered, 'please only look. If you do more than that, I will be in grave trouble with your father. He will banish me. I will have no work and my family will be without rice.'

So from that point on, my boy left behind the tools and camaraderie of the workshop. The men and women there, whenever they saw him pass by, whispered among themselves that he seemed to have lost the serene spirit he had always displayed with them. I felt it too. Looking back, I wonder if perhaps it was more, a quiet kind of despair.

All this occurred sometime before I fled the Capital for the Temple of the Trinity. But, about two weeks into my stay there, Heaven deigned to open for Sovan a path that was entirely new.

One morning word reached my husband that the Brahmin Subhadra would visit a minor prince whose land lay a short distance south of the Capital. Nol decided, on the spot, to make an exception to his rule that his son would serve only the King.

'Go along and oversee the bearers for the Rajaguru,' he told Sovan. 'And when you get to the estate, make sure you keep your ears open.'

Sovan welcomed a chance to get away from court – he never felt comfortable with that duty. But he knew there was some special reason for his father's instruction. 'What should I listen for, father?'

'Just listen, discreetly. As they say, "catch the fish without making the water muddy." Then come tell me what you heard.'

At the appointed hour the next morning, Sovan arrived at the Brahmin's house with six parasol bearers and an eight-slave palanquin. Presently Subhadra emerged, and if he felt any curiosity as to why he was being paid the honour of Sovan's attendance, he didn't show it. He offered greetings to the young man, then took his place in the conveyance. It was hefted to eight shoulders and the trip began. Sovan walked silently to the side, his feet raising tiny puffs of dust. It was late in the dry season. He was perspiring already.

Right away, Sovan broached the subject of my situation – such was his devotion to me. When might it be safe for me to return to the Capital? The Brahmin gave a morose look in reply. Unfortunately, he explained, there is no news at all. His Majesty simply will not discuss it.

An hour later, the party reached the destination, a rather small estate house that stood to the side of an ancient gum tree. The young prince who was its lord was waiting at the door with an unsettled air about him. He went to the dust for Subhadra, who thanked him and bade him get up. The slaves and bearers were directed to the back for food and water; Subhadra and Sovan and the two bearers were shown up the steps through the house's main door, then down a hallway with floors that seemed just to have received a polishing. At the end was a small audience room.

Subhadra and the prince took places on the mat. Sovan sat to the side; the prince's own fan bearers would take over now.

'How nicely your fields are being prepared for the rains,' Subhadra began. 'It was a pleasure to pass down the road and see people working with such energy. And in such heat.'

'We try our hardest,' replied the prince. 'His Majesty has entrusted this land to us and we can only do our best to keep it at its full potential.'

Two maids entered the room, walking on their knees in the presence of such rank, and put out tea and cut pineapple.

When they had withdrawn, the prince said earnestly: 'The land has been very productive in the past two years. We have more rice and animals than we can use here, in fact. If it's not presumptive of me, I would like to propose that we increase the estate's contribution to the royal grain stocks. I believe that a sixty-forty split would be appropriate.'

'That's kind of you,' said Subhadra, puzzled. 'But it's not necessary. His Majesty's stores already have all they can hold. As you may know, fields in the Empire as a whole have become productive with the peace that has set in under His Majesty's blessed reign.'

The prince seemed not to hear. 'We have served His Majesty to the best of our ability. We fought in the northern campaign. My own brother died there, and I received a wound from a Siamese arrow. Right here.' He twisted to show a scar above his left hip. 'We have served, and we believe that under our guidance the land can produce far more than it could under another family...'

'Please!' said the Brahmin. 'What is this about?'

The prince took a moment preparing his answer. 'Sir, with your permission, I will speak plainly. My message is that whatever I have done that has disappointed the palace, I will undo. Whatever the mistake, I will correct it. I ask for a second chance, to remain on the land, to show His Majesty my love and devotion.'

'And why do you think you have disappointed?' Subhadra had no idea.

'Because...because...because there have been men from the palace inspecting the land, sir. They don't even ask permission to come...'

Now Subhadra smiled with a father's affection. 'Don't worry,' he said. 'His Majesty is entirely pleased with your stewardship. There is no problem. In fact, the work of the men you have seen may result in a remarkable honour for you and your family.'

'Whatever this honour might be, we don't deserve it.'

'Let me explain,' said Subhadra. 'In fact, this is the reason that I am here at your estate today. The King has been on the throne for five years now. It is time to begin the great project that anchors every great reign, construction of a mountain-temple. The Temple of the Eighteenth Reign will be dedicated to our Lord Shiva and, as you can appreciate, will contain countless lingas reflecting Shiva's great generative powers. The temple will be His Majesty's citadel on earth, his place for private devotions and the conducting of an annual cycle of rituals. Now, the palace geomancers have been conducting investigations to determine the perfect site for the monument. They have drawn lines on charts, in consultation with the texts and priests, they have made observations of the sun and stars and their movements in the sky during the annual cycle. There are different ways to carry this out, you might know, and from different ways come different results. But what I have come to tell you is that by one formulation, the lines of divination intersect at a point on your estate.' He paused to let this sink in. 'That's why those strange men have been coming here – they are surveyors, seeing if they can confirm on the land what the charts show on palm leaf. They could not, of course, announce to you their purpose in coming.'

My son was paying special attention now. This was the news his father had predicted and to Sovan it was interesting in its own right.

The Brahmin continued. 'If your land is selected – and that decision has not been made, I must tell you – then the first ground will be broken early next year. Foundations will be dug, great stores of building materials will be brought.'

Now you can imagine how the shock that the prince's face had been displaying turned to elation. Then his head went straight to the mat, hitting it with a bump that made my son suppress a smile. 'I thank His Majesty, sir,' the man murmured into the straw. 'I thank the lords of Heaven for an honour of this sort.'

'We expect that the mountain-temple and its moats and outer walls and lands would occupy about a quarter of your estate,' the Brahmin said. 'It might become necessary for you and your family to vacate this house. You would of course be compensated, with silver and comparable land and residence elsewhere.'

'I would need no compensation, sir. The honour would be enough.'

Subhadra had lived in the Capital long enough to know that this young prince might come around to the idea of being paid.

Then the priest turned quite serious. 'This information must remain entirely confidential. If it becomes known, there will be the most serious kind of trouble for everyone involved.' He cast an intimidating glare toward the fan bearers and my son. 'You may know that when word of this gets out, land around the edges of the site that will be needed for construction staging, huts for the workers and things like that. This land will tend to change hands and to rise very quickly in price. There is even a family in the city whose fortune began with a bribe given a man in the palace surveyor's office for advance word on the site of the temple of a previous reign. These people bought the site and everything around it. When it came time to build, they sold it back to the crown at a very high price, which they negotiated with the very man whom they'd bribed for the information in the first place. No doubt he got part of the sale price himself. Anyway, we are determined there will be no repeat of that sort of thing.'

'I give my sacred word,' replied the prince. 'There will be no disclosure from this side.'

'I'm glad to hear that. I'm told the site is a place the local people call the Field of Three Spirits. His Majesty's chief architect is on his way here to have a look.'

My son was excited at that news – he was going to see the man who created temples.

Presently the bells of an approaching procession were heard. The men rose and went to the house's front door. A covered palanquin carried by slaves had come into view, and on it sat the Architect. He was at this point already getting on in years, but he retained a lean face and physique that showed few effects of age. Sovan took note of everything about him and his entourage. At the door, he hopped to the ground in an impatient way, as if he'd have preferred the quicker transportation of his own feet. He traded quiet words with two young men who'd followed his palanquin in. They carried woven-straw bags and long-bladed knives and seemed to be assistants.

The young prince crouched and made an offer of refreshments, but the Architect waved it off, despite the heat. 'What I'd like,' he announced, 'is to see the site.'

The prince pointed the way, a narrow path that ran south from the estate house. In hardly an instant the Architect was striding down it, in the lead. He moved so fast that bearers whom the prince ordered along with a couple of small parasols had trouble keeping him in shade. The Brahmin chose to stay behind; it was too hot for this kind of exertion.

After ten minutes of this brisk pace, the prince called from behind for a stop. 'This is it, sir. The Field of Three Spirits.'

Now my son felt some disappointment. The place seemed

nothing special, just a collection of rice fields like any other, dry, barren, awaiting the rains, broken here and there by copses that had never been cleared and by the piled dirt of termite nests.

The Architect looked to a small promontory, covered with thick weeds and bushes. He turned to one of his assistants: 'Hack us a path up that thing.' The young man took out a long-bladed knife and began slashing.

Sovan was last in line, and when he reached the top, he turned by himself and looked again to the fields.

He would always remember what happened next – he told me many times about it. From this new height, from this different vantage point, Heaven caused something remarkable. Paddy dikes, stretching toward the horizon, seemed to my boy to hint of a broad avenue. Fallow fields to the right and left evoked sacred moats. A distant tree line, shimmering due to the heated air, seemed very much like a body of stone, with five gently curving peaks atop it, shaped like lotus blossoms. What he saw might have been man-made, my boy told me, or it might have been placed there by the gods. He closed his eyes, and everything came into even sharper focus. He was standing at a great gate, looking down a long avenue that gave onto a great stone citadel, larger than anything he'd ever seen. He was looking at Heaven on earth.

Then, he opened his eyes. Before him was dry paddy land again.

He glanced about, a bit frightened, I think, wondering if anyone else in the group had seen. But no. They were all looking in the opposite direction, in fact, following the Architect's lead.

'It's a fine site,' the man was telling the host prince in his gruff way. 'I thank you for showing it to us. Now we're going to look around for a while.' There was an awkward pause. The prince was being dismissed, on his own land. My boy sensed that it wasn't really his anymore.

The prince turned to descend from the hillock, but one of the assistants spoke up to him – what forwardness that was, but such was the honour and responsibility of assisting the Architect that they could break the rules. 'We will need a parasol. Not a ceremonial one like this, but a real one, for real shade. And a bearer.'

Sovan said instantly: 'I'll take care of it.' He too felt invested with this man's authority.

He hurried back to the prince's house, got a servant to show him the shed where the shades were stored, then returned to the site with a large white one. By now the Architect had left the mound and was standing alone, in thought, in a patch of ground that had never been cleared for cultivation. Those two assistants hovered nearby. One was holding a wooden box taken from his shoulder bag. It was a sort of portable desk, and on it was a piece of slate for writing.

'Thank you,' said the man when Sovan raised the parasol over him. 'There are times when you actually need these things.'

Then he surprised my son by dropping to a squat, right there in the dust, like a farmer. A small spade was in the left hand of this great man. He drove it firmly into ground, turned some soil over, then placed a pinch in his right palm. He brought eyes close and explored the sample with index finger, flicking away a pebble and a dead root. He sniffed. He touched finger to tongue and reflected on the taste for a moment. All this Sovan watched as closely as he dared.

The Architect tossed the dirt aside and shuffled on his haunches to another spot, Sovan doing his best to keep him in shade. The process of examination began again.

Finally, the Architect turned to the assistant with the slate: 'Medium solid, some lime. No signs of clay at the surface. Quite good, all around.' The words were written down with a piece of chalk.

'All right. We'll walk a bit now.'

He repeated this procedure in four other places around the fields. Then he called to his assistants. 'Now show me the holes.'

The party moved to a circular pit, dug by the men whose presence had so concerned the young prince and, you will now understand, the people of the village my husband and I owned to the west of the site. The pit had the diameter of an outstretched arm and went a bit deeper than a standing man, with clean, sheer walls inside, and some water at the bottom. The assistants lifted their master by the arms, and lowered him in. Another remarkable sight! He spent some extended time down there, squinting close-up at the walls, running fingers over them, muttering, probing the mud beneath him with his toes. He called to Sovan. It was either 'Boy, shade me, will you? It's hot down here.' Or 'Boy, move that parasol out of the way, I want the sunlight to fall directly on the wall of the hole.'

Later the man began a walking inspection of the entire site, tramping through bramble bushes, up and over more mounds and termite piles, past a nearly barren stream where a pair of turtles sunned themselves seemingly unaware of the great disruption that might be visited upon their home. Nothing escaped the man's attention. At a gully baked dry and cracking, he ordered the assistants to run a long cord from one side to another, then pull it tight and measure the length of another cord that from the middle of the first hung down to the ground. Sovan watched every step. A King subdues enemy princes and armies to create an Empire. This man was going to subdue land, trees and water to create something which – who could say? – might last longer than an Empire.

The work concluded in late afternoon. On the walk back to the prince's house, my boy summoned up some courage and asked: 'Is the soil solid enough to build here, sir?'

The man at first seemed annoyed, but then he replied. 'Yes. It will be very good. It's a lot better than what's under some of the previous reigns' sites. They should have checked more closely and chosen somewhere else.'

'That gully will have to be filled in completely, won't it, sir?'

'What, are you an architect, young man?'

'No, sir,' said Sovan. 'Only a boy who is interested.' Others would have wilted in the face of such a remark. But such was my son's engagement with this subject that he was not afraid.

'Interested in the business of building?' said the Architect. 'You don't like carrying parasols for famous men?'

He grinned, and Sovan realized there was a hint of self-mockery in his words.

'I do find value in the work, sir. It's my family's station. But I also love temples – not so much what goes on in them, but what they are. They give me peace of mind and proof of Heaven. But I've never understood how temples are conceived and built. There are just too many pieces.'

'You don't believe it's the gods who build them, then?'

'No, sir. Not the gods directly. But the gods making their will felt through the labour of human beings.'

Now Sovan thought a moment, and decided to share what had come over him four hours earlier. 'May I tell, you sir, that at the top of the mound, when we began, I felt that I could see the new mountain-temple in place already. It was like the gods created the site just so that men would come along and discover it and build.'

'You think so, do you?'

'I do, sir.'

'And what form did this temple take, the one you saw?'

The man was teasing, but he seemed also to want an answer.

'Sir, it had five towers, the five peaks of Mount Meru. Each was gently curved at the top like the closed blossom of a lotus. There was a long causeway approaching the main entranceway, with two stone libraries on either side. And a great moat. The temple was larger than any I've ever seen. '

'That does rather sound like a vision from Heaven,' said the Architect, suddenly serious. Then his former tone returned. 'But I'm afraid you saw the wrong temple. The one that will be built here will have three towers, and they will be straight and square at the top. A pyramid form. No curves. This is the temple that the King's priests have seen and that His Majesty has now seen, drawn out on palm leaves by those same priests. Though I must say that five towers would be beautiful and pleasing to Heaven. You say they curved like lotus buds?'

'Yes, sir.'

They had reached the estate house. The Brahmin had returned to the city, but the prince was waiting attentively at the door. He voiced an invitation to food and water, and this time the Architect accepted.

It was well past dusk when Sovan arrived back at our family house. He bathed, then went to see his father in the main room.

'So, tell me about the day,' my husband said. 'But first let me speculate – Subhadra went there to inspect the place as a possible site for His Majesty's mountain-temple.'

'Yes, father, that's how it was.'

People sometimes said that Nol heard more with one ear than anyone else heard with two. They never said it in front of him, but he would not have minded if they did.

Responding to questions, my son described the Architect's visit. But Nol didn't seem to care about the details. He just wanted to know whether the visitor had settled on this site. My son was quite sure that this would be the place, but he replied there was no clear answer.

Nol would not accept that: 'It sounds to me like this is the place,' he declared. 'The family's going to do very well by this – I figured it out right!'

'Heaven has favoured us, then.'

'Sovan, be sharper than that. What people say is the gods' favour is usually something that's been thought up right here on earth. All of us in court have known that a decision on the site was close. So I've been asking people...'

'Only asking?' Sovan asked dutifully.

'Well...' And a sly look crossed Nol's face. 'I did go to the Architect's office and tell one of the draftsman there that I'd secured a place for his daughter in the royal dance school. And, do you know what? He let slip that the selection had been narrowed to two possible sites. So I went out and had a look, and then last month, when word came that our family was going to get a couple of tracts of land, I went to see a man at the royal land office, and presented some blandishments that persuaded him to recommend that we get two particular sites.'

'And both happened to be near a place where the temple might be built?'

'Why yes! One of them is the land of the village your mother visited. Just to the west of the place you were at today!'

My husband always preened when talking about property in the family's hands. Sovan thought a moment and I think took secret satisfaction in asking: 'But father, isn't there a problem?

A temple's entrance is always on the east. Isn't that where you'd want your land to be? That's where the markets and public shrines and hostels for pilgrims will go up.'

Nol frowned; the boy had put his finger on the one weakness of his scheme.

Later, Sovan walked in the dark toward the jars for a final bath of the day, but halfway there, in the middle of a courtyard, he stopped. The temple was again presenting itself in his mind's eye. Five glorious towers. The Architect had said three, but Sovan nonetheless saw five, each with the gentle curves of a lotus bud.

30: The night festival

At this time of the year, the only place in the house where the air was bearable was the veranda, and so Sovan sat down there that night to eat his final rice. Then he went to his room, where his mosquito net had been strung. But he didn't lie down. He picked up three sticks of incense, stuck them in his waist and stole silently down the back steps.

My boy passed quickly across the Naga bridge to leave the royal sector. There he dropped his pace a bit, relieved to have departed without questions being asked. He kept to the avenue that led toward the Pre Rup mountain-temple. People passed him in the darkness, laughing, already tipsy as they headed for a festival that had begun that night across the city.

At the shrine by the mountain-temple's east gate, he approached Bronze Uncle and lit the incense he'd brought. He knelt, and whispered prayers for my safe return, confident that through the god his words would be accorded a special hearing in Shiva's court. He raised his head and looked toward the old temple, whose outlines loomed high against the night sky. Here and there lamps burned on its heights, like new stars in the Heavens, just as they did when we lived as a family of commoners in the little quarter on the other side.

He walked quickly away, not wanting the acolytes to recognize him.

Prayers for me, of course, were very important to my boy – such was his devotion. But what he was to do next, well, it was very important too. Do not ask me to guess which one was the more so in his mind.

He headed for a temple near the city's southern edge, following the revellers he had passed earlier. The occasion was the Festival of Heavenly Fertilization. The miracle of rain drawn from barren skies! The heat of dry season in retreat, dried, crumbling leaves blowing away, parched paddies welcoming water again, the Freshwater Sea expanding its domain. So it is that life becomes possible for another year. As you know, any number of temples put on variations of this festival, but in those times people travelled for days or even weeks from every province to the one to which my son was walking. Part of the reason was that this was not a royal temple, and ordinary people could pass inside to say devotions, at least at some of the lesser shines. More important was that some years earlier the temple's priests had persuaded men from the Upper Empire to conduct the festival in the particular way of their home villages, only on a much more spectacular scale. With the help of Chinese merchants, who provided special powders from their native country, the festival at this temple was each year more of a show than it had been the previous year.

As Sovan neared the temple, the streets became busier. Vendors who couldn't afford the high rent that was charged on its grounds had set up along the approaching street instead. With fruit snacks and coconut milk laid out on brightly coloured cloths, they called out to people passing by to come have a look. Sovan did, and at one lamp-lit cloth he found what he wanted – dried banana sweets. He bought some, thanking the old vendor woman as she wrapped them in leaf. He rejoined the flow toward the temple.

He passed a wine stall. In front was a girl who caught his eye and refused to give it up. He looked away, but she countered by falling in step alongside him. 'What, no girlfriend for a handsome boy like you? I can do something about that.' I can imagine that she did something like stroke his forearm as she spoke, or perhaps she was even more direct with her hands. It is sad truth that women enter this profession, but once they are there, it is only natural that they do what they can to get business.

My boy would have found it hard to say anything at all to this sort of thing, I think. He would have shaken off that hand and quickened his pace, she calling after him: 'On your way home, maybe? You know where to find me.'

Outside the temple's main gate, torches illuminated other people who had set up for business – a fortune teller plotting the future of a shy young couple, a vendor selling charms he swore had been blessed personally by the holy hands and voice of the temple's founding abbot a century earlier. Atop a tiny stage – it was a market crate actually – pranced a monkey wearing a tiny sampot, drawing smiles from a clutch of children. Sovan's eyes scanned the faces around him, then he moved to the gate, where people were crowding in to make offerings of the evening. Sovan had already made some elsewhere, of course, but he joined the throng anyway and edged through the entranceway. He went to each of a dozen separate shrines and images to look over the people who were kneeling and lighting incense and placing garlands around the necks of images. Then he passed back out the gate.

To the side was a large field with another crowd, and more torches. Sovan stopped, wondering what would be the best strategy. Then, ahead, two young women, their backs to him. They were on a festival stroll. An older servant walked behind, keeping an eye. He thought: a chaperone, a sister brought along – it might just be possible! He hurried forward, murmuring apologies to people he jostled. When he got ahead of the promenading group he turned as casually as he could to look. No! These were two young women well into the age of motherhood; the maid was no one he'd ever seen.

He stopped, oblivious to the crowd. I think it was now that the thought sank in that it would be so much easier, so much more dignified, to find a wife in the usual way. And so much faster, which would be a blessing. He had to marry; he was past the age. His father was demanding it. As for me, I was not pressing him, but waiting out this period with some impatience. His own soul and body craved it, I'm sure. Is it possible for a young man to go on forever this way, never giving in to the wine-stall girls? Perhaps only if he takes holy vows, and even then... But each time my boy prepared for a possible match, putting on his best sampot, calling on the latest well-bred girl nominated by priests or parents, or sometimes ones he'd become aware of on his own, he never got beyond the preliminaries. Nol complained many times – to him, to me – about the string of break-offs, saying that people were starting to talk, that parents weren't going to risk letting Sovan add their daughter to the list. My boy did tell me once that he felt he'd behaved unfairly toward these young women. But he knew why nothing was working out. I did too – it was a secret we shared: No one measured up to the standard, the standard of the girl at the stone-edged pond in the country house six years earlier.

It was more than his memory of that encounter. One night, he told me, a spirit had planted confirmation in him. He had been tossing and turning on his mat, and then his eyes closed, and opened again and there she stood before him. She had grown to young womanhood. Her hands were together, there was that same faint smile of mischief on her lips. She was not doing anything – she was not even looking at him. She was just *being*. After a moment, she sat down, on that same grass, and Sovan saw the same stone-edged pond behind her. With that same reed she stirred the water gently.

Do you know, for years he believed that Heaven did not intend them to be joined. It had created them of quite different social ranks, after all. He had always worried that her invitation to call at the estate house that long-ago day was meant only to spare his feelings. It was given with the expectation he would not act on it. Heaven had not allowed him to hear her name, nor even the name of her estate. It had led the prince to leave the district the very next day for the Siamese border, taking his entourage along, Sovan included. On this last point, however, my boy felt that his father had played a role as well – he had dismissed a very strongly stated request to stay behind a day or two and then catch up.

But a dream has the power to clear away all uncertainties. When Sovan woke up, he knew he must take the initiative. A young man in search of a wife is like a bee buzzing about a garden – the flower does not come to him, *he* must go to *it*. But where would he go to find this particular flower? That was something his father would know how to answer, but Sovan didn't want his help. Instead he got up his courage and went to the market to talk to one of the men there whose specialty is confidential assignments on hire. Sovan told him as best he could remember how to find the little house in the forest and the girl's estate. Four weeks later, the man reported back. He had located both houses, he said, and both were empty. Local villagers remembered the noble family but said they'd moved away some years earlier. To where no one could say, the man said. No one knew the lord's name, just the title by which he was referred. As for his daughters, the people did offer some help, three names. Of them, Sovan settled on Suriya, because he liked its sound and its meaning – the sun, which had shown on her so fetchingly that day.

Were the villagers really so ignorant of where this family had gone? I wonder. Perhaps Sovan's agent was holding out for more silver for what was of course the crucial piece of intelligence. But he got no more silver, and Sovan got no more information. As far as my boy was concerned, Suriya could be anywhere.

But that was cause for hope. Perhaps this girl, this now young woman, was living right in Angkor, a short walk from our house, or perhaps she was visiting from the provinces on this very day for this festival, as gentry often did. So here he was, searching through tens of thousands of people, with a bag of banana sweets to offer should the miracle occur and Suriya come to be standing before him.

A gong sounded. Sovan turned to see novice priests shooing merry-makers away from the temple's gate. Soon four men with drums emerged in procession, followed by a torch bearer and a dozen priests. Then came the thing the crowd was waiting for. It was a thick wooden shaft, as long as four men lying down in line, an arrow-straight, hollowed-out tree trunk, painted bright red. It was carried cradled in a large yellow cloth by ten stout bearers on each side. The crowd, men and women alike, let out a collective gasp. No one had ever seen one so large. You can imagine the kind of lewd jokes that people were soon making about the bearers' burden.

Two priests of senior rank splashed it with holy water. Then it was carried in procession across a field toward a tower made of bamboo scaffolding. The crowd followed in excitement, Sovan included. Below the tower, the thing was laid down on the grass. Village men tied it with ropes that hung from the tower, then pulled on the ropes. The great shaft began to stand up – and there was another round of joking in the crowd. The crowd drew near for a better look. 'Keep that torch back!' shouted a Chinese man who was helping set up. His strange accent made people laugh; the torch moved back only a bit, because without it no one could see.

Then, on cue from a priest, the crowd knelt and put hands together as other priests splashed yet more holy water and chanted yet more prayers. May Heaven accept this gift, may it be impregnated, and in due course grant the gift of water to us people below, so that the soil in the Empire's paddies might again be soft and fertile, that rice might grow anew and all people eat, that those people pledge to be eternally grateful and respond in myriad ways that would please Heaven.

Now the crowd was pushed back, sometimes physically, by burly men hired by the temple for the purpose. Quiet was called and a priest held a small torch to the sky. He blessed it, then threw it to the ground. From that spot, fire raced in a line across grass to the base of the holy implement. Fire and smoke burst out there, creating a roar louder than any storm or waterfall, louder than anything Sovan had ever heard. The holy implement quavered for an instant, then came to life, leaving its bamboo berth, racing toward the Heavens, gaining speed and leaving a shower of flame and sparks behind it. People crouched, frightened and amazed, keeping their eyes toward the blaze of light moving up and across the bowl of night, still creating its din. It veered left and right, and people found courage to stand up straight and squint and raise hands to brows the better to see. Then it burst apart in a remarkable spectacle, sending great flames in every direction. There came a clap of thunder. So loud and sudden was it all that spectators dropped to the ground, hushed in wonder.

As the last sparks drifted across the sky, shouts of Heaven's glory echoed from the crowd.

That was it. My boy got to his feet with everyone else. People began drifting toward the streets to go home, but Sovan went back inside the temple walls. There he said prayers at an image, one with a record of granting wishes to deserving supplicants. He left the banana sweets before it, untouched.

On his way home, two things happened that bode well. The first was that he had no trouble walking past the girl who called to him again from the wine stall. The second was that when he crossed the bridge into the royal sector, he felt a drop of rain on his brow.

31: Exile

At the temple on the hill, I now had a routine. Each day I rose before dawn, bathed, then said devotions at the foot of Vishnu's tower as the sun broke forth over the paddies to the east. I took the first rice of the day alone. The food brought to me was what the abbot imagined to be city-quality (I had spotted a new cook at the fire), but in fact it was not much different from what I'd eaten as a child and that became another reason why I took to this place.

In late morning most days, I walked down the hill to the town. Sometimes I passed a line of slaves making the ascent, carrying thatch and lengths of bamboo for work on the ruined guesthouses. The trip was easier now. Workers hired by the Chinese merchants had repaired the washed-out sections of the path.

In the port, I checked in with Sergeant Sen to show that I was in good health and to chat a bit – truth be told, I did get lonely up that hill. Then I strolled through the open market and bought whatever minor things I needed. Sometimes I stopped at the merchants' hall. Tea was brought out and Mr Chen and other of his countrymen sat down and passed the time with me, maybe opening with talk of the shadow puppet show at a shrine up the road. Of course the talk usually turned at some point toward the palace's purchasing plans and the best source of such-and-such commodity.

One day, I said: 'You know, Mr Chen, if the palace is going to contract with a firm for the long term, we like to have seen its facilities.'

'Then why don't we go and visit mine?' he replied, as I'd hoped he would. 'Our main rice storage depot is just a short distance from here. Shall we call for your cart?'

'Actually, I would prefer to walk.'

We set off, Sergeant Sen trailing behind. A Chinese ship was tied up at a dock. My eye could not leave it. No matter how many times I saw these things, they seemed unnatural to me. Floating buildings! Water craft should be small, controlled just by a paddle.

'You must be brave to go aboard that, Mr Chen. I can't imagine staying on it for an hour, let alone the whole day it takes to get to China.'

'A whole day?' Mr Chen seemed amused, in his usual good-natured way. 'We stay on it a lot longer than that, Lady Sray. The trip to China takes about two months.'

'Two months! How can that be? China is just on the other side of the Fresh Water Sea.'

'Perhaps the person who told you that did not quite understand, Lady Sray, and meant to say the Salt Water Sea. To get to China, first you sail the length of the Fresh Water Sea, then you enter the Great Dual Vector River and follow it to another river that is even larger, which brings you to the Salt Water Sea. Then you cross it – China is in fact on the far side of the Salt Water Sea. You don't follow the shore, but head straight across the water. Sometimes you can't see land for days and days at a time.'

I couldn't imagine that. It wouldn't be this earth if there weren't land.

Mr Chen hastened to explain. 'You can't see land, but you always know it's there, just out of sight. It's like taking a long trip on land. You can't see the village you're going to – isn't it so? But that doesn't mean it isn't there. At the end it always shows itself.'

'Still, two months is such a long time.'

'Yes, but knowing that home's up ahead keeps us going. And out on the sea on a calm day, with the sun shining down and every patch of the sky open to see, well, you can't feel much closer to Heaven.'

That sun was warming my head even then. I asked, cautiously: 'Do you ever actually see Heaven out there?'

'In the heart you do, Lady Sray.'

I wondered briefly if for me it would ever be any other way. Then I put aside the thought. 'Is China like the Khmer Empire? Same blue sky overhead?'

'Oh, yes, it's the same sky. But a different kind of people. For one thing, they wear clothes over their entire bodies.'

'Really!' It wasn't entirely a surprise, though. I had seen figures dressed in that way on the teapot that my husband had sold in the first days of our new lives. But I'd never understood why. So I asked.

'Partly...well, it's just the custom, Lady,' said Mr Chen, showing a bit of embarrassment. 'You get so that you don't feel yourself if you're not covered up. But it's also because it can get very cold.'

'Like here, then! Not so different. Like on those nights after the winter solstice when the wind blows.' In the heat of this day, it was hard to imagine that such nights existed.

Mr Chen laughed again. 'Consider, Lady, if the air were ten times or twenty times colder than what you just described. Sometimes it gets so cold that water turns to stone and white powder falls from the sky instead of rain.'

'I can't be!'

'It is in fact like that. People shake and shiver like they have a fever. But they're not really sick. They can solve the problem by covering their bodies, or by keeping moving so that their bodies make heat.'

I looked to Mr Chen and thought that indeed I was talking to someone experienced and wise.

We reached a large wooden building, with its own jetty in the back. Inside, Mr Chen showed me bag upon bag of rice stacked in neat order, too many to count. In an adjacent building, I was invited to inspect wooden boxes filled with chinaware, tea, bolts of silk and a few things I didn't recognize.

'It's very impressive, Mr Chen. It must all generate a good flow of income.'

'Yes, we can't complain. We are blessed.'

'And what type of charity do you support?' I must confess that I wondered if he would now dissemble. The Trinity Temple had after all been allowed to fall into such disrepair. I had heard it said that Chinese loved their money like Khmers loved their children and wouldn't ever part with it.

But he answered: 'Different kinds, Lady Sray. Hospitals, an orphanage. I will take you to one of our projects.'

He led me a short distance through streets to a large pavilion at the port's edge. At the door, a man who seemed to be in charge greeted Mr Chen in a most respectful way. The merchant knew his way around inside, and he gave me a tour. In one area, people from local villages laid on mats, tended by a Brahmin physician. In another, people stood in line to receive rice soup from a large pot.

As we walked back, I said: 'Mr Chen, I think it's possible that the palace might give your firm rights to supply a quarter of its rice.' I laid out possible terms.

He listened, thinking, and I could tell something more was on his mind. 'Those are very fair conditions,' he said. 'But I must tell you that we are often not able to move things to the Capital freely. The local magistrates put a tax on each sack we load on a boat. Sometimes they just hold things up, for no good reason.'

'Why is that?'

'Because we're foreigners, I suppose, and we have money. And no real rights to be here other than the magistrates' forbearance.'

'Mr Chen, I will see if I can do something.'

It was time to return to the temple. Ten days earlier, the year's rains had begun. Most days they fell late in the afternoon. For that I liked to be atop the hill, alone in the guesthouse.

That night, I laid down on mats the novice had shaken free of dust when I was below. My mind turned toward what might have happened in the Capital in my absence. I was quite sure now that the King did not remember me from the estate those many years earlier, that his interest in me grew only from who I was now. Perhaps his interests would burn itself out naturally, perhaps the Brahmin would bring about a change of mind with teachings from scriptures. And of course there was the other question of the sensations that paraded through me uninvited.

Whatever resolution was to come, it would take time, that was certain. I might have to stay here in the guesthouse indefinitely, both to wait out the King and to correct my own failings.

I closed my eyes and fell asleep to chimes from the temple's inner courtyard.

I awoke to a presence in the guesthouse, somewhere to the side. It was curious – I felt no fear, and merely looked up into the darkness, wondering if this was how one met a divinity and how one should respond. This god moved very gently, with near-silent steps, and I felt a gentle surge of gratefulness, for family, for health, for wealth given me for no reason I could comprehend, for my existence at this time in the cycle of creation and decline.

'Don't you move!'

The words were whispered, yet they sounded like a shout, and they paralyzed me. I waited tensely for more words, but I heard only more steps, this time heavy, making their way toward me. The god didn't glide through the air, but made the house tremble like a human.

I found my wits and got quickly to my feet. I felt more safe that way. In the gloom before me, I saw a young man.

'Why are you here?' I demanded.

He sprang. His hands roughly twisted me so that he was behind me now, holding me immobile, a forearm against my throat. I went limp. What terror I felt! I had been seized and held this way only once in my life, that day in the clearing.

'Take what I have,' I whispered. 'It's there, in the bag, by the mat.'

There was a pause. He seemed to have a knife in his other hand and to be summoning an awful kind of courage.

Nol could not come to help this time. I knew suddenly I must act myself. 'You would harm a woman in a holy place? So near the abode of the Blessed Trinity?'

'Be quiet!' It was a rough city voice.

'Heaven teaches that no person has the right to take the life of another unless in war or in payment for a serious crime.' He squeezed harder, but some spirit showed me how to keep going. 'May the gods find it in themselves to have mercy on you for what you intend to do. May your next life not...'

Then he mouthed a single, pathetic cry and his grip loosened. I was tossed to the side, and he fled down the steps.

Two minutes later, I stumbled weeping to the door of the priests' sleeping pavilion. The abbot emerged, shocked, and I blurted out the basics of what had happened. He told the other priests to go quickly and search for this man and he sent a boy down the hill to fetch Sergeant Sen. By the time the soldier arrived, breathless from racing up the path, I had regained my composure and was sitting on a mat, drinking from a cup of tea.

He was nonetheless horrified, and went straight to his knees. 'I have failed in my duty, Lady! I will never again let you out of my sight when you are entrusted to me, on my honour!'

Though the man with the knife was never found, I felt physically safe in the days that followed. Sergeant Sen was never more than a few steps away. His soldiers kept watch at various corners of the temple grounds. I felt safe, but the peace of mind I had come to associate with this place did not return. My mind wandered when I said prayers. I studied the words of my holy texts, but they made no impression. The sergeant would not let me go down to the port; I began to view the temple not as a haven but a jail.

32: The precepts of Kingly congress

All during this time, my husband was appearing in court on his usual schedule, but he was deathly worried. The King had not contested my departure from the Capital, indeed, had made no mention of it to anyone, but nor had he expressed acceptance of it. What was to be the permanent solution? This was on my husband's mind each waking minute, and in some of his dreams too. There was, of course, the option of flight. We had done that almost twenty years earlier, and the tricks of the resulting existence had not been forgotten. But there were complications now, very large ones. For a start, there were our children, who would be unhappy in life on the run, and held to account if they stayed behind. Moreover, Nol's parasol bearers would lose their livelihood, his artisans their work. There might even be blood retribution against those associated with us – such things were hardly unknown. And of course wealth and standing would have to be given up. I am sure Nol was honest enough to admit to himself that this was a consideration, though his many inner monologues on the subject would have noted that it was only one of many.

The Brahmin too was anxious to put this issue behind. And then one day, Heaven chose to place an idea in him.

In times past, the divine realm had handed down the Ten Kingly Virtues as a set of broad principles concerning royal probity. It was up to the senior priests to draw up the precise, detailed rules by which these principles would direct the King's daily activity. With each reign, the rules were refined to assure that they in fact reflected Heaven's will. There was, for instance, a principle that the King's body must be clean. Therefore, obviously, he must bathe only in pure water. But what constituted pure water? How far above the point in a river at which the royal bathwater was drawn could villagers be allowed to wash themselves? Or, dare we ask, urinate? Priests drew up rules on this principle and quite a long list of others: the King must avoid untruth and deception, he must provide for the sick and dispense justice fairly. He must revere the gods. And he must shun improper carnal practices.

I have told you about the law that he must treat another man's wife as a sister or as poison. But holy law is not only about the forbidding of things. For everything denied, a King must be granted something else. It was on this duality that the Brahmin's idea rested.

Now it happened that at this time thirty aged priests were about to open a convocation at a palace annex to discuss rules of daily royal existence. In previous months they had made their way through questions of cleanliness and happened now to be taking up the principle concerning carnal practice.

Novice priests take the vow of celibacy but of course many of them allow those vows to expire when they grow older so as to marry and father children, for how else would they beget new generations of Brahmins? Most of the holy men at the convocation had chosen that route; they were patriarchs of some of the most powerful priestly families of the Empire. Thus they could discuss carnal practices with the authority of experience. I do believe that Subhadra was the only one in the group who could not. He had renewed his vows annually through his life as a priest. Perhaps this made him the most able to consider these questions objectively, to weigh a particular practice between King and Queen or concubine solely in terms of textual authority.

Some priests who take the chastity vows have difficulty sticking to them. But I will tell you that I believe that Subhadra did not. I believe that he was that rare human being who is left cold by the idea of lying entwined in the limbs of another, be it female or male. I never saw him cast toward anyone a glance that even hinted of that sort of interest. And certainly I never heard whispered stories of secret night-time assignations. One can never truly know motivations on such a question, but could it be that as he grew older the vows were for him in part a way of turning aside inevitable questions from parents and siblings as to when he would take a wife?

So, the meeting began, those thirty aged men sitting on mats arranged in a circle. They spent long hours discussing the issue and consulting the Vedas and commentaries, with Subhadra directing and sometimes, I think, controlling the discussion.

After eight days, they reached agreement and called in a scribe who wrote out the revisions on a cured deer skin. Now by tradition, the rules and the divine logic underlying a new ruling on royal behaviour are explained in some detail to the monarch. So the King came to the meeting hall. He took his place on a dais, legs folded, as four fans moved the air overhead. He said nothing, but every priest in the room could sense that he was already suspicious.

Incense was lit, prayer were chanted, and then the Brahmin began.

'It has been discovered, Majesty, that in the procreative sphere the gods in fact approve of certain practices that were previously barred.'

The royal visage lit up. Do you recall Subhadra's observation that at times our King was like a handsome young village man strolling through a festival, inspecting the local girls as he goes? There was truth in that.

'Majesty, the controls have been too restrictive for many years. We offer apologies that you were subjected to them for so long.'

'Well, what are the changes then?'

The priest began to describe them in detail. Must I specify? I suppose yes, at least somewhat. I promised to tell you all I know, though I may blush in doing so. It was like this: simultaneous encounters with up to six partners, rather than the previous limit of four, were permissible. Certain carnal positions that had been treated as an affront to Heaven were not in fact so, were even encouraged by the deities as a celebration of strength. The priests at the gathering had listed fourteen such positions and scribes had drawn diagrams. The Brahmin passed these to the King, who examined them with what was recalled as a close and sometimes disbelieving kind of interest.

'Do you accept these changes, Majesty?' the Brahmin asked.

'I accept them.'

'Very good. Now I will proceed to explain to you the rest of the rules in this portfolio and I am sure that you will take them to heart as graciously as you have the ones I have presented already.'

When a King enters into a new carnal relationship, it must be with a virgin, the Brahmin said. It would be an offense against Heaven for the monarch's organ to visit a place where an ordinary man's had been before. There must be in all of these relations the maximum opportunity for the royal seed to unite with a female counterpart, so that royal issue would result. The chances of this occurring decrease with increasing age of the female. Therefore, only the youngest of females who have reached the age of monthly blood must be chosen. And to take into the concubine pavilion a woman who has earlier established married relations would also be an offense against the societal order that Heaven strives to engineer on earth. Because no matter how high the compensation offered, there would remain the risk that the recipient might feel it insufficient, yet feel unable to turn it down. In addition, to bring in an older concubine might cause discord among the other concubines in the pavilion, because there would be a conflict between age and seniority.

The reading, including supporting scriptures, continued through the afternoon and, after lamps were lit, into the evening. The King grew increasingly unsettled. Twice he instructed that the session be suspended, but the Rajaguru bravely pretended not to hear.

In the end, the King gave in and withdrew.

The next day, His Majesty took the scribes' diagrams with him into his sleeping chamber. Concubines joined him there. I will not try to imagine the things that went on in that room. But I will say that from the standpoint of divine law, whatever happened must only have strengthened the writ against any intention to call me as a concubine. The King could not accept one part of the new rules and ignore another.

Some days later, Subhadra was kneeling in the private chapel of his house, working his way through midday prayers, when an attendant announced that my husband was outside. The two men took places on mats, across a table of polished teak.

'I've come to express my gratitude for what you did,' Nol said. 'There is nothing more dear to me than my wife.'

'No thanks are needed,' the Brahmin replied. 'It was a privilege to help. In any case, what we did at the convocation was merely to bring about deeper understanding of the laws of Heaven. But let's not talk about that any more. It's settled.'

It soon became clear that what the priest really wanted to talk about was something else entirely, the war with the Chams. He spent some time recounting the last dispatch from the front. The Khmer forces had failed to advance as far as planned and had suffered high casualties. Dysentery had rendered a third of the soldiers unfit to fight. The remaining soldiers risked their carts and chariots bogging down in rainy season mud. In the meantime, the Chams had opened a new front to the north and burned a Khmer border town – the local prince there had changed sides and given over to the enemy two fighting boats moored at his estate's docks.

It was the Brahmin's belief that the time had come to talk peace. But the King had to be persuaded. 'It could be presented to His Majesty as a temporary holding in place while we built up forces for a later offensive,' the priest observed. 'As you know, on many subjects he changes his mind if given the time. After a few months he might forget about resuming operations and when we...'

Here my husband broke in: 'No! We have to keep on with the war. We've suffered losses, yes, but the Chams have suffered much bigger ones. We can gain the initiative now. We can reach the enemy Capital before the start of the rainy season, I'm sure of it...

But Nol stopped there, because his mind had caught up with the reason why this subject was being raised now.

The Brahmin let the silence develop. 'My friend,' he said, 'we have worked together for the sake of your wife's safety and freedom. Let us work together on this other subject as well.'

Nol left an hour later, having agreed to take up the case with the King but also with Rit and the other senior commanders.

I can imagine that the priest, watching my husband depart, felt that things had turned out not so badly. The King had been steered away from a morally defiling liaison. And a bad war was going to end before it got worse.

33: The corral

A messenger with word of the king's acceptance of the new rules reached me just as I was finishing evening prayers. The next morning, I descended the hill to where the cart awaited. The journey home began, Sergeant Sen staying very close at hand, as he always did now. We passed through villages where boys led buffalos and women fanned stubborn coals. The sights, the sergeant's presence and the measured plod of the oxen's hooves made me feel that life was swinging back to a more normal course.

We stopped for the midday meal at a roadside teashop. As I returned to the cart, an aged man in tattered sampot stepped forward, begging a word. Sergeant Sen tensed, a hand going to the knife in his waist, but I could sense that the old man was harmless. I signalled that I would listen.

'Great Lady, I have come to ask that you help us,' he said in a raspy voice. 'We have a project of benevolence that might interest you, involving certain animals. It is not far; I beg to take you there.'

He led our party along the main road a bit, then onto a track that crossed paddies now fed by rains. We were brought to a rough wooden gate, a very high and strong one. Sergeant Sen insisted on going through first. Then I followed.

'Be careful with your steps,' advised the old man from behind. Here and there were ankle-high droppings.

It was an elephant corral. Four of the great animals were half-submerged in the water of a dirty pond a hundred paces away; others were picking through an already picked-through pile of wilting foliage. Their grey flesh sagged, their ears flapped too slowly to keep insects at bay. My eyes examined each of the animals, but I did not see the one I now dared hope for.

'How hungry they are,' I said to the old man, though I knew it was not his fault.

'We try our best, Lady, to give them a decent place to live out their years. But they eat so much. We have a hard time keeping up.'

Then I turned and saw Sadong running toward me. He went

straight down at my feet, face to the dust, and when he looked up, tears glistened on both cheeks. 'It is in fact you, then!' he cried, putting a hand to my foot. 'The Lady Sray and our old friend the duck egg vendor are the same. But I'm sorry – I should not speak in such a familiar way...'

'It's all right, Sadong. You may speak as you want. And you may stand up. I wish you would, in fact.'

He did, gratefully. 'Lady Sray,' he whispered, with pride, 'your piece of jewellery was used as directed.'

'Oh, Sadong, there was never any doubt it would be. But I am so happy finally to see the place.' Then I paused and whispered too, not wanting the sergeant to hear: 'And a certain elephant. Is she still with us, or has her soul passed to her next life?'

'Oh no, Lady. She remains with us, and in good health. She is just over there, do you not see the one? Behind the other animals. You might not recognize her. We have applied dye, to hide, you know, the holy mark on her forehead.'

As we approached, the elephant was browsing through scraps of straw that lay on the ground. The diamond was there, visible if you knew to look for it. With strangers around, the beast seemed to realize a need for discretion. She paid no particular attention when I stopped just an arm's length from her face. She did not trumpet nor offer her trunk to nuzzle. But each time that she brought straw to her mouth, an eye turned and met mine in the former intimate way.

Old friend Kumari! I began to speak to her in thought. Blessed friend Kumari! To think I had always believed that you went to some far corner of the Empire. And yet you were hardly half a day's journey away, all this time.

I wanted to formally pose a question to the animal like in past days. But the sergeant was there. So I strolled with the keeper out of earshot. 'Your conditions here are difficult, but you have cared for her well. Do you think...do you think that the spirit of the former Majesty still resides within her?'

'A man like me is not capable of sensing such things, Lady. But I can tell you that she still has powers of divination. When I heard that the Lady Sray was staying at the temple by the port,

I brought out the old sticks with text on them and asked if this might be the same Mrs Sray who had been so kind to us. I had heard some people say that the Lady had risen from a humble life. And the elephant chose a stick that told me yes and that we would see her again. So I left word at the tea shop on the road that if ever her procession were to pass by the shop, that someone must run here to inform us. Our fortune was better than that – her procession stopped at the shop. By the powers of the holy elephant, she has arrived at our corral.'

How could I not be touched by that? Tears began to form.

'How do you support this place now? The money from the neckpiece must have run out a long time ago.'

'I do as best I can, Lady.'

In the next ten minutes, I learned that Sadong sometimes hired out the elephants for labour, though at a discount because most were lame. The priests at a nearby temple sometimes sent over a bit of silver, and the teashop let Sadong take away its refuse as feed. Sometimes the local villagers pitched in too, but relations with them were not so good just now, because a week earlier two of the elephants had escaped the corral and fed at a cucumber garden, trampling it.

I wandered back to the elephant, this time alone. When I was close enough to feel the breath and to smell the body, I whispered: 'Kumari, it fills my soul with gladness to know that you are here in safety. I assure you that you will always have food to eat. So here – please take this.'

I bent down and took in my hand a piece of straw. This I held out, knowing that what mattered was the sincerity with which a gift, however insignificant, was presented, and sincerity was something I had at that moment in large supply. The large eyes regarded me with empathy. Then the trunk rose; its tip took the offering gently from my hand.

That evening, Nol welcomed me home with effusive words. We ate a dinner of rice, grilled prawns and papaya, favourites all, to celebrate my return. He seemed entirely calm and peaceful, so unlike when I had departed, as if he had forgotten even the pain in his back. I decided I would not disturb him by mentioning the attack. Later, we sat together at a window, the final drops of a monsoon shower sounding on the roof, a lamp burning between us. I put an arm around him and pulled myself close. We remained together, as crickets called to us from the darkness outside. Then I led him to the mosquito net. I wanted to show him, and perhaps myself, that my loyalties lay with only one man.

The next day, I went to see Mr Narin. He was now, as before, chief scribe. I told him about the temple. He told me I was very generous with my money and that it was a shame there weren't more people like me. I replied that in fact there were more such people – he had given me an opening for the subject I wanted to discuss. I explained about Mr Chen and the other merchants and how they would have more money for good works if the local magistrates would stop demanding bribes. Mr Narin listened, then sighed and told me that this had been a problem for many years.

'The Chinese come here from their country to trade,' he said, 'but they have no formal status in the Empire, because our Empire has no formal relations with theirs. So Khmer officials look on them as a source of quick money. At times the magistrates stir up the local people against the Chinese, but sometimes the people don't need any stirring.' At that he paused. 'When I was just at the age of starting my studies, it got out of hand in my town, and twenty or so Chinese were murdered. Right on the street and in their homes.'

'How awful!'

Mr Narin explained that the same kind of things had happened sometimes to Khmer people who live in China. It would be so much smoother, he said, if the Empire had some kind of agreement with China, so that each would treat the other's people with fairness. The Brahmin Subhadra, he said, had written to the Chinese authorities with such a proposal, sending his missive on a merchant ship, but had never received an answer.

I said: 'Perhaps someone will one day work it out. In the meantime, do you think you could raise the issue of the bribes with the Brahmin? I feel that the merchants deserve some relief.'

He said that for me, of course he would. That was his way, always willing to help.

'And Mr Narin, if I may ask one more favour...'

'Of course.'

'It is that you might convey to the Brahmin my deepest thanks for his role...his role in the adoption of the, the new rules.'

'I will, Lady Sray.' Then he lowered his voice. 'And may I make a suggestion, as a friend? If you have business outside the city, why not take care of it now? The priests have devised rules that are very strong, but still it would be better if adherence to these rules is never tested.'

That seemed to be wise advice. So the next morning I got things ready and sent a servant to the barracks with word that Sergeant Sen and his men would be needed again.

34: A new avocation

Shortly after the rains ended that year, six priests of the Council of Brahmins strode in procession toward the site of the future mountain-temple. Members of the palace household turned out to watch their departure. Across the Naga bridge, so did many tens of thousands of the Capital's people. When the priests reached the temple site, all was hidden and private, between holy men and Heaven alone, but later on we learned in detail what happened. The priests erected a wooden altar at the precise spot at which the central tower would rise. They put flowers and fruit on the altar and blessed it to the fullest of earthly authority. And then they moved to the side, anxious like at no other time, because for that brief period they had been kneeling at the precise centre of the universe, the very pivot of creation.

A few hours later, the Rajaguru Subhadra arrived in separate procession. He dismissed the six priests, who went to make devotions at a place in the forest where slaves had set up shelters. Then he spent extended time checking the materials, size and orientation of the altar. That evening, he bathed with water placed there in a large sacred jar, said prayers and lay down to sleep, his head aligned to the east, his thoughts as serene as was possible for a man on whose shoulders the Empire's spiritual security rested. He awoke at dawn, and began a six-hour rite witnessed by no one but himself and whatever deities chose to look on. As he made his way through the chants, I would guess that he felt that quite a few gods did gather, and that they were sympathetic to his plea for support in an endeavour that would consume the time, wealth and energy of an entire generation of the Empire's people.

At midday, Subhadra sniffed at the lingering scents of incense, murmured a final verse, then rose and walked out through the forest to where the other priests waited. There he declared that everything had been done exactly as Heaven would have it.

As soon as he and the others left for the Capital, another spiritual job got underway. This one Subhadra never acknowledged, to me or to anyone else, as far as I can say, but he did nothing to stop it, no doubt knowing how uneasy the local villagers, and quite a few Brahmins as well, would feel if it were left undone. It was carried out by men whose garments were frayed at the edges, who were missing eyes or fingers or some basic trait of human decorum, but who had shown that they had power to reach into the supernatural realm. These men – you have seen their kind, I'm sure, begging by the roadside, or in trance at a forest refuge – had the assignment of calming the paddy and tree spirits who would be displaced from land they had always inhabited. It was all very unfortunate, but these spirits would have to take up residence elsewhere. At the same time, it was of course important to make sure that they left on the best possible terms. Otherwise, what mischief they might cause! What if they were seen to hover at night in the workers' encampment in hideous glowing form? Labourers would drop their tools and run, no matter what orders were issued to the contrary. What if they chose to befoul the drinking water? So these tattered holy men built tiny shrines on dikes, beside the largest, oldest trees, sometimes even in the waist-deep water of ponds. They burned incense, a cheaper variety than what the Brahmins used. They made offerings of rice and sometimes they fell to the ground in one of those trances. Villagers watched from a respectful distance, hands together, to show they were concerned over the spirits' plight, even if the reason for the eviction was a legitimate one, creation of the greatest mountain-temple the world would ever know.

In the end, it was concluded that most of the spirits were duly assuaged and made their exit. Now an army of labourers could move in. Numbering more than five thousand, they were all volunteers, some from settlements a short walk away, some from the far reaches of the Empire. There had been quite some competition for spots in this throng. Every person in the royal compound had heard in recent weeks from some relative or acquaintance hoping for a place in this first labour team. Nol, I believe, personally placed more than thirty from the parasol village. For people who lacked such connections – well, there were other ways. I am sure some paid bribes to local priests and headmen who made the picks for labour quotas that the Capital had assigned. The work would be punishing, yes, but when else in their lifetime would they get a chance to accrue merit of such inviolable purity?

The chosen men were given a few days to build a bamboo shantytown on scrubland to the south and to dig slit trenches. Then they laid down for what would be their last night of peace for a very long time. In the morning, they tied on loincloths and lined up to be issued shovels, saws and long-bladed knives. Then there began a full-scale attack on the land, because it would have to be ravaged before it could host Heaven on earth.

In ensuing months, I passed the site several times on my journeys in and out of the Capital. What activity, what energy there was, no matter how hot, no matter how strongly the sun shone down from the sky! Sometimes I had trouble seeing through the raised dust. The men levelled paddy dikes and hillocks, they filled ponds and depressions. They cut down trees, using elephants to drag away the logs. Grass and reeds were ploughed under. At times, the site put up fearful resistance, the work of a few recalcitrant spirits. One day, a mother boar, surprised in her lair, bloodied a boy who was bringing drinking water to a shovel team, and then fled snorting into jungle cover with her two young. On another day, a saw blade snapped, opening the belly of a man who had arrived only a day earlier. He died within the hour.

But try as they might have, these few spirits could not obstruct the flow of events. After eight months, the ground was flat and clear. Priests blessed this first team of labourers and sent them home. The Architect, trailed by assistants, spent a week walking the site, memorizing every feature, though now there were far fewer of them. But there was one more important rite to be staged before actual construction could begin.

On a sunny afternoon, His Majesty was carried to the site in a gilded palanquin, twelve parasols overhead, in the company of many Brahmins and nobles. Members of the palace household followed behind. The procession ended at a teak altar that had been placed on raked soil at the precise centre point of the future central tower. The King took up a position facing to the east. There began prayers by the Brahmin assemblage, the lighting of incense.

My husband and son sat down just behind the altar to oversee the bearers who shaded His Majesty. I was not present – I avoided all gatherings that His Majesty attended.

The Brahmins worked their way through a very lengthy liturgy, now picking up the speed and volume of their chants, now slowing down. The rite's peak came perhaps an hour along: The priests stopped, abruptly, and cued the King to raise his right arm to the sky. With a bleached white cord, two of the holy men took a precise measure of the distance between royal wrist and elbow. They now had the basic unit by which the mountain-temple would be laid out and constructed.

With the ceremonies completed, my husband got to his feet and began forming up the procession for the journey back to the palace. Sovan, however, remained on the ground, peering away from the holy altar.

Nol was annoyed. 'I can use your help, boy.'

He got no response.

'Get up. What's the trouble with you?'

'What? Nothing's the matter, father.'

'Well, come on then – pitch in.'

But even then he did not get up. Nol prodded my boy with the staff of a folded parasol and finally he stood.

I later learned that the trouble with Sovan was that during the ceremony he had had a flash realization: His Majesty, indeed everyone, was facing the wrong direction.

When Sovan had arrived at the site, he had looked all around and tried to match what he saw against his memories of that day when he had tramped around virgin ground with the Architect. It seemed impossible that this was the same place. Termite nests, paddies, swathes of tangled forest – all gone, as if the builder god Visvakarman had cleared them with a single swipe of a giant forearm.

That disbelief was to be expected. Had not thousands of men, if not a god, worked to transform this site into something entirely different? But then there began something that was entirely a surprise: In the midst of the ceremony, strange tinglings arose in Sovan's heart. They were slight; they escaped his notice at first.

When he became aware of them, he in no way felt they were due to illness. There was placed in him a conviction that the cause was some force that was outside his body, but resonating inside. His eyes moved about, seeking an explanation. He examined the altar, the sun, the lie of the shadows of the parasol shafts, the lazy motion of a distant bank of clouds. In stages it came to him: There was something wrong in *orientation*. He was sitting behind His Majesty, and yet this supposedly subordinate place was invested with the greater cosmic energy. He was sure of it. He could feel that the future temple's emanations flowed toward the west. Yet everyone here was aligned toward the east, creating a conflict. It was as if many men were pulling on a rope in one direction, and many others pulling in the other. The rope would grow very taut, and it would vibrate – that is what my son was feeling.

It was a breach of protocol, but he turned his back on the ritual and did what he had done on that long-ago day when he first came to the site. He looked in precisely the opposite direction from that which had the attention of everyone else. The tingling subsided. He gazed down this western axis and an image appeared again to him, but with new clarity and truth. He saw a great holy mountain of stone with five towers, each with the gentle curves of a closed lotus blossom.

Then he looked back to the ritual, seeing His Majesty raising his arm for the measurement, oblivious to the mistake.

Sovan finally came out of his reverie with the help of that poke of a parasol handle. He said nothing to his father, who would only have laughed. And Sovan was modest enough to wonder how it could really be possible that so many learned people – virtually the entire elite of the Brahmin community was present that day – could make so fundamental a misjudgement and feel nothing of what he was feeling.

Nol stepped away to tend to something at the front of the procession. Then, from behind – a voice.

'The young would-be builder! Still working with parasols, but I see he's come up in the world. He's not bearing but supervising.'

It was the Architect. Sovan blushed and looked to the ground, but at the same time, I don't think he felt he was being mocked.

'Tell me something,' the Architect said. 'Can you read and write?'

'Why, yes, sir. Of course. Keeping the records of the parasol pavilion requires it.'

'And how about numbers? Can you work with them?'

'Yes. I do it most every morning to keep the accounts.'

Just then, over the Architect's shoulder, Sovan caught sight of two young women standing far away, at the edge of the cleared ground, no doubt waiting for His Majesty to leave before they would make their own exit. My boy was still unmarried and such was his abiding hope of finding the girl from the house in the forest that he allowed his attention to wander in the very presence of this great man.

'Well, then,' said the Architect. 'How would you like to help build this temple?'

'Sir..?' Sovan's attention returned in a flash!

'Help build it as one of my assistants.'

My boy gasped. The Architect folded his arms, seeming amused by it all.

Occupations are of course determined by birth, but there was something I did not know at the time – exceptions were made for a few lines of life work, architecture among them. The innate talents were so rare, it was said, that the Empire's chief builder could induct people into his group regardless of their station of birth. A call from him was assumed to carry the authority of the King, because it was in his name that the work was carried out.

'It's not what you were raised to do, I know, or what your family expects. But one of my assistants, he was a very promising one, died last week – a snake, actually, it got him in that stand of trees just across there.' He poked a finger in its direction, but his eyes remained on Sovan. 'So I need a new one. I'm willing to take a chance on you. Will you do it?'

Sovan answered: 'Sir, you know I was born a canal dredger?'

'I do. And I would be counting on that to mean you know how to do a real day's work.'

Sovan took a breath. This was a sign if ever there was one. First a repeat of the vision, then this great man standing before him.

'Then, yes, sir. I will join your team. If you will have me.'

'Then be at the plans pavilion at sunrise tomorrow. It's just beyond that same tree line. We get started at first light.'

'Tomorrow, sir?' Sovan was trembling now.

'Why, yes, tomorrow. Do you want the job or don't you?'

Nol reappeared. The Architect broke off the conversation and walked off.

On the way back to the city, Sovan resisted his father's urgings to tell him what the man had wanted. Yet, back at the house Sovan came right to me and spilled it.

I was as shocked as any mother would be, and said so. How could his years of work with the parasols simply be cast off? And what would be the effect on Nol? 'Do you know how people will laugh at your father if he has no son to take over when his soul departs? You know, it's been a very long time since people have laughed at him. It will hurt him deeply.'

'Please, mother, I will have prayers said. But don't you think his shock, and yours, would pass? He has an apprentice, Veng. He's good. Really, he's better than I am. He can take my place. He likes the work. I wish I did but I don't. I hate the waiting, I hate the palace gossip.'

'You'll grow accustomed...'

'I won't!' His voice had actually risen – I had rarely seen this kind of emotion in him. 'There are times...there are times I think of killing myself, rather than doing this for an entire life.'

Now he pled for my help, and, how could I stand up to that? I embraced him and promised to speak to his father.

It was no surprise that however gently I broke the news, my husband reacted with cries of anger and betrayal. What I didn't expect was that he would run outside for a stick and then go after my boy, who was waiting in his room.

The first blow caught him across the jaw.

'Leave the family, will you?'

Sovan retreated unbelieving to a corner. There would be less room to manoeuvre the stick there. I rushed in; Nol fended off my attempts to restrain him.

'Father, I'm sorry! I only thought...'

'Leave behind everything we've built here? Everything I've done for you and the family?'

'I only...'

'You want to rise above the place I've given you? You want to shit as big as an elephant, do you?'

'Father...'

His voice was cut off by the stick. With no room to swing, Nol was jabbing its tip hard into Sovan's belly.

I placed myself between them.

'You will not kill our son, husband!'

He backed off, swishing the stick through the air. 'I will do whatever is necessary to put an end to this ridiculous idea.' He gave one more hard poke, then stared at his son. 'I expect your apology and your immediate rejection of this request. A servant will deliver a note.'

He left the room. I stayed with Sovan. Some time later, Nol returned, still holding the stick

'Are you ready to apologize? Answer me!'

'Father, I want to work with the Architect. I'm sorry, I'm sorry...'

Again Nol struck him!

'The parasol hall's not for you? It was the parasol craft that nurtured you, that got you your rice, your education, your place in society.'

'Please, father...'

'I'm not finished. It's the craft that got us out of that slum we lived in. Do you remember that? You were just a naked boy, running around with all the others, nothing to set you apart.'

That was it, for that night at least. But Sovan was not deterred. He left the house early the next morning. He later told me that when he presented himself to the Architect the man joked about the bruises on his face and informed him that he was worth a full evening banquet for ten at the new inn, the one that had just opened just behind the morning market, with wine and music and dancers. Nol, you see, had come to speak with him the night before, and opened with this offer if the invitation were withdrawn. When that didn't work, the terms were raised, by quite a bit: fifty weight of silver, twenty paddies of rice land outside the city, one hundred oxen, the use of a cart and driver for six months. And so on. The Architect turned it all down, saying that life had brought him material wealth, but the thing in which he was truly poor was that which he valued most, talented, inspired assistants. When he had finished recounting this to Sovan, he declared that he liked it when his assistants had to make a choice. Do you really want to do this? He gave Sovan one more chance to back out. Of course Sovan did not.

It was all work for the rest of the day. A young man a few years senior to my boy entered the pavilion and was introduced as Pin, the Architect's nephew. Sovan would start as his helper and be shown the basics. Pin led Sovan silently to another pavilion, which contained a row of tall shelves. On these, Palm leaf diagrams were stacked lengthwise. Pin pulled one down in a hurried kind of way. 'Study this,' he said. Then he left him alone.

Sovan is the kind of person who prefers it that way. He would have all the time he needed to examine the diagram, without worry of someone hovering around and thinking him stupid for taking time. He took the sheet to a table, and unfolded it. On it were lines and shadings and circles, all coming together into a cohesive form, a holy stone. In ten minutes he had figured out that he was looking at the plan for the lower parts of a library. The laterite blocks which would make up the base in the soil were marked with tiny patterns like the strands of a fishnet, sandstone blocks resting atop them were rendered in shaded form. To the side, drawn in the margin, was a rough outline of a divine guardian that would be carved on its upper edge. This, then, was how buildings began the journey from thought to solid stone.

An hour later, Sovan looked up to see the Architect.

The man asked: 'Where's Pin?'

'I'm sorry, I don't know, sir. He left.'

'Just as well. Now, I need to see how good your hand is. Can you make a copy of this?' He held up a small, simple diagram of a doorway. 'Take one of those slates. You'll use the chalk and a bronze edge. And don't get too ambitious. You're not designing a temple yet, just copying. Now here's how you start.'

He put the bronze edge down, drew the chalk along it, then lifted the edge. It was some kind of magic – on the sheet now was a line as straight as any sun ray emerging from any cloud. He drew three more to form a rectangle.

'Now look here, I'll show you something. Draw a line like this. It's called a...' I think the word was 'diagonal,' or something similar. There were many technicalities tossed about that day. But in the end he revealed some more magic by which the drawing of straight lines allowed a rectangle to grow or shrink and yet retain the precise same proportions with which it began.

That evening Sovan returned home exhausted. In the main room, his father waited. I stood to the side. I did not have to physically intervene because I knew that something different was coming.

'Sovan,' said Nol, 'you have not responded to arguments of duty, or to force, so I will now try to buy you off.'

'Father, I don't want an offer...'

'Sovan, I will place you in full charge of the work of ordering and maintaining His Majesty's parasols. The storage hall will be yours alone to direct; I will never enter. You may work on them yourself if you wish. You are very young for such responsibility, in fact I can't think of any man your age in the Capital who would have anything comparable to it. You would be in charge of relations with the village that makes them, and you would direct the thirty artisans who work here.'

'Father, please, but no.'

'All right, then! You've made your decision. Tomorrow morning I will begin proceedings with a magistrate to adopt Veng as my son. He will take your place in every way, in the family rolls, in temple ceremonies, in occupation. And in inheritance. You will get nothing from me. Do you understand *that*?' The last words he shouted.

'I don't want a conflict, father.'

'Clearly you do.'

Nol called out the names of two male servants. They entered behind Sovan and took him each by an arm, whispering apologies as they did.

'Put him out the door, and don't ever let him back in.'

The servants pulled at Sovan, lightly at first, then a bit harder, whispering more apologies. He gave in and let them propel him to the compound gate.

There one of the servants said, as I had told him to: 'Master Sovan, it would be good if you went around to the back...'

He did, and there he found me. At my feet was a large straw bag.

I embraced him. 'Take this, then,' I said. 'Your basic things and garments. And go. It won't be for long. Your father will get over this, I know it.' That is what I said, but it was only to convince myself. 'There are quarters awaiting you in the inn just behind the marketplace. That is, if you still want to go ahead with this. I would prefer that you come back inside, as a parasol bearer again.'

'I have to go on with it, mother. Today the Architect let me draw. It was like there were entire buildings in my head waiting to be put down on the slate. He showed me how to...'

I put a stop to this talk by hugging him again. Then I sent him on his way. But I had a servant trail along behind and report back to me. I was comforted to learn that my son had in fact settled in at the inn, and that the proprietor had pledged bath water and a good meal every evening.

As it happened, my plans for his comforts came to nothing. The very next day, the Architect told my boy that he would live at the construction site, in a hut with the other assistants. Sovan dutifully packed up his things and moved. I took heart in knowing that he was in the hands of a good master, who would teach him many things and leave little opportunity for getting into trouble.

35: Envy

When our family was poor, I was always touched that my husband worked so hard to buy me shiny things, even if they were things I did not want. Whatever he brought home, I was grateful. But in his mind, that which he could provide was never enough. This trait did not abate as we rose in the world. No matter how much silver, how much property we amassed in those years, it seemed to him only a prelude to what we deserved. He was forever comparing to himself our holdings with those of other members of the court.

With me safe from His Majesty's attentions and his son banished, concerns of money rose again in his mind.

Most of all, Nol wondered why he had ever seen value in owning land that would be behind, not in front of, the King's new mountain-temple. It was true that there was some immediate gain after ground was broken. A few of the masons and foremen who arrived to take part in the great project built huts on our land and twice a year they paid rent that was split evenly between Nol and the village down the track. A small market began to operate, and each woman laying out her wares there paid a fee to him and the village. But it was not much and in any case there was no permanent arrangement. One day the mountain-temple would be finished, and all of these people would leave, and everyone would know that what Nol One-Ear owned had gone back to being just ordinary land, disadvantaged land, in fact – the mountain-temple would in perpetuity be turning its back on it.

As for the land east of the temple, it was Nol's great frustration that it was already mass-producing income for its owner. The majority of people involved in construction chose this place to build their huts. There was also a thriving market and shrines for offerings. Four hostels had opened, so that pilgrims could sleep near the temple's future entrance, enjoy the excitement of the coming and going of elephants and building materials, and absorb some of the holy energy that priests, regardless of what my son might think, said was already radiating from the eastern portal. Within a year, this area was practically a city in its own right.

Every few weeks, Nol's duties took him through this bustling new area and each time he came back dispirited at what he saw.

So after a while, he came to a decision. He would buy the eastern land.

It was owned by the family of Kiri, keeper of the King's sacred cattle. Now *there* was a simple job, Nol used to say. Basically all this man and his family have to do is feed and groom the animals, and then once a week splash some holy water on their hides and lead them in a herd around the palace! There could be trouble, of course, if any of the animals died, but Nol felt that ultimately a cow was just a cow, and that if the gods saw fit to call one from this life, it could quietly be replaced with another, with no one the wiser but Kiri and his scribe.

One day, Nol consulted with his financial clerk about how much silver he could raise, on his own, not counting whatever wealth I might have. (Generally he avoided thinking about my numbers, and in conversations with him I always found it wise to understate what I had.) The clerk took some time doing the figures, combining the estimated value of houses, rice fields, jewellery, carved teak tables, silver vessels, a honey farm, stored rice, spare parasols, pig sties and various other assets. He gave Nol a summary written on a slate. The equivalent of twenty-eight hundred laks of silver! A hand at his heart, Nol gasped in delight. I happened to enter the room at this moment, and saw the enchantment that lingered on his face. He had not thought the sum would be anywhere near that, and before I knew it, he was taking my hand and leading me to the household shrine. There he said a prayer of thanks addressed to any god who might have played a role in assembling the fortune.

But, you know, within an hour misgivings settled in. The land he had in mind was going to be quite expensive; it would be hard to part with a big chunk of his money.

But a week of fretting led him to conclude he had no choice but to proceed. In his view, his standing was at risk. He served the King, close up, every day, and yet it was another man who owned the land so near the place that would host His Majesty's essence eternally.

So he sent word to Kiri's household that he would like to pay a call. The next day he ordered up his best palanquin, with two bearers and the clerk to walk alongside. I saw them off. Two hours later, he came back, in a sour mood. This man Kiri had treated the offer of four hundred laks as a joke. Coarsely spitting betel as he spoke, Kiri had said that that was what his family took in in a single day. Surely it wasn't, but I can imagine that the man was enjoying taunting Nol. Offer twenty thousand, and maybe we can talk, he said. No, forty thousand!

In ensuing days, Nol recovered his spirits and began to plot a counter-move. He had his clerk do the sums again to figure if his worth really was twenty-eight hundred laks. 'Only' twenty-eight hundred was how Nol expressed it. The man did manage to get the figure a bit above three thousand, by marking up the presumed value of farmland and some of the jewellery and by assuming that the coming harvest would be larger than any before. But that was nowhere near the figures that Kiri was talking, of course. So, Nol decided to try other ways. He hired an agent to approach Kiri's people on behalf of 'a client who wishes to remain anonymous,' in case the high price was motivated by jealousy of closeness to the King. But Kiri wasn't fooled and he stuck by his impossible figures. Later Nol sent a man to the land office to have a look at the rival family's title documents. He was hoping they'd contain some legal error that would allow a challenge to ownership, but there was no such thing. Other inquiries into the background of the Kiri clan turned up nothing useful for discrediting them.

By now there was more bad news: those few tenants on Nol's land were beginning to move away, saying it made more sense to be in the settlement on the eastern side, even if the rents were higher there.

Then came word of an outbreak of dysentery in the eastern settlement. A terrible one – it hit everyone at once. The privies were mobbed by frantic people, some of whom couldn't wait and unburdened themselves right there on the street. Brahmin physicians were called urgently from the Capital's hospitals, and they dispensed their chants and powders, but other than that they merely looked on in dismay and predicted that the problem could only but go away, with patience. But it did not. Week after week, people suffered incapacitating pain in the gut without warning. Pilgrims began staying away. Word began to circulate that there was a hex of some kind. It was not on the site itself, which was holy in a way that could not be denied, but on the people who owned it. It became advisable for members of Kiri's family to keep out of sight there, and when they did come to collect rent or to see to some building project, they brought bodyguards.

There was no such illness in the western site, on my husband's land, and a few people moved there, built houses and regained their health. The little western market picked up. Nol happily collected some extra rent.

At the height of the illness, Nol left again to call at the house of Kiri. He returned without a deal, but with some satisfaction. Kiri had lost his smug demeanour, he said, and had actually grown angry in Nol's presence and threatened to file a petition with the King.

'On what grounds?' I asked.

'This Kiri thinks I have something to do with the illnesses.'

Oh! He said that, and I saw that now it was he who had a smug look on his face. I walked away, unsettled.

It was a long time before I learned what had been going on. Nol was in fact behind the illnesses, but not directly. What he'd done was to tell his new son Veng to go to the market one night and have a word with the men there who took on assignments to deal with embarrassing problems in a confidential way. Tell them, Nol said, that there would be a fair sum of silver for them if suddenly it weren't quite so pleasant to live in the eastern settlement. Veng looked askance at this instruction, but he was anxious to prove himself an enterprising son, so he steeled himself and went. When he came back he reported it was all taken care of. The men never said exactly what they were going to do, but Veng left thinking they might pick fights in the settlement and maybe bloody a nose or two. The next day Veng went to the market again to hear it from them, and he came back shocked. They had picked up a spade and gone to a privy, and there the youngest of them had been told to hold his nose and scoop up a bag-load of what was at the bottom. Then that young man was told to take the bag to the settlement after midnight and drop some of the contents into each of the eight drinking wells there. He did, and the gang's members were amazed at how quickly this worked. The next day they strolled through the settlement, watching people in agony and found secret pleasure in knowing the cause. This gave them such a feeling of power that they sent the young man back three nights later to contaminate the wells again. The following week they sent him back yet again.

But by this time the young man was growing careless. He neglected to do one of the wells. One of the Brahmin doctors noticed that people who lived near that one recovered, while everyone else remained sick. The Kiri family caught on. Three of the cattle keeper's sons armed themselves and hid near one of the still foul wells to watch and several nights later, they saw a man approach and drop in something from a bundle he carried. They jumped up, seized him, and tore open the bundle. Gasping at the stink, they knocked the man around some. In the course of that, some of the muck got onto one of the son's face, and this so infuriated him that he took out his knife and waved it around and asked the prisoner if he'd like to get *this* in the stomach, and when the man didn't immediately beg for his life, its point was thrust straight in. There was tremendous bleeding, and before long, the sons had a corpse to show their father, not a prisoner.

I learned all this, but I did not report any of it to the magistrates – how could I do such a thing to family members? But what a tragedy! A young man dead, even if he was a hooligan, and hundreds of people subjected to the worst kind of physical agony. When those pains begin, coming and going in waves, it can be as bad as child birth.

The young man's death of course was good luck for Nol, because otherwise he would have been exposed. But it put an end to his plot. Guards were placed around the wells and soon everyone in the eastern settlement was feeling fine. The few people who'd moved to the west gave notice and returned their things to where they'd been, and Nol felt angry all over again.

His back began to hurt. He asked that I give him a massage. By now I knew what had happened. I held up my hands and said that I had strained them, that he should call someone from the market.

36: Jugglers and balladeers

Bopa never learned of her father's frustrations about the land. That was because in those days she rarely saw him, or anyone else in the household. Myself included, I will confess it.

How did I allow this to happen? The reasons I gave to myself back then seem absurd now: I had the distractions with His Majesty, I had my duties for the palace pantry, I was often traveling. And at those times that I did think to worry about her, I told myself that her dear heart and the scriptural teachings that she had absorbed (or so I thought) would help her find her way past temptations.

Our family owes so much to Yan, Bopa's maid. It was she who finally laid the true state of affairs before me.

You will appreciate what an awkward position Yan was in. Any servant girl must think long and hard before making any judgment, any comment on the behaviour of her mistress. It is so much easier to pretend not to see. And what to do if there are two mistresses, each with a different view? Yan tried to be loyal to us both – I was the lady of the house and paid her wages, of course – but there were times that she found herself in conflict between the two of us.

So early one afternoon, when Bopa was not to be seen, Yan came to me as I sat in my room going over accounts. I sensed immediately that something was wrong.

'Yan, what is it? Are you not well?' That was how I was, choosing until the very last to refuse to see. I knew very well that Yan would not come to me to complain of an illness.

'Lady Sray, my health is fine.'

Presently she came out with it: 'It is about your daughter, Lady.'

'Oh!'

'As the Lady knows, her daughter spends much time these days at the concubine pavilion.'

'Yes, yes, I do know that.' I said that but in fact I did not really know. I knew only that Bopa was out of the house for long periods.

'I am not sure that the Lady would approve of some of the

things that go on there.' She looked down, troubled. I began to worry what was coming.

'Bopa sits with Rom and whatever junior girls are on hand and they gossip and laugh and play board games. Sometimes Rom brings in jugglers and acrobats, hired from the market. Or balladeers, who sing songs of country girls finding love with city boys.'

'Oh! That doesn't sound so bad.'

But Yan was a strong girl and now she refused to let me bat aside the message she had come to deliver.

'There is always honey wine, Lady.'

'But everyone drinks some of that from time to time.'

'It is more often than some, Lady. And at all times of day. Morning even.'

'I see...Well, I will speak with Bopa when she comes back.' I looked away from Yan now. I confess that I was thinking of myself as well as my daughter. It was shameful to be told this, and by a young girl.

'Lady, I am sorry to say, but the Mistress Bopa is not out now. She is lying on her mat in her sleeping area. She is in such a deep sleep that it's impossible to rouse her...'

Together we hurried to the other side of the house. It was just as Yan had said: my little girl, sleeping, her mouth wide open. Snoring, drooling onto the mat! There was an awful stale smell of honey wine in the air. Ever since that day, I have been unable to tolerate that smell.

Yan whispered: 'Please, Lady. Please, you won't tell her that I brought you here...'

'I will not. But you did the right thing. This cannot go on.'

I told Yan that she could go, but she was not finished. There was more to tell. This was not the first time this had happened, she said. Usually Bopa slept it off at the concubine pavilion. But on this day, there had been a shocking kind of trouble there. One of the younger concubines, perhaps jealous of my daughter's favour with Rom, had begun having her idea of fun once Bopa fell asleep. She had been poking her with a stick, laughing that there was no response. Then she began to draw patterns on her face with ashes from a cooking fire! Touching her head! Yan tried to shoo her away, and was shocked when this concubine, younger than she, turned and slapped her on the face, saying how dare a servant behave this way. So do you know what Yan did? She lifted Bopa and helped her stumble her way outside! There was an empty oxcart there, and she laid her in the back and pulled closed the straw shades, then went and found a driver. She told him not to look in the back, just to drive to our house. It was not a long way, and at the house she made the man go away and she helped Bopa inside, laid her down and washed the ashes from her face.

Yan was weeping by the time she finished telling me this. I know she felt terribly remiss for not coming to me sooner. But, she explained, she had had hope that Sovan would straighten things out. He had lately been spending some time with his sister, despite his responsibilities at the construction site, taking her to places in the market, trying to entertain her so she would not go so often to the concubine pavilion. None of this had I noticed.

I put my arm around the maid and pulled her close. How I wished sometimes that my daughter had this maid's character. Yan told me much more that afternoon, as we sat near the sleeping Bopa, speaking in whispers. She had recognized that the pavilion's society was poison. It of course had Rom at its centre. And increasingly, her son Darit. He did not live there, but when he arrived for a visit, everything came to a stop, and it was best that any other concubine who'd given birth from the King's seed make scarce of her own child. Darit's mother would take his hand and display him left and right, and there was competition to say nice things about him. Sometimes he deserved it, other times he ran riot, shouting, overturning bowls, tracking mud onto mats and sometimes right onto the laps of startled junior concubines. There was always that armed man staying close, but to Yan it seemed more and more as if Darit was in charge of the man. Rom approved of that; in fact, she declared one day that she had given the man instructions that he was to obey the boy in all things, unless there was a question of immediate danger.

And do you know, Rom often made stinging remarks when comparing her son to Crown Prince Aroon, the child now five years old who had been born to the King's consort in the second year of marriage. She would note what a horseman her own son was turning into, how he was fearless, had taken the reins from age two, while the prince...well, the prince seemed almost afraid to mount. It was widely known that the boy had been thrown several times. Some spirit, perhaps, had decided that horses would be a challenge. But the prince, lacking bluster, did not take it up. Rather, he had taken to pretending that he was not interested in riding. Rom would laugh over this. The concubines would join in. This was of course dangerous behaviour. I asked Yan: and Bopa, does she laugh as well? The maid hesitated, then replied 'no.' I think that was the only lie of the afternoon.

Yan made a final point to me. 'Rom has invited your daughter to sit with one of the pavilion's own maids when Rom leads the parade of the concubines at the New Year festival next week. Lady, I am sure there will be honey wine...'

She didn't need say anything more. 'Yan, she will not go as the guest of Rom. She will sit with the people of our own household.'

I sat by my girl the rest of the afternoon. In truth I must say I felt not only concern for her, but anger. A girl with so much rice to eat, a clean place to sleep free of mosquitoes, and yet behaving this way! A girl who did not have to work in the sun in some market. A girl who had the best religious teachings. Even if no one knew of her drunkenness now, the word would surely spread. I turned all this over in my mind, but as one hour became two, some blessed spirit came into me, silently instructing that for now my own feelings were not important. This spirit bade me enter into the feelings of my daughter. I began to think that perhaps she lacked the stamina for the life here. Me, my husband, my son, we all had found roles and places in the palace compound. We were busy. But Bopa? She was not one who could find her own way. She would follow the example of whatever person took an interest in her. She would not say no, that's not right, I won't do it that way.

Marriage was of course the usual route that a girl of her age took. She was well into marriage age, in fact. But who could deny that even that would be hard? Those nice young men from the old neighbourhood no longer came calling at the house. I suspect they felt she had risen above their hopes. Yet boys who had been born into palace life would probably see her as lacking. Her accent betrayed she had grown up on the outside. She had learned only a few of the skills of running a prominent household.

By evening, my daughter was stirring, whimpering in her sleep. I lay down and took her in my arms. She murmured something heartfelt – I couldn't understand it, I could only sense that she was welcoming me.

I began to whisper. 'Bopa, darling, you and I will spend so much more time together now...You will not be afraid of life here, I will help show you the way...You will not want to go to the concubine pavilion any more...We will do fun things together and we will also fill your heart, your soul with the virtue of the scriptures.'

Preparing Bopa for the New Year's parade was of course no simple matter, but that was good. It gave mother and daughter a task to share. For a start, there were special sampots to be purchased. A man came from the market with sample fabrics, and my girl giggled over the selection laid out on the floor, finally settling on this one – no, that one. A seamstress sewed them to order for both of us and fitted us, Bopa standing up and trying on the half-finished garment, asking for a change, more flare at the waist (I wondered where she had seen such fashions). On the day of the celebrations, Yan helped her dress, tucking in those flares – they now seemed like the wings of a great bird. The maid painted red colour on her mistress's palms and cheeks. Jewellery, a bronze headdress and scent were added. Yan held up the polished metal mirror, and Bopa smiled at herself. Do you know what that smile was like? It was like that night after the Brahmin came to our old little house, when Nol told little Bopa that she would paint her palms red, like the palace girls, and she looked at those palms and could already see the red and she smiled the biggest of smiles.

At the appointed time, I saw her off to the royal terrace, tended by Yan. It was a doleful moment for me. I was proud of how beautiful she looked, yet I could not go. His Majesty would be in attendance. The terrace was big, but not big enough for there to be sufficient separation between us.

Everyone talked about the event for days afterward. Bopa

took a place on a mat that Yan laid out with cool water and fruit. She was in good company, surrounded by the parasol pavilion's foreman and several elders from the parasol-making villages, invited by Nol as a reward for good service. After a time, gongs sounded, then a conch horn, and everyone put foreheads to mat as the royal fire was carried out of the palace main gate, followed by His Majesty, the Queen and their son the Crown Prince, all on foot, beneath a forest of parasols. The royal family took their places on a dais. The boy stayed very close to his mother.

Servants strode this way and that making final preparations. Then the parade began. First came fierce-faced commanders atop elephants, then men with spears, then priests and then the parade of the concubines.

What a sight that was. At the fore was Rom, and she caused a collective gasp from the men on the terrace. Atop her head was a silver diadem with three filigreed points rising impossibly high. Coconut palm flowers and lotus blossoms adorned each one. Silver pendants dangled from cords beneath her shoulders; silver bracelets enclosed her wrists and upper arms. Around her neck, were three strands of set pearls, each one seeming to catch the sun's rays. Her sampot was of bright green silk, edged in silver. Its sashes, starched, flared out like the wings of a bird. Of course. She walked in a prancing way that generated sexual longing or envy the length of the terrace. Her face was as smooth as any temple image's; her breasts like those of a village girl who has yet to bear children. Behind her walked the two deputy concubines, and then behind them, the full corps of women, each one striking and fabulously dressed. But you know, I think that all of them were unable to draw eyes away from Rom.

Before long, the concubine passed out of sight down to the right. People looked back to the parade, not expecting much now, but they saw a marvellous sight of a different kind. It was a boy not more than five, his neck and chest adorned with silver and precious stones and an amulet, atop a very powerful horse. Most boys of that age would have feared losing control of the animal, a war mount, but there was not a trace of diffidence in this one. The horse had recognized who was master.

The King was wearing a look of absolute delight. He stood up, so quickly that his parasol bearers were caught unaware and scrambled to keep the shade on him. He took a step forward for a better view, and the boy on the horse turned and looked straight into the royal eye. People gasped at that effrontery, but the King was not. He smiled, watching, until the boy too was lost from sight.

I was sitting at a window that evening when Bopa returned. A surprise: a young man – I could not see him clearly – was with her and made his good-byes at the gate.

As Bopa passed inside, I asked, 'Dear, who was that?'

'No one, mother. Just a boy who walked with me.'

Of course a young girl would answer in that way. I did not press her. Then Yan came in and whispered that he held a senior position at the royal horse stables. He had approached after the festivities broke up and asked Bopa if he might escort her home. He drew a laugh or two from her as they made their way toward our house. Yan seemed not entirely approving of him, but everything she described sat well with me. Here was a young man taking a proper kind of interest in our daughter. His family was of our rank. Who could say but it might lead to something good?

Yan was not willing to let it rest there, however. The following day, she made more inquiries, then came to me to share the information: He is the crown prince's riding instructor. And he is a cousin of the concubine Rom.

I did not sleep well that night.

37: The Architect's queries

When Sovan departed the house, my husband of course forbade me any contact with him, and for quite a few months I honoured that. But how long can a mother accept such an unnatural demand? Whether a child is infant or adult, it makes no difference – that child is part of her being, her flesh. I dreamt of my boy, I imagined him at mealtime sitting on the mat beside me, I felt resentment when I saw other women walking with their sons, carefree. And so I finally resolved that I would see him. Nol would not have to know. As long as I did not flaunt my decision, I felt, it would be all right.

I sent a message to the assistants' hut at the construction site. Our first meeting was at the inn by the market. We embraced; we sat down over tea and soon it was like old times. Except that his air of moroseness, of dissatisfaction, had vanished. Never mind how taxing this new life was. My boy spoke with animation about his work, about the people, about the fantastic thing that was slowly taking shape on the former rice lands south of Angkor.

'You must show me this thing, Sovan,' I said.

The request came from my mouth before I could give thought to whether it was proper. It would be an unusual thing indeed, a woman being received at a place that was for men alone. But my boy did not treat it that way. He said he would get permission.

So it was that a week later I found myself at the entrance to the site, at dawn.

My boy, I learned, had acquired a daily routine. Rise from the mat before the sun showed itself, creep out of the hut so as to not wake the other assistants. Bathe at a jar in the dark, taking care to keep the noise low as he scooped water with a coconut shell. Feel with his hands for his garment, then dress quickly, find his chalk and slate and walk to the building site, following a trail tramped out by the feet of a thousand labourers. He had done all this by the time I arrived that day.

'We'll walk the perimeter of the site, mother. Anything unusual I'll mark down here.' He held up a slate.

I am sure that this was his favourite part of the day. The

site was largely deserted, mist hanging in the air in places. Everything was silent, still, as if awaiting his private inspection.

We walked.

'The eastern bridge, mother.'

'Oh!' I had expected things to be further along. What I saw was a rough earthen causeway, though I know that in my boy's mind a stone bridge, carved with deities large and small, was already visible.

To the right and left we could see where men with shovels had begun excavating the future Sea of Creation. So far, they'd made a pair of broad, shallow holes that were as dry as any village fishpond at this time of year. The hole on the left, focus of the previous day's spadework, had grown by perhaps half a cubit, my boy said. That was not so much, he added, but the team digging it had been short a few members the day before, due to an outbreak of fever.

We crossed the causeway, the soil pleasantly cool against our soles. At the other end was a series of ropes running long and taut along the ground at right angles to our path's direction. Another mystery to me, but to Sovan all was clear – they were outlines of the future perimeter wall, he explained. A few steps further he showed me how with each end secured by an iron stake, the ropes stretched taut and would guide the start of foundation digging here. 'One set of labourers will sink the trenches to clay level, another will pour in basketfuls of sand to prepare the bottom for the first blocks of laterite that will underpin and stabilize the sandstone walls.' Such big words he was using.

Looking again, I began to comprehend patterns and planning, all for the noble purpose. I told Sovan as much, that it was a salute to the hard work of him and everyone else. Such a design – how long it must have taken to think out!

He smiled. 'Yes, but thankfully we don't have to devise it all ourselves. In his work pavilion, the Architect has holy texts that give us guidance.'

'Ahh...'

'They require that moat and walls be built first, so as to mark off a zone of Heavenly earth fit for a mountain-temple. That's what we're doing now. But you know, my master has shown me that in insisting on this sequence Heaven is giving some practical benefit to us down here.'

'I don't think I know what you mean.'

'Well, we excavate the moat first, and it will be linked by a canal to the Capital's main river, because that's how it will get water. And when the main construction begins, we'll have a water route all the way from the quarries in the north right to a place on the moat. We'll need to drag them just a short distance.

'And sometimes the help in these texts comes through what they *don't* say, mother. Nowhere in them, for instance, do they say that the mountain-temple's eastern gate, nor lesser ones that will face the three other cardinal directions, have to be erected at an early stage. So on each of the four sides, the perimeter wall will for years have a broad gap through which elephants and men will be able to haul stones to their final places in Heaven's design.'

We reached what would be the southeast corner of the outer wall, then turned right to walk along its future southern edge. My son was happy; everything seemed in order this morning. Further on, he pulled on a rope to check tautness and smiled at what he found. Over on this side, the digging had already begun. Neat spade marks were visible.

'But where is the soil?' I asked.

'Carried away in baskets by the labour volunteers, mother. Their children trail behind to pick up whatever clods drop to the ground. This is one of my master's abiding principles – the labour that builds a mountain-temple must be as precise and ordered as the finished monument itself.'

Just then something caught Sovan's eye, and for a moment he forgot me. He stepped quickly to one of the holes. Rocks, three of them, were visible at the bottom. He hopped down into the hole for a closer look, and, standing there, made some notes on the slate.

'You never know how big they are – they may be showing just a tiny part of themselves,' he said. 'Removing them may be a huge job, provided the priests let us do it. Every time we find something like this, they come in to make a determination as to whether Heaven has intended the stone's removal or its incorporation into the design.'

We passed on to what would become the temple's rear wall, on the side of the setting sun. I could not but help notice that Sovan glanced not entirely easily out toward the trees beyond the site – our trees, our land, owned by our family.

We had not talked about his father, on this or any of our other meetings. But now he brought him up. 'Sometimes, mother, I imagine that I'll see him out there, between one of those trees right there, staring at me. Sometimes I imagine him holding that stick again.'

My poor boy. He hadn't forgot that evening at the house.

'Sovan, you will be reconciled with him. I pray for it daily and in those evenings when his mood seems right, I bring up your name.'

An hour after we'd begun, we were back at the future entry bridge. From there we went to a communal drinking water bowl. As we stood with cups in our hands, I heard a voice.

'Hey – we've run out of lamp oil at the hut.'

It was a male voice, speaking in an almost abusive kind of way. I turned to see another young man approaching. It seemed he was ordering my son to go the market to get some oil. Then this man saw me, and his tone changed in a flash. He put hands together, he inquired after my health and my tour of the site.

Sovan later told that this Pin was one of the few problems of his new life. Though my boy had been on the job a year he was still the junior-most of the assistants. The petty ordering around had become more common, it seemed, in the three months since the Architect had assigned the morning inspection to Sovan.

Work was beginning in earnest all around us. It was time for me leave.

I had no idea of how important the rest of the day would turn out to be for my son. The following morning, I knew all about it. My boy came all the way into the city just to tell me.

Shortly after I had left, Sovan had gone to the design pavilion for a regular morning meeting. Pin and the other assistants were present. Soon the Architect strode in, leading a servant who carried a wooden case, and the assistants began giving their reports. One described efforts to lease another ten oxcarts to carry food and other supplies to the labourers' camp. Another outlined plans for a trip to a quarry to the north to inspect a new outcrop of sandstone discovered there. Sovan spoke of the moat diggers' need for a doctor, and the rocks that had been partially uncovered.

The Architect listened to all this, then moved on. 'I've got something to show you all.' That was the cue for the opening of the wooden case that the servant had carried in. The Architect took from it a large sheet of palm leaf and laid it with some flourish on the table.

'Here we are, then – the outline of the future mountain-temple itself. It was approved by His Majesty last night.'

Sovan and the others pressed quickly close, jostling each other. The plan was drawn in the Architect's own flawless hand. It was a stepped pyramid of five levels. From each cardinal direction, stairs led to the top, with a pair of sculpted lions standing guard at each level. At the top was a square platform, a large tower at its centre and four smaller ones at each corner.

'The dimensions at the outer enclosure,' announced the Architect, 'will be three hundred ninety cubits.' He paused to let them take that in, because this was larger than anything built before, the proud promise the palace had made so many times.

Pin declared: 'It will be the greatest creation of the Empire, sir. You will be blessed for having drafted it.'

The Architect's eye went to Sovan and he knew he had to speak.

'It's excellent, sir.'

'That's all you know how to say?' The Architect, it seems, enjoyed putting him on the spot.

'Well, sir, the proportions seem to my amateur eye to be perfect.'

'Yes? And why is that?'

I cannot pretend to give you Sovan's exact language. But it was to the effect that the base level seemed to anchor the temple to the earth. The angle of slope leading up toward the top was a bit sharper than at other temples, and this would communicate the fact that His Majesty's connection with Heaven was close. And the level area at the top marked the highest presence, the highest possibility of human work on earth, before the central tower, pointing skyward, showed the way to Heaven and, again, His Majesty's affinity with that place.

'Thank you, Sovan,' said the Architect. 'I see that you understand.'

My boy wished that that hadn't been said in front of the other assistants.

Now the Architect spoke for close to an hour, giving details of planned engineering and materials and making assignments. The inner core, hidden from view, would be composed of soil and laterite blocks, and one assistant would do nothing for the next week but work out the numbers of those blocks, and the ideal dimensions of each and in what order they would be carved from the earth and transported to the site over the coming years. A second assistant would calculate the precise surface area of wall that would be available for holy carvings and begin consultations with the palace priests as to which scenes from the myths would be depicted and where. Other assistants would be assigned to particular labour teams, to schedule their movements so as not to conflict with others. Pin was one of them – he got the elephant tenders.

'And you, Sovan, you will work directly with me to assure that the design is executed precisely as His Majesty wishes.'

'Sir!'

'That's all, then,' said the Architect. 'Each of you will continue to report in here daily on your progress. You have permission to consult with me directly if you have questions.'

They all stood to await the Architect's departure. Sovan ignored the glare that Pin had fixed on him.

Pin and the other assistants knocked off work earlier that afternoon. They would go to the market to celebrate the start of the new phase of construction. After some wine, I'm sure, they would visit the girls at the lamp-lit stalls, as men do at such times. Sovan remained behind in the assistants' hut, I'm sure feeling the burden of abstinence. But before he could devote much thought to that, a messenger arrived. The Architect, Sovan was told, summons you to his house in one hour's time.

That was a surprise – the master had taken over the house of the anxious young prince whose land this once was, but no assistant had ever been invited there. One hour later, Sovan arrived there. Another surprise – it was no longer the one the prince had occupied. Of course, thought Sovan. Our master would never live in something as ordinary as that. It had been replaced by a large teak residence of ample windows and soaring eaves. Even in the failing light, Sovan could sense design and craftsmanship of disquieting precision. He stopped outside the gate, and took some time studying it.

A watchman appeared, seeming to know that Sovan was coming. He was an older man, but he treated Sovan with some deference, informing him that the master had been called to the kilns and had asked that the visitor be shown there. My boy followed him around behind the house, along a rectangular lotus pond which at its centre had a pavilion on stilts, a sort of house on the water. Then came a path into forest. After a bit, a clearing, with the strong scent of charcoal signalling the firing of tiles and ceramics. To one side was a collection of potter's wheels, to the other a half dozen domed dirt kilns as tall as a man. Each had a hole in its front and a chimney in its back. Quite a few people were busy at the kilns, potters kneeling at the holes to place clay tiles inside for firing, slaves feeding charcoal to the hidden flames.

The Architect was there, in conversation with a man who seemed to be the foreman. My son was called over. 'We've finally figured out what was making the tiles come out bad so often,' announced the Architect. He gestured to a pile of fragments to the side. 'Every single one was cracking after it cooled, so we had to throw them away. But it turns out the clay contained a contamination. We've switched to clay from another spot and things are working out fine now. Have a look here.' He led my boy to a kiln. By it were ten roof tiles, cooling. 'Flawless,' he said.

'I had no idea you operate kilns, sir.'

'Just a hobby, boy. After we moved here, we discovered there were good clay deposits on the land – most of them good, at least

– so it seemed fun to try our hand. Well, then, come back to the house with me.'

It was getting dark now, and when they reached the grounds, torches had been set burning on poles around the pond. Candles flickered inside the pavilion that stood over the water. The Architect led the way along its access footbridge.

Inside, he said: 'Sit down then, boy. Make yourself comfortable.' Sovan did, wondering when the purpose of this visit was going to become clear.

'Do you like this pavilion?' the Architect asked. He didn't wait for an answer. 'It's the only place I can get peace and quiet. There's a very strict rule – no one comes across the bridge unless I say it's all right. Not my wife, not my daughters, not my servants.'

'I'm honoured that you let me enter, sir.'

'Never mind that.' He took out a palm leaf and laid it close to a candle. 'Now, tell me what you think of this.'

It was the same leaf he'd presented that day. Sovan cleared his throat, and began to repeat his words of a few hours earlier.

A frown stopped him. 'Sovan, if we're going to work together, you must speak your mind with me. At the meeting today you were saying what you felt I wanted to hear, and you're doing it again now.'

'Sir, I'm only an assistant, the most junior, in fact.'

'Yes, and if you retain an assistant's timidity, you'll be one all your life. Now, look. This is not the King's court. It's not a meeting with the other assistants. It's just you and me. Well, go on!'

Sovan took his time. 'Well, sir, it's just that...I suppose it's that...that this design seems to be mainly a larger version of what has been built in previous reigns.'

'I agree.'

Sovan at this point might also have mentioned his belief that everyone had been facing in the wrong direction on the day of the cubit ceremony. But he kept that to himself; it would be too big a challenge to his master, who after all had been facing that wrong way along with everyone else. Instead, Sovan focused on the design.

'I feel, sir, that to show our devotion to the Absolute, we must at all times be striving to perfect our understanding of the appearance of Heaven and how a structure here can replicate one that is there. Each reign's construction should advance us along this path, seeking harmony with both earth and the motion of the sun and stars, until we create something that is indistinguishable from what is found in Heaven – in fact, *is* that thing.'

Do you see? When speaking his heart, Sovan could be like an orator.

The Architect took a moment to smile. He tapped Sovan on the shoulder. 'You do understand, then. Now let's look at the paper again.' He moved the candle closer. 'What you see is what I drafted based on a drawing by His Majesty, a man of great abilities in war, but whom Heaven has given lesser abilities in the appreciation of the aesthetic realm of life. His Majesty has seen the temple of our late lord Udayadityavarman, has picked up a piece of chalk and imagined his own temple looking not so different than that one. Bigger, of course. He has set his mind on this design, and so has the Brahmin Subhadra, who is happy that the King has shown an interest in something that doesn't involve weapons or concubines.'

Sovan had never heard anyone speak this way about our monarch and it made him uneasy. But it did sound like truth.

'So,' the Architect concluded, 'this is what we have been given. Except...except in a project of this complexity, the Architect has certain authority to make changes as the work goes along, and it's not necessary to report to the palace about every little one of these changes, because people there don't want to be drowned in details. And they know, as you and I know, that some number of changes will always be necessary to achieve the full effect of a design, because not everything can be foreseen in the initial plan.'

'I think I'm starting to understand, sir.'

'I would hope so. Now, if ever we're challenged, you'll appreciate that there's a fine line between a change that retains the spirit of the original design and one that takes things in a new direction altogether. It's often something that can only be settled by debate, and the person who is the more familiar with the vocabulary and aesthetics and theory of this kind of thing can usually prevail in such a debate.'

'Sir.'

'Now, this will all remain confidential between you and me. But I can already see refinements that should be made to the design, and I will begin sketching out some changes and we will not tell anyone about them. That would just create confusion. There will be times when I will rely on you to convey word of a change to the team working on a particular element of the project, and you may need to be very diplomatic, and maybe not convey the real reason why you want them to, say, make a trench twenty cubits longer than is shown on the plan they're working from.'

'I understand, sir. You can count on me. And I...I deeply appreciate the trust you are placing in me. I am the most junior of your assistants.'

'Most junior, yes, but least capable, no.' The Architect shifted his legs to relieve some ache. 'You know, it was clear to me from the day I first met you, when I came out to have a look at the site, that you had something in your soul for this craft. Who knows? Perhaps the builder god Visvakarman had reached down from Heaven and touched you. Just a bit, mind you. Everyone else was swatting at flies or griping about the heat, but you, you looked and you saw a mountain-temple.'

'Sir, I'm nothing as you...'

The Architect put up a hand to stop him. 'Down the road you may wonder why you ever agreed to this. It's going to be endless work for the next twenty or twenty-five years. Now listen. There are going to be changes in your schedule. You'll continue to do the morning inspection, but for the next few months I will want you to spend three hours each afternoon refining your drawing skills. You will come to the design pavilion out at the site. Sometimes it will be a draftsman instructing you, sometimes it will be me.'

'Yes, sir.'

'Well, then – that's settled.'

'Thank you, sir!'

Sovan expected to be dismissed. But the Architect cleared his throat and looked again to him. 'Now, Sovan, I need to ask you a few other things. Let's start with: Do you pray on a regular basis?'

'Yes, sir.'

'And give offerings?'

'Often enough, I think, sir. My life is blessed.'

'A good answer. And do you have debts?'

'No, sir.'

'Do you have any...unmentionable disease?'

'No, sir.'

'And do you go with the girls in the marketplace, the ones who become a sweetheart for a night?'

'Why *no*, sir!'

'There's no need to be offended. But maybe then there's some girl who's especially dear to you. The daughter of someone on the palace staff, perhaps.'

'No, sir,' my boy said again, reddening. 'It didn't happen before I moved out of my former father's house. And in my current situation, I hardly have the opportunity to meet such a girl.'

That brought amusement to the Architect's face. He said: 'Well, then. That's all you and I have to talk about for now. Good-night.'

Sovan stepped along the footbridge, puzzled. There was too much to sort out here. A new position, a new design, whose course he might conceivably affect; questions about health and marriage. He came to a stop. That last one he suddenly figured out, standing still in the light of the pond's torches. The Architect had daughters, but no son. Everyone knew that. No one to teach the craft to. Under the laws of Heaven and Empire, a son can be born into a family, or he can be brought in, just as Veng became son to my husband with Sovan's expulsion. And sometimes, sometimes, a son is brought in as husband to a daughter. Sovan swallowed. Things could become terribly awkward very quickly now. But then a spirit placed a humbling thought in his mind: this perhaps is why your own father, having only one son, was so angry at losing you to a man who had none.

An old servant woman waited at the end of the footbridge. 'This way please, sir.' As she led him along a path, he found something to wonder about in her too, and the answer was starting to come to him as she led him up the back steps of the house and into its main chamber.

There a young woman stood waiting. Her face and hands bore the rouge of the well-bred; her hair, pulled back, was secured by a bronze clasp. This time, a lamp shone on her rather than the afternoon sun.

She asked: 'Do you remember me?'

'Of course!'

'And I remember you. I saw you talking with Father the day His Majesty came to bless the building site. I knew right away it was you and I told Father. He made me wait. But now you're here. Would you like to sit down?'

She didn't wait for an answer but called out. 'Nang, could you please bring some water for our guest? And please put out the banana sweets I bought. I think he likes those.'

So! My son's problems of marriage were past. For love and for life, Heaven had delivered to him this girl, this young woman, just as his dreams portended.

When he told me, I embraced him, tearful. Happiness for Sovan! Grandchildren! I felt such a sense of celebration, even as I worried over the other things he had confided, that he was now part of a secret challenge to the authority of King and Brahmins.

38: Nol's dream

My husband had almost come to accept that he would not get the land to the east of the temple. Then the fires were lit in him all over again, by the royal cattle tender Kiri and, I must admit, by me, though I of course had no such intention.

It happened on the first day of the water festival in the shrine that stood behind the central market. Scores of vendors had set up on its grounds. Dancers and fortune tellers had come in great numbers. Now common folk were thronging in, and so were heads of prominent families, who presented offerings to the priests or risked people saying they were miserly with the wealth that Heaven had settled on them.

Nol and I walked with attendants toward the grounds, me carrying, wrapped in silk, a silver bowl that we were going to donate. Nol believed it was too valuable a thing, but I had convinced him that the priests were deserving of it. As we drew near, there was a commotion on the road ahead. People were stopping, going up on their toes to see better and soon it was impossible to get by.

Nol called to a soldier standing guard on a rise by the roadside. 'What's going on here?'

'The royal cattle tender Kiri is coming this way,' the man replied. 'And his palanquin is fabulous!' Such a sight it was that the soldier had failed to notice that Nol was someone notable too.

Nol fumed; I think a new wave of pain began passing through his back.

People were now stepping out of the way to let the palanquin pass. I should have taken Nol by the arm and propelled him elsewhere, but it was too late. The palanquin sailed past us, like a boat borne on a sea of humanity, and it was in fact a marvellous thing. It was silver-plated top to bottom, with dozens of carved deities on its sides. It was upholstered in blue silk and decorated with fresh lilies and orchids. And at its centre: Kiri, accepting greetings left and right.

Nol turned away, worried that Kiri would see him.

'Husband – please, you mustn't be angry.'

'Why do you think I'm angry?'

'It's plain to see. But please, do your best to put it aside. It makes me grieve.'

The crowd broke and we walked on a bit, slowly. Then Nol stopped again, right there in the road. 'How much would such a thing cost?'

'The better question,' I replied, taking his arm, 'is why does he spend so much on something like that, when there are so many people without food, so many shrines to be built?'

'It's unfair. He has so much. That property by the mountain-temple's east gate – how much must that generate?'

I tried again. 'Husband, you lose standing in Heaven's eyes when you allow such feelings to build up in you. We have more than we need.'

'That land is going to be mine! I'll get it, and I'll buy an even larger palanquin, and you will ride on it.'

The next day, I left the Capital on a trading trip. When I came back two weeks later, there was a stunning surprise. My husband had triumphed over Kiri! He had not acquired the east land; rather, he had caused its value to move to ours.

I will explain to you, though it took some time for me to find out how it had happened. Nol at first would not discuss it, but after a while, he did. You know, I think he was so pleased with how he'd managed it that he simply had to tell someone and I was the only person who could be trusted to keep the secret. It was that repellent.

Things had begun the very day I left for the provinces. Nol saw me off that morning, then turned to a major job at hand, replacement of the parasol pavilion's roof. During a monsoon cloudburst some weeks earlier, water and broken tile had come cascading down without warning. Eight new parasols had been stained beyond repair. A slave sent up to inspect had reported that the supporting timbers had gone rotten. Nol gave an order that the entire roof be replaced.

After I left, he went to the pavilion and paced in front of it, waiting for another cart, which would bring the first load of new tiles. When he committed money to something, he liked to see with his own eyes that the materials were of the quality promised.

The cart appeared. The driver stopped it with the oxen facing a door through which the tiles would be taken. Nol inspected them; they were good. He stepped back, gave an order, and a couple of slaves began to unload, from the back of the cart. They carried armloads past the cart, then around the oxen, ducking each time to avoid the animals' horns. They were taking many extra steps just to get past the cart.

'Why haven't you turned the cart around?' Nol demanded. 'Place it so the back is by the door. The job will go much more quickly that way.'

Nol swore under his breath, thinking that people had to be told the simplest things. And right there the idea came to him. It was so frightening that his legs began to tremble and he had to sit down to consider it.

The following day, Nol was shown into a rear room in the palace. The King sat on a dais. A new concubine was an arm's reach away.

Nol pressed head to mat. After preliminaries, he put on his best worried face and said: 'Majesty, I ask permission to tell you something.'

'What is it?'

'A dream, Majesty.'

'Ahh – a dream.' The King was always intrigued by dreams.

Nol took a breath and pressed on. 'It was a very short one, Majesty. But when I woke up I remembered it so vividly that I felt it must have some special significance. People have advised me that I should not share it, that I should not bother you...'

'And you have ignored them. Good. Now what was it?'

'A simple dream, Majesty. You were standing at the foot of the steps to your mountain-temple. It was completed, in its full glory. You were...'

'You saw the completed temple?'

'Yes, Majesty. And words fail me to describe it. It was the largest and most beautiful in the universe. Its spires glittered with gold, it rose so high in the sky that clouds had to make way for it. It was on the earth, and yet it was not, it was part of Heaven itself.'

'And I was there, in this dream?'

'Yes, Majesty. You were dressed in silk and gold and with the

302

largest sword, and you were standing at the foot of the steps with the royal flame burning at your feet. You were facing down the entrance causeway toward the outer gate, Majesty. I was not there, Majesty, There was no need – your parasols floated of their own accord above you. But somehow I was able to see you. Or perhaps just sense your presence.'

'Go on.'

'And down the causeway, beyond the entrance gate, was the sun, and it was low in the sky.' Nol paused, and said nothing, waiting for the King to speak.

'That's everything?'

'No, Majesty, not everything. But I have hardly the standing to mention what I saw. Down the causeway, just before the entrance gate, stood our Lord Vishnu.'

'But the temple will be dedicated to Shiva.'

'It will be, Majesty, but it was Vishnu I saw. To his side was his consort Lakshmi, she who in her devotion massages his feet in eternity. And behind them was his mount the Bird God Garuda and one hundred attendants. And I think it was very significant that Our Lord Vishnu was not above Your Majesty but at the same level. Our Lord Vishnu was beckoning that Your Majesty should come commune with him. He was speaking words that were soft, but somehow they carried the entire distance between Your Majesty and the divine party with no trouble whatsoever.'

'What did Our Lord say?'

'Majesty, I cannot answer – the words had no meaning to me. They were in the language between King and god. But I think that they had meaning to Your Majesty, because the royal feet began carrying Your Majesty down the causeway to join the divine party.'

'Right toward the divine presence?'

'It was that way, Majesty. And then as Your Majesty walked, the sky began to grow dark, and on reaching the divine party, Your Majesty was entirely covered up in this darkness. There was nothing to see anymore.'

I do believe His Majesty must have been very concerned at this point. But Nol quickly followed with words to fix that.

'But then, Majesty – it was like many hours passed in the snap of a finger. Your Majesty was back at the temple and had even more power and vitality than before. And the sun was rising from the other side of the temple.'

The King was wearing a rare expression of contemplation. 'I feel it's a very meaningful dream...'

'Yes, Majesty. I felt that I had to relate it.'

'You are to be commended.'

'I should tell you, Majesty, that there was in this dream a mood of great optimism, despite the interlude of darkness.'

'Darkness, yes, darkness. Now, you say the sun was low in the sky, and then there was darkness?'

'Yes, Majesty.'

'The sun rose...and then it set. Then there was darkness.'

'No, no, Majesty, it was not like that!' For a moment, Nol worried he had overplayed his case, but it was too late to stop. 'The sun did not pass high and set behind the temple. It was low in the sky when I first saw Your Majesty, and then it went down and vanished. That's what caused the darkness.'

This startled the King.

'And you say that Our Lord Vishnu and the divine party had entered the temple grounds and were standing with their backs to the main gate?'

'Yes, Majesty. It was just behind them.'

The King thought this over some more. Then he said: 'You're sure about these details?'

'Yes, Majesty. Is there something that troubles you about them?'

'No, no...only that what you recount would seem to suggest that the temple was facing to the west.'

'Majesty?'

'Facing to the west.'

'But temples don't face to the west, Majesty. They face to the east, every one I've ever seen. But yes...you have helped me understand! This temple, the temple in my dream, must have been facing toward the setting sun, toward the west.'

'What could that mean?'

'I am not an interpreter of dreams, Majesty. But I wonder...No, I mustn't say.'

'Yes, you must!'

Nol swallowed, to give time to frame his words carefully. 'Majesty, I wonder if Our Lord Vishnu was communicating that the temple of the greatest King should show the King's glory in a special way. That though most mountain-temples honour Shiva, Vishnu is signalling that he has chosen a special association with Your Majesty, in this life and the next. And that though it would be wrong for other kings to build a temple facing the west, it would be wrong for this King to build one facing east.'

'But the temple is being built facing east!'

'Yes, Majesty, it is, it is! Forgive me, forgive me!' Nol put his head to the floor again. 'My interpretation must be wrong.'

The young concubine drew near, anxious to regain the King's attention, but he showed no interest.

Just then Subhadra entered the room, looking like he'd come in a rush and slowed only at the door. Nol felt dismay.

'Majesty! Is there some difficulty?'

'There is none.'

'But as I was entering, Majesty, wasn't the parasol master saying something about the alignment of the temple...'

The King was caught, and so he told Nol to repeat the dream. He did, and the Brahmin listened and then made a show of giving it deep consideration. 'I think, Majesty, that you can ignore this dream. The Lord Vishnu would not deliver such a message through someone outside of holy orders, someone uncertified as a vessel of spiritual communication. And such a remarkable message would come many times, not just once.'

Nol looked to the King, and he could see that this was not what the ruler wanted to hear, that in this brief time His Majesty had been taken with the idea of his temple and his divine affinity being different than the others. Nol said: 'The Brahmin is more schooled in these things than I am. I'm sure his opinion is correct. With the King's permission, I will leave now.'

Outside the palace, Nol's legs almost gave way at the thought of what he'd done.

But an hour later he was back at his parasol hall, looking up at the workmen on the roof, and he felt glad for that monsoon downpour and the damage it had caused. His mind had conjured up a theory that he was only functioning as a tool of Heaven, that for reasons he could not fathom the orientation of the temple had to be changed.

Ten days later, one of Nol's informants came to him with news he had expected: the blind shaman has been called from his distant retreat. In a closed oxcart, he arrived at the palace with the boy who led him by the hand. He spent two hours in private consultation with the King, then departed in the same clandestine way.

Before long, Nol was summoned to the palace. He arrived thinking he'd be shown to the King's private chambers for some more questioning. Instead he was directed straight to the throne room. There the King sat in full regal glory atop wooden dais whose legs were the curved bodies of Naga serpents. Fans and fly whisks stirred the air overhead – theirs was the only motion in the room. The Architect knelt to the side, along with various palace functionaries. Everyone was silent, waiting. It hit Nol all at once that this was a formal court session, that he and his dream would be its focus, and that the King's thinking had progressed very far very fast.

'Go ahead, parasol master. Recount what you saw.'

The Architect listened, and as the story progressed, scepticism grew ever plainer on his face. When Nol finished, he shrugged. 'Majesty, my skills are in building, not in interpreting dreams. But even so, this dream seems unworthy of serious consideration.'

'Why is that?' The King's eyebrows rose an intimidating way. 'It is my belief, and this belief has been confirmed by people skilled in interpretation, that this dream means that the current orientation of the temple is wrong. That it should face the west – toward the realm of Vishnu.'

'But Majesty, how can that be? All mountain-temples face east. We have been working for three years with that orientation.'

'All temples but mine. Heaven desires the reverse orientation for mine. The *correct* orientation.'

'Majesty, I don't think...' This man was among the few who dared stand his ground in a disagreement with the King.

'You should show a more positive outlook, Architect. Now, what would be the loss of time and the extra cost to proceed with a western orientation?'

'Majesty, I would have to do quite a few calculations. But the waste and delay would be enormous. We would have to remove the eastern bridge. We would have to shift walls, dig new trenches. We have begun work on a pair of libraries; they would have to be taken down. And all of this assumes that the soil at the western entrance is up to the job.'

'But construction of the main temple has not yet begun, just walls and moat and ancillary buildings. That is correct, is it not?'

'Yes, Majesty, that is correct.'

'That's the major part of the job. I will ask again. What would be the delay?'

'Three years, perhaps, Majesty. Three years.'

'And what if we increased the levy on the estates, to make them send more volunteers, more material? Could we then close the gap and finish in the same amount of time?'

'Yes, Majesty. But the estates are already heavily burdened by the existing levies. It would be difficult to raise them further.'

'You are suggesting that some of the princes would resist? Tell me, who are they?'

The Architect took a moment. He now realized what he was facing. 'No one would resist, Majesty. All live to serve you and will welcome whatever chance you give them to show, even more, their loyalty and devotion. That is true of the rural princes and of every one of the people on their estates.'

'Good. Architect, you will begin drafting plans for the change. You will tell no one for the moment. You will return a week from now with detailed estimates of the time and the cost and when the new levies should begin. The temple will be the greatest in the world, and it will show from its orientation that it occupies a different realm than all the others.'

'Yes, Majesty.'

'And you will be remembered as the man who built this great thing.'

One month later, at a time selected by the palace astrologers, the King went to the construction site, and Subhadra led a ceremony that announced that a wonderful thing had been discovered, that the King's Heavenly counterpart was in fact Vishnu, that the new temple should be aligned as the starting point in the King's journey toward the next life, that when his soul left his body, it would pass down the causeway and out the main gate into the sunset realm of the dead. The rite lasted all day, and, by torchlight, into the night, lengthened by pleas to Shiva to recognize and welcome this shift, which, the chanting priests averred, would in no way detract from the devotion felt for that deity by King, priests and subjects at large.

The following night, a man arrived at the parasol compound. Nol received the man, then signed leafs that turned over ownership of four hundred weight of silver that was on deposit with merchants in the main market. The servants dared not ask who he was, but the night watchman had one clue, a few overheard words in the accent of Chaiyapoom.

Even before labour teams began dismantling the temple's unfinished eastern gate, the hostels, shops, houses and stables that had stood nearby were removed. People knew that now the place to be was on the temple's western side. Salvaged materials were taken by cart to that area, where trees and undergrowth had already been cleared for a settlement. Nol's steward sat in a small pavilion, newly erected for the purpose, and in it he received new tenants one by one to discuss the terms under which they would build, reside and engage in business.

Nol had one more triumph. He sent his steward to see Kiri and offered him and his family rights to provide food for guests of one of the newly constructed pilgrim hostels. A trembling Kiri replied that the offer was declined. Nol made the steward repeat the story over and over, and each time he laughed.

But what wickedness this was, inventing a dream, invoking the names of our lords in Heaven, to bring about such a selfish goal. The only comfort I could find was the thought that perhaps

Nol was unknowingly functioning in some way as temporal agent for the divine vision that our son had had, that the orientation of the temple was in fact wrong and should be corrected. But Nol knew nothing of that vision! He never spoke with his former son and in theory neither did I, so I had never conveyed it. No, Nol's motivation was entirely his own aggrandizement. And his act meant that he and I now had not one but two secrets that could bring our arrest. I wondered, when would come the day in which we could live our lives in the open, with full honesty and no deception?

Of course I remained silent about what Nol had done. I reported nothing. He was my husband. But my anger glowed like coals in a fire. It gave rise to more than one quarrel between us. My frustrations were all the deeper because I could almost never say out loud what I felt. I had always to speak in circumlocution, in metaphor, because in palace life there were always servants near.

Mostly I protested silently. I began staying away from our sleeping chamber again. Sometimes I spent the night in lamp-lit vigil at the shrine of Bronze Uncle. The god must have felt disappointment in me, wondering why I came so rarely when my life was in order and so often when I had specific needs.

Nol passed the nights alone too. But perhaps he consoled himself by picturing in his mind the account records that showed his fortune growing by the day.

Part Three
Temptation

In the following years, the reversal of the mountain-temple's orientation made us wealthier than anyone outside the immediate royal family. Close to thirty thousand people came to be living on our land at the western approach. Each paid rent to our stewards, and with that money Nol acquired other land in the Capital and as far away as the Saltwater Sea to the south.

By his order, our house near the palace compound was torn down. A new one, of twice the size and ornamentation, was built in its place, with ponds and gardens of its own. Forty priests came to chant blessings on its day of completion. Nol also expanded his collection of money-generating properties. Among them were stables for horses and elephants, a copper mine, rice lands and a set of villas in the capital at which visiting gentry put up at enormous rents.

And he got his new palanquin. It was larger and more elaborately decorated than the one that Kiri the cattle keeper had owned (but no longer did – the collapse of his businesses forced him to get rid of it). Nol's was inlaid with jewels, its carrying shafts were tipped with bronze Naga serpents and hefted by not twelve but sixteen slaves. When he rode around the city in it, people pressed their faces to the dust.

How he loved that palanquin. How I detested it. There were times I longed to set it on fire as it lay in its storage shed behind our house. But of course I did not.

Male and female are opposites, and thus Heaven places them together. But in addition to this duality of flesh, I was coming to feel that Nol and I were opposites in most every question of judgment and values.

39: All the reds and yellows

However questionable the benefits of the temple's reorientation for our family, there was no doubt that it brought much good to the village we owned, Veya, a half hour's walk down the track from the future western gate. Perhaps that was why Heaven allowed my husband's ruse to stand. The village's people now sold rice and vegetables to shopkeepers in the burgeoning settlement being built on our land. They rented out carts and oxen. Daughters served food in restaurants, sons became messengers and labourers and night guards.

I continued to visit the village and make minor gifts – water bowls for the shrine, herbs and powders for the clinic, a new rice-storage facility, and fifty weight of silver to endow a hermitage headed by a priest who was cousin to the headman. I suppose I saw my gifts as a silent rebuke to my husband. See how these people are not greedy, they want only enough of life's bounty to be comfortable, grow their rice and raise their children.

One day, returning from a provincial trip, I arrived at the village under the escort of the sergeant and his squad of soldiers.

The official reason for my presence was a ceremony to mark the first year of the hermitage. Yet as the rites were conducted, I could sense that everyone was waiting for something that would come afterward. And sure enough, when the priests were done, the headman told me there was something he'd like to show me. And so I went with him, leaving behind my maid and soldiers. We walked along a paddy dike to a copse at the far side of the fields, me still having no idea what this was about. From behind us, villagers watched, and I could feel that they wanted to follow but dared not.

Beyond the copse, we crossed a stream on a bamboo footbridge that seemed newly built. There began a trail, edged with white stones, that wound its way up a thickly forested hillside. This brief climb brought us to a sunlit clearing on a slope and a small wooden house. It looked toward distant trees that seemed a gentle blue.

'Goodness,' I said. 'What a pretty place.'

'It is for you, Lady Sray.'

'What can you mean?'

'It is for you to use whenever you wish. Our gift to you, as Heaven would have it, for your so many gifts to us.'

The headman's tone was a shade diffident. I could guess why. He was worrying that he had miscalculated, that a woman of my standing, whatever she might say, could never sleep in a place like this, without servants, without the soft mats and mosquito nets of the city.

I turned to look at the house again. I had so much already. How could I accept this?

'You are so kind, headman, but really...' When I saw the disappointment on his face, I softened a bit. 'But...but may I go look?'

'Of course.'

First I stood a moment at the pond, gazing at the mother duck and her brood. Then I climbed the steps. Inside was a loom. How charming, I thought.

And then...and then, a mother duck emerged from some foliage with four ducklings hurrying behind her. Straight down to the water this happy party went and presently they were all bobbing up and down.

I broke down in sobs right there. The headman must have heard, I was so loud.

When I stepped back to the door, he was all confidence. 'You'll find the sunrise is quite striking from here, Lady Sray. It reflects off the water in the paddies. It's as if the gods have decided to put all the reds and yellows of creation in one place, right out there, and let us watch and marvel how there can be so many.'

What a beautiful thing to say. I felt that a kind spirit had put the words right in his mouth, as a signal that I should say yes.

'Would you allow me to stay here tonight?' I asked. 'Just for one night?'

I spent that night at the house, and the next one, and then I sent a messenger back to the city with word that I would be away for a while longer, but that no one should worry.

Those next days I have never forgotten. At dawn I sat on the steps and watched the sunrise, which was just as the headman had described. Later I sent the ducks out to forage. I gave each one a name. I worked the loom, I prepared simple rice and fish for myself on the brazier, using supplies that were left at the edge of the clearing, overnight so as not to disturb me.

Of course, I was not really alone. I became aware that there was a jungle path that made a wide circle around the hill and ended at a leafy spot down below that was meant to be a hidden look-out. There from time to time I spied village men and women, looking up in my direction, and sometimes Sergeant Sen, no doubt concerned I was on my own up here, though I had come under no threat in many years.

How many days passed before the message came, the one that set my life in a new direction? I cannot remember. Such was my bliss in life on the hill.

40: Channary's dolour

All human events, good and bad, are connected in some way and influence each other, don't you believe? The change that was to come for me was set in motion in part by an admirable, benevolent quality: the love of orchids that resided in the heart of His Majesty the former King. In the final years of his reign, he spent much of his time at an orchid farm on a small lake just north of Angkor. After his death and the rise of our new King, this place fell into disuse, until one day the concubine Rom decided to go have a look. She promptly claimed it. It was not the flowers that she found attractive – her first act of proprietorship, in fact, was to order the beds and trellises dug up and a new cooking hut built in their place. Rather, what she liked was the large teak house, with its mats and carvings and veranda that gave onto the lake. By the water's edge was a dock with two small sampans for lazy paddling across the still surface and through the reeds and lilies that lined the far shore. So, when her monthly flow began, and there was no chance of receiving a call to the King's chamber, Rom often decamped to the lake. Sometimes she took along a group of concubines. Who went and who was left behind was one of the measures by which the girls judged their standing with the woman they all addressed as Elder Sister.

One evening, at the time I was staying in the hilltop hut, Rom named six to go with her on a trip the following day. One of them was Channary, a quiet beauty from a village near the city. She had come to the concubine pavilion six months earlier, nominated by her district's headman, and had caught the King's eye from the start – her trips to his sleeping chamber now numbered fifty-eight, according to the pavilion's log. But the girl, to everyone's surprise, showed no pride in this distinction. An air of dolour hung over her at all times. Often she laid down to sleep in the evenings before the others did, and rose while they still slumbered. They would awake to see her sitting outside by the lotus pond, alone with her thoughts, or kneeling at the shrine whispering devotions that went on longer than other girls'. Anyone who tried to draw her out came away with very little, only the feeling that Heaven had taken her from home but chosen to deny her a vocation for the new life.

No one but Rom had ever been called so frequently to the royal chamber, and so for weeks the junior concubines had been watching to see whether the Elder Sister would respond with spite. Yet she showed no discernible ill will. On the contrary, warmth and generosity were on display. She called Channary to sit with her in the afternoons. She fed her from her own basket of cut fruit, she invited her to play with the boy Darit. And now there was this suggestion that she come to the lake house.

Rom rarely invited outsiders, but for this trip she sent a messenger to the parasol compound. Who was she inviting but Bopa! My girl accepted, though she hadn't been to the pavilion in months. You see again what a poor judge of character I was – I had believed that it was safe for me to go on a trip, that her pavilion days were behind her. Love and instruction from the texts, I was sure, had destroyed any interest in going there. In my daughter's defence, I'm sure the invitation was hard to resist. For so long she'd been sitting at home tended only by the maid Yan. Poor Bopa had few friends of her own.

So as soon as Rom's messenger left, Bopa told Yan to prepare her jade pendants and armlets for the trip. Yan didn't like the idea, but – again, what can a maid really do? She made up her mind to speak to me immediately when I returned.

The next morning, two covered oxcarts waited in front of the concubine pavilion. By the first one stood Rom and Channary and two bodyguards, by the second were the other concubines chosen for the trip.

'Hello, Bopa!' called Rom. 'Come ride with us.'

I doubt that Bopa noticed, but Yan, at her side as always, sensed unfriendly eyes among the girls in the second cart – probably the girl who had once painted ash on my daughter's face was among them. Cart assignments on these journeys were another form of the Elder Sister's slights and favours.

Rom chattered as the vehicles crossed the city, Yan walking alongside with the other servants, bodyguards going ahead to part the crowds. Beyond the north gate, the drivers turned onto a curving road that passed through paddy land and villages. Rom kept up her talk, telling Channary how much she would like the lake, how new drapes had been put up in the villa only the previous week.

But it seemed that once they left the city, the young concubine was paying less and less attention to the conversation. 'My goodness, Channary,' Rom was heard to say. 'I feel we've lost you! You keep gaping at things we're passing. What's so interesting out there?'

And a bit later: 'Come on! You've seen something special, haven't you? Share it with us.'

Finally Channary answered. This village, the one the cart was passing through, was her home village.

'*Really?*' said Rom, and now her voice had quite a lot of concern in it. 'I wouldn't have brought you if I'd known! Come on now – turn your face away. We can't have anyone seeing you. People from the old place always make a fuss over a concubine and if some man takes an interest in you, even if it's just a look, there's always the chance that word will get back to the palace and there will be terrible trouble.'

But the young concubine protested, showing life for the first time on the trip. 'Please – I want to see. Just the little shrine that's coming up on this side of the road. That would be enough. It's been so long....'

'Impossible,' declared Rom. She took the girl by the shoulders and eased her to the mat. 'Now lie down and pretend you're sleeping. No one will know it's you.'

The girl did not resist. She lay on her side. Bopa saw the glint of a tear on her cheek.

The cart was passing the village's market now. One of the bodyguards fell back and knelt down at a fruit vendor's mat. Yan watched the guard – her attention was drawn because she thought it strange that a stout fighting man would break ranks in this way. Soon he stood up, fruit in a banana leaf bag. His eyes went left and right, left and right and then he saw what he was looking for, a young man selling amulets. The soldier approached this man and delivered some kind of message. Whatever it was, it seemed to shock the young man.

At the lake, the party was welcomed with water and sweets by servant girls who'd been sent out from the palace in advance. Rom announced that she would lie down for a while in the resthouse, but that the others should go have fun on their own. Most everyone made for the dock. Without Rom on the scene, some unseemly competition broke out for spaces on the boats. Bopa did not get one, which was no surprise. In a situation like that, she always relied on someone speaking up for her. She turned away and went off to look around, on her own. It was better to stay away from the house, lest Elder Sister be woken. So she poked around a small annex pavilion that stood across a wide yard from the resthouse. She looked into the cooking hut, then walked along a gravelled path that followed the shoreline, feeling boredom setting in already. Ahead she saw Channary, seated alone by the water's edge. Even from this distance, it was clear that the girl remained in low spirits; Bopa thought it better to turn around.

That evening, the girls gathered in the house's main room. From the cooking hut came the scents and sounds of food being put to flame in iron vessels. Food and honey wine were put out and everyone partook. When they were done, Rom suggested some song singing. Girls let out delighted squeals and moved close together, snuggling like a litter of puppies. Rom gestured to one: you go first. Flattered, the girl began a ballad about the gone-away sweetheart of a buffalo tender.

Channary sat alone and seemed hardly to hear. When her turn came, she did her best with a song that was meant to be happy, about the joys of harvest-time flirtation. But her voice cracked half way through, and in the end the song sounded only mournful. When she finished, silence set in, and everyone thought the contest was over, but Elder Sister insisted that it was beautiful and that Channary should give the group another song. And then another. Finally, after that third one, Channary asked. Please, Elder Sister, please, would it be all right if I go lie down alone in the annex across the yard? I'm so tired. Rom said of course, that would be fine, and told a maid to set up a mosquito net.

Bopa fell into a doze a few minutes later – she had swallowed more than a cup or two of the honey wine. Yan was there to cover her up with a cloth. Bopa awoke some time afterwards to find that the party was over, that all but one of the lamps were out and the concubines were settled in all around her in the room, on their mats for the night. Rom was still up, however, sitting by a window.

Later, Bopa was awoken by a scuffle somewhere outside. There followed male shouts, then a piercing scream.

'What is it?'

Yan, who was lying nearby, already knew. 'Elder Sister heard a thief outside and told the bodyguards to go see.' Rom had followed them, it seemed.

First one girl, then all of them, found courage to go to the door to look. Whatever it was, it was happening in some woods beyond the annex. Then, one by one, though no one had given them permission, they spilled out the door and hurried across the yard and through some bushes and trees, where they saw a torch burning. Rom's two guards came into view. They were standing over a form on the ground. Rom was beside them, holding the torch.

When she saw the concubines approaching, she raised her hands. 'Go back, girls, let's all go back! This is no sight for your eyes to see.' Bopa strained to see anyway, and made out a young man's body on the ground, motionless, bleeding from wounds around the middle.

Rom renewed her demand, and the girls began picking their way back through the darkness. At the annex, they came upon Channary sitting in the doorway, trembling. Several girls moved to comfort her, but Rom called them off. 'Go back to the resthouse. I'll stay and look after her.'

Of course no one could sleep after that and they passed the hours until dawn trading stories of who had seen and heard what. One girl voiced a thought: do you think it's possible the thief came in here first? Everyone scurried to check their things. But nothing was missing.

When morning rice was served, Rom returned to the house.

Their sister Channary was unhurt, she said. She was resting and the guards would stay with her for now. Rom announced too that officials were coming out from the palace to investigate. Several of the girls traded significant glances over that. Bopa was puzzled – a thief was just a thief.

In early afternoon, they were surprised to see the Brahmin Subhadra approaching outside, accompanied by two scribes and a group of soldiers. He went straight to the annex, posting his soldiers outside it. After a while, the girls were certain they could hear their sister Channary weeping. Maids put out more food, but no one touched it. After more than an hour, the Brahmin and Rom came back to the resthouse. Rom announced that he would question each girl, separately. Bopa was frightened to hear she would be first.

The priest took her down by the dock, away from the house, and there they sat on a mat someone had laid on the grass.

'You will recount to me everything you know. You will speak with the understanding that Heaven is listening and that everything, everything you say will be the truth.' I can only imagine the terror my daughter felt on being addressed in that way.

How, he asked, did she, who is not a concubine, come to be here? Who rode in which cart? Were there any stops? Sometimes he cut her off even before she finished answering.

'Now, Rom has told us that Channary asked many times to come to the resthouse here. Is this true?'

'Yes, sir,' said Bopa, though she could not recall such a request. But if the Elder Sister had said so…

'And that Channary was quite interested when the cart passed through that village on the road, that she kept looking out, as if she were trying to catch sight of someone.'

'Yes,' said Bopa. She felt on more solid ground now, because she had a clear memory of that.

'And at this point Channary admitted that this was her home village and Rom then insisted that she lie down, out of sight.'

'Yes.'

'And she told her there that she must have no contact with people from her old village, especially any young men.'

'Yes. She said all of those thing.'

The Brahmin seemed unhappy with these answers, but he went on. How long did the party last? How much wine was consumed?

'Now,' said the Brahmin, 'did Channary herself suggest that she sleep in the annex, or was it someone else's idea?'

'It was her own suggestion, sir.'

'Don't lie! Don't repeat what someone else has told you to say!' Bopa was stunned. She began to cry, but this got no sympathy.

'Now listen to me carefully. Rom has told us that she was awoken by a sound outside, near the annex. She called to the guards to go check. They say that when they came near the annex, they could see through a window that your sister Channary was inside her sleeping net with a man, in an embrace of love. The man saw the guards and leapt out of the net, ran from the annex down the path that leads into the woods. The guards caught up to him and brought him to the ground. He pulled out a knife and tried to slash them. They were forced to kill him. Now, is this what happened?'

'If the Elder Sister says...'

'I am not asking that. I'm asking what you saw, with your own eyes.'

'I couldn't see anything. I was inside sleeping.'

Now the Brahmin shared with her something very interesting. It had been determined, he said, that the young man was from Channary's home village. Did she know that before being called as a concubine, Channary had been engaged to a young man? It was *this young man.*

'Let me tell you, Bopa, that Channary says that there was never any man with her in the mosquito net, that she was sleeping on her own, that suddenly the guards began chasing someone outside. You are acquainted with this girl Channary. I ask you now – do you believe she is capable of such terrible betrayal of His Majesty, or would you believe her version of events? Or is it possible that this young man was lured to the resthouse, perhaps told by someone that his former betrothed was in danger and had urgently begged that he come?'

You can see what had happened, I'm sure. But I'm afraid that my daughter, close as she was to it, was not able to. She felt only confusion and anxiety. I suppose it was for the best that now she broke down, weeping, and was not able to offer an opinion on this question either way, and at least did not suggest that this poor girl Channary was guilty of anything.

The Brahmin let her go after that, and she slunk back to the resthouse. She drank water while the next girl's questioning began. Later, she closed her eyes and drifted off. When she awoke, from troubling dreams she could not remember, she ate some rice. Rom passed close by several times. Bopa sought her eyes, hoping to convey that she had stood up for her, but each time the woman was looking somewhere else.

The concubines were all kept in that room all night, while the questioning continued. Bopa looked for Yan, but she had disappeared.

Late the next morning, a servant girl approached with a message: Sovan was waiting outside. Yet again, Bopa was stunned. She went to find him, and without preliminaries he announced he was taking her back to the Capital.

They walked silently from the house, Sovan carrying her things. Ahead, a hired oxcart was waiting in the failing light. Yan jumped down from it – it was she who had summoned Sovan.

By the time they passed through the city gate, Bopa felt able to talk about what had happened.

'It must have been upsetting, sister,' said Sovan when she was done. 'And perhaps for the Brahmin too. He must be sure of the evidence. It's a very serious accusation that's been made against Channary, with a very serious punishment.'

'What would that be?'

'It is what you would guess, sister. Let's not speak of it now.'

At the gate of the parasol compound, Sovan said good-bye, so as to respect my husband's edict. Yan helped my girl bathe at the jars, then took her to her room. 'Lie down, mistress, lie down,' she whispered, holding open her mosquito net. Yan blew out the lamp, then sat down to wait for sleep to overtake her charge. Bopa lay still and pretended to fall off. After the maid left, she crept out of the net and to a box in which garments were kept. In it, hidden, there was also a small wine jar, her secret friend. Yan returned to the room to find Bopa upending the jar.

Bopa had got enough down to sleep. The next morning, Yan brought rice and fish to her mat. Bopa ate, then, when the maid was away washing the bowls, she stole away to the concubine pavilion.

41: The heavenly sister

So that is what finally forced me from the little house at the village.

Before my son went to fetch my daughter from the old orchid farm, he dispatched a note to me. 'Please come back immediately,' it read. 'Bopa needs your help and guidance. I will wait for you tomorrow afternoon at the south gate.'

He was there as promised when my cart arrived. During the ride across the city, he recounted the events as best he understood them and Bopa's subsequent disappearance into the concubine pavilion.

We fell into silence. I upbraided myself for having left my daughter alone. So, right there in the cart, I made up my mind. I would go to the pavilion and take my daughter back. If I had to confront Rom, I would confront her.

An hour later, I arrived at the pavilion's gate. With a sentry looking on, I called through. A maid listened on the other side, then went away without answering. After ten minutes she came back and opened the door, offering no explanation for the delay. I felt offended, but said nothing – my purpose was to retrieve my daughter. The maid led me around a lotus pond, across a footbridge and then into a large but empty pavilion.

There I was left, again without explanation. I stood; sitting would imply I meant to stay a while. Some minutes passed; footsteps and whispered words sounded from a doorway that was covered with a drape.

Then the cloth was pulled smartly aside and a woman entered, wearing a green silk sampot, silver necklaces, bangles and armlets, in general more jewellery than I was used to seeing on a person in a private setting. Two maids trailed behind.

'Good morning,' she said. 'I am Rom, chief concubine to His Majesty. I am sorry you were kept waiting so long.'

'Thank you for receiving me,' I replied evenly. 'I am Sray, mother of Bopa.'

'Yes, I know who you are. Who doesn't? But please, please sit down.' She gazed on me in a way that made me look aside. She sat down. And I? I felt compelled to follow.

'The beautiful merchant woman,' said Rom, in a not unfriendly way. 'Or is it the beautiful devotee of Heaven? People say it both ways, did you know?'

'I am not aware that people speak of me at all. But in your presence, it becomes quite clear how plain I am.'

'Such modesty! Heaven smiles on that.' She gave a short laugh. 'Just like your daughter. You have brought her up very well, if I may say so. She has the most lovely of faces. It's quite like yours, really. As perfect as a lotus blossom. I can see her in you right away.'

'She and I are not like you describe...'

'But you are! And you know, your daughter is not the least bit vain about it. It's good to have someone like her at this place. She's an example for everyone, and not just in beauty. If something unsettling happens, the girls turn to her instinctively because they know she'll know what to do.'

Was that an allusion to something that happened at the orchid farm? If it was, I hoped I could believe at least this much of what the woman said. I replied: 'You are kind to say that. But really, I do not want to take up your time. I have come for my daughter, that's all. She is needed at home.'

Rom clapped her hands twice. Another maid appeared at the door. 'Bring fruit for our guest.'

'Really, really that's not necessary,' I said, trying for firmness. 'I've only come for my daughter.'

'I'm sorry, but she isn't here. She's gone to one of the other pavilions across the compound, with some of the younger concubines. I'll have someone go get her.' She glanced to a girl by the door, and it was remarkable how quickly that girl set off.

'So,' said Rom. 'Bopa tells me that you travel quite a bit. You've just come back from a trip?'

'A short one, yes. I was in a village to the south.'

'Oh! Those places are so pretty – away from the strains of life here. Which one?'

I told her, then wished I hadn't.

Fruit and tea were served, and Rom insisted that I eat. When we finished, she said: 'Now, I know your daughter, so it's only fair that you know my son. Come see him for a minute – I hope you won't be bored.'

She rose and I could only follow. We passed across the pond's bridge, then down a long wooden arcade. At the end, just before a corner, Rom stopped and signalled for silence. 'Please,' she whispered. 'Let's just look from here. Otherwise he'll stop. He hates for me to watch him.'

We moved ahead two more steps so that we could just see around the corner and into a small courtyard. At one end was a straw target. At the other, a boy of about ten, holding a bow, a dozen arrows at his feet. By him was an instructor, in the uniform of the palace guard. The man voiced a command, and the boy snatched up an arrow from the ground, strung it, pulled and let fly. It was a single, smooth, practiced motion. The arrow went straight, piercing the target barely off centre.

Rom gave me a silent look of delight. 'Let's go, then. Before he sees us.'

As we walked away, Rom said: 'I'll tell you a secret – he's going to give a demonstration for His Majesty next week.'

'You must be proud.'

'A bit, I will admit,' she said. 'His Majesty is quite interested in him. Sometimes I think...'

Her silence demanded what I said next: 'Think what?'

'That perhaps he's becoming a favourite.'

Back inside the pavilion, relief – my daughter was waiting. The girl put hands together in bashful greeting. She and I would have a talk later, away from this place.

Rom walked us to the compound's gate. There she made an elaborate good-bye. I began to feel my distrust returning. But then she stepped to the side and Bopa and I passed through the gate together. We had made our escape.

But then, an enormous shock: Not five paces away stood His Majesty! All I could do was go to the ground, face down.

Why had I not thought of this danger when I came strutting over to the pavilion, so filled with righteous purpose? Had he come to seek me out or was this just an accident? How could I withdraw? I wish that I could say that these were the questions that coursed through my mind as I crouched at his feet. But no, my thoughts were of the blood that filled my cheeks, of whether he noticed or could at this moment see it, of the workaday sampot that I was wearing, of my instant's glimpse of him, facing me full on, and that he seemed, for that instant at least, to be as much at a loss as I was.

I remained on the ground, and he remained standing before me, a gap of silence lengthening. Then he took a step closer.

The dust of a sovereign's feet. We are taught from childhood to revere even that aspect of a King's sojourn on earth. I was close enough now to sense this dust, and I will tell you that I was struck with the feeling that it seemed no different than that of any other man's feet. And that somehow I took this as a signal that perhaps there was no barrier to speaking to him as I would with any other man.

Then Rom's voice broke up my thoughts. 'Majesty! We were not expecting you.' That drew no response so she pressed on. 'Let me take you inside. We will bring tea for you in the pavilion.'

My head was still down. But right then I chose to raise it. Our eyes connected.

'Lady Sray...' He could get nothing further out.

Not a word came from me. But I dared get to my feet and face him. There came another silence.

Rom broke in again. 'Majesty, the Lady was on her way home. She will continue and I will take you into the pavilion.'

Again, the King seemed not to hear. 'Lady, it has been too long since I have seen you.'

'I am sorry it has displeased you, Majesty. But the work that Heaven has chosen for me takes me out of the Capital often.'

'But now you are here.'

'Yes, Majesty. I have come to take my daughter home.'

The King's eye went to the girl. For the first time now I remembered she was there. 'My daughter, Majesty. Her name is Bopa.' She was behaving according to protocol and remained on the ground. The King gave an appreciative nod to her. 'Whatever your business,' he said, turning back to me, 'I am happy to have found you here. Perhaps we can have tea in the pavilion before you go. Can you spare the time, Lady Sray?'

It would still have been possible to beg off. But no, with a dip of my head, I acquiesced. He led the way, slowly, lest I be forced to walk too quickly. My eyes went down, and there they came upon the taut back of his calves, sinews moving in outline below the skin. My gaze rose and came to rest on his shoulder blades.

He entered the pavilion, and as he did he gave me a glance over his shoulder, then smiled and looked away. In that gesture I saw confirmation of what I had seen in that first instant of our meeting, the same nervousness that I was feeling. This also confirmed the sign. A King behaving as a King would show no diffidence in dealing with one of his subjects.

I passed inside, and I noticed now that no one else had followed us from the gate. 'Please, please, sit,' he said. He motioned toward a mat laid out in a spot obscured from the outside by a hanging drape. We took our places.

'You are comfortable?'

I nodded yes, and attempted to still my breathing.

'Do you recall, Lady Sray, the last time that we met?'

'I do, Majesty.'

'I came to your house. You kindly received me, but our visit was cut short by my Brahmin. There was much more I wished to ask you about charity and other works. And...'

He paused to collect his thoughts. 'I will admit something to you, Lady Sray. It is more than that. Sometimes when I am passing through the streets of the Capital, or walking across the palace compound, I look for you. Yet I have never seen you, until just now. I must ask – do you avoid me?'

'My duties keep me elsewhere, Majesty.'

'You say that, Lady. But is it the only explanation?'

A maid appeared, bringing porcelain pot and cups on a tray. She set it down between us and withdrew.

I poured for him.

'Lady Sray, please, you did not answer my question.'

'Majesty, I have given an answer. But you choose not to accept it.'

'Because I sense that there is more to say.'

'Majesty, you know as well as I that there has been an issue of holy law.'

'Yes.' He hung his head for a moment.

I poured again, this time filling my own cup. He watched me intently. 'There is that,' he said. 'But surely it does not prevent us from drinking tea together.'

With two hands, I raised my cup. There it remained, at my mouth. I was suddenly disquieted – the cup now seemed something to hide behind.

Then the King's hand moved slowly toward me. He put it forward as an offer, to be accepted or turned away. There was nothing in the gesture that hinted of force. Now his index finger came to rest atop my cup, then moved it down, gently, to reveal my face. Then that finger, inverted, found its way to the skin below my chin and brought my face up so that my eyes met his. His were pleading. I swallowed, incapable of looking away. But then his eyes left mine. They followed his finger as it travelled first the slope of my neck, then the ridge of my shoulder, then down again, tracing the flesh of my arm. It came to rest on my wrist. My wrist, the one part of me that he had touched before, by candlelight that night as I laid in my sleeping chamber.

At this precise moment, the spell broke. I turned away, ashamed. I at once sensed that in this room was present the ghost of His Majesty's brother, gleeful over the harm it was accomplishing.

'Majesty, you mustn't...' It was all I could do to get that out in a whisper.

'Please don't say that.' He took my hand.

'Heaven does not intend me to unite with the blessed monarch. It has united me with another man already.'

His hand tightened on mine just slightly. 'Please! For years I have hoped that Heaven might choose to change that. And when we met outside, I had a sense that it had.'

'Majesty, I thought just now that it had, but I am sure I was mistaken. It was a trap.'

'What, what do you mean?'

'I cannot say. Only that we must resist. Both of us. We must resist.'

'So *you* too feel the need to resist. You have said it!'

'No!'

'Whatever the law, if it has not been put aside, then we must be put it aside ourselves. Please, Lady, I have waited so long...'

'*Majesty*!'

It was not my voice but Subhadra's. He was crouching by the door; he had dared enter the pavilion.

The King's fierce character returned in a flash.

'Leave!'

But the Brahmin did not. Rather, he spoke again, addressing his words to the mat. 'I cannot, Majesty. My duty, the Empire, the future of the reign all require that I remain.'

'I said leave!'

'Majesty, if I could, I would be gone. But I cannot, I cannot.' He went back to a full crouch and continued talking in a voice barely audible through his whiskers. 'If I leave, Majesty, I will live a while longer, but I will be delivered straight to hell when I die, and I will be tormented by flames and scorpions and rats and I will be reborn as a slug. That will happen, Majesty, because I will have allowed worse to happen to you.'

The King gave no response, and this gave the Brahmin courage to go on.

'If you complete what you wish to do with this woman, Majesty, it will mean the end of the reign, the collapse of the Empire, the Chams dancing on the smouldering ruins of this great city. It will have that result, Majesty, because this woman has the potential to be your destruction. Bringing her into your fold will set off a revolt first among your own women, then among your soldiers, then your people at large. The gods will pass your mandate on to another, Majesty. Your temple will never be completed, your name never inscribed on the holy tablets in Heaven.'

'How is that possible?' His Majesty shouted.

'It is because she is not like any other, Majesty. The proof is in your interest in her. For all monarchs, there must be things that are forbidden.'

'But look at her!' said the King. He strode to me and took me by the shoulders, turning me to face the priest. 'She is not the incarnation of some demon. She is purity, she is virtue. Anyone can see!'

'You are right, Majesty. She is the incarnation of....of your heavenly sister.'

'*What*?'

'Your sister, Majesty. In Heaven. It is taught that a King must treat another man's wife as if she were a sister. But in this case, she is in fact your sister. In Heaven. Your Majesty exists there in divine form, as does this woman. You are brother and sister there. The deities would be incensed were carnal relations to occur between your earthly avatars. You must live apart. But Heaven is merciful and just. It has seen that this woman, your sister, is well provided for on earth, that she has a home and children and wealth.'

The King sank to his knees, his determination faltering.

Subhadra came closer and whispered. 'Majesty, Heaven sends trials for all its children on earth. While an ordinary man can fail the trial, it can never be that way for a sovereign of the world.'

The King was rocking slowly on his heels, his head down.

'Majesty, you must send this woman away. It must be by your own order, and it must be because you have decided that it is best.'

The King waited a moment before answering. 'You are certain about this, there is no doubt?'

'I am certain, Majesty. I have known of this woman's identity in Heaven for many years, but have not wanted to trouble Your Majesty with it. The principles of conjugal life that the holy men devised for you served the purpose for a long time. But now it is time that you know the truth.'

'Then let her leave!' he cried, looking away.

I moved for the door. I ran to the gate and found Bopa, waiting with a clutch of concubines and servants. I took her arm and marched her off. I resolved that I would do whatever was required of me to never come together with His Majesty again, to remain faithful to my husband, to respect holy law.

At our house, I left my daughter in her room in the care of Yan, then went to my own and closed the drapes. I lay down, and for close to an hour I wept. For so many things. My anger with myself, my frustration, my betrayal, and for a very selfish concern, my inability to know how long the Brahmin had been at the door before he spoke up, how much he had seen and heard. There was one thing of which I was certain, however: the priest had invented on the spot this notion of the Heavenly brother and sister. Had such a link been real, I was sure I would have felt some inkling of it long ago.

Later Nol came in. He had heard what had happened, at least an account that portrayed me in the kindest possible light. We embraced. I wept again and did nothing to correct his misunderstanding.

The following day, Subhadra called on me at the house, unannounced. I was of course apprehensive as we sat down over tea. But as we spoke, there was nothing in his words or manner that conveyed disapproval of anything on my part. I took this to mean he had seen nothing. I knew that had it been otherwise, he would have said nothing but his convictions about personal probity would have brought a certain coldness into his demeanour. However cordially we might have behaved, my friendship – I think I can call it that – with this man who had been only a force for good in my own life and the life of the Empire would have come to an end. So there it was – my secret safely locked up again. I could continue to pose as the virtuous female wanting only for the attentions to end.

No, the purpose of the visit was to inform me that the King had decreed I must leave the city. I immediately thought of the hut in the village, and suggested it, but Subhadra said no, much greater distances would be required and an absence of a considerable length of time.

'The Empire will soon be sending an embassy to China,' he said. 'There are many things to discuss with the authorities there. Trade is one of them. Lady Sray, I urge you to go with the group. It will be far away, and certainly you know well the things that the Empire can offer for sale.'

Had I not just promised myself to do whatever was required of me? I could only submit. 'I will go. And I will take my daughter.'

'That...that I'm afraid would not be advisable.' He seemed to struggle with his next words. 'There are many young men on the ships. It would not be an appropriate place for a young unmarried woman.'

'But...'

'Furthermore, I am prepared to oversee her safety in your absence and give her instruction in the texts. I pledge that no harm will come to her, that she will in all ways lead a moral life. She will be very well seen to.'

In the end, I gave in to this too. I asked myself, what success have you had in setting your daughter on the right path? Surely the Brahmin will have more.

But before I took my leave, I had a request. 'Could you see to it that she spends no time with Rom?'

'Lady Sray, your daughter will have no contact with her, of that you can be absolutely certain. I recognize as well as you the character of the concubine. The incident at the orchid farm made this once again very clear.'

'Do you mean, sir, that the concubine Channary is not to be punished?'

'She will not be punished – His Majesty agreed to that this morning. On the face of it, the evidence was against her, but I feel that the hand of the senior concubine was involved in the incident at the farm. Channary will not remain in the pavilion; she will return to her home village and take up residence with her parents.'

'His Majesty is merciful.'

'Yes...' He looked to me as if to say something more, but did not.

Our meeting was over. 'I will go to China, with peace of mind. Thank you!'

The following morning, I left the house with a maid. Sergeant Sen and a small guard detail awaited us at the city's south gate, prepared like us to be gone for a full year.

42: A house that floats

When my maid and I arrived at the port on the Freshwater Sea, Mr Chen was waiting in his solicitous way at a wharf where a very large ship was tied up. He helped us females along the boarding plank, talking all the way to allay the nervousness that I'm sure he could sense. Preparations for the voyage are proceeding on schedule, he said. You'll find the ship to be safe, and comfortable too. On what other kind of travel conveyance, he asked, can you have your choice of food, and room to walk around when your limbs get stiff?

But the first thing I saw on deck was cause for shock: two very large wooden cages. Inside each was a bulky grey animal, its body the size of a horse's, but with short, stocky legs and on the snout the strangest sight – a horn. One of the beasts lay on its side in laboured sleep, the other stood feeding from a basket of leaves placed between the struts of the cage. I stared; I had never imagined such beasts could exist.

'Gifts to the Chinese emperor,' explained Mr Chen. 'They run loose in the forests in the far west of our Empire. The Chinese monarch has a menagerie, and they will join it.'

He led me through a tiny door, then helped me down a set of very steep steps. I had imagined a great open chamber below; instead there as a narrow corridor. Mr Chen told us again, don't worry. He opened a door. Inside was a room brightened by scented flowers and light from a tiny window; mats had been laid on the floor for sleeping. There was a teak box for storing clothes and a small table on which sat my portable shrine.

'Your home for the voyage, Lady Sray.'

I did feel better now, and thanked him for seeing to everything so thoughtfully.

Then he showed me a smoky compartment in the rear where food would be prepared. A cook was sorting through bundles of rice, fruit, spices and vegetables bought in the market. There were live chickens too, in wicker cages. The supplies would last quite a few weeks, I could see, and Mr Chen explained that in any case the ship would be stopping during the first part of the voyage at waterside towns and fresh food would be bought in markets there.

I returned to my cabin to find my maid on the floor, weeping.

'I'm so afraid, Lady,' she whimpered. 'A house can't float on water! When I was a girl, the river next to my village rose, and carried away all of the houses. We watched from the top of a hill. They broke into pieces and disappeared in the water.'

'That won't happen here, Da. The ship is not a house. It's a very large sampan. It has gone to China many times, and it is blessed by the gods, Mr Chen told me. We must trust the gods, as always, and we must trust him. He is a man of his word.'

I sat beside the girl and put a hand on hers. She was new to the household staff, young and energetic – on land, at least. I had never seen tears.

An hour later, gongs rang to signal departure. We went up on deck. Chinese crewmen were running this way and that, wielding ropes and strange metal implements. Yet we remained at the dock. The ship did in fact seem too big to move. But, then, without Da or me even noticing, it edged away – our sleeping ship was taking up! We soon saw how: In the water up front, at the end of a long rope, was a sampan with six stout men, each paddling furiously. Somehow their small boat was pulling this large one, advancing it majestically down a narrow channel at what was even less than a walking pace. Ahead was open water – the Freshwater Sea, explained the always helpful Mr Chen, who had silently appeared at my side. Soon the sampan broke away, its men shouting farewells, and our own crewmen hoisted large sections of rigid bamboo matting up a pole, thick as a tree trunk, that grew straight up from the deck's middle. They did the same to a second, smaller pole up front. Wind took the matting suddenly in its grip, and the ship lurched ahead, slicing through waves with the strength of a wild animal set suddenly free. I scurried to the centre of the ship. The motion was making me feel ill.

From behind, Sergeant Sen shouted. I hadn't seen him come up. 'Mr Chen! Please slow the ship down. The   Lady is experiencing discomfort!' He said it for me, but I could see that he found the speed disorienting too.

Mr Chen called in his language to the captain, who called out orders to the crew, and the boat settled down to a tolerable pace.

The merchant came to me. 'My apologies, Lady Sray. I think the crew wanted to show off what their ship can do. You'll feel better quickly, I promise. Everyone has a bit of trouble at first. But you will get used to this and quite a bit more. When we're out on the sea that tastes of salt, the waves will be quite a bit higher, sometimes higher than the ship itself.'

This was hardly reassuring. 'They don't flood the ship?'

'They don't. Otherwise, we would never see Chinese goods in the Empire. It's like the ship and the sea are talking to each other, like they're good friends. The ship knows exactly how to rise and fall to keep the sea happy, and the sea is careful that it never rises or falls more than the ship can manage.'

I took comfort in that, and went back to the railing. Ahead was a second ship, a near copy of ours, which carried a minister from the Council of Brahmins who would act as representative of the King.

I walked to the ship's rear and from a railing there said good-bye to Hanuman's hill and the towers of the Temple of the Trinity atop it. Pennants, tiny at this distance, were flying from poles up there, lashed to guesthouses I had rebuilt. I looked back to the water. My stomach was calm now, as Mr Chen had promised. For the first time in days, I felt at ease.

'Lady.'

It was Da. I turned to find her holding out a straw bag.

'I'm sorry, Lady, but I forgot to give this to you. It was delivered to the house last night by a runner with instructions that it be handed to you personally.'

She left me. Inside the bag was a small filigreed box made of tin. I opened it and let out a small gasp. Two golden bangles, resting in silk, lay inside.

What a shock! What did he mean by sending these? Did he too remember that my wrist was the place he had first touched me? Were I to wear these things, I would forever be feeling his hand on me again. My calm evaporated; I tried to push aside the memory of lying before him that night in the lamp's glow.

How long I stood at that railing turning this all over I don't know. But then the idea came that I must not keep these things. They were a link between two people who rightfully had none. Had I received them at the house, I could have sent them back to the palace by runner. But what about here? There was of course the water. I peered down into the swirls of the ship's wake and wondered what spirits lived down there. How might they react to seeing golden jewellery sinking past them into the murky depths? Would they have powers to know they were gifts from His Majesty?

Perhaps just the box, then. I let it fall. It sank quickly as I said a prayer to the spirits not to be disturbed.

Five minutes later, I was down in my cabin again. Thankfully Da was not there. I opened my own jewellery box and placed the bangles carefully in it, underneath other silver and gold.

I went back on deck with a holy text. I found Da and for an hour we sat together, I reading aloud, a passage about protection that gods afford to deserving travellers. All the time I was trying not to think about those bangles.

Later the cook appeared with bowls. 'Rice and grilled fish for the lady and her maid!'

As we ate, Mr Chen returned.

'The food meets your approval, I hope?'

'Yes, Mr Chen. Very much so.'

He motioned approvingly toward the text. 'The Lady pays much attention to the life of the spirit.'

'You are kind, Mr Chen. Not as much as I should. But I can see there will be lots of time on this voyage. And in China too, I hope. So tell me – in China, will there be a temple near the place where we stay?'

'Yes, Lady Sray. There will be a temple, but it won't be exactly like what you know in the Empire. In China people worship gods with different names than the ones we know in the land of the Khmers.'

'But how can there be different gods? There are only the ones in Heaven, known to us all.'

Mr Chen took a moment to sit down next to me. 'Lady, I have

travelled to many places, and I have found that in each place, the people worship gods that, if not actually different from the ones you know, are at least known by different names. There are islands on the east side of the Salt Water Sea where people worship only the spirits in the forest. There are no temples, no priests, no texts of any kind. Yet still the people worship. And they seem quite content. Their gods help them to lead moral lives, as yours do for you.'

'Still, how can there be other gods?'

'I think because people believe in them, Lady Sray. That is all I can say. In China, you will find, there are some that are different for every family. They are the spirits of those who came before us. We have a place in the home for images that commemorate the deceased, and we pray to these images, and if their spirits look on us and feel that we are deserving, they cause things to happen in our favour. And of course, they can make things go in the other direction as well – so we have to be careful in what we ask.'

'Now,' he continued, 'as I said, we do have temples in China and inside each one is a large image, but this god is not really a god. Rather, he was a human like us, but he found the way to achieve a state of perfect harmony with the universe. We believe that before he devised his teachings, men and women were imprisoned by ignorance. But now, if we pray and study his texts, we can learn the way. It's up to us to take it or not.'

'Yes,' I replied, a memory stirring. 'There are people in the Empire who have similar beliefs. Did you know there is a special temple on the east side of the Capital – perhaps you've been there? Several years ago, I stopped in. The priests said that a King of many reigns past had worshipped there and that later Kings allowed the temple to stay, out of respect to their forebear. Inside there was a large image of a sacred being, sitting and meditating. They called him the Lord Buddha. I had never seen such a likeness – his face was so calm, as if he was shutting out all the worries of the world.'

'Yes, perhaps he is the same being whom we honour, in our way, in China. And in the Khmer Empire there are others that seem quite familiar to us. In your country, you have the Naga, in our country we have the dragon. It has a frightening face and scales like a crocodile's, but at the same time it can be quite friendly toward people. Like the Naga.'

For two days, followed the shore of the Freshwater Sea, leading toward the sun in the morning, away from it in afternoon. We called at a small port. There slaves carried tied-up bundles aboard our vessel for stowage below deck. The cargo, I was told, included silver utensils, spices and many bolts of silk. Selling them in China would help pay the cost of the embassy.

As the loading progressed, I walked in the waterside market, buying fruit as a gift for Da, who was feeling better about the journey now, and for Sergeant Sen and his men. Do you know, I had the bangles in my bag as I walked that market. I had thought I might come across some place fit to deposit a gift of a King – the pristine water of a fast-running stream, perhaps, in a hidden spot where no one would happen upon it. What foolish thoughts. The bangles came back on board with me. They took their place again beneath my own jewellery and there they remained for the rest of the voyage. But let me say that whenever I opened the box I did my best not to look at them.

The ships resumed sail, making good time beneath clear skies. I had also bought some sugar cane in the market, and now I asked the cook to cut it into sections. These I gave one by one through the slats of the two cages to the great horned animals inside. They chewed gratefully. Poor animals – their travel would be so much more confined than mine.

Late that day, I noticed I could now see both sides of the Freshwater Sea at once. The far shore came closer and closer and after a while the ships seemed to be not in a sea at all but in a very wide river in which the current was barely perceptible, but nonetheless helpfully carrying us travellers along with it. Here and there on, villages and temples showed themselves. Children swam naked in the water and called to us.

Three days later, the river widened so much that the shores were again barely visible. The water began to change in colour, from the familiar bright brown to an almost glowing blue hue that I had never seen, with swaths of gleaming white where waves broke.

'We are near the Saltwater Sea,' Mr Chen announced. 'We'll turn north and sail along the coast for a few days, then head out to open water.'

Two days after that, I awoke to a strange stillness in the ship. It had stopped. I went up on deck and was surprised at the sight there: to either side rode a large vessel, flying strange red and green banners. Men in helmets moved about on the decks.

'The ships are Cham, Lady Sray,' said Mr Chen, from behind me. I hadn't seen him approach.

'Oh! The enemy.'

'No, Lady Sray. The Chinese Empire and Champa are at peace, so there's no reason to worry. The Chams treat these waters as theirs, that's all. They require all Chinese ships that go through to carry documents issued by their authorities. Sometimes they stop us to check the documents. Sometimes they even ask us to bring our vessels to one of their ports for a bit and there they always find something to tax.' He made a resigned laugh. 'But don't worry, it's all very routine. We'll tie up and negotiate what taxes we will pay on the goods we're carrying, then we'll be on our way.'

With the Cham vessels in escort, our ships turned west toward shore. After a few hours a port became visible ahead. We reached it at mid-afternoon, with coolies securing the vessels with thick ropes. Mr Chen had spoken very confidently, but I could not put aside my concerns. I watched from a hidden place on deck. The coolies wore dirty loincloths. Soldiers in strange caps paced up and down the wharf. Beyond the waterfront warehouses rose a spire of a style I had never seen.

Mr Chen went ashore. An hour later, he returned to say we would stay the night, but that no one would leave the ship. Tomorrow morning we would put back to sea.

I came up on deck the day next day to confirm to myself that preparations for departure were underway. But I saw none. Instead, I saw the King's minister leave his ship and walk to a small building near the dock. He was escorted by Cham soldiers.

Concerned, I found Mr Chen. He was dismissive of the whole

affair. 'They say there's a problem with our passage document, that's all. They say it was signed by a Cham maritime official who's been transferred and so it isn't valid any more. This kind of objection is always being raised to open a path to a payment. We'll get it cleared up soon.'

I went below to Sergeant Sen. 'Come look, please,' I said. 'I'm a bit worried. They've taken the minister into a building on the shore.'

'I would like to, Lady. But Mr Chen says it's better if I and my men stay down here, out of sight.'

That did nothing to calm me. Later, with some prodding, Mr Chen explained that the Cham authorities had raised another question, the presence of soldiers on our ship. There was nothing in the passage document allowing that. But I shouldn't worry – the minister was going to point out that these men were not fighting men, merely members of a ceremonial entourage. Mr Chen hesitated, then told me that the Chams were also being told something else to prove that this was not a military mission: that traveling on this ship was a renowned holy woman, a Lady of great devotion and benevolence and spiritual powers, who was going to China to teach people about the faith that Khmers and Chams shared.

I wished he had not told me. There flashed through my mind an image of a jungle clearing, where a young prince lay bleeding. My tongue touched the gap in my teeth. I wondered now if the ghost was able to cross the sea to follow me.

Three days passed. The King's minister shuttled back and forth from his ship to the building, surrounded by a clutch of Cham soldiers who on each successive day seemed to treat him more like a prisoner. Sailors began to whisper among themselves, and the maid Da became timid again, rarely leaving our cabin. On deck, the two horned animals shifted restlessly in their cages, as if sensing danger.

On the morning of the fourth day, I awoke to sounds of commotion. From deck I was shocked to see perhaps one hundred armed Cham soldiers lined up on the shore. On the other side of the ship, floating a short distance off, were sampans filled with more.

An order was shouted, a signal drum beaten, and an officer

wearing a helmet with a feather plume led soldiers from the wharf onto the ship. Mr Chen ran up to the officer – and was rudely shoved aside. The man drew his dagger and moved toward the steps that led below deck.

I knew in a flash what I had to do. I placed myself in the man's path.

He frowned and barked an order in his language that clearly meant to get out of the way, but I did not. Instead, I began speaking.

'You must not pass through here, sir. This is a holy place and it cannot be defiled by the presence of men of arms with violence on their minds.'

The officer turned to Mr Chen and shouted something more. Mr Chen replied, in a meek voice, and the officer shouted once again, but then they both stopped. I had begun to chant and rock back and forth and roll my eyes in a way I'd seen a spindly limbed ascetic do at a temple festival.

'Lady Sray!' cried Mr Chen, fearful, and at the same time puzzled. 'This man says that if you don't get out of the way, you will get, you will get the point of a dagger!'

I paused in my chant, but not in the motion of my body. 'Please tell him, Mr Chen, that there is no reason for him to go below, that the men are no threat, that they are simple men who honour the deities and want no trouble with anyone.'

He translated, and the officer listened at first, then made again to move.

'Tell him also that I have here' – I lifted a text – 'the words of the most powerful, the most unbearable curse that the gods have ever allowed to be used on earth, that it brings boils on the face and on the private parts, bleeding from the ears, and foul breath that no one can bear, and that the next time that he has relations with a woman, provided he can find one who is willing, there will be a sharp-toothed demon inside her private parts, waiting... And then, after his death, will come torture and torment as a spirit, before rebirth as a lizard.'

Where did I get such words? To this day I have no idea.

Mr Chen seemed terrified to translate this, but he began to, and as he did I continued to chant.

'And tell him that I saw him on the dock, and I knew what he was about to do, and that I have already placed this curse on him, and on his sons, and that if I die, there will be no one to remove it and the boils will begin to break out immediately and that will be just the start.'

Mr Chen bravely translated. The officer blanched. His eyes went not to me but to the text in my hand, and I knew I had reached him.

At the door leading up from below, I saw Sergeant Sen climbing up, knife in hand.

'Sergeant!' He stopped. 'You must stay out of sight. I will handle this.'

'I cannot allow you to.'

'Sergeant,' I said, as calmly as I could, 'if you do, I will die and you will die. There are many, many more Chams here than you could ever overpower. It will be all right. Now go! Get back out of sight!'

Thank Heaven, he did. Then Mr Chen spoke up. 'Perhaps, Mrs Sray, if we gave the Cham gentlemen a bit of honour with which to withdraw? The men below might turn over their weapons. They can easily be replaced later on the voyage.'

That made sense to me, and so Mr Chen proposed it to the officer. Heated discussion between the Chams followed. The officer gestured at the text, and Mr Chen responded. Then the officer went to the edge of the ship and called in very assertive tones to soldiers on the dock. After more consultations there, an answer was called back, and Mr Chen looked suddenly relieved.

'Lady Sray,' he whispered from his spot next to me. 'A decision has been made that the men can remain on the ship, if they give over their weapons. And if, of course, the curse is removed.'

A spear and a knife were passed up through the door. Then Mr Chen suggested to the officer that before any more came up, some of the Cham soldiers should return to the dock. They did. Then came more weapons, and the rest of the soldiers left, all but the officer.

He spoke with Mr Chen. 'He says, Lady Sray, that now you must remove the curse. But I would suggest that we only do that when we are underway.'

Mr Chen told the man that, and got a furious snarl in response. His hand went to his knife.

But then I thought to say: 'Why not tell him that he is welcome to come along with us for a bit to confirm that I remove the curse. That the word of the holy woman is that he will not be harmed and that our men will remain below until he has left the vessel. He may have one of his own men follow in a sampan to take him back.'

For the next half hour there was a lot of scurrying and shouting in Khmer and Chinese and Cham. Then the ropes at the dock were untied. It was a miracle – the two ships were edging toward open water.

I had the officer kneel before me and remove his helmet. With his face fully visible, he seemed like a decent enough man, and I felt remorse for frightening him this way. I raised my right hand and chanted a prayer calling for health and prosperity and a wife with a womb that would bear many children.

I called for some water, prayed to make it holy, then splashed some on the man. 'Tell him it is done, Mr Chen. His life will go on as before.'

The man rose, and put hands together in thanks. Then he climbed down the side to a Cham sampan.

Our ship picked up speed. No Cham vessels followed us; we were free. Presently Sergeant Sen came on deck, and his men too, all laughing in relief, but then they went respectfully silent while I said a prayer of thanks. A gong sounded from the ship ahead and standing on its stern was the minister. He looked to me, and like the Cham officer had done, he put hands together, conveying across the water a thank you of his own.

Later, the sergeant approached.

'You appear flushed, Lady Sray. Let me get you some water.'

I didn't need any, but I waited while he went below for a cup and brought it back, filled.

'Thank you, Sergeant Sen,' I said. 'Any problem that I have, this water will cure. I am fine. The gods protected us.'

'They did and so did you.' He was quiet a while, then said: 'All these years, Lady, I've been with you with the job of assuring your safety. Yet I missed the man with the knife in the temple atop the hill, and now I have missed again with the Chams – in fact it was you saved me. It's not what was intended when I was assigned to you.'

'It is as Heaven deemed,' I said. 'But you know, having you close has always made me feel safe. So I think you have done your job.'

'Thank you, and thank you for your courage, and, I suppose, for my life. You are right – we could never have stood up to so many of them. If you say that I make you feel safe, I will accept that and find honour in it and hope that I will continue to have that effect. But let us pray, Lady Sray, that there are no more situations where protection is needed.'

We looked to the shore again, and after a while, I said, 'You know, Sergeant, I misused the text back there. There was no curse, no magic, and yet I terrified that officer into thinking that what I held contained instructions for casting spells. Do you think I sinned against the texts?'

My husband would have laughed at this question, but the sergeant took a moment considering it, and then said: 'I think that Heaven would smile on what you did. May I suggest too that Heaven may have placed certain words in your mouth – I know that they are not there naturally.'

I blushed.

'And the text, Lady – you were using it for a holy cause, the saving of lives and the prevention of violence. And if it was an unusual way that you used them, well, the result was the same as if you had recited prayers at an altar.' He laughed. 'In fact, what you did was probably much more effective in achieving the holy goals, Lady Sray!'

'Thank you, sergeant,' I replied, smiling too. 'To hear you say it reassures me. You seem to have a mind for sorting out questions of this kind. May I ask, were you ever in the holy orders?' I felt it was all right to ask. It was just a superior showing a benevolent interest in one of her people.

'No, Lady. Nothing like that. I grew up like most of the boys in my village, praying at the wooden shrine beneath the village's largest tree. Sometimes we went to festivals at the temple of the lords of our estate, but I certainly never went into holy orders, though I recall one of the priests there suggesting that I come for instruction before my wedding ceremony. But I didn't go. I felt that the gods of that temple were for our lords, and the spirits of the forest and fields were for us the villagers. So, I had no instruction. But as for the rights and wrongs of things, like what you did at the port – well, often they seem more like just a matter of common sense. Consulting texts can merely put things into confusion.'

He had never given me any hint of having a wife. I felt now the most intense curiosity. 'Sergeant, I didn't know that you are married. I feel regret for taking you away from your family for so long.'

'It's all right, Lady Sray. My wife in fact is no longer among us. Her soul was carried off by an epidemic in our village a long time ago.'

'I'm so sorry, sergeant.' Now that I knew, I felt intrusive for asking.

'Please don't be, but let me tell you it all. It was the same for our three children, Lady. I was away at the time. My estate's lord had sent me as a soldier and I was serving at a garrison on the Cham border. It was quite peaceful there, though everyone had warned me it would be a very dangerous place. It turned out that the real place of danger was my village. Altogether, thirty-eight people died.'

I could think of nothing to say.

'I can see that this troubles you deeply, Lady. But please...It was the wish of Heaven, and we have no right to question. My wife and children had good years on this earth. Our village was in a district just below the mountains that mark the start of the Upper Empire. We had fertile fields, with water for two crops a year. Every house had chickens and ducks and most had a pig and buffalo. Every month there was a different festival. War and rebellion never came close. After the epidemic, well, the bodies were properly seen too. I have prayed for their souls many times, and the priests assure me that they have gone on to good new lives. You know, even without being told that, I knew it was true.'

'I'm sure it is, sergeant.'

'And I've been provided for, so how can I complain? My home is now my barracks and my men are my family, Lady Sray. I eat well and though I'm a soldier, war doesn't come close any more.'

'I will pray for your lost family, sergeant.'

He left me then, and I looked to him as he walked away, and wondered more about that wife and those children. Did he dream about them, did he wish he'd been carried away as well? What had been their formal names, their names of affection? Had that village truly been so idyllic, or was he trying to spare my feelings? And I wondered if there would ever come a time when he did not call me by my title.

43: Induction

Normally many weeks, even months, pass before a new concubine is called for her initiation with the King. First a scribe comes and asks detailed questions concerning prior experience, so that a certificate can be drawn up showing that there is none. Then a Brahmin physician conducts an exam. After that, the newcomer receives instruction in etiquette of the court, and in techniques of carnal union as practiced by Kings. There follows a series of prayers and baths. Then she is sent to the pavilion to join the other women, who give a lot of practical advice that may conflict with what the priests have said. Then the wait begins.

I know these things, I know them now, because in the case of my daughter, many of them were ignored, or compressed into just a few hours.

Do you understand? This is what the Brahmin had meant when he assured me that Bopa would be well seen to in my absence – she was to be the King's consolation. He would lose the mother but gain the daughter. The priest kept this from me that night, sending me off to China in ignorance, though I can now see his logic in doing that. This was the King's condition, I was later told. But I have always wondered if it was in fact something that the Brahmins proposed in hopes of dulling the King's frustration. Whoever's idea it was, Bopa's transition to the concubine state was rapid and smooth. She was of course not married, so no social stricture would be broken. And though the Brahmins had declared that I was Heavenly sister to the King, they ruled that Bopa by some quirk of cosmic alignment was not his Heavenly niece.

On my girl's first day in the palace she was first shuttled from place to place, now a small shrine for prayers, now a pavilion where she was prepped and purified. One after the other, priests, maids, perfumers, jewellers and seamstresses fussed over her. Everyone seemed in a rush to finish up. They managed that just as the sun was disappearing over the tile rooftops. A priest splashed on some final holy water, maids applied powder and perfume, and she was declared ready.

But nothing happened right away. Bopa was left to sit, as instructed, wearing a green silk sampot with flaring sash. Perfume's scent wafted up from her palms and breasts, silver jewellery lay heavy on her neck and arms. She smiled to herself, but after a while stole a look toward the door. Poor girl – she was wondering when Rom was going to arrive and join in the fuss over her. But Rom did not appear. Rather, after some time, the priest with the final holy water did. He led Bopa toward the King's quarters and the other girls lined up on either side of the gravel walkway, hands together, and she felt all but overcome with pride, even without the Elder Sister witnessing this moment.

I have told you that I swore to stay away from the King. Yet I never mastered the art of staying away from thoughts of the King. Gurus teach the skill in certain of the Empire's temples and several times during my past life I accepted instruction from them. But it was to no avail. So, I will ask you, what kind of mother is jealous of her own daughter's assignations? Jealous is what I was – there is no other word for it. When Bopa shared the details with me many months later, I swallowed hard and tried to give no sign and avoid imagining what it would have been to be in my daughter's place. I am quite sure the girl never suspected.

So it is difficult for me to recount what followed that first day as a carnal partner. But I will present it to you in as objective a form as I can.

In the royal sleeping chamber, the King was waiting, his back turned. Bopa had thought she'd have time to prepare herself, but before she knew it, the drapes had closed. The King turned to face her. She was meant to put head to the floor at this point, but this slipped her mind, and the King did not correct her. Rather, he asked her in a voice that surprised her with its gentleness if she might move to the middle of the chamber and stand there. Then he circled her, eyes taking in every detail, as if he was looking for something hidden, taking so long that she began to feel uneasy, especially when he was behind her.

'The garment, please – can it be removed?'

Bopa trembled at those words, but before she knew it, two maids had stepped in from behind and done the job. Bopa stood naked, save for her jewellery. She felt briefly ashamed, but she tried not to show it, keeping her eyes to the floor, while the King continued his walk around her, seeking out some quality that she felt suddenly sure she did not have. He came close and let his finger travel down the side of her neck, then across her shoulder and down her arm. There came from him a sigh, and then he eased her toward the mat with more of that unexpected gentleness. She tried to recall the proper position for the initial encounter, but her memory failed. In any case, His Majesty seemed not to care. His hands moved to other parts of her body and the business of carnal union began.

Afterward, my girl lay curled on her side. He stood over her and whispered: 'Sweet Bopa, almost...almost the same.' Then he left.

A priest she'd never seen came with a new garment and a silver implement, with which he recovered a spot of royal seed that had spilled. He kept his eyes away from her at all times, but spoke to her, instructing her to remain lying down and to try to retain whatever seed she could. She stayed on the mat, eyes closed, hoping for some sign from him that she had pleased the King but none was offered. After a while, the priest told her to stand up. He splashed her with lustral water, looking to one side or the other of her as he did, and then told her to dress and return to the pavilion.

There the other concubines were lined up to greet her and this revived her spirits. They led her to the bathing jars and took turns pouring water over her while she stood hands together. Then they returned to the pavilion, where a table was piled with flowers and cut fruit. One by one, the concubines approached with private gifts meant to commemorate the initiation – small things of no great cost, because most of the concubines had no money. One gave a scented garland, another a shell necklace from the market, another an amulet. But no one touched the food on the table or asked what happened. They were awaiting the arrival of Rom.

When more time passed and she did not appear, they grew braver and began to nibble at the food. One of the girls volunteered that the soldiers must still be keeping Rom away.

'Soldiers?' Bopa was confused.

'You didn't know? Some soldiers from the palace came,' the girl said, following with a bite into the milky flesh of a rambutan. 'It was an hour or two before you arrived for your preparations. Their commander asked to see Elder Sister. She kept him waiting, and then let him in. At first we couldn't hear what was going but then she began showing her temper. She was shouting at him that she was the King's favourite, that her son was too, that the officer would regret carrying out an assignment like this. And the commander shouted back that he would not, that this was an order direct from the King, that he was told to take her out by force if he had to. She quieted down after that and left with her two maids.'

This was added to so many things that day that Bopa couldn't make sense of. Later she lay down to sleep, and when she awoke, she had a headache and called for some powder. When she was feeling better, she sat up, to wait for Rom's return. But again she did not come. Rather, her father did.

He entered the pavilion, and he astonished her by going to his knees and putting head down and hands together.

'Bopa, sole daughter,' he said, in a very formal tone, 'you bring the most profound merit and honour to the family. I have come to tell you that your father and mother recognize your accomplishment and service, that what you are doing here will be recalled for generations. I will do all I can to support you in your life.'

Then he motioned to a servant who knelt to the side, and the man put forward a box. Bopa smiled and forgot the pain in her head. The pride of a few hours earlier came back. I do believe that this was the first gesture of respect she could recall her father ever paying her. And she liked presents more than anything. Inside, wrapped in double folds of white cotton, was a silver box. On its top was an inscription, in Sanskrit. She couldn't read it, but her father right away did, aloud. 'On the occasion of the ascension of Shining Gem Bopa, daughter of Nol the Parasol Master and the Lady Sray, to the position of conjugal partner of His Majesty King Suryavarman, whose arrows darken the sky.'

I believe now that this state had been my husband's intention for Bopa from the beginning. I had been too busy with other things to take notice.

Later that evening, the Brahmin Subhadra appeared. He led Bopa out of the pavilion, she wondering why she was not first bathed and perfumed. But he took her not to the King's chamber, rather to a far corner of the palace compound, where there stood a newly built house, with a tall wooden fence enclosing it and a small garden. A soldier stood guard at the door. Bopa passed inside with the priest and found another surprise – the maid Yan.

Bopa was incredulous. 'May I know, please, sir, what is this place?

The priest replied, 'Mistress Bopa, you are so highly valued by His Majesty that he has deemed that you deserve better than to live with the other concubines. You will live here, alone.'

'But, there will be nothing for me to do!'

'It is by His Majesty's order.'

'Well, please, I'll go to the pavilion during the day.'

'I'm afraid you will not do that, Mistress. You are to stay here in this place until His Majesty calls for you. I will come every day to take part in your spiritual instruction. I must tell you that the soldier at the door knows the orders and will enforce them if necessary.'

He left. Bopa collapsed in tears. Yan knelt by her, whispering comforting words. She brought drinking water and got her mistress to sip some of it and to allow a linen cover to be pulled over her. Then Yan sat down and hummed a country lullaby until her mistress was asleep.

The King called her that night and again the night after that.

44: The distance from earth to Heaven

There were equally big changes in my son's life at about this time. I have sometimes wondered why Heaven chose to send me away before it went about re-ordering my children's affairs. Perhaps it felt I would interfere – any mother claims such rights when her children are involved. But for close to a year, all through the visit to China, I was in ignorance, believing that my son and daughter were in the same situations as when I had left them. Each day I prayed for them, picturing them in the only way I knew. And it was all illusion.

When I departed for China, my boy was high ranking in the design pavilion, son-in-law of the Architect, chief assistant, sharer of confidences, father of one baby son. But all of this did not make him immune to undermining by jealous assistants. The man Pin in particular.

Let me give you an appreciation of his character. One morning – it must have been shortly after our ship went free from the Cham port – Pin reported at the daily meeting about two minor princes who'd come in from a near province to see how the bamboo they'd sent was being used. He'd taken them to see it and they'd been quite disappointed, he could tell, though they lacked the nerve to say anything. Their bamboo had gone not into scaffolding for the central sanctuary, abode of the gods, sacred peak of Mount Meru on this earth – that work wouldn't begin for years – but instead had become part of a shantytown for women who called themselves entertainers. Split lengthwise, the bamboo now formed the platforms on which these unfortunates lay with labourer men who came calling at night with a few pebbles of silver.

'Unholy women they are,' said Pin. 'But without them a holy place could never be built!' Such a cruel thing to laugh about, but Pin had no difficulty.

Now the Architect asked him: 'And what about that shipment of timber, the one from the south? Is it on schedule? We're going to need it for framing at the two libraries.'

'Sir, we expect it in four days' time.'

'Good. Can you give Sovan a list of exactly what's coming?'

'Of course.' He turned to Sovan. 'I'll see you get it this afternoon.'

Pin was no longer openly hostile. Any undermining had to be conducted out of sight.

The Architect raised a hand. 'All right, all of you, get on with your work, please, and I'll see you back here tomorrow. But you, Sovan, stay back a moment, will you?'

When the pavilion was clear, he said, in a conspiratorial tone that he now often adopted with my son: 'I've finished something, something important.' He went to a case that lay on a low table and removed a palm leaf. 'The new elevation,' he said.

'*Really*? May I look?'

'Of course.'

Sovan spread the leaf flat on a table. He grasped the changes right away. The pyramid now had six levels, not five. The centre tower at the top was dominant, the two to either side were like younger smaller brothers to it. Guardian images on the steps leading up were of a larger scale. And at the base was something new, two small towers, one on each side at the start of the main steps.

'Remarkable, sir.' My poor boy! He was praying that he sounded sincere.

'It feels good to be done with this – like giving birth. The same pain, if not the blood.'

Sovan said: 'The proportions are correct, pleasing. This line here, and this one here – they form axes that cross in the right place, sir, up here.' He indicated a spot in the air. He was finding it difficult to keep up this kind of talk.

'I've worked on it every night for the past four months,' the Architect said. 'Out in my pavilion on the pond. When no one's around. Now, the foundations we've already built – if we extend them out at this point here, can we make them long enough to accommodate the extra cubits in the base level?'

'I think we can, sir. The excavation team has dug the foundation trench but hasn't started laying rice husks yet. That's meant to start next week. We can have them make the trench longer, then apply the husks. If you can draw up an order, I'll deliver it to the foreman there. But tell me, sir – the stress at the base. Won't it be much greater than with the old design? How will we compensate for that?'

'We'll have four extra levels of sandstone on the inside, replacing laterite. I've done the numbers and four will be more than adequate, and accommodate any other changes later that increase the weight. Now, do you think there's enough stone left in the north quarry, or will we need to open a new one? But... but don't answer that. I can see we're both playing a game here.'

Sovan could not disagree, so he said nothing.

'You know,' the Architect said, turning away from the palm leaf, 'when I first showed you the original plan those years ago, you behaved just like you are now. 'Brilliant, sir.' 'Inspired by Heaven, sir.' You didn't say what you truly felt.'

'Sir, at that time I told you...'

The Architect cut him off. 'You know, I call you boy, but I don't really think of you that way. Partly it makes me feel younger and I need that now that my hair is white. But you're not a boy. You're how old? In your thirty-second year, I think?'

Sovan nodded.

'Thirty-second. You've had quite a bit of experience now. You've done very well, of course. You learn faster than any assistant I've ever had, faster than I ever did. That sketch you did for the facade of the west gate – it's better than anything my old brain could produce. Now I've been working on this new master plan for months and each evening when I sit down with it, I think, this is the evening when the builder god Visvakarman will reach down and touch me. He will impart true inspiration. My wrinkled hands will finally know what to draw. But that inspiration never comes. I've become more and more convinced that I haven't got the design right. And now, seeing you confirm those suspicions, I suddenly wonder why it's got to be me. It's true that I'm the one the King expects to do it, the one the priests blessed and sprinkled with the holy water they put so much faith in. But I have to ask, why would Heaven bother sending inspiration to me, with my imagination hamstrung by fifty years of doing things the old way? If the grand idea were somehow implanted in me, I don't know that I'd recognize it. But then I think, there's someone right here, who even as an untrained boy, a boy holding a parasol to keep the sun off my head, had a vision of what this place should be. You've never talked much about it, and I've never asked. But each time you look at these plans, I can sense that you see the shortcomings.

'I believe, boy, that Heaven has placed in you the true design for this place we're tasked to build. I can sense there's something remarkable in you, something waiting to break out.'

Sovan's only reply was to hang his head.

'If you can't speak, perhaps you should go back and be a parasol bearer.'

Sovan blinked, startled.

'Got your attention, did I? Now, I'm serious. I want you to sit down and make some sketches. Keep it secret, of course. But you mustn't limit yourself to trying to improve on what we've already got. You must behave as if you're starting from scratch and put down your full vision. I want to see it, not just hear you describe it.'

'Sir, it's not my place to...'

The Architect sighed. 'Do it, boy.'

Four days later, the Architect died.

Sovan heard over midday rice at his usual place, a rice stall outside the west gate. A slave came running, out of breath, and called him urgently to the design pavilion. The others had already assembled there. A Brahmin physician was present too. He suggested that they all kneel. He mouthed a prayer, then announced that their master had been walking toward his house with a servant when suddenly he fell down, clutching his chest in great pain. The servant rolled him onto his back to make him more comfortable, but was otherwise helpless. The physician arrived quickly, but by then the master was still. His heart had stopped, his breathing as well.

Sovan went outside. He wept, for the first time since he had been expelled from his house. Then he found the chief foreman and ordered that all work at the site be suspended, that slaves and craftsmen alike go to their own shrines, burn incense and pray for the soul of the master, that it would wander for only a brief time and then would find its way to a new, higher incarnation (though Sovan could not think what that might be). Then he walked toward his own house. Only then did he realize he had no formal authority for what he'd just done. He had done it anyway.

Two days later, the Architect's body was placed atop a mammoth pyre built just inside the future gate of the temple. His Majesty officiated and put flame to the aromatic wood that soon was popping and crackling, liberating the master's soul. Sovan and Suriya looked on as chief mourners. When seven days of mortuary ritual had passed, Sovan got up early and returned to the building site, uncertain of what to do for the first time since the death. No word had come from the palace.

At midday, he was arrested! There was no warning. Six soldiers simply showed up as he ate in that same rice stall where he had received news of the death. They bound his hands and marched him to the palace. There his face was pushed to the mat before the King.

A voice barked: 'We demand that you confess! You have tried to ruin the design of your monarch's mountain-temple.'

It was not the King's voice, but that of a man to the right. A magistrate.

Sovan managed to speak. 'I've done nothing like that, sir. I've only worked with my late master, the chief Architect, to build the finest temple in the world.'

'That's a lie! You were overheard talking with him at the design pavilion about changes.'

'I've never...'

'Speak the truth! Your monarch is listening!'

'I know only that my master was proposing some refinements.'

'You blame it on him?'

'I place no blame, sir. I have no right to do that. He was the greatest builder ever to serve the Empire. I can only tell you what happened.'

'Look here.'

Sovan raised his head a tiny bit. The man thrust in his face the new elevation the Architect had drawn.

'Is this not the so-called refined design?'

'It is, sir.' It was only now that Sovan saw that Pin was in the room, standing to the side. His face showed a wicked kind of glee.

'And do you approve of this new design?'

Sovan hesitated.

'Do you approve of it? Yes or no.'

'I do not, sir.'

'Yet did you not express admiration for it at that time? Did you not say it was remarkable and had perfect proportions?'

'I did say those things, sir.'

'You were lying to your master?'

'I was.'

'Your master, who took you on as apprentice, who trained you, whose rice you ate year after year, who brought you into his household as a son, husband to his daughter? You were telling lies to him?' He turned to the King. 'Majesty, we have heard enough. He acknowledges he knew of the new plan, that he praised it. And we know that he did not report it.'

Then Sovan heard the King's voice. 'You – the prisoner. How can you explain this? You say your master was the greatest builder the Empire ever had, but you also say you did not really admire his plan.'

Sovan hesitated.

'Answer!'

'Majesty, it is, it is...because when I was a boy, I believe I saw the finished temple, just for a moment, in a vision. And it was very much different from what we have been building and what my master the Architect drew in the new plan.'

There was silence. Then the King spoke up, wearily. 'This family. How many of you have visions of the temple? So what did you see? Tell me!'

Now Sovan talked without reservation. 'I saw a great mountain, with five towers, Majesty. But it did not rise steeply and sharply, with rigid angles, fighting with the ground beneath it. It rose as real mountains do, gently when seen from a distance. Each of its peaks curved like a lotus blossom. Majesty, the current design and the Architect's changes are in line with all the knowledge we have about what form a temple should take, that is to say, it is a variation on the other temples in the Capital here. The plan is better than the others, yes, but it is...it is nonetheless only a better way of doing what I humbly submit is the wrong thing.'

The guards, the priests, the magistrate even Pin tensed at such a shocking claim. But the King did not. 'How can you say that?'

Sovan's head went back to the mat. 'Because I am foolish,' he mumbled to the floor. 'Majesty. It has no value, this view of mine.'

'I'll decide that. Go on.'

'What we are building now has straight lines and sharp corners and it bursts up from the horizon. It announces that it is different from this earth.'

'But it's a template of Heaven. Of course it's different.'

'Yes, Majesty. But is Heaven really so different? Did not the lords create the earth that we walk in an image of their own? Do not the holy mountains, the Himalayas, which our texts describe, have gentle foothills? They demand a long journey of any being who wants to ascend, even a god. It's only toward the summits that they become great towers with shear sides.'

The King was trying to picture this, Sovan could see.

'There is another problem, Majesty, with the current design. The scale, Majesty. The temple as it's now being built is too small.'

'But it will be larger than any we have,' the King countered. 'The Architect showed me that.'

'It will be larger, but not as large as Heaven wishes. Majesty, the base of your temple should fill the space that is now designated as the total grounds of the temple, marked by the outer wall. We would need to build a new outer wall far out on all four sides.

'So the land it covered would be what? Four times bigger?'

'It would be at least twenty times more. But Majesty, I am telling you only what I saw when I was young. I am sure that my vision had no value.'

'Go on.'

'Majesty, when I was young, I saw this temple from a great distance. There was an avenue leading all the way from where I stood, in the secular realm, to the holy realm of the temple. The distance between earth and Heaven is great, but in temples of past reigns, this distance has been expressed in symbolic terms only – from the gate to the temple itself is in fact only a few steps. I believe it should be a long one, so that as His Majesty processes toward it he will experience the journey of life. There would be a grand gate at the entrance. Other temples have what is essentially a ditch to symbolize the seas of creation. The moat circling this temple would seem as wide as a real sea, with a glorious bridge to carry your blessed feet across to the gate. Majesty, on the scale in which this temple appeared in my consciousness, it would take you close to two hours to process the full distance around the moat.

'And inside this temple, Majesty, there would be three levels, each representing a higher level of divinity. There would be long, long galleries sheltering bas reliefs of Heaven and hell, of the epics, of the deities. And, Majesty, many many apsaras, the Heavenly nymphs, would greet you there as well.'

'How many?'

'Majesty, mountain-temples your predecessors built might have ten or twenty. This temple, this greatest temple, would have – it would have close to eighteen hundred.'

The King gave off a small gasp, and Sovan began to feel some hope.

'They would gaze out from pillars, from walls, from hidden alcoves. Your Majesty, walking the temple corridors, might have difficulty becoming familiar with all of them. You would come across a new apsara and be startled with delight of unknown beauty.'

Sovan let that sink in a moment. Then he put his face down again: 'Majesty,' he said, 'That is my vision. I feel that only a King as great as you could warrant such a place, or cause it to be built in this way.'

There was silence, then the King broke it.

'Years ago your former father had a vision about the temple. Is your vision related to his?'

'Majesty, I never told my former father what I saw.'

'Then tell me. The temple as you have seen it – it faces west, does it not?'

Sovan knew how important this question was, to the King and to himself. He closed his eyes and pictured the great edifice one more time. Yes, all was as he had remembered – it faced toward the direction in which the sun departs. It always had. That day when he had first met the Architect, during the scouting of the construction site, and again at the ceremony of the royal cubit.

When his former father caused the reorientation of the temple, Sovan had seen this as confirmation of his vision. But I hadn't told Sovan that his former father's vision was faked, and I never did. Yet when I learned of my son's interrogation in the court, and his steadfast description of the temple he had seen, I became convinced of something of which I had formerly only hoped. It was that when Heaven sets events in motion, the purpose might become clear only many years later. Nol had become wealthy through his cynical machinations, but that result was insignificant in comparison to the other – the primary – effect of his action, that the orientation of the greatest holy edifice of the world had been set right. The Empire had been saved from the immeasurable harm of building it in a way that would resist and obstruct the energy of the cosmos for all eternity.

Sovan opened his eyes. 'It faces west, Majesty.'

'Then you may raise your head. Your master stated to me before his death that he wished you to be his successor, and you will be. As chief builder of the Empire, you will build this temple in the way you have seen. You will be provided all the materials and workers that you require.'

Sovan's strength fled straight out of him at this point, both from relief and elation. He collapsed flat onto the mat. Two retainers helped him from the throne room.

My husband was furious when he heard – furious that his former son had received such an honour, that the villa Nol had ordered built two hundred paces from the future mountain-temple's gate would now have to be dismantled and moved back a thousand paces, to make way for enlargement of the grounds. But then he realized that all his tenants would have to do the same, and that he could rent them the carts and hire out the slaves they would need for the move. At the new place, they would squabble among themselves for the better locations and drive rents up.

Sovan never saw Pin again. The assistant was also escorted from the audience chamber, but by two guards. At his sleeping hut he packed up his things in a hurry and was put on the road. Two months later, word came that he'd begun work as an assistant at fortifications being constructed at the Cham border. The previous assistant there had died of mosquito fever.

45: Its own kind of land

When our embassy's ships went free from the Chams, Mr Chen declared that no more chances would be taken by sailing close to shore. So a course was set to open sea. Land receded behind the vessels, until sky and water squeezed it to nothingness. At day's end, Da and I watched the sun set in land's former place and begin slipping below the water. It would be all right there, Mr Chen assured us. The divine energy with which it burned was so intense that no amount of water could quench it.

Soon the ships were pressing through misty blackness, leaving luminescent ribbons in their wake. I grew anxious again, over so many strange sights and sounds, and fears of what kind of spirits might inhabit these waters. Da seemed unsettled too, and even Sergeant Sen, standing a respectful distance behind us, seemed out of sorts. So I suggested that we all say prayers at the portable shrine.

'Would it be all right, Lady,' asked Da, 'if we prayed that the gods create some land in the ship's path? Not much, just enough to be a place to stop and let us get off for a while.'

'Yes, we can pray for that,' I replied, though I felt that was asking too much. The more realistic thing to request, something Heaven might actually provide, would be a safe passage to the foreign country.

Still, on the following morning I went up on deck to look, just in case Heaven had shown special generosity. I saw no land, but Mr Chen was up and about in the day's first sunlight, his former cheerfulness restored. From the railing, he pointed out a group of fish skimming just below the surface a ways off the bow, each as long as a man. They breathed air like animals of the land, he said. Just then, one leapt from the water, and I tell you, it smiled at us! By midday, my worries had faded. The rise and fall of the ship, the wind that put the smell of salt in my hair, had begun to be comforting. I sat on deck most of the day with Da, reading texts, and I came to think of the ship as its own kind of land, safer in some ways than the kind I knew, because it could not flood. It was as Mr Chen had said. No matter how high the salt water rose, the ship rose higher, keeping us safe. Our prayer had been answered.

That evening, we ate fresh meat and vegetables with our rice, and the next day too. But in days that followed, those foods began to run out or go bad. The sailors put nets overboard for fish, and if that brought up nothing, the cook served up strange types of preserved meats and greens taken from barrels. Da and I exchanged sceptical glances, then ate. But it was not so bad as that and in any case the rice was always good, cooked in a pot above deck.

Later the fresh water in the ship's jars ran low. The men began to bathe in water raised in buckets from the sea, with Mr Chen insisting that Da and I use what fresh water remained.

Then one warm sunny afternoon, the captain ordered the bamboo sails to be pulled down. The ship slowed to a stop, and one by one, sailors launched themselves overboard. The brightest bubbling foam appeared wherever they struck the water. I watched. This was bathing, but it was also amusement, it seemed. The Khmer men looked on too, curious. Mr Chen assured them there were no crocodiles here to drag swimmers under, though at the same time it wouldn't be wise to try to touch bottom. Sergeant Sen and two of his men went below and returned in old loincloths. They too threw themselves merrily over the side, making another round of large splashes. Da was too shy to join; I stayed put because I knew my presence in the water would change the tone of everything – Mr Chen would have a ladder put over the side, sailors would forget their antics and help me down and fuss over me in various ways, worrying that I found the sea water too warm or too cool. And of course I might be at quarters too close with the sergeant.

Ten days later, as I sat on deck reading a text in the afternoon's final light, a sailor called out from the mast. Others hurried up from below, showing special energy, and crowded together at the bow to look. I joined them. There was the outline of something far ahead. Gradually it became clear. It was land, but like no land I had ever seen – a mountain that came right to the water, a mountain so tall its top was obscured by a cloud! I wondered if the gods that lived in that cloud would be friendly if the ship passed underneath.

After the evening meal, Mr Chen came to me on deck, carrying something wrapped in paper.

'We are close to the first land of my country, Lady Sray. Tomorrow, we will call at a seaside village to take on provisions for more sailing. But our Capital is many days further sailing to the north.'

He paused, having something more to say. 'I would ask, Lady Sray, that when you set foot in my country, you wear this on the top of your body. At all times in public.' He unwrapped the paper. 'We call it a blouse.'

It was a fine piece of silk, red and silver and blue, with embroidery and a series of loops on the front.

'I don't understand, Mr Chen.'

'It's simply the custom in my country, Lady Sray. My people will wonder and stare if you don't wear it.' He held up the garment, showing that it had holes. 'Place your right hand, please, through here. See? Then the other.'

I followed his directions.

'Now,' said Mr Chen, 'please close it up in the front. You can place these knots through these little loops to hold the fabric closed.' He did not seem to want to help me with this.

'Must I? It's not so bad if the air can enter.'

He laughed kindly. 'I'm afraid you must, Lady Sray. And this other blouse is for your maid. She must do the same. When we land, we'll be able to give you many more, for wearing on different days.'

I remembered something. 'It's like on my old teapot.'

'Pardon me?'

'Before my husband was called to service with the King, Mr Chen, I owned a Chinese teapot, with four little cups. The set was blue and white, and one of the cups had a cracked rim. And on the pot was a picture of some Chinese people. They looked rather happy, and they were all covered top to bottom in garments, like these that you gave us. Well, all right. So it will be with us.'

And then I felt suddenly nostalgic, even resentful. 'You know,

Mr Chen, I liked that tea set so much. But I'm afraid it's gone – my husband sold it to raise money to establish the parasol pavilion. I've always wondered what happened to it.'

'Probably it is making some other family happy, Lady Sray. And I expect that you have many more now.'

'Actually I don't. Not like that one. But it's nothing.'

Later Sergeant Sen happened by, and I showed him the blouse. 'Strange,' remarked the sergeant. 'He's said nothing to me about wearing one.'

We stepped to the railing for another look toward the land in the failing light. 'Well,' I said after a bit, 'I never felt I'd feel attached to this ship, but now that we've reaching this strange place, I feel it will be hard to get off. It's China that now seems the foreboding place.'

'I will stay close.'

The lamps of a village burned in the blackness. I said: 'It looks just like a settlement on the Freshwater Sea at night, doesn't it? Maybe the people there are the same too, do you think?'

'I think, Lady, I think that they are the same – some are kind, some are not, some can be trusted, some are thieves, some are strong, some are weak. It is the same, but it will take us a while to recognize that, because the people will look different, they will speak in strange words that have no meaning to us and their houses will resemble nothing we know. Even the smells in the air will be different.'

'Oh – you've been to China before, sergeant?'

'No, Lady. But I have been to foreign places. Champa. On campaign.'

'Oh, yes. And the strange things that you encounter in a foreign place, they don't frighten you?'

'They do at first, Lady Sray. But then after some time you become accustomed to them, and to the ways of the people there. It's an odd feeling – almost as if you are released from your contract with the gods. The gods, our gods, seem not to be present in a foreign place, and therefore the rules that they teach us seem not to apply either. At least there is no penalty.'

'That could be harmful, I think.'

'Yes, with some people, Lady. Sometimes men who at home seem to be normal and decent – well, in foreign places I have seen them do horrible things you would not care to know. And then somehow they become normal and decent again when they return home.'

'Sergeant, you said some people. I'm glad it's not everyone.'

He laughed. 'Lady Sray, it's not possible it would be that way with you.'

'Nor with you, I think.' I thought a moment, then said: 'You say that sometimes men do terrible things in foreign places. But is it possible also that release from the rules of home can result in something good?'

I stopped, unsure what I meant by that. The sergeant did not answer. Then he excused himself, saying he had to return to his men.

46: The Chinese sleeping mat

Our ships made their way along the Chinese coast for almost a month. Then one morning, I stepped up to deck to find that our vessels had turned toward the land, and were on brown water. That colour was welcome, rich earthy tones so like what I knew from rivers and canals at home. Far ahead to either side were low hills, but they revealed no sign of habitation. By early afternoon, the land was closer, off both sides now, and offering hints of life – tiny houses, planted fields undulating up hillsides, a horse and rider, the smoke-haze of unseen cooking fires. The Chinese crewmen grew animated, pointing out things across the water to one another. The channel slowly became narrower; I now realized that it was in fact a river. Hours later, around a bend, there came into view a most astonishing sight: a city, with tall white walls for protection and brightly coloured pennants flying from towers. At the waterfront were masted ships too many to count. I watched spellbound. In my imagination, China had always been a collection of villages along a winding clay road, different from home mainly in that the people had pale skin and spoke in the strange tones of Mr Chen.

Then he was right there alongside me. "It is Hangzhou, Lady Sray, seat of the Chinese monarch. We have reached our destination."

Presently our ships drew near. On a wharf, soldiers dressed in bright red stood in formation, spears pointed to the sky. Before them was a man with long stringy white whiskers. Blue robes covered him head to foot, just like on the long-lost teapot. I felt warm in my silk blouse, but I wondered how this man could bear being entirely covered like a moth in a cocoon. Then, before I had time to gather my thoughts, the ship was making contact with the dock. Men threw looped ropes back and forth; the vessel shuddered as it came to rest against the piers – perhaps it was its spirit letting out that sound, its long labour of transporting us completed.

Strange sounds of gongs and chimes wafted to us from the wharf. From behind me, Mr Chen appeared one more time, dressed in the same bright and suffocating clothing that all his people wore. He greeted me. In just a few minutes, he pointed out, he would send a few men ashore, then I would step down a plank onto solid land. But Sergeant Sen, standing nearby in his own ceremonial garb, the blue sampot of the palace guard and bronze neckpiece, declared firmly but politely that he would go before me. Mr Chen came around to the idea. But you must not unsheathe your knife, he counselled, because people might think it unfriendly.

So the grey-haired soldier stepped down the plank before me that day, drawing the curious eyes of the Chinese guardsmen and the many townspeople they now held back. But, I must confess that attention left him when I stepped into view – perhaps this was Chinese custom, paying greater honours to women guests. I recall a great collective gasp; people jostled for a better view. I looked down, feeling unworthy as I always did in the face of such attention. I began to descend the plank, worried I'd tumble right into the water, but then Sergeant Sen stepped quickly back up and led me by my hand.

Mr Chen followed us down. He approached the man in silk robes, voiced some words to him respectfully, then turned to me.

'I present Commissioner Lee, minister of tariff collection and commerce in the port. He welcomes you to the Capital of the Empire of China.' The man made a low bow.

'Would you please tell the commissioner,' I replied, 'that I am delighted to make his acquaintance and hope that he is in good health.'

Mr Chen reported back that the commissioner was in fact well, and that he requested the privilege of showing the Lady to her accommodations.

I assumed that this would mean walking. But now I was directed toward a large wooden box. It took a moment, but I realized that it was a palanquin, yet covered. Men were waiting at either end to lift it. There was nothing I could do but get inside. I and the box were immediately lifted and a journey through the streets began, the commissioner in the lead in his own conveyance, Sergeant Sen thankfully walking beside mine, a hand on his knife hilt. The city had the oddest feel – most everything was brick or stone.

Could everything be a temple here? It would mean the people must be quite devout. But for now they seemed mainly to be enjoying themselves. They lined the street to inspect us; from windows, they leaned out and stared, or talked in loud voices, though I could of course comprehend not a word. Everyone did in fact look like Mr Chen, with narrow bodies and pale skin. They wore their hair drawn up at the back, and had coverings even on their feet, so that they did not step directly on the ground.

The party reached the guesthouse. It was bright red, standing without support of stilts. I wondered how it was possible to sleep in such a thing, with no space for spirits to pass underneath. Perhaps Chinese spirits went *around* things.

The commissioner bade me an elaborate good-bye. Then Mr Chen led the way through a gate that was another sight to behold – a giant circle, nothing else! My room was in the rear. Lit by large windows, it was, thankfully, bright and breezy. Invisible hands had set out fruit and tea. My apprehensions softened; this seemed familiar to me from visits with Chinese merchants home in Angkor.

Across the room I saw a large carved wooden thing that seemed a house within a house, with its own roof.

'That is a bed, Lady Sray,' said Mr Chen, noticing my surprise. 'In China the well-to-do sleep on these things, not on mats on the floor. This is a rather elaborate one – the commissioner insisted on it. You see the surface there, with the fabrics? That is where... where the sleeper lies.'

'Oh!'

'But we will provide mats for the floor if you would be more comfortable that way.'

'Thank you, but that's not necessary.' That seemed the polite thing to say, but I instantly wished I hadn't.

'And where will the sergeant and his men be staying?'

'The men will go to a garrison nearby. The sergeant will stay in a room in front of this house. I told him you'd be well protected here by Chinese who will stand guard at the gate, but he insisted that he be right at hand.'

'Mr Chen. I'm sure he didn't mean to suggest this place isn't safe. He is sometimes overprotective, that's all.'

Mr Chen left. Da and I took some time inspecting the rooms. We opened a cabinet and found that it contained ten silk blouses. We dared to lie down and test the feel of the bed. We agreed it was too soft to sleep on.

Then came a riotous hubbub from the front – shouts, the banging of gongs. We went to look. The cause was the two horned animals. Men were hauling the cages on carts through the streets, the occupants snorting in a way that showed more fright than aggression. Quite a few people had come to gawk.

Dinner was brought in baskets by Chinese servants. The rice had a different taste and texture than rice at home, but we ate it anyway. That night, feeling I must try to please my hosts, I lay down on the bed and eventually slept, but not well; I felt I was floating all night, and it was disconcerting to be off the floor. The next morning, I bathed at a jar outside. With Da's assistance, unneeded but provided nonetheless, I put on my finest silk sampot and a bright red blouse chosen from the cabinet. The maid spent time arranging my hair and applying jewellery and red powder. Normally, I was impatient with lengthy preparations, but today I welcomed any delay. It was the day of the audience with the emperor.

At the circular gate, my bodyguard was waiting.

'Sergeant,' I whispered. 'I'm so glad you're here. Your presence will give me courage for the ceremonies that are coming.'

There followed another covered palanquin, another journey through teeming streets, another brick gate. Rows of Chinese soldiers in red uniforms and caps stood waiting. When we Khmers had all arrived, a Chinese who seemed to be some kind of master of ceremonies formed us up into a procession, the minister at the front. Sergeant Sen was directed to the rear, but he affected not to understand and stood instead behind me.

Inside, the palace was like a mountain-temple in size and symmetry but the resemblance ended there. So many things were painted in the bright red that I now associated with China. (And I will confess I was finding the colour a bit unnatural and disturbing.) Roofs curved at odd angles, strange creatures of stone looked down from eaves. Following an arrow-straight walkway, we embassy members passed through inner gate after inner gate, then into a stone-paved courtyard filled with more soldiers in formation. The two cages from the ship had been placed to either side of the walkway. Both animals were on their feet, unhappy with the presence of so many strange people.

'I was told,' whispered Sergeant Sen, 'that the emperor requested to see the animals right away.'

On cue from the master of ceremonies, we passed up steps to the door of a large wooden hall. A gong sounded, and a strange, solo voice began an undulating chant. We stepped through. It was gloomy inside, with just a few candles burning and the smell of many bodies mixed with still air. Perhaps there was not sufficient water for bathing here. Huge red columns held up roof and rafters; I had never been in such an enormous covered space. Straight ahead was a piling-up of gilded platforms. It seemed to be a throne. Atop it was – a boy of perhaps six, wearing an embroidered gown that was too big for him, and a cloth cap.

It was hard not to stare. Even our minister did, taking a moment to ascertain that he saw what he saw. Then the man went to his knees and touched his forehead to the tiles of the floor three times. Mr Chen appeared at his side, ready to translate the statement whose time had come.

'Separated by the Salt Water Sea,' intoned the minister, 'two great Empires exist in friendship, both beloved of Heaven, both centres of learning and martial prowess, strengthened by trade that...'

That was as far as he got. Because the boy on the throne had sprung down from his perch, and was running to the door, shouting, pursued by half a dozen courtiers.

Sergeant Sen and I exchanged glances, amused for the first time. 'I think,' murmured the sergeant, 'that he wants to see the animals. In that way, boy emperors are no different than boy villagers.'

We walked to the hall's entranceway to look. Down the steps, the young Majesty was having second thoughts. He hung back from the cages, clutching at the robes of a courtier. The animals had taken notice of him and were huffing and grunting in a menacing way. Where was his mother, or nursemaid? No sign, only half a dozen of these courtiers, wearing the clothes of men, yet seeming somehow different than men.

So I hurried down the steps to the boy. 'The animals won't hurt you,' I told him, stooping down to his level. 'They're just a little nervous. It's best to be still. They'll get used to you faster that way. Then you can go closer.'

A breathless Mr Chen translated. The courtiers received this idea with scepticism, tossing comments back and forth in their language.

The emperor and I stood and watched. I thanked Heaven that, just as I'd promised, the animals calmed down.

'Now, would you like to feed them? They would like that.'

I took his hand – the courtiers gasped. A Khmer keeper by the cage provided two lengths of sugar cane. I gave one to the boy and stepped to the cage with the other. 'Like this,' I said. 'Gently. Put just the end through.'

The boy followed my example, giggling as the beast took the cane, grinding it between mammoth stained molars. The courtiers relaxed. The second animal was fed too; I explained to the emperor that Heaven smiled on fairness. Soon I led him back up the steps and the welcome ceremony resumed. At the emperor's insistence, I stood next to the throne. But when the last official word had been intoned, two of those courtiers stepped forward and re-asserted control. With firm insistence they led the young emperor off, one to each side. I felt doleful at the sight. Just before they disappeared through a door, the boy managed to turn and look to me with an expression of yearning.

That evening, we went, this time on foot, to Commissioner Lee's residence for an official dinner. A young Chinese man who'd been on the ship lit the way with a torch, and at windows there were again those many curious eyes. Da, at my side, had regained some courage in this new place, and walked proudly. I was sure she'd begun making eyes at the young man with the torch. No, I realized now, sifting through some memories – that had begun on the ship.

Inside, the commissioner waited in an expansive dining hall of polished beams and white plaster. To the side, something large was covered in red cloth. Mr Chen joined me. I was shown to one of the tables with him and a group of clearly prominent Chinese men. It was all very awkward, because I could feel eyes inspecting me at every opportunity. Then servants brought bowls of steaming rice and spiced meat and vegetables, and the men looked to the food, and I felt less the centre of things. How glad I was that I had learned at home how to use the small lacquered sticks with which Chinese eat. Over the next two hours I tasted many things I had never tasted before, even in the Chinese places at home, and I sipped at a strange wine that was placed in front of me.

Sergeant Sen stood by the door, and every so often my eyes sought his out.

Later, servants cleared away the bowls, and the commissioner made a speech, Mr Chen translating to me in low tones. Again the subject was the happy relations between the two great Empires. The Khmer minister responded in kind. Then one of the Chinese posed a long question about whether ivory truly came from an animal that weighed as much as twenty horses and had a great snake growing from its lip, and, whatever the appearance of that animal, where ivory could be bought and at what price. I waited for the minister to answer, but Mr Chen whispered that no, the question was addressed to me. Indeed, everyone was looking my way. Some friendly spirit came to my aid just then. I shed my self-consciousness and answered that question and others that followed.

Later two men came to me and presented a fancy carved box. I had no idea what was inside, and the commissioner voiced a few words. 'It is a gift, Lady Sray,' said Mr Chen, 'one by which we hope you will remember China. Please open it.'

Inside, packed in straw, was a brand new blue and white teapot, with matching cups. I took the pot in hand and turned it slowly. Remarkable! It had the same kind of patterns I remembered, the same colours. And a painted scene of people drinking tea. Not quite the same as the old one at my house, but close.

'I will take it home and treasure it as a memento of my time here.' Translated, this caused general delight around the room. Then two servants stepped to the large thing covered by red fabric and, with a flourish, pulled it off. Underneath were stacks of boxes resembling the one I held.

'One thousand sets!' declared Mr Chen. 'To take home for sale in Angkor. Of lesser quality, of course – only you deserve one as fine as the one we have given you.'

When it came time to return to the guesthouse, Da was missing. As was the young Chinese man from the ship. We waited a bit, then a servant from the commissioner's household was assigned to lead the way with a torch.

At the guesthouse door, Sergeant Sen said his good night. Pensive now, I passed slowly down the corridor to my room. A lamp was burning there. I removed my jewellery and splashed water on my face from a bowl. Then, for no reason I could discern, I sat down on the floor, facing a window open to the stars. I blew out the lamp. I gazed at Heaven's lights, but at the same time my mind turned over another question: the room to which Sergeant Sen had retired – did it have windows, did it look out to the night sky in this same way? I pictured him settling in for the night on one of these bed things, tossing, unable to find a comfortable pose. Just like me. Or maybe he would just sleep right on the floor, mat-less. He would not have asked for one; he never worried about his own comfort.

Then there came to me a particular thought, one that had been hiding in my consciousness for how long I didn't know. Now it had been brought to the fore, by some spirit, surely, perhaps a friendly stow-away on the ship. Was it one of Bronze Uncle's assistants? Was it the one that had helped me find my voice at the dinner? I was certain that it was now suggesting that a certain course of action was something Heaven would accept, even approve in this far-away place.

I rose and stole down the corridor toward his room.

'Sergeant,' I whispered from the door. 'I have heard a strange noise in my room. Will you come and look, please?'

'Of course, Lady!'

Lamp in hand, he hurried past me. I followed him back down the corridor, feeling bad, but not too bad, for alarming him in this way. I spied on him from the doorway as he looked in his diligent way behind drapes and furniture.

'It's all right, Lady. There's no one here. But I'll check outside as well.'

'Sergeant. I...I have a confession.'

'Yes, Lady?'

'I deceived you.' I took a breath. 'There is nothing. I deceived you...so that you would come here and we would be together, alone.'

I was unable to say more, because I felt suddenly terrified. The meaning of those words was unmistakable, and with it I might snuff out the quiet friendship on which I had depended for so many years.

He was speechless as well. Then, looking down, he said: 'My place is in my own room, Lady.'

I found my courage. 'For tonight, please make it here. I ask as someone who has...who has...felt – I must say it – the deepest kind of love for you for many years. And I dare to suspect that you have something similar in you. We have felt this way since the day at the prince's compound, have we not? And yet there is a terrible distance between us. Does it always have to be so? There are different principles that govern life in China. You said so yourself on the ship. I think that different principles can sometimes bring a good result.'

When he answered, there was despair in his voice. 'Lady, all these years I have felt a craving to hear what you have said. I have carried this burden with me every day. I recognized the goodness in your heart on that first day, when you worried more about food for the other people than for yourself. I saw it again today – you were the only person who felt compassion for that poor little boy who has been made emperor. I worry that when you left the palace today he suffered the same disappointment that I have for so many years, Lady Sray.'

'Don't call me that – please! I deserve no title. On the ship, you told me of your past. Mine is the same, can't you tell? I was born in a village like yours. I lost my family, not to disease, but to war. I grew up in a house for orphans. I raised ducks and sold their eggs in the market. I never prayed for anything more than a simple life. But Heaven chose to elevate me to a station where I don't belong, where I have never felt contentment.

'For just one night, I would like to be again what I was brought into this life to be, to know what I might have experienced. To be as wife to the man whom I wish Heaven had placed with me from the start. For tonight, I want the Lady Sray to vanish and the simple village woman Sray to take her place. Please, won't you allow it to be that way?'

There was another silence, and I felt I had lost him, that he would leave without another word and send one of his men to occupy his room. But then he pulled me gently to him. I laid my head on his shoulder.

'Do you know,' he asked, 'what I imagined today at the palace?'

'Tell me.'

'That you and I and the boy were transported by some deity to a village, one of those that we passed on the ship, and we were set down and became a family, no different than any other there. We remained there after our ship departed for the Empire again. I worked the fields, you took your place at a stove, fanning the coals. The boy grew up as our son.'

'And we had more children, I hope?'

'Oh, yes, many more. They cared for us in our old age.'

I became aware now that I couldn't feel his skin against mine. I stepped back and unfastened the silk blouse.

'There!' I laughed, throwing it aside. I sank back into him. 'How do people wear this all the time? I can't understand it!'

'Nor can I. But for now, let's pretend that we can, because the dream about a Chinese village requires that you wear the garment. Except at night...Sray.'

And I called him Sen, for the first time, and many more times before first light appeared those names went back and forth between us.

I told you when I began this story that the last moments of peace I ever knew came just before the Brahmin appeared at our door in the little settlement so many years ago. But that is not entirely true. For the few hours of this night in China, the burdens of family, of wealth, of fear of vengeance by a ghost and discovery of a terrible secret – all these things were lifted from my heart.

47: The boar-hunting ground

I have told you of the startling changes that came over my children's lives during my absence. There was also an important change in the palace. It had to do with the succession.

Most every person who lived in Angkor in those days belonged to one of two camps, those who felt deep affection for Aroon, Most Excellent August Royal Prince, and those who wished the title had been settled on Darit, born of the concubine Rom. As the two sons of the King grew up – Darit had reached his sixteenth year before I departed for China, while his half-brother was a year younger – their every move and expression was noted and analysed and discussed, whether in palace annexes, homes or marketplace noodle stalls. Disagreements on this subject sometimes ended even in brawls and the break-ups of long friendships.

Aroon's proponents were in the majority and, of course, had convention and blood line on their side. The prince had been born to the first and only official wife of His Majesty. He had inherited a fine sense of duty and decorum, and was known for selflessly shouldering the many obligations that his birth entailed. He took part in lengthy temple rites, he walked in procession, he attended court, never arriving late or seeming impatient once he was there. It was true that he had rather a plain face and he did not seem over-blessed with innate abilities, either of body or mind, but he worked diligently to develop those he did have. He became a competent archer, for instance, by drawing his bow against a straw target each morning without fail, rain or shine. He had worked, with signs of success, to overcome a fear of horses. He was generous, endowing hospitals and hermitages. But what was most remarked on, at least by females in the city, was the devotion that he displayed toward his mother, Her Serene Majesty Queen Benjana. He called on her often at the teak house outside the Capital where she passed most of her time. Some days he took her out for air in her palanquin, walking to the side with the humility and attentiveness of a servant.

All of this added up, and each year the palace Brahmins accorded Aroon a new rank that confirmed, again, that he was progressing down the path of succession as Heaven's choice. The latest such marker was his betrothal to a princess from a large estate south of the Freshwater Sea.

Darit was an entirely different sort, to the point that people wondered how it was possible the two had the same father. He had been born, it was said, with a leer on his face. He passed through life protected by the magic amulet around his neck. Patience and approbation were foreign concepts to him; he was known to slap courtiers, servants, girlfriends, anyone he believed failed him, and in at least one case, a priest. But he was quite pleasing to look at, sharing his father's solid chest and square jaw, and there were already two young women in the extended palace household, one a wash maid, the other the daughter of a carpenter, who made proud and credible claims that their infants were his.

As a boy, he had learned in a single day to shoot arrows to within a finger's width of a bull's-eye. And horses – Darit had an affinity with the animals that people said could only be divinely accorded. A horse with Darit on its back became an inspired animal, racing faster and farther than its grooms thought possible, sensing its rider's commands before he gave them. Darit was possibly the best horseman in the Empire. And wouldn't that be a fine skill in time of war? This was the kind of point his proponents kept coming back to in those sometimes violent arguments. Whether he's worthy of love or it, it's as simple as that, they said – Darit has the bearing and bullheadedness of a King. He would secure the Empire's borders or expand them, as his father had. Men would follow him into battle; with Aroon they would feel the need to close around him and protect.

From the day of that parade a decade earlier, in which a small boy atop a large war horse had made such an impression, His Majesty's favour had gone in the direction everyone expected. At least once a week, the King ordered that the Darit be brought to him. With his mother watching from a discreet distance, they played at various battle games with swords, clubs, bows and of course horses. Whatever bad the budding young man did, His Majesty was of a mind to forgive – this business of slapping servants and seeding the palace with superfluous children could only remind him of his own youth.

Over the years, the King wondered aloud many times whether some formal honour ought to be bestowed on Darit. A title, something not terribly high-ranking to start – Sacred Celestial Crystal, perhaps? The Brahmin Subhadra, alert to anything that in future years might cloud the rightful path of succession, invariably responded with a long, concerned face. He dared not mention that these suggestions usually followed the King's nights on the mat with the concubine Rom. Instead, he offered long and complex theological arguments, backed by scriptural passages read aloud by a scribe called to the room for the purpose. The Brahmin's teaching was that the continued turning of the cosmic engine – for King, for Empire, for the universe in its unfathomable vastness – required an heir recognized clearly and indisputably from the very start.

As the two boys approached full manhood, putting aside toy weapons for real ones, the Brahmin began adding another line of reasoning. It must be acknowledged, he pointed out, that the Empire has a history of violent succession, each case tragic and despised by Heaven, save His Majesty's own. (For wasn't it true that in those days the Chams and Siamese were practically at the gates of Angkor?) But it mustn't be forgotten that Prince Aroon has shown the sense of proportion necessary to wait out the great number of years that by Heaven's design must pass before the sun sets on the current reign. It was pointed out that though the prince was in the presence of His Majesty often, sometimes even with a sharp knife in his waist, he had done nothing to try to hurry that unwanted time's arrival. His Majesty can turn his back – can he not? – and even lie down in his presence and sleep, without the slightest concern. The prince's devotion is absolute.

At first, the Brahmin's arguments exasperated the King. But as the years passed, he began to reconsider. The charm of Darit's impetuous ways was somehow diminishing. The King became aware that so much of the boy's rebelliousness was directed at things that a King, by virtue of being King, had to value. Why is it, His Majesty began to ask the priest, that the boy cannot summon at least a trace of interest in the audiences and the ritual that occupy so much of a monarch's day? At these times, the Brahmin did his best to suggest, without ever saying it openly, that contempt for these things might disguise contempt for the person of the King himself.

One morning, an argument broke out between Darit's two girlfriends in the palace household, resulting an hour later in one of them, infant in arms, daring to throw herself at the feet of His Majesty himself as he walked to his palanquin. Bodyguards dragged her off, slapping her across the face, the baby screaming. The King looked back on her, appalled. People said later that he seemed to be feeling disgust that his son should be party to creating such a scene.

Rom, of course, could sense that Darit was losing his father's support, and so she did everything she could to bring them together in favourable circumstances. One day, when she learned that the King and Prince Aroon were to go to a boar-hunting ground, she insisted that she and Darit go too. The contrast between the two sons would be on full display. With impressions of the young man atop a horse fresh in the royal memory, she would renew her private petitions for a title.

The hunting ground was not so much a ground as an arena. A pavilion built for royal spectators of a previous reign gave on to a broad grassy field. Everything was enclosed by bamboo fencing capable of resisting the charge of the fiercest, longest tusked boars, brought here so that royal hunters would be saved the bother of tracking them for hours or days through forest. Palace huntsmen and their teams of slaves got that dangerous assignment, following droppings and trails and tree rubs to find and capture the beasts alive. They bound their legs with rope, then released them one by one inside the fenced grounds to be chased and killed. Plans called for the hunting party to gather at the palace gate the morning of the hunt, then proceed to the grounds together. Prince Aroon arrived early. By departure time, Darit had not appeared. His Majesty frowned; Rom did what she could to delay, but soon the procession began, with a pair of servants left behind with urgent instructions to find Darit and get him to the grounds on his own. Prince Aroon rode alongside his father; my husband walked behind, happy that things were already developing favourably for Aroon.

The hunting pavilion had been polished and swept by servants who went out in advance. Inside, a dais awaited, with sweets and water laid out. His Majesty took his place. There was still no sign of Darit. Rom paced, growing more perturbed. There was still some time – priests had yet to chant the elaborate pre-hunt prayers that would assure Heaven that the animals to be killed were in no way associated with the third incarnation of Vishnu, the giant boar Varaha, which rescued the Earth Goddess from the floor of the primeval sea. The priests began. Then – the sound of hooves. The gates to the grounds were thrown open, and Darit came through, atop a powerful galloping horse.

He faltered slightly in getting off his mount. People felt that a hint of wine breath crossed the air. Rom frowned.

When the prayers were done, he rose, barely acknowledged the King, and remounted his horse. A groom handed him an iron-tipped lance. At the far side of the field, a small door in the fence opened, and a snorting boar was forced through by quick-handed slaves. The animal took an instant getting its orientation, then raced to the right, seeming to think that escape lay in that direction. Darit urged his horse forward, its hooves raising dust. Soon it was clear to everyone that they had in fact smelled wine. The boar ran right past its stalker! Left and right, back and forth, all around the field it raced, Darit struggling to follow. The animal was in charge; the scene became almost comic – the famous amulet was doing Darit no good at all. He flailed with the lance, each thrust missing by a wide margin. Then he lost his grip on the weapon and had to dismount to pick it up. The boar stopped a few paces away, grunting, as if unwilling to charge an adversary so pitiful.

The King closed his eyes, a hand to his forehead; Rom left the pavilion. My husband, of course, was enjoying himself.

The chase continued until the boar was worn down by exhaustion. Finally Darit impaled it, but in its neck, not in a clean way. It flailed, it thrashed. Now truly angry, it charged Darit's horse, drawing some blood from the mount's legs. Then it contemptuously turned away, bleeding. Darit came near; it charged once more, leading him to spring back. Then it lay down and its spirit departed.

Cheers normally followed a kill, but everyone in the pavilion, including the King, responded to this one with shocked silence. Darit turned his horse back toward the royal party, showing no shame. He got down and came inside the pavilion, sweating. He gulped from a bowl, then splashed some of its water onto his face. People winced at this show of bad manners. His mother seized his arm and led him away from the pavilion for a talking to.

Now Aroon rose, pretending he'd noticed nothing amiss. What breeding the prince displayed! He bowed to the King, crossed his arms in salute, then mounted his horse. This time there was no hesitation. Aroon sped straight for a newly released boar, keeping his horse deftly on track, anticipating the zigs and zags of the prey's attempts at evasion. One thrust of the lance – that was all it took. The point entered the racing boar's torso just above the right front leg and pierced the heart. The animal went into a dust-raising somersault, the kind that hunters love, then fell heavy and still.

The cheers that erupted were too loud for such close quarters to the King. But no one had ever seen Prince Aroon ride this way. Fearless, entirely in control, practically like a god atop a magic mount. As he returned toward the pavilion, His Majesty rose. He stepped outside and he embraced this son wholeheartedly – it was said this was the very first time for such a display. Tears flowed from the young prince's eyes.

The party began the trip back to the city, Nol on foot. Before long, Rom came up to his side.

'I know it's you who put her up to it,' she hissed. 'My son told me about the girl at the drinking stall!'

'I can't imagine what you're talking about.'

That was true so far as the details went. But Nol knew the basics. A startling young beauty from a village, newly installed at the drinking place that Darit visited most every night. Secret payment to her to entertain Darit the night before, but to delay the wine, to assure that it started only after midnight and kept up straight through to sunrise.

'Don't lie, parasol master!'

'I wasn't there, so how can I lie? But if there was such a girl, I imagine she didn't have much trouble getting him to drink till dawn. He's got some experience at that, I hear.'

'Don't taunt me! I'm going to His Majesty about this. We'll do the hunt over again!'

Nol smiled. He had been waiting for this opening. 'I wouldn't advise that,' he said, 'because I might have something to tell His Majesty too.'

She shot him a withering look; it only increased his satisfaction.

'The prince's riding instructor – his former instructor, I should say. A certain Mr Ton. I believe you got a message a while ago saying he was making a visit back at his village...'

'What of it?'

'Well, Ton didn't go back there. That message was a fake. He's in custody, in a cage at one of the palace guard barracks. Because one of the hands in the royal horse stable came to me and recounted that he'd overheard a conversation between the instructor and a certain senior concubine. The talk about money and riding accidents disturbed him deeply and he felt it was his duty to convey it to me.

'I've got your attention now, do I? Well, let me continue. The timing of all this was quite interesting – this came to light just the day after you persuaded His Majesty to take your boy on the hunt. Well, do you know what this Mr Ton has told us, after a guardsman threw a rope over a rafter and hung him by his right arm for an hour? That in all the years he's been with Prince Aroon, his goal has been to make him afraid of horses. Imagine that! He has put thorns under the saddle cloth to cause the prince to be thrown. He has matched him with horses too powerful, some of them not trained at all. Once when the prince was in a stable stall, he spooked the horse to make him kick the prince. The prince was laid up for almost a week by that – it was lucky there were no broken bones. Do you know that this man even confessed to having put drugs in the water of the horses that the prince rode in public, to rile them up?

'Now, why would this man Ton do such things? Why, it turns

out that someone was paying him! Someone was sending him a bag of silver at the end of each month. He's confessed that his village is the village where a certain senior concubine grew up, that his family owes a great deal of money to the family of that concubine, that it was that concubine who brought him to the Capital years ago.

'Well, as I said, this Ton is no longer the prince's instructor. The prince has a new one. Wasn't it remarkable how his riding has improved? All it took was a couple of weeks with the new man. Think what it'll be like in a year!'

Nol turned to look to her, but she was gone. She had fallen back in the procession, joining her maid, and was silent the rest of the trip back to the Capital.

She lay with the King that night, as scheduled. I am sure there was no mention of any provincial beauty at a drinking stall. Instead she would have stuck with her entreaties for a formal rank for Darit, but to no avail. Her son, meanwhile, returned to the stall and found that the beauty was no longer there. He slapped the proprietor around to try to learn where she'd gone, but then three burly men with clubs came in and he had to withdraw.

Two weeks later, the palace priests settled another title on Prince Aroon. He became Aroon, Great Secondary King. He was now officially the heir. Crowds turned out to kneel at streetside as he made his way from the temple where the rank was conferred; he took collective breath away with the quiet dignity he showed in walking by the palanquin of Her Serene Majesty, Queen Benjana.

Everyone believed that the Empire's future was now secure. When the time finally came for His Majesty to depart this life, he would be followed by this gracious prince, favoured of Heaven. Why do humans persist in thinking they can see the future? Darit's disgrace in fact would bring on turmoil of breadth and intensity the Empire had not known in decades.

48: The Great Dual Vector River

We are taught that all rivers in the Empire are holy but the Great Dual Vector River is the most holy of all. This was the channel we sailed on our departure for China. I have told you of the venomous words with which I helped turn aside the Cham boarding party that day and how they were perhaps placed on my tongue by a spirit. Would it be vain to wonder if that spirit was the river's spirit? For a brief period, I became precisely the person I am not, at least the person I strive not to be. It was a realignment of left to right, top to bottom. This spirit, as you know, alters its character in an equally dramatic way, first nurturing us, the Khmer people, giving us the water of life, but then taking it back, to teach us a lesson, a sometimes painful one, that if the world is to know bounty, it must also know privation.

How perfectly the spirit carries out this plan. For half the year, it directs the river to flow to the northwest, feeding the Freshwater Sea. Have you been at the sea in that season? In later years, I always tried to time my travels to place me there at this time. The sea bursts its banks and sends waters out to dry paddy land, garden ponds and canals. The sight is unforgettable. With the flow comes silt in which rice seedlings thrive. So do catfish, in numbers beyond counting, seeming determined to swim into the bamboo traps that villagers lay for them. Soon the waters begin arriving from the Heavens as well. Late-day rains turn soil from hard and crumbly to soft and fertile, quick to catch in the toes of people who walk through it. Streams ran fast and clear, feeding the sea even more. Wildflowers bloom bright in jungle clearings, fruit grows large and heavy on the bough. In air that becomes refreshing, even cool, people – most people, at least – work hard and sleep well.

But in not so many months more, the spirit will change its mind. At its command, the river will reverse course and flow to the southeast, sucking life and water from the Freshwater Sea, causing it to contract to a fraction of its former size. The rains will end. It will be a time of unhappy events. Vast expanses of parched wasteland will come into being, strewn with dead fish, shrivelled plants and other reminders of bygone fecundity. Paddies will go dry, soil will crack, crumble, even turn to dust. At temples, fragments of fallen leaves will fill the cracks between paving stones. The air will become so hot and oppressive that people will avoid going out and at night lie sleepless for hours on their mats.

We Khmers know such times will come, yet we are not angry for it. That is one of our great virtues, do you not think? Each year, at the time when the river's feeding of the Freshwater Sea comes to an end, we don't rue the change. Rather, we celebrate. Many of us flock behind His Majesty to a sacred place on the river banks to bid farewell to the waters, to thank the spirit residing in their depths for having been so generous for so long and to give assurances that we have made every effort to put the gift to greatest use. To the chanting of vedas, to the scattering of flower petals, our monarch stands at the river's edge, then raises hand and golden sword. He announces to the spirit below that we the Khmer people are humble, pious and deserving of a future reprieve. He issues a call: Show us your benevolent power again, spirit of the Great Dual Vector River. Let the waters now go, but let them come back and repeat their regenerative wonders.

You know, I'm sure, of the celebrations that follow. Nol took me to them several times. Boats powered by forty paddlers racing each other across the water's surface. Soldiers duelling with blunted spears, with heavy betting on the outcome. Royal dancers dipping and swaying in groups of a hundred or more, and the royal concubines parading, each wearing her finest green sampot and headdress.

Except, of course, that we don't see the concubine chosen that year as Woman of the Great Dual Vector River. She remains out of sight. After His Majesty restarts the Empire's cycle of life, she will couple with him to do the same on a personal scale. Did you know that the honour is so great that some of the concubines lose all sense of rectitude and compete for it? The boldest of the women try to influence His Majesty directly, through whispered pleas and special carnal techniques, while others feel that attention is better directed toward the palace Brahmins who make the pick.

But in the year that my story has reached, the year when I was still on my trip to China, the outcome of any such competition was known in advance. The one honoured would be my daughter Bopa. It was simply that she'd been summoned so many times from the house in the far corner of the royal compound, where she continued to live with the maid Yan. The priest who oversaw preparations for the river rite had come to the house three times with an assistant and asked questions, about the health of her womb, the timing of her flow, the state of her spiritual development. Everything that she said was taken down on a slate by the assistant, then discussed by the full Councils of Brahmins.

The signals were strong enough that even my girl picked up on them in the isolation of her house in the compound. She began to feel hope. Not out of love of being singled out, I think, though of course she felt such love. The fact is that she was deeply lonely. She began to believe that winning the honour would somehow mean she could leave her house, her prison, and go to live with Elder Sister Rom in the concubine pavilion.

One morning, as she sat in her enclosed garden, two concubines passed on the other side of the fence and she overheard words that made her certain the honour was coming.

'I was told His Majesty asks everything about her, what she's thinking, what she's doing,' one was saying.

'But how can there be news? She's so far away.'

'Of course she is! But now the shaman has arrived. He can sense everything. Yesterday the answer was: 'Now she's sleeping, now she's waking to the sound of a temple bell, now she's watching a mango being cut for her breakfast.''

A mango! Bopa had eaten one for breakfast just three days earlier. She'd been sleeping when Yan prepared it with a knife, yes, but this shaman could not be faulted for not knowing that.

That afternoon, a priest came to the house and escorted my girl to an unfamiliar room in the palace. On the floor was a sleeping mat, in a corner a Chinese table. She looked around, confused, but before she could ask what this place was, the priest whispered: 'You will lie down right there' – he gestured to the mat – 'and look as if you are sleeping. Close your eyes. Be quick, please.'

She did as told and the man left. After a moment, a bell rang somewhere outside and the priest whispered from the door: 'Now, get up, as if you've awoken from sleeping all night.'

What game was this? She did as instructed, rubbing her eyes for effect. In a moment, a female servant entered, carrying a tray set with mango and knife. The woman began to cut away the fruit's skin.

'You will watch,' the courtier whispered, still at the door.

Bopa obeyed and then she was given the mango to eat. As she did, she suddenly felt that the royal eyes were on her, had been from the moment she'd arrived, through a hole in the wall to the side. She dared not look. When she finished eating, she waited, trembling, and got no more instructions from the priest. Footsteps came from outside, then the King entered. He stood back for a moment, wearing what she felt was a mournful expression. Then he turned and studied her with an intensity that she found both exciting and humiliating. After that, the King knelt by her, then made their union, gently, and when it was done she lay back, breathing hard, hoping to hold in his seed, and he studied her again, with such a strange, tragic look on his face that she turned her face to avoid it.

In subsequent days, she was summoned to this same room again. Each time this same priest told her to carry out some routine domestic task. One day it was eating, the next it was bathing – a water jar had been brought inside and bathing without splashing water everywhere on the mats was quite awkward. Another day it was reading holy scripts (this she could only pretend to do). And the day after that, yet another surprise. A man with a pale face and wearing strange silk robes that covered him top to bottom was in the room when she arrived, and he addressed her in a strange language. Then there were words from outside the door and His Majesty entered.

Then one morning, Bopa was sitting in her house's main room, tended by Yan, when the Brahmin Subhadra brought official word. Bopa would be the river rite partner. She would leave for the site the following day on a royal barge.

The rest of the day seemed like a repeat of her first time with

His Majesty. Two aged seamstresses came to make the special sampot, followed by a priest who instructed her in the ceremony, then assistants with bath water drawn from the river and blessed, then a woman who spent more than an hour arranging her hair.

At the port on the Freshwater Sea, Bopa and Yan boarded a barge that would take them down the coast. The two were directed to a pavilion at the stern. It was an odd thing, closed on three sides, open only to the back, so as to hide the females from the rowers' eyes. Inside were sleeping mats, a small shrine, and a teak chest, which she'd been told in strict terms not to open. Inside would be garments and jewellery for the rite.

After three days, the boat tied up on the river bank, connected by a narrow plank, and all the rowers went ashore. A priest appeared. He explained that the site for the ceremony was just a short walk away, but that Bopa must remain on the barge until instructions arrived. Evening came, but no instructions, and then night and morning and another full day of waiting. Servants brought food and left without a word. Bopa picked at it, growing more and more bored. She told Yan to open the teak chest. It couldn't hurt just to look. But Yan frowned and said, please, mistress, we must not.

That evening, a boy arrived with a message. Yan was to come with him to receive instructions for the rite. The priest had said nothing about that, and the maid resisted. But Bopa, fearful they'd get a scolding, urged her to go.

She lay down for another nap and was awoken by a voice. It was Rom's.

Elder sister was standing on the shore, smiling across at her. 'You look absolutely stunning, Bopa! His Majesty will be delighted when he sees you.'

Really it was Bopa who was delighted, so much so that words failed her. Rom hurried across the plank to join her. 'Oh, Bopa,' she said, clasping both of her hands, 'you look a bit concerned! Don't tell me you're worried about those silly rules that we can't see each other. They don't apply down here, don't you know? We can spend as much time together as we want.'

Rom sat down beside her and in an instant Bopa was

blubbering like a child, embracing her friend around the waist. 'I've missed you so much, Elder Sister!'

'And I've missed you,' she said, stroking Bopa's shoulder.

'All day I sit in that house with the silly maid Yan. There's not a thing to do, and I think of how much fun we used to have in the pavilion.'

'We'll make up for it down here. When the ritual's over, we'll go out together into the festival. In the meantime, I've brought you something to eat. I hear that what they've been giving you is terrible. Priests have no idea at all about food. But look – it's your favourite.' She held out sweetmeat wrapped in a banana leaf.

Bopa grinned and took some. It did taste fabulous.

'Go on!' laughed Rom. 'Eat as much as you want!'

She had some more, and before long she was sucking the meat's juice from her fingers like a village girl, which seemed to her quite funny. Rom watched, and she thought it was funny too, and laughed and said it was so good that Bopa should finish it all. Rom could go get some more. That was the last thing the girl remembered: Rom holding out a morsel, and Bopa wanting it, but feeling unable to raise a hand to take it.

And thus was my girl cheated out of the river honour.

When she awoke, Rom was gone. But sitting close to her, wearing an expression of very great concern, was Yan.

Bopa sat up in a start, confused. Her hand went to her head, which was pounding. She grimaced and fell back to the mat and slept again, though she did not mean to. Later, she awoke, this time her bladder insisting that she get up. Helped by Yan, she stumbled to the edge of the boat, where she hung her rear over the edge, not caring if anyone saw.

But there was no one to see. The boat was empty, save for her and Yan, who was relieved that her mistress was awake and moving around. But then the maid began to cry.

'Mistress, I'm so sorry – I should never have left you. I came back and that woman Rom was here. You were sleeping and you wouldn't wake up! Then the priests came to dress you and get you ready and still you wouldn't wake up. Oh! I should never have left you alone.'

'It's all right. I'm awake now. We can go.' Bopa's head began to throb again. She lay down, afraid she would faint.

'Mistress, the Brahmins saw that you couldn't go, and so they made a ruling, right here, that in an emergency, when the King was waiting and the selected concubine was not up to the task, for whatever reason, they could choose someone else. They chose Rom.'

Bopa's head pounded all over again. She had to ask: 'And they dressed her in the garments from the chest?'

'They did! There was a sampot with two green sashes and a three-pointed headdress, and very fancy red dye for the palms and feet. And there was perfume and lots of armlets. They put them all on her. Mistress, I know you treasure her, but she's not your friend! She brought you something that made you sleep. She planned this, don't you see?'

'Of course I see!' cried Bopa, and indeed I think she finally did.

'Mistress, you're awake now. Maybe there's still a chance. Let's go to the festival area ourselves and see.'

The idea of confronting Rom frightened my daughter, but she allowed herself to be led off the barge. The two women moved along a trail that followed the water's edge. Around a bend, they saw soldiers and pavilions and banners, and Bopa lost her nerve.

'You go find out. I'll stay here.'

She sat down beneath a tree and leaned against its trunk. She sank to her haunches. How comfortable it seemed – she fell asleep again. But then Yan was there again, gently shaking her awake. 'His Majesty performed the ceremony,' she said. 'I'm sorry, it's too late for you. But Rom has been disgraced!'

'I don't understand...'

'The priests chanted and they threw lotus petals and His Majesty gave his blessings and thanks to the water. I arrived just as he was doing that. But when he was processing to the pavilion to be in union with Rom, one of the courtiers came running up and told him something, and he just stopped, right there. He stood there, still, like an image in a temple, looking down the river, like he was searching for something. And then he gave some orders. Rom was ejected from the pavilion! She was screaming, protesting, but His Majesty simply turned his back on her. Nobody could understand what was happening. But then the word spread. His Majesty had just been told that the ships from China were not far down the river and are coming this way.'

'Ships from China?' It was a powerful drug Rom had administered; my girl's head still was not clear.

'Yes, mistress – China, the embassy. Your mother is part of the embassy. She's on one of those ships.'

49: Plea for peace

At the time, I knew nothing of the events concerning Rom and Bopa. How could I? As they unfolded, I was up the river, standing on my ship's deck, also peering into the day's final light. I was having the most hopeful kind of thoughts. The long journey was near its end; I would see my girl, my boy, my husband, I would sleep on my own mats again, I would eat rice from my own bowls. Then, with sunset approaching, a crewman at the bow called out that we were near the site of the river festival, that it seemed to be underway even as we approached. Soon we could all make out torches ahead. No one had timed our arrival this way. Rather, Heaven had chosen to give us winds that delivered us at this very moment.

It came to me that my gaze might be meeting, invisibly, the gaze of His Majesty. I looked away, and thought of the golden bangles, which still lay in my jewellery box.

Two hours later, our ship was riding at anchor in darkness off the bank. We could see many more torches on shore, their light glinting off a profusion of polished head pieces and jewellery. There was no doubt that His Majesty was present. I thought, this is starting again so soon? I have yet to even set foot on Khmer soil. Yet I understood. Our embassy could no more sail past His Majesty than some minor god could pass Vishnu and give no obeisance. The King would not be meeting with me so much as meeting with a member of the China embassy.

So I put on a ceremonial sampot and stood still while my maid dusted my hands with powder and applied jewellery and holy scent. Presently I took a place on a sampan, sitting behind the embassy's chief minister. I recall above all how quiet it was, that none among us spoke, and that all on shore remained hushed as well as our boat drew near. The loudest sound was paddles stirring the water's surface, signalling our passage to the great spirit below.

On dry land, crouching courtiers showed us forward by torchlight. People knelt left and right as we passed. Then I caught sight of my husband ahead. Our eyes locked. His face displayed his unquestioning devotion, his long readiness to protect me. What a faithful spouse he had always been! It was a breach of court etiquette, but I put hands together to greet him, right there, before I had acknowledged the lord on the dais.

I kept my eyes down as we approached the King. Then I went to the dirt, along with the minister.

'Majesty,' the minister announced, 'we have completed the blessed mission on which you dispatched us.'

'We welcome you back to the Empire,' the King replied. 'We are happy to see that you are in good health.' The voice was the same, deep and melodious, captivating me even before the second word was out, blocking out consciousness of my husband, who was so near.

'We have conferred with the Emperor of China, Majesty, who sends his greetings and best wishes and hopes of good health, as well as gifts...' And then he spoke at length, in the most elaborate and grandiose terms, as officials do, as if their education is for nothing but such times. The subject was the Khmer people and the Chinese people now united as brothers. For me, hardly a word sank in. But then there came a murmured interjection from off to the right: 'We will see.' I glanced up. The words had come from Commander Rit. His tone led me to force my mind to back up and recall what the minister had just been saying. It was that this new unity as brothers would also bring peace with the Chams.

Now it was the King who spoke. 'Lady Sray, please tell us, did the voyage go well for you?'

I dared look up again. His eyes were on me alone. And I am certain that for just an instant they went to my wrists, hoping for things there that were not there.

I found my voice. 'The voyage did go well for me, Majesty. As for us all. Not one of us was claimed by the sea or disease or violence. We made prayers at our shrine on the ship. In this way, we reached our home again safely.'

I looked down, hoping that no more would be required of me. But the King turned to a courtier. 'Hurry – have water and rice and fish brought here for her, no, for everyone in the embassy. Make it a good meal.'

'You are kind, Majesty. We do not deserve it.'

'Now, Lady Sray, please tell us, what things will we import from China?'

'In our ship, Majesty, are more than twelve hundred bolts of silk. There are wood carvings, as well as porcelain and large jars. We will offer them for sale in the market here. People will see the benefits of our new friendship with the Chinese Empire. And we will provide things in return. The Chinese have had bad rains this year. They need rice and we have agreed to send them twenty shiploads. We will send them live animals as well. They are very fond of pork, and a single pig will fetch three times what it does here.'

Two slaves hurriedly put a table in place; others, right behind them, placed bowls of rice and fish on them. I had imagined a very different first meal at home. Certainly not one in which absurd thoughts about a law in suspension returned.

We members of the embassy ate, very self-consciously. My eye fell again on Commander Rit. There remained a malevolent smile on the man's face. And then it came to me, suddenly, a thought placed there by some god, I'm sure. Our ships had passed safely through Cham waters, so now war could begin. My eating came to a stop as I considered that.

The King asked: 'Are you truly well, Lady? Is something troubling you?'

'I am in good health, Majesty. I am happy to see my family and home soil.'

'There is nothing more?'

'Only, Majesty, that I hope that...' Why had Heaven placed this responsibility on me? But I knew I must find courage and go on. 'I hope that our relations with the people to the east will remain peaceful.'

'Lady, do not worry. You and your family will be safe. Whatever happens will be swift and decisive.'

'Majesty,' I murmured. 'I have no fear for our safety. The Empire's armies will see to that.'

'The Empire will become larger. All of us will become more wealthy. Perhaps you will have a new house on land along the Salt Water Sea that the Chams now occupy.'

'But my family and I have houses enough. There is no need for another.'

The court fell silent. Only the chirping of insects from the jungle darkness was heard. I do believe that the King had begun showing a touch of perspiration on his brow. He said: 'Parasol master, your wife is an unusual woman – turning aside royal gifts! I am lucky that she agrees to eat my food!'

Poor Nol. He had to make a large smile to indicate that this was both an excellent joke and a kind comment on my virtues. With his eyes, he told me now that I should not speak again. But I could not stop.

'Majesty, I cannot help but feel that our Empire is now precisely the size that Heaven has ordained. It has rice and fish and fruit enough for every person and for every image in the temples. It has water, for drinking and bathing and bringing life to our fields. It has ample stone and bricks and wood with which to build. It has silver to make into bowls and boxes and yarn for cloth.'

'Lady Sray, we seek only what is ours by right, to guarantee a future peace.'

'But by sending soldiers, Majesty, do we not guarantee future wars? The families of those who die at our hands will not forget. Anger will live on in their hearts, fuelled by evil spirits, and they will seek their vengeance, even if not right away.'

'I understand your concern about war but you are a woman, with no experience in it.'

'Majesty, I do have experience. I was born in a village near the eastern frontier. When I was not even a year into my current life, there was war with the Chams. My village burned, my mother and father, brothers and sisters – their souls all departed. I was the only survivor.'

'Your experience was tragic,' said the King, his voice now not fully steady. 'But surely, it was part of a divine plan for your progress in society. You are now one of the Empire's most prominent ladies. Without the war, you would be an ordinary village woman. Heaven had a plan, and it was successful.'

'Majesty, without the war, I would indeed be a woman in a village. In life we have no right to choose, but were it different, I would have chosen that.'

'Over all your wealth, your servants and houses?'

'Yes, Majesty. In the end, nothing of merit comes from wealth, nothing of merit comes from war. As we are taught, Heaven is most pleased with the man or the woman who does good to others, who never utters abuse, calumny or untruth, who kills only for food, who desires the welfare of all creatures.'

'You believe that, you truly live by that?' There was no rebuke in the question, I believe, only genuine inquiry.

'I do, Majesty. Whether I successfully live it, that is for Heaven to decide. But I have spoken enough. I have taken time that Your Majesty could have devoted to others.'

Subhadra spoke up now. 'Majesty. Please sit back and we will show a sign that what you have heard here is indeed Heaven's truth.'

How was it that the priest so often would step in to support me, unbidden? Now he went down to the shoreline and spoke there with a man from the ship. Other priests approached and they sat in a row near the water and began a chant that carried far into the darkness. When they reached the final stanza, a gong sounded and across the river there was the most astounding sight.

A fountain of fire, with embers of red and orange and green, shot into the air like a luminous liquid. People gasped and then two more fountains, larger even than the first, erupted to each side. Then came a series of crackles. Then, things that no one there that night ever forgot. Vishnu's pillar of fire, spraying so high into the night sky, then breaking open with a flower of brightness, and booms louder than thunder. One by one, people fell to the ground and put hands to ears, and felt the gods speaking.

Even the King crouched, holding a hand to the sky for protection.

When the noise and light subsided, Subhadra declared: 'Heaven decrees it, Majesty. With this display, it announces that this is a time for peace, and that there is a proper place in society for everyone, whether beggar or King, and that everyone, beggar or King, desires things that he cannot have.'

Later that night, I sat down in a lamp-lit pavilion with Nol and there came another surprise. My daughter, and my son – my son in the presence of his father for the first time in twelve years. Sovan had come with the court to the festival, and I think that the emotions of my return melted Nol's enmity toward him. This is not to say that all went smoothly. I only now learned that my daughter had become a concubine and I began an indignant protest, though of course I didn't say half what I was truly thinking. But Nol jumped in with a list of reasons why this was a welcome thing – Bopa lived apart from Rom, there was no longer a question of finding a husband for her, the loyal maid Yan continued to watch over her. He knew me well enough not to mention that our family's ties to the palace had been strengthened. Then Bopa spoke up to say she felt pride in her station, though I'm afraid that shortly afterward she was expressing anger over losing the chance of the elevation. Nol suggested she should not have overslept; she shot back with an account of the trick that Rom had played. That was new – she had acquired the confidence to speak back to her father. Now Sovan took sides with her, noting how hard she'd tried to abide by the ways of the palace. He spoke in such a persuasive, sympathetic way that Nol fell silent and listened. Then, a miracle of reconciliation. He asked Sovan about his wife and their three sons.

I looked on, just listening now. It would take time for me to accept my daughter's new station. But now my mind offered a silent prayer of thanks that my family had come back together. I looked again to my husband, now listening intently to his son, and I felt a tremor of the deepest affection and respect for the little man, who had always protected me, who had never taken a minor wife even in those long periods when I slept apart from him or even (I was certain) when I had gone abroad. His love was so strong that he could feel no suspicion about me. What had happened in China would never be repeated here. Here, among our own gods and spirits, it would be a grave sin. But it would also be a betrayal of the man who now sat at my side. I decided then and there that I would endow a new shrine for a purpose that would remain private, even from the priests who would serve it. Kneeling there, I would say prayers seeking health and happiness for the fine village man who remained on the ship this night and now would again be only my bodyguard.

The next morning, the court awoke to find that the river was flowing away from the Freshwater Sea. Under Subhadra's direction, the priests consulted the records, then reported to His Majesty that the previous rite in which this had happened so quickly presaged a year of peace, a harvest never matched, and the unearthing at a distant temple of a lost golden image of Vishnu.

Part Four

A secret unravelled

The empire's soldiers did not go to war that year, or the next, or the next. A thousand thousand mothers were spared the agony of losing their sons. No smoke of pillaging armies blackened the skies. Rice continued to grow, eggs to hatch at frontier villages that otherwise would have been swallowed up by conflict.

Some people have said that this peace was due solely to my words by the river that night. Truly, it could not have been that way. One women speaking for a minute or two could not have such broad effect. More likely the cause was the long and diligent teachings of the Rajaguru Subhadra. Still, I will admit that in the years that followed I sometimes allowed myself to think that perhaps I did have at least some small effect on our King. We were to be always apart – I accepted that – but in this thought I had the comfort of knowing that something of me lived in him. And I had the golden bangles. They stayed with me.

For my family, there began a time of domestic peace. My son and husband were reconciled. I no longer had to make secret visits. With me near at hand again, my daughter was given freedom to leave the house in the palace compound where she had been confined. She found, I think, a good measure of contentment in life as a concubine, though I never quite gave up wondering how she would have fared had she married one of the boys who used to come calling.

Things were well too between Nol and me. I no longer slept apart from him. We took rice together, we confided, we went for walks in the evening. When he began to develop pain in his joints, he slowed his pace on those walks and I slowed mine. Back at home, he lay down on his mat and I massaged his places of pain.

I was wise enough by this time to know that such tranquillity cannot last forever. But I prayed that when change did come, it would come subtly, through things barely noticeable, giving us all time to adapt. That was not how it happened.

50: The apsaras

Eighteen hundred apsaras. My son had told the King that this number was part of his vision, but I can tell you that prior to the moment when he knelt in the audience room, bound and pleading for his life and permission to build the mountain-temple in the proper way, he had had no idea how many Heavenly nymphs should brighten its stones. The number floated by in his mind as he crouched, and he reached out and plucked it, sensing that for the King the chance of eternity amongst such a host would close the question.

Now, the number he promised was approximately the same as the number of sculptors at the construction site at the time. For the time being, they were concerning themselves only with ornamentation, carving symmetrical grooves onto door frames, Capitals onto column tops, flower patterns onto lintels. They were waiting impatiently for the Brahmins, who were rarely quick about anything, to work out the precise roster of gods and epic scenes that the temple's stone would depict and the sequence in which they would be carved. But from the moment that Sovan was helped from the audience room, one part of the plan was settled, whatever the Brahmins might say – there would be apsaras everywhere.

A few months later, I was sitting in the design pavilion with him, drinking tea, when an assistant announced that the chief concubine to His Majesty the King had come calling.

Before he could respond, she breezed in, trailed by two maids. She sat down, saying nothing, not acknowledging my presence – I doubt she would have chosen to come had she known I was there, but now she was too proud to withdraw.

She began by letting a silence build that was supposed to convey that he could guess why she had come. Avoiding her eyes, Sovan called for tea for the visitor. It quickly came; she ignored it. She was still looking at him, sizing him up now – he told me later that this was the first time they had ever met.

Then she made an announcement: 'I have come to pose for your master sculptor.'

'Pardon me?'

'You don't know, Architect? The Brahmins have ruled that my face and form will be the model for the mountain-temple's apsaras.' She took a breath, and held still for a moment, as if posing, daring him to say there was beauty that could outshine hers.

I must say that she did have beauty, but in my opinion it was a baleful, spiteful kind that would not fit with the spirit of the edifice.

'We might as well get started,' she said. 'His Majesty is already asking when he can see the first of his eighteen hundred.'

Sovan parried. 'Forgive my ignorance, but no one has told me the Brahmans had made the decisions you describe.'

'If they haven't already, they will. Perhaps you'd know if you spent more time at the palace, not as a hermit out here. Everyone knows.'

Sovan replied that the chief sculptor was away at his home village; I could sense that he was inventing this, playing for time. A posing was simply impossible for now, he continued. She protested, saying she would settle for the chief's assistant, but Sovan countered that a woman of her rank could be sketched only by the top man himself.

Slowly she gave in; an aide showed her out.

Sovan let out a long breath. 'Mother, there's always something like that. I have so little time left for the actual work of building this place. The question becomes whether to build the best building I can or appease someone's demand.' He broke off there, because he was contemplating something, a finger to his cheek. Then he said: 'Theological interpretation is not my specialty. But tell me, mother, may I pose some ideas to you? I am not sure they are valid.'

'Of course.'

'The human world is in many ways a reflection of the supernatural one, is it not?'

'Certainly it is.'

'Heaven has day and it has night, as we have here on earth.'

'Yes, of course.'

'On earth, some people do good, some do bad, some people do good and bad, just as it is in Heaven with the gods.'

'Yes, it is like that.'

'On earth we have scenes of great beauty, such as mists kissing a river's surface at first light, and we have scenes that are foul beyond description, such as, well – there is no need to name any of them. It is that way in the gods' realm, is it not? Mount Meru is a place of divine perfection, yet there is also hell, where the air rings with the screams of tortured sinners.'

'Yes, yes.' I was anxious to hear the point.

'Now, on earth, we have many kinds of women. Some are beautiful – like my mother. And please, don't protest! I say that not only because I am your son. Some are plain, some are...well, there is no word but ugly. Some are a mixture of both – a beautiful face and shoulders, perhaps, but hips that are more narrow than the ideal. In any case, each woman has an appearance different than any other.'

'Yes, yes. We can see that every day.'

'Then, can we not conclude, drawing inference from these analogies, that these women we see reflect the nymphs of Heaven? That therefore nymphs come in all kinds, that they do not all have perfect physical attributes?'

'Why, I suppose so.'

'And would it not match Heaven's will if the nymphs we will carve at the temple were to reflect this eternal truth?'

There were so many aspects to my son's brilliance, can't you see? The next day he went to see the Brahmin Subhadra. First, he found that the council was nowhere near a decision of the type that Rom had claimed. And second, he found that Subhadra was willing to put to the council the approach that he had outlined to me.

A formal decision was issued four weeks later. Rom quickly went again to Sovan's workplace, this time to demand that she at least be the first to be sketched. The chief sculptor was duly called. She stood for him, and he began to record her likeness on a slate. Several times he told her, using the most diplomatic words he could muster, that, please, it would be good to relax, to contemplate the Vedas, perhaps, that her face should reflect Heaven's flawless harmony. Instead, her face tightened! The sculptor gave her no more of those words, trying to achieve the desired effect on his own. But when she had gone away, and he looked at his drawing, he announced to my son that he had succeeded only in part.

The chief sculptor went on to carve an apsara in Rom's image. But she was to be just one in a holy host. Every one of the eighteen hundred sculptors got the right to select one woman – wife, minor wife, sweetheart, drinking-stall companion, coveted village beauty – to serve as model for one apsara. This was as my son had proposed to the Brahmins. It seemed a good way to bring in a sampling of all the Empire's women, however many million they were. It might also put an end to recent grumbling among the masons that their skills made them deserving of more silver and larger rations than other workers.

The sketching and carving took place over many years, because when it began only a fraction of the walls and columns that would be homes to the apsaras existed. The chief sculptor told a scribe to maintain a list of the men and select from them as new walls and columns were completed. The scribe chose randomly, except, perhaps, concerning those men who paid him bribes. In some cases, this was not entirely dishonourable – construction progressed so slowly that some of the older men worried that they might be dead before their turn came around. Each man on whom the good news was settled got one cycle of the moon to make his pick. His chosen woman, bathed, purified by her local priest, put on her finest and processed proudly to a masons' work yard to the south of the temple. She was directed toward a wooden platform decorated with flowers and bright drapes. This was of course a special occasion, and family, friends and the hundreds of sculptors and assistants stopped work to watch. The female of the day climbed the platform and stood there proudly, perhaps holding a lotus blossom to her cheek. She might smile with a hint of provocation, catching the sculptor's eye; she might gaze to the earth with modesty. The sculptor sketched the image on slate, then held it up to the crowd for admiration (and sometimes good-natured derision). Later, the image was recopied in charcoal on the designated place in the temple. Then the real work began. The sculptor first chipped away stone that lay outside the outline, to create a niche-home. As days and weeks progressed, his nymph took form from the stone that he had left untouched. With that work complete, painters came to apply gilding to her jewellery, hues to her flowers and cloth, and a gentle pastel to her skin. Her eternity of glorification of her monarch began.

As the years went by, the dress of the women posing on the platform came to be more and more elaborate. Sampots acquired starched flares like the wings of birds. Jewellery was worn around ankles, wrists, upper arms and necks. Headdresses were the real field of competition. They grew taller and taller. Silver filaments, lotus buds, coconut palm blossoms were added to create the most elaborate ensembles. The masons couldn't believe that a woman's hair could rise so high. But it could, if reinforced with hidden bamboo strips and if the woman beneath it was careful to walk with the tiniest, most careful of steps. The main marketplace, in fact, now had shops whose only business was outfitting women who were heading to their posing sessions and coaching them in how to present themselves to the best effect. Not a few family fortunes, large and small, were depleted in these places.

Being the model for an apsara marked a woman for life, in a very positive way. But none ever got to see her own likeness in stone. The Brahmins saw no reason to open the holy construction site for the sake of female vanity. So each woman made do with whispered assurances from her sculptor husband or boyfriend that her Heavenly twin inside was unique, her face so lovely and smooth, her chest and hips so alluring, her headdress so glorious and jewel-studded and tall that the King, when he came on inspection, could but only pause and gaze in admiration and think yearningly of that time in Heaven when he might encounter this being, in the playground of the heart's desire.

You know, I am told that the husband or boyfriend always followed up with a plea. Beloved, tell me that when that time comes, I'll at least remain in your heart. Don't worry, that woman always replied. My devotion to you will never be broken.

Let us hope that she actually meant it, and that had the woman been me, I would have meant it too.

51: Parental inspection

Two, perhaps three, years passed. One day, it was arranged that Nol and I would come to the unfinished mountain-temple to see our son's work.

It was late afternoon when we arrived at its western bridge by palanquin. This form of travel was ostentatious, but on this day I did not object to it. My husband's pains had spread to his knees now; he could have extreme difficulty walking. I knew that he would refuse to be carried around as we toured the temple, so it was good that his joints be spared the strain of the trip out from Angkor.

The slaves set down the palanquins at the bridge, but there was no sign of Sovan. It's unusual, I thought. It is his way to be on time.

But after a bit came a squiggle of motion at the far end of the moat that extended to our right – a cantering brown horse, and on top of it, our son. Nol saw it was him before I did. His eyes, at least, were still good.

Sovan kept the horse at a canter but the moat was so long that it took some time to reach us. Finally he jumped down from his mount, perspiring, and knelt. 'Please, please, father, forgive me. I have no right to keep you waiting.'

'Oh, get up, boy. It wasn't so bad to sit for a few minutes. I got to take in what you've been up to out here. It looks like you're making good progress with that tower on the entrance complex.' He cast a hand its way.

Entrance? I had thought this was the temple itself!

'Yes, father. It should be completed in about two years.'

'You do plan ahead.'

'It's a skill I learned from you, father.'

I said nothing, just enjoying watching the two engage in this way. Then Sovan put out a hand to help his father up from the palanquin, but the old man shook his head. Grimacing, he got to his feet himself.

'So,' Nol asked, when he was finally standing straight. 'What was it that delayed you?'

'A problem at another construction site, father. You know it – the temple we're building just beyond the eastern reservoir. I've been trying out some new design concepts there, on a smaller scale than what we will have here at the main mountain-temple.'

'The designs didn't work out?'

'No, I think they'll be all right. The problem has to do with people.'

'That sounds like a parasol pavilion.'

'Very similar, father.' He laughed. 'There's a feud between two men who should be working together to make a balustrade. Did I tell you about that last time? On both sides of the entrance causeways at the temple out there, we'll have long balustrades, made of the bodies of stone Nagas. They'll be about as thick as a large coconut tree's trunk. They'll be held up off the pavement by a line of stone posts. One team of masons is making the bodies in sections, and another team is making the posts. The pieces have to fit together just right – the tops of the posts have pins that go into holes in the undersides of the Naga bodies. So the holes have to be chiselled in the right places, at the same interval as the posts.'

How intense my boy was just now, how proud he was making his mother. The Empire could have no one better in charge of this work.

'The team making the posts and the team making the Nagas are headed by these two men who don't get along. Apparently it goes back to having come to blows over a girl when they were young – they're from the same village out east. I split them up a couple of years ago, had them work on opposite sides of the site, and didn't realize they'd be paired up again for this job. It turns out the feud continues and they don't even talk to each other and don't let their men talk either.'

'I'm getting worried,' Nol said. He was feeling nothing of the sort, of course – he was enjoying the story.

'Yes, and I should have been. This morning I was at the site for a ceremony, the first union of post and Naga on the causeway. The posts had all been carved nicely and put in place the full length of the causeway – it's quite a long one, though not nearly as long as what we'll have here. Then an elephant dragged out the first section of serpent body. The pin holes had the wrong spacing! A full cubit off! And the holes were too small for the pins. A priest was there to bless the first union, and you can imagine how horrified he was. He began chanting prayers to frighten off the bad spirit that must have caused the mix-up. I told the Naga man, well, don't make any more sections with the pinholes spaced like that. The posts are already up, so you'll need to accommodate them. And he said, sir, we've been making Naga sections for the last twelve months. They're all done and they're all like this. He started to get a bit worked up. He pointed at the holes. We did them like this, he said – and now he was almost shouting – because this length is the standard separation for pinholes. This man, he says – now he was pointing at the other foreman – never told us about any change. Now the other foreman became riled and there was almost a fight. They had to be pulled apart.

'So I went to the stone-cutting yard and spent an hour looking over the Naga sections the team had made and thinking out what to do with them. We'll manage something. Maybe we'll send them out to a temple that we're doing in a district a couple of days' travel to the east. But it won't be easy getting them there – there's no stream to transport them. So, that's the story. All this made me late leaving the site to come here. I had to borrow this horse.'

We crossed the bridge, the sun behind us, two parasols overhead. Sovan followed his father at a creep, as if that pace was his usual. I walked behind.

We entered the entrance complex's left gate – only His Majesty could use the centre one – then passed down a corridor where the air was cool and wood shavings littered the floor. Carpenters, sweat-dampened kramas wrapped around their foreheads, had been fitting the first panels of the wooden ceiling overhead. But now they knelt, hands together.

We emerged again into daylight. We were at the western extreme of a stone-paved causeway. How far did it stretch? I cannot say. A thousand paces, perhaps. At its end was the emerging mountain-temple, covered in bamboo scaffolding, for now just two towers rising in stubby form from the outer left and right. In the air was the pleasing clink-clink of a hundred masons' hammers.

'We're focusing on giving them a bit of height, now,' said Sovan, his eyes on the towers. 'All the stone that's floated down the river and into the moat goes to them.'

We began walking again. Poor Nol – for him it was a forced march. His objective was to reach the end of the causeway without assistance. But part way down, our son stopped our party again. He motioned to either side of the causeway. 'Here and here, father, we'll be building a pair of annex buildings, for astrological instruments and records. And some secondary '

Nol asked: 'When will that begin?'

Sovan assumed the earnest look that I remembered from childhood. 'If we keep to schedule, we'll break ground four years from now.'

'It's been twenty-two years since work began on this place. It would be possible to assemble an entire Empire in that time.' In his mind, if gods were going to inhabit this place, then gods should do the work, applying some magic to make things move more quickly.

'Yes, the work goes slowly, father. But I can't complain. The estates have only so many workers to contribute, only so much stone and bamboo. Many of them are already sending slaves to supplement the volunteers. That's the only way they can meet their quotas. It's gruelling work and sometimes the conditions are horrible.'

I knew what he was describing – the previous month, my cart had stopped for directions at one of the quarries north of the Capital. The conditions in which people were living were shocking. Several lay in troubled sleep on grubby mats unrolled in the open, shoulder to shoulder. They were dirty, they seemed to be surviving on nothing but rice and fish paste. I sent word back to the city for my people to send some bamboo so they would at least have proper huts.

Sovan continued. 'Many of our people, father, aren't stone workers by trade. They're ordinary farmers. They have to keep it up for months at a time, then they go home just in time to get started on a new rice planting. The work gives them merit for the next life, but there needs to be balance so they can take care of the obligations of this life.'

Sovan was caught in a trap, I could see. What builder does not want more men, more stone? Yet my son's heart could not ignore the human costs of infinite supply. My own thinking was somewhat different. This was not merely my son's project, it was Heaven's. Through a series of visions and transcendent communications, the gods had made known the form and scale of our King's future monument. What better purpose for sacrifice than seeing to a divine wish? And how much better than devoting this sweat and treasure to war.

Nol said: 'Everyone must give, Sovan. In fact, soon everyone is going to give more.'

'What do you mean, father?'

'Let's finish our walk.'

Ahead were stone steps that took the causeway to a higher level. They were hard to climb, but climb my husband did, again turning aside our son's offer of a hand. At the top was a mat, shaded by a parasol and tended by a servant who had laid out flowers and refreshments.

'What's this?' Nol said. 'Let's go on. We didn't come here to rest.'

'Please, husband,' I said. 'It's hot and I'm a bit tired. Let us sit down, just for a moment.'

He acquiesced. It was for me, after all. We sat shaded by the parasol, and the water did Nol some good. Sovan let a few minutes go by, then asked, 'Father, you were saying people would have to sacrifice more?'

'Don't look so worried, Sovan. It's good news for you. The palace has decided that construction must proceed more quickly. No, it's not that they're unhappy with you. I've heard it said very clearly that the problem is that you don't have enough to work with. So a proclamation will be drafted that will increase by one half the levies on the estates. All other stone construction in the Empire will be suspended, so that the materials and labour can be diverted here.'

'I see.'

'The provincial princes will be called to Angkor to hear the decision personally. They will sign documents agreeing to it and will renew their oaths of allegiance to His Majesty. This is a secret for now, do you understand? His Majesty will inform you officially soon, but I thought you should know in advance.'

'Thank you, father.' Sovan looked down, his face still showing concern. Nol saw it.

'Boy, don't be foolish! That is why princes and farmers and artisans and slaves exist – to serve the King. Just as you and I do.'

'Some of us give more than others, and some are better rewarded.'

'Of course. The world everywhere is that way.'

'Can you say, father, is this a decision of the Brahmins, or of His Majesty?'

'I would say both, though His Majesty is not the direct source of the order.' Nol took a sip of water. 'No, it's coming from the priests, but they sense what is going on with our King and want to accommodate him. He has passed his fiftieth year, like your mother and me. He looks to the future and for him this life no longer seems to stretch forward without limits. Each time the rains begin, he is thinking, "I will see only a certain number more wet seasons in this existence." Now, were some other man to feel such concern, I would say that the reason is that he feels death approaching, and he wants to make sure that everything is in order for the cremation rite, for the passage to the next incarnation. But in the case of our King, I would say something different. He is a man who can never sit still. He wants the temple to be completed so that he will see it in completed form. He wants to know that he did in fact build the greatest the world has ever achieved. He wants to watch people come from all over the Empire to see it. He wants to look at it and tell himself that in seven, eight, nine centuries from now, people will still be coming to this place and they will marvel too and know the name Suryavarman.'

I affected to listen to all this as if it were mere palace gossip. I had not been in His Majesty's presence since the night by the river.

412

'Whenever construction is sped up,' observed our son, 'the rate of accidents, of falls from high places, increases. We say the proper protective blessings, but there is only so much we can do.'

'Sovan – it is better not to resist. It will be an instruction to you direct from the palace.'

'I will remember that, father. Thank you for the advice.'

'Yes, sometimes an old man knows a thing or two...'

Sovan smiled and got to his feet. He put out a hand to his father, and this time it was accepted.

For the next two hours, we toured the site, slowly. First we walked around the lower galleries of the temple. Sovan pointed out a long, bare stone wall which would become the Churning of the Sea of Milk, in which gods and demons worked in union, pushing and pulling on the body of the Naga Vasuki to create the nectar of immortality. Another lengthy wall, our son explained, would become the epic battle of the Kaurava family against the Pandava line, who were undefeatable because they grasped the Way of Higher Truths.

We passed up a half-finished stairway, stepping around tools and stone chippings, to reach the temple's second level. There we came to the foot of a very steep, very tall staircase. Nol looked up to the third level, holiest of holy places, knowing he was incapable of the climb.

But then two labourers approached, carrying a plank.

'This is how we go up, father. Let me show you. Now Mother...'

'I will stay here. You go with your father.' I had come high enough; I did not feel I had a right to go to the top.

Sovan sat on the plank, his back to the steps. The labourers lifted it, then put their strong legs to use to carry my son up the steps. How quickly they went! Sovan held his hands out to show how safe it was. Nol smiled at the sight. Then it was his turn.

I walked now to the point at which the east-west axis passed through the level on which I stood. I gazed west. My son and husband did the same, but from the third level, directly above me.

What I saw made me truly grasp the greatness of this place for the first time. The causeway on which we had approached ran straight as a ray of sunlight. To its left and right were square pools of water, beyond them great rectangles of manicured grass. Further on, the entry complex in perfect symmetry, and beyond that, hidden by the walls but there nonetheless, the bridge and the moat and a road that ran straight and true, like the causeway, further than the eye could see. It was the view from Heaven to earth. Everything made perfect sense in scope and resplendence.

All this was the work of my son, who as a boy had run naked in the old neighbourhood. Above me, I could sense that my husband was feeling the same stirrings.

Nol later told me that he had turned to his son and said: 'You have created something that has no equal on the face of the earth. I have the deepest pride in being your father.'

And Sovan dropped to his knees and put his head to the stone at his father's feet.

We reached the gate of Sovan's residence at dusk. Suriya welcomed us, then led us to the bathing area. Servants helped us there. Later they showed us up into the house for evening rice. The three sons, waiting in a line, greeted us their grandparents. By lamplight, everyone ate and talked and traded views and opinions. There were moments when Nol and I thought the boys laughed too loudly, or were too quick to challenge their parents – our eyes seemed always to meet at these times. But I found myself reflecting on how different life might have been had talk flowed so freely in our own house.

52: Parade of the princes

My husband was not mistaken concerning what the King was about to do.

Some weeks after our visit to the temple there began a grand spectacle on the streets. Everyone was talking about it, and so I went to look myself. Princes of the Empire were entering the city one after the other, borne by gilded chariots. It was odd, as if each prince had decided to put on a different kind of show for the adults squatting at roadside and children darting close on dares to touch the wooden spokes of the vehicles. One prince made his horse prance, one stood so straight that people thought he was an image, one pretended to cast a spear, wearing so fierce a look that he seemed genuinely in battle, one tossed bits of silver, causing a rush by children and adults alike.

I later heard the servants trading views on which prince had a posture that was truly royal, the fruit of Heaven, which prince looked like, well, the son of a whore, which prince would speak well and get the King's ear, which would be ignored. And how it looked so unnatural that no prince was at the head of a long column of soldiers, but that each instead had a puny escort of not more than a dozen men, and those dozen lightly armed, because this was the Capital and here only the King and his guard could wield real weapons.

When the princes reached the bridge to the royal sector, they sent their escorts to find places to sleep in the market, then drove their chariots across the bridge, iron wheel rims clattering on the pavement. On the parade grounds in front of the palace, they drove their vehicles up and down, tearing swathes in the grass, not yet willing to stop while there remained an opportunity to show the other princes their skills and equipment. A few of them got down and sparred with wooden swords. Of course. They believed themselves to have been called to a council of war.

The next morning, the new lord of Chaiyapoom called at our house to pay respects, due to my husband's links to that estate. He was a stocky young man, quick to declare his ambitions.

'I'll be leading two thousand men when we attack the Chams,' he told us. 'I intend to be first into the Cham Capital.'

What could be said of this man? Heaven had settled so much on him, and yet he found no satisfaction in any of it. He wanted more. And he felt the way to obtain this more was to squander what he already had. Scythes and chisels would be converted into implements of war; farmers and artisans who had laboured long and selflessly for their prince would become makeshift soldiers facing death on a distant battlefield.

The prince looked to my husband, I suppose hoping for a word or gesture that might reveal some specifics of the King's plans. He got none. Nol was not one to share court secrets with outsiders, even one who came from the Chaiyapoom estate.

Rumours circulated that the King would address the princes on the second day, but that day came and went with no such event. Instead there was more of the same – waiting and talking and driving chariots up and down. Some of the princes took to flirting with the servant girls who tended the pavilion in which they were staying. On the third day came something different. Messengers from the palace began summoning the men through the palace gate, one by one, alone.

What shock they endured beyond that gate! Each man was led into a darkened room, where various Brahmins stood. Each man's palm was cut to draw loyalty blood. Then he was led in the recitation of a long and frightful oath to His Majesty which assured the most awful kind of death for him and his family were there any violation of its terms. This is how loyalty is thought to be created. And then he was presented not with a war plan, but with a long list of men and materials that his estate would deliver to the construction site in the Capital. I can imagine each prince stumbling back into the light of day, rubbing his eyes, unsure whether what had happened inside truly *had* happened.

Three days later, the princes were told they were free to leave the city for their estates. But the young prince of Chaiyapoom first came again to our residence. We listened at some length to this newly humbled man – at least he seemed that way to me at the time. He had been willing to all but strip his estate if war were the purpose, but faster construction of the temple? Now he outlined at length why Chaiyapoom should be exempted from the new levy. Surely, surely, it was only fair, he said. The estate had played a special role in the ascent to power, so people there could not be faulted for expecting they would have a new bridge to span its river. They would think that its great house should be maintained and expanded, its temple given new stones to replace ones that were cracking.

When the speech was finished, Nol responded that he understood the burden and sympathized. The call for new levies did not originate with him, he assured the prince, and he could do nothing to change them.

'But sir, your son...'

'My son,' replied Nol, 'is concerned with carrying out the orders of Heaven. Those orders have arrived through the words of His Majesty.'

Then he called for drinking water for the prince and bade him a safe journey home.

53: Darit's request

Over the years, I continued to travel the Empire in my oxcart, seeing to charitable work and my trading business. How I would have preferred to carry it all out in anonymity. But when I arrived in a place, it was not uncommon that people would come to ask this favour or that. Might I find a minor post for a nobleman's son in the palace? Could I put in a word with a local magistrate in a case concerning a broken marriage contract? Once I was even asked to settle a theological dispute among the priests of a monastery. Whoever came to me, I felt an obligation to listen and do what I could if the cause was legitimate, but the truth is that as the pleas increased, so did a craving in me for solitude. So as I approached the Capital on my return from a trip, I would often call out to the cart driver. 'If you would, please turn down the track to Hamlet Veya.' I always tried to make it sound as if it were on a whim, but I think now that I fooled no one. Soon the cart would be spotted by some child or farmer, who would run ahead to the hamlet with word of our arrival, as had happened on that very first visit, and people would turn out to greet me. The headman would offer me water and fruit and too many other things, and tell someone to carry my things to the house, and as soon as I decently could, I would set off up its trail, alone. Rice and charcoal and other essentials would be waiting by the door, placed there while the headman entertained me. Ducks would be nibbling at greens in the pond – perhaps the ducks were not doing that each and every time, but such is my memory.

Whatever my initial intention, I would often stay for an extended period, sometimes even for weeks. There was an understanding, with my husband and children, with my staff in the city, with the people of the village, that once in this house I would not be disturbed. There I read the Vedas and recited lengthy prayers. I cooked for myself, kneeling at the charcoal stove. I did my own wash, though I knew this horrified the villagers. When work was done, I sat contented on the porch, experiencing the simple pleasures of breeze, of the rays of late afternoon sun on forehead and breasts.

One morning late in the rainy season, after a ten-day stay, I left the house to walk back toward the village centre, a bag of possessions over my shoulder.

As I drew near the village, I noticed some unusual sights – three fancy horses, one with a silver bridle, and a pair of retainers squatting beneath a palm.

Sergeant Sen hurried toward me, with something on his mind. 'Lady Sray, the son of the concubine Rom has come and wishes to speak with you. I advise against it.'

My beloved Sergeant Sen – without complaint, back in his role merely as protector, and always worried about my safety. And sometimes with good reason. Why did I not accept his advice that day? Perhaps that certain ghost was hovering over me just then, planting resistance in my mind. I found out later that the concubine's son had arrived a full day earlier, requesting to meet with me in the village pavilion. The sergeant had done his best to make him leave, variously telling him I was not there, was indisposed, or did not meet with people such as him. I am sure this last claim was dressed up in some tactful language. It was quite a thing for a bodyguard to say, but Darit did not take offense. Nor did he leave.

My life was not my own once I left the house by the pond. How could I say no to someone respectfully seeking a meeting? This was what I told myself as Sergeant Sen stood before me, awaiting my decision. I suppose too that I was curious to meet this man who was son of the concubine – and yes, I admit it, son of the man who had given me two golden bangles that even now went everywhere with me in my travels, hidden in my jewellery box. At this moment box and bangles were in the bag over my shoulder.

So I turned and walked to the village pavilion, the sergeant trailing behind me disapprovingly.

Most everyone knew the reputation of the man, even me. Now near his thirtieth year, he had wealth but still no clear place in the world, no estate or commission. He still spent nights on the prowl at wine stalls, the cockfighting rings, and on sleeping mats where he didn't belong – he had graduated from servant girls to the jaded wives and daughters of noble families. Everywhere he went, he was noticed, and he had a following, ranging from young men with lesser titles to boys who held the reins of his horses outside wine stalls. He had a temper, these people knew, but as long as it was directed at others, I suppose it was part of his appeal. Around his neck he wore that mysterious cloth-wrapped amulet. Certainly it continued to protect him. It was said that wine pots thrown during drinking-stall melees sailed harmlessly past his head, that no aggrieved husband, fiancé or father had ever bested him in a fight one-on-one.

He held his head pressed to the mat as I approached, murmuring. 'Lady, it is an honour that you find time to receive me.'

'The honour is mine.'

Then he raised himself up to face me, and I was at once taken aback, because he bore such a resemblance to his father. There before me were the same broad shoulders, the same sculpted face and knife-edge confidence. He wore the sampot and jewellery of a nobleman, a knife in his waist, and around his neck that cloaked amulet.

'I have come,' he said, after more preliminaries, 'to request permission to assist with the hospital that you have begun building in the Capital. If it pleases you, I would like to provide thirty slaves for labour and, when the place is completed, funds for four physicians.'

'How generous is your offer.' I was caught off guard. I had certainly never heard of this man giving charity. 'You will earn much merit for your next life.'

Sergeant Sen sat nearby, his hand close to his dagger, and I could tell from his stony look what he made of Darit's offer. Various of the village's people were hovering around beyond the pavilion as well, watching without appearing to. I wondered what they would make of it, but they were not close enough to hear.

'Lady, it is my hope,' Darit said, 'and I have conveyed this to a priest, that any merit accruing be settled not on me but on the patients in the hospital.' He smiled in a disarming way; I wondered if I had misjudged him.

For the next five minutes we discussed details of what the

contributions would consist of and when they would arrive. The business came to an end, but Darit did not leave.

'May I ask something else of you, Lady Sray?'

'Of course.'

'May I ask that you bless me?'

This was one of those requests that I received from time to time. 'But I am not a priestess,' I replied. 'Any blessing from me would have no value.'

'I ask that you do it, Lady Sray. I plead for your help. I have done things for which I have special need of a blessing.' Before I could answer, he put head to mat and held it there. So, I had no choice but to place hands together and say a brief prayer over him. By now almost the entire village was looking on.

On the trip back to the city, I turned the encounter over in my mind but could make no sense of it. I put the question to the sergeant, who still wore his troubled look. 'With a man like Darit,' he said, walking to the side of the cart, 'there is always some motivation other than what is presented. You must be on guard, Lady.' The sergeant would be too, I could tell.

My husband was not in when I arrived at the house, so I decided to go see Mr Narin. The chief scribe's eyesight had gone bad enough that he no longer worked with manuscripts and ledgers. But he still went to court every day to preside over the compiling of these documents by younger men, and there he learned all sorts of things.

Receiving me on his house's terrace, he took some time asking about my trip and the people and places I had visited. When I broached the subject of Darit, my real purpose in coming here, he frowned instantly.

'Lady Sray,' he said, 'it is always difficult to speak ill of someone to you. But I should tell you that on one thing at least this young man Darit told you the truth, that he has a particular need to make merit right now. He has committed a very serious crime.'

'Oh?'

'I would prefer not to go into the details, Lady Sray. Someone such as yourself should not be exposed to such things.'

But I felt I had to know, and with some coaxing Mr Narin

gave me a version. Two days earlier, Darit had stopped into one of the night establishments of the central market. He was in a bad mood – he had just lost a large sum at cockfighting. The son of a provincial lord was sitting with one of the establishment's girls, one whom Darit had taken to an enclosed place in the back a few days earlier. Now he perceived an insult in this other man's attentions to her. He strode over and demanded he give her up. Witnesses later agreed that the man got no time to comply. Instead, a knife came out from Darit's waist and in an instant the lord's son was lying bleeding to death on the floor, slashed across the throat. Darit seized the girl by the arm and pulled her toward one of the booths, she horrified, blood on her forehead and belly, straining to look back at the dying man. The stall's proprietor stepped in Darit's path, and received a slash across the shoulder, though not a fatal one.

'He is a vicious man, Lady Sray, as if some demon drives his actions. I am sure you were safe in his presence – neither he nor the demon would dare harm you – but the fact is that he has become a danger to people in general.'

'Perhaps the King will do something?'

'He has already, Lady Sray.'

It was due to the Brahmins. They saw the crime as a Heaven-sent chance to secure real action against Darit. Subhadra reported it to His Majesty, whose reaction was merely to throw up his hands and turn his back, as if to say that what the Brahmins must do they must do. He loved his son, I know, but he knew also that the time had come. But Subhadra wanted His Majesty to be part of what action would be taken. So first he spoke with various figures of the palace, Nol and Commander Rit among them, and secured their support. Then he sent soldiers out to round up witnesses. Late the following afternoon, when the King was unsuspecting, Subhadra came to court with a magistrate, a scribe, the drinking-stall girl, the proprietor and two other men who had been present at the crime. The priest applied elaborate oaths to the witnesses and then had them tell their stories. When they left, Subhadra declared to the King that the real issue was not Darit's guilt – that was firmly established – but the King's response. People in the market were starting to say that Darit's continuing freedom was a sign that he could not be controlled, even by the King, and that the palace might even be afraid of him and so did not arrest him. The Brahmin left unstated the implication that if the King could not control his own son, close at hand, how could he control the princes of the outlying provinces? Subhadra then ordered one final witness brought in. This one was a labourer who worked for a Chinese merchant, loading and unloading baskets of rice. Two soldiers brought him in, bound, with bruises on his face from interrogation, and pushed him to the floor. Subhadra led him through his story. The man had heard what happened in the drinking place, had he not? He knew that Darit had not been punished, did he not? Was this something everyone knew? And what was his own remark about it? Please, please, the man whimpered, trembling, it is too terrible ever to repeat. The priest declared: Then I will be the one to repeat it! Did you not say to a neighbour that His Majesty was afraid of this Darit, as a small dog fears a big one? Now the man only wept. He did not deny it. Did the neighbour not think that remark funny and spread it around his workplace? Again, there was no denial.

The prisoner was taken out, and a silence settled over the chamber. The King turned his back and stood there, thinking in his intense way, and for a while Subhadra did not dare speak. Then he found his tongue and assured the King in a whisper that everyone who had heard this remark had been arrested, but that the proper way to deal with this was to eliminate the cause of such talk. We must arrest *him*, the Brahmin said. The King waved his hand to say, all right – do it.

Two hours later Darit was brought to the audience room, by the same two soldiers, who held either arm and looked worried that this assignment would end badly for them. He was not bound, because the Brahmin knew that this might trigger some reaction of compassion in His Majesty. Darit knelt at his father's feet, the guards keeping hands on him, and before Subhadra could say a word, Rom burst into the room. Her first step was to pummel the soldiers, screaming that they must take their hands off her son. They looked to the Brahmin, who signalled to hold firm. She turned then to the King and demanded he be released. Five men had set upon Darit, she declared, and all he had done was defend himself. To everyone else's most deep relief, His Majesty was not swayed. The Brahmin told her in a settled voice that only compounded her anger that there had been detailed testimony establishing something very different. Then she said that the dead man had provoked her son, in a way that could only result in death.

It went on like this – Rom shouting and stamping and to everyone's amazement, the Brahmin starting to shout back. Practically the whole palace could hear. Finally she was reduced to throwing herself on the mat alongside her son, pleading for mercy for him, and reminding His Majesty of her own help in the ascent to the throne, the hidden bow Gandiva, the hidden arrows. The King was showing signs of wavering now, and in the end, she had some effect. His Majesty demanded silence. He announced that there would be no execution. He looked down to his son and shouted: Get out of the Capital! Go to a station on the border with the Siamese territories. Serve me there! As a common man at arms! Sleep on the ground, eat that bitter food, leave wine and girlfriends behind. See if you can take it. The soldiers released their grip, and Rom hurried her son out of the room. The Brahmins could only watch. Not one of them believed that Darit would live like a real foot soldier. But with luck a Siamese spear point would find its way to him.

'He has been banished, Lady Sray,' said Mr Narin. 'I would guess that when he stopped to see you he was on his way out of the city.'

I recalled Darit's gentle smile, the request that any merit from his charity be allotted not to himself but to the patients' accounts with Heaven. 'Perhaps,' I said, 'perhaps he has had a change of heart. Heaven's wisdom has entered him.' I did believe it.

'Let us hope so, Lady Sray. That is always a possibility. Your blessing, even if you bestowed it reluctantly, could only have a good effect.'

I walked back toward my house. At the gate, a servant conveyed word that the Brahmin Subhadra was inside, waiting to see me. In the next hour, he asked question after question about Darit's visit.

That evening, a messenger arrived at the house with some more troubling news: the previous night, thieves had broken into the elephant corral near the road to the port. They had tied up Sadong and another keeper and made off with not all but just one of the beasts.

54: The country pilgrim

The next morning, I went to the shrine of Bronze Uncle to say special prayers for Darit and the elephant Kumari.

I have not told you – the shrine was quite different from the old days, unrecognizable, I would say. Bronze Uncle now inhabited a chamber in a stone tower. His door was protected by a pair of sculpted lions. One priest or another officiated in his presence all day long. I had paid for all of this; if I could not come to say devotions every day, I could at least show my reverence in other ways.

The attending priest welcomed me when I arrived in my oxcart. Then I knelt before the god for close to thirty minutes, seeking his pacifying intervention in whatever untoward events lay ahead concerning Darit and the holy animal.

When I stood up, the priest had a question. 'Lady Sray, would it be too great an inconvenience if you stepped to our pavilion for a moment? We have prepared refreshments.' My mind was still troubled, but I could not say no. So I allowed him to show me along a paved path to this pavilion.

Ahead, a group of men and women rested on mats in the shade of a banyan tree. Aged pilgrims, they looked to be. The shrine was now a stop for many who made the holy journey to the Capital.

There was a general shuffling and putting of hands together as I approached and in me this kindled an old sense of undeservedness. Blessings were murmured, and I returned them under my breath. I was just passing when my eyes fell on a white-haired man who sat on his haunches by the trunk of the tree. He was looking toward me in a curious, sympathetic kind of way.

He had grown old, but I recognized him immediately. He was the cart driver Sao, the kind man who had brought me from the home for girls without parents to the estate where I was first married.

It had finally happened, then. So many years, and no one from that old estate, until now.

I hurried on, terrified. In the pavilion, it was all I could do to keep my composure while I drank cool water put out by an acolyte and traded pleasantries with the priest. When it was time to leave, I returned to my cart by a way that did not pass the pilgrims. I climbed aboard, then said to the priest, in a voice calmed as best I could: 'The people beneath the tree – they look quite fatigued. They must have travelled a long distance.'

'Why, yes, Lady Sray. It's the late years of life for them, as you can see, so they make the effort.'

'Yes. And would you know where they are from?'

'From a province to the west, Lady.' I waited. Would he say more? Out it came. 'Some of them, I am told, had a connection to His Majesty in his youthful days, service on his birth estate. So it's quite an honour that they visit us.'

When I got back to my house, I hoped that the sight of familiar people and things would settle me, but they did not. I sat in silence on my terrace, as a servant told me that things were ready for my bath. I scarcely heard.

My husband was away, so I did not have to put on an act for him. I devoted my full attention to replaying the encounter at the shrine in my mind. It was over almost as soon as it began, so, surely, there was no time for the man to recognize me, assuming that at such advanced age his mind was clear enough to recognize anyone. He must have been well past his seventieth year. Perhaps his eyes were bad, or simply held on anything that moved. Or maybe he remembered, but not who I was, just that I was someone who had had some presence in his past. Or his mind was so feeble that even if he remembered me and made a mention to others, they would pay no attention.

Surely the ghost had planted in his mind the idea to come on this particular pilgrimage, knowing its course would intersect with mine. Did this ghost also have the power to bring clarity to his old mind and make him remember and act on what he saw? I could not say.

I slept badly that night, and when I awoke I said prayers at the shrine in my room. A maid brought rice and water spinach. I ate, but after a few bites the food turned sour in my belly.

I sat before the unfinished meal, and a thought arose: cart

driver Sao was very old – whatever the ghost intended, he might drop dead before he could say anything.

I closed my eyes, suddenly weeping. I had wished death on a man who had shown me only kindness, who had sensed my sorrow on the long ride that day to the estate and from his own purse had bought me a coconut.

55: Martial games

For weeks after that, I was sure that soldiers would come and take me away. I passed every waking moment wondering, what if it happens *now*? But day after day, the soldiers did not come, and I began to calm down. My mind turned elsewhere. But I paid scant attention to the approach of an event that would set in motion drastic changes for me and my family, and, I should say, for the Empire as a whole.

It was the annual martial games, a week of competition in swordplay, elephant duels, horse and chariot racing, the casting of spears, the shooting of arrows. For the King, lacking a war, there was nothing closer to the excitement of combat – not a few of the competitors expired on the field. For Crown Prince Aroon, I think the games were something different, a chance to ride with his father and demonstrate progress in martial skills. He would take part in two events of horsemanship. And he would see, for the first time, the estate where the rise to power had begun, because the honour of hosting the games had fallen to Chaiyapoom this year.

We all had heard that this choice had been enabled through pledges of silver by the estate's young lord to the private charities of certain palace Brahmins. This was a common-enough method of securing the games. Each lord of the realm of course stood to gain from the resulting recognition, the flowery mentions in court. And having the ear of the King for an extended period allowed for the talking-up of private agendas. Nol suggested to me that the young lord, having gotten nowhere with his appeals to us that day, planned to plead to the King that because the cost of hosting the games was so high, his estate should be exempt from the new levees for construction of the mountain-temple. He would not volunteer that these would amount to three to four times the expense of the games. His Majesty wouldn't know – he never took interest in details like that. And in any case, Nol said, the King would be distracted watching for Darit. The Upper Empire was the region to which he'd been banished, and there was wide speculation that he might show up at the games to seek forgiveness from his father. No one expected Darit to remain banished for long.

The departure for the games was a great ceremony in itself. Following tradition, King and Crown Prince mounted horses, then led a cohort of two hundred royal guardsmen in parade before the palace. The column passed the reviewing stand, which was crowded with retainers, and kept right on going, heading for Angkor's north gate.

Falling in with the column after it left the palace vicinity was the usual tail of retainers, cooks and washerwomen. And the oxcart of my daughter Bopa, designated concubine for the four-week excursion. She was sleeping, tended by Yan, as the cart rattled through the city's avenues. Nol was not to be seen – those aches in his bones had continued slowly to increase and limited his duty to the Capital.

Ten days' travel brought the column to the boundary of Chaiyapoom's lands. By a marker stone, four horsemen in the red sampots of the games waited. My girl eyed them through slats in the cart's side, relieved that the estate and its cool-water comforts – she had heard there was a waterfall – must now be near. Yan cooed sympathetically. She produced a damp cloth to moisten her mistress's forehead.

Finally, the caravan reached the estate house. King and prince were received by the young prince of Chaiyapoom. Bopa and Yan watched from the edges, then an estate retainer showed them to a small guesthouse.

The next morning, an estate retainer appeared at the guesthouse with word of where and when the games would begin. Presently the two women walked the forest path he had mentioned. They emerged into the sunlight of a large open field. Ahead was a newly built bamboo platform, a forest of red royal parasols over it. His Majesty and the Crown Prince were there already, seated on a gilded double dais, tended by the estate's prince. A phalanx of the King's guard surrounded the pavilion. But its members knew Bopa and her maid, and so they stepped aside to make way. Bopa took a place behind the King, Yan beside her.

On the field ahead, lines of soldier-competitors, all in the special red garments of the games, stood waiting. Behind them were ranks of war elephants and horsemen. Near the pavilion, referees, guardsmen and servants all hurried about making last-minute preparations.

More rows of men in red sampots, more war elephants, moved into place, from every direction it seemed. Finally there came a general quieting – opening rites were about to begin. The young host rose and the guardsmen made way to allow him to the centre of the field. There he stood a moment, facing the pavilion. But he did not announce the start of the games. Instead, he gave way to a man of broad shoulders who stepped from the ranks.

Everyone recognized him immediately. Darit.

The whole world has heard of what came next; there are many versions of what happened. I will tell you what I know direct from the mouths of Yan and Bopa.

'Fellow Khmers of the palace guard, welcome!' Darit shouted. 'You have travelled a week to be here. We salute you!'

Yan knew that no matter how he'd come to be here, Darit should not be acting as master of ceremonies. She felt uneasy. But not the King. He listened, smiling, his pride plain for all the world to see. He was just a father now, delighted that a long-lost son had reappeared. He seemed the only person who failed to notice that Darit had not crossed his arms at his chest in salute.

'You are highly skilled in war arts,' Darit continued, 'We know how far you throw your spears, how straight you thrust your daggers, how fast you run and ride. I saw it many times during my years in the Capital. So many times we practiced together, do you remember? There is no military force like you in the world.'

His Majesty put hands to mouth and shouted: 'Perhaps you'd like to concede all the prizes right now?' He thought that was a wonderful joke.

Darit paid no attention, yet still the King's suspicions weren't aroused. 'We have come here to confront you, fellow Khmers of the palace guard. But the truth is that we would rather not. We have come here not for sport, but to save the Empire. The current reign has surpassed all limits of respect! It has squandered the bounty of Heaven. All over the Empire, in your own home villages, people are oppressed. You face demands for so much rice that your families go hungry. You face quotas for so much building material that you are left with nothing to honour the deities of your own districts.'

The King was on his feet, staring, finally understanding.

'We will fight you if we must,' Darit continued, looking again to the guardsmen. 'But we will win. Because we have the support of Heaven. Here is the proof!'

He gestured toward a far-off tree line. There, out of arrow range, stood an elephant, a rather old one, draped in white, its tusks in gold sheaths.

'It is the holy elephant Kumari, favoured beast of the former, rightful King.'

Cheers and the mass shaking of weapons sounded from Darit's lines. The King's hand went to his dagger. Yan's hand went to my daughter and pulled her to her feet. 'We must go!'

Bopa was up, trying to comply, but she was stopped by Darit's next words: 'Kumari, my fellow Khmers, has remained alive these years through the courage and benevolence of the great holy woman of the Empire, the Lady Sray, endower of hermitages, feeder of the poor, healer of the sick. It was she who on the day the usurper seized the throne led Kumari out of Angkor to safety, because she knew that in the beast resides the spirit of legitimate rule. Before I left the Capital, I called on the Lady at her village retreat, and she blessed me and all who would join me. Anyone who does not believe may ask my retainers, ask the villagers there.'

You see, then, his purpose in calling on me that day! What wickedness, to use me in the spilling of blood, the advancing of selfish ambition.

Now the King bounded forward, right through his guards' line, sword in one hand, dagger in the other.

The soldiers' ranks, so straight and organized, dissolved straightaway into the confusion and din of combat. Men swung swords wildly, shouting, cursing. Some quickly fell bleeding, their souls already departing. A war elephant pushed close to try to ram the King's pavilion. Arrows and spears pierced the roof and sides.

It was only due to Yan that my daughter got out of there. The maid held her firmly by the wrist, pulling, pulling, not letting anything stop them. They ran right past grunting men swinging blades at each other. Ahead was the forest, which would provide cover. Just as they entered it, Bopa looked back. Men in red sampots were inside the royal pavilion now; His Majesty was to the side of it, still with sword and dagger, half a dozen enemies closing in on him. And Prince Aroon – bravely standing firm, right there with his father. The last sight she saw, before she turned and ran headlong down the trail, was a royal parasol falling.

Somehow they reached the gate of the estate house, exhausted, their garments splattered with mud and water. The retainer they'd met that morning ran up to them, in a full panic. Don't gather your things! Just get out!

Even here, everything was happening too quickly to comprehend. Three soldiers in red sampots suddenly appeared. 'Look at this!' cried one, seizing Bopa by the arm. 'I get my prize before the fight's even over!'

Yan stepped forward and slapped him hard across the face. He sputtered in rage and reached for his knife, but then arrows were striking all around – the ground, the gate, the thigh of the blustering soldier. Bopa ran again, but fell face down after a few steps. Tasting dirt, she rolled over. Fire arrows were streaking across the sky toward the estate palace. Then Yan was pulling my girl up again and together they fled the compound. There was smoke in the air. And then ahead, their oxcart. The two beasts were hitched to it, but there was no sign of the driver. Yan hurried her mistress aboard, then seized whip and reins and got the animals moving. From behind, the din of fighting carried in through trees and brush, seeming to chase them. Bopa pleaded that they go faster, but Yan replied that oxen know just one pace.

Horsemen appeared ahead. They were no threat – they were flying the standard of the King's guard. They passed, offering no protection, just shouts of slogans of loyalty to His Majesty. Bopa felt better on hearing that, but a minute or two later the cart passed two of those same King's men lying dead in the track, eyes vacant and mouths open. She looked away and mumbled a prayer.

All morning and afternoon, Yan and Bopa bumped along this jungle road, passing unfriendly spirits, meeting no humans. Bopa worried they were lost. At dusk, they reached the crest of a hill and saw that ahead the jungle ended – there was grassland, a stream, and on its banks, where the road crossed the water at a ford, a small fort built of logs. Yan argued for going right on past. But Bopa said no, they should stop. There would be food and water, and protection. As it happened, they had no choice. The fort's commander, seeing that this was a palace vehicle, stepped into the road. He voiced an elaborate welcome, showing no surprise at the strange sight of a woman driving an oxcart. One of his men stood behind with bowls of water. Clearly, word of the rebellion hadn't reached this far. Yan whispered to her mistress to stay in the cart and say nothing. But Bopa sat up and blurted out the news. She began weeping, pointing at her torn sampot and speckles of mud still on her arm. Shocked, the commander helped her down, then questioned her, like a servant, it seemed to her, right there by the cart, and at length. Yan got the same treatment. A dozen or more men emerged from the fort and pressed close, weighing every word, fingering their daggers in a way Bopa found frightening. The promise of water was forgotten; no one seemed to care that the two women had almost been killed.

Later they did get their water, and some food, by lamplight in the commander's hut. They ate hungrily, though the meal was coarsely milled rice and the flesh of a mole. Soldiers whispered in the shadows among themselves, and Bopa felt afraid all over again. Later, four of the men grudgingly cleared out of a hut and turned it over to the women, but took its only lamp with them. Bopa lay down in the darkness. The mat stank of old sweat, and all night her mind replayed the leering soldier and his grip on her arm. And the things that Darit had said about me. None of it made sense.

When morning came, she was offered rice and more of the mole. The men eyed her like they had the night before; she turned away, recalling again that grip on her arm.

Then came a shout and everyone went to the fort's gate. Horsemen flying the King's standard were approaching. But not at a gallop. Even from afar it was clear that this was a procession of defeated men. Wounds and torn clothing and damaged spears began to show. The fort's commander, frowning at the sight, stepped forward and traded a few words with a weary officer who had a gash across his shoulder.

When the commander returned, he had grave news. 'Prince Aroon has been killed. The Chaiyapoom estate house has burned to the ground and its prince is dead too. About His Majesty – they don't know.'

Yan asked: 'So what should my mistress and I do?'

He looked to her with some irritation. 'Do whatever you want.' Then he turned back to his soldiers.

The rear of the column was still in sight. Yan told Bopa they must hurry and join it. Five minutes later, the cart was fording the stream, water up to its axle. But the beasts, as always, refused to move any faster than a plod. The cart could not catch up to the horsemen, and soon the two women were traveling alone again, through another stretch of foreboding jungle.

Ahead, a wild boar darted across the road. Frightened, the oxen stopped. No matter how hard Yan flicked the whip, they refused to move. Bopa lay down in despair, arms folded tightly to her chest. She no longer believed that Heaven was charting her safety.

56: Captivity

So the soldiers finally did come for me. It was at night. I was at home at the time, sleeping, naked under my linen. I was awoken by footfalls on the polished teak floor, by the flicker of a lamp that one of the men carried.

I sat up, heart pounding.

'Lady Sray,' said the soldiers' leader. 'You must come with us.'

Through my mind flashed images of the long-ago prince lying dead.

'I will. Please do me the courtesy of stepping back while I dress.'

'Yes, Lady Sray.'

Presently I emerged from the net, a prayer on my lips. It was peculiar – in the face of the reality of arrest, I was far calmer than I had been in merely worrying about it. The soldier in charge led me down the steps of the veranda and across the courtyard to our compound's gate. Servants peeked from windows and doorways, weeping, whispering protective prayers in my direction, but unable to do anything more. Outside the compound walls, more soldiers waited, and they fell silent too when I approached. They formed up around me at a respectful distance and walked me in silence through darkness to the palace.

There I was led along a long wooden arcade, to a door. Beyond it a lamp burned, revealing a chamber prepared for a lady, with full comforts – mat and linens, gilded frames on the windows, silver cups of water, a small shrine.

I entered. Behind me, a drape was pulled across the doorway and I was alone.

I knelt at the shrine. 'Lords of Heaven, let whatever penalty has resulted from my life be exacted on me alone. It was I who failed to keep away from the young prince. It was I who led my husband to run away without facing the consequences. Let me pay the price for these acts, let it fall to no one else.'

I sat back. My calmness, I think, grew from relief that the wait and dissembling were over. I would now salvage some small measure of honour by admitting to what I had done. The encounter with the aged cart driver had brought back to me a truth that I had sometimes put to the side, that one's past cannot be escaped, that the sum merit and transgressions of a life's every thought and action carry forward with that life.

Later, dawn began to colour the small patch of sky visible through the window. Footsteps sounded outside the door. Two servants entered, poking heads through the drapes. They set trays of food on the floor and left without a word. I ate a bit of rice and plum.

Later there entered a stone-faced Brahmin I didn't know and a scribe, who carried a small writing stand.

'I have come to question you,' the priest announced.

He settled down opposite me, his eyes declining to engage.

'You are, are you not, the Lady Sray, wife of Nol the parasol master? Mother of Bopa the concubine and Sovan the architect.'

'I am, all of those things.'

'And endower of charitable works, most recently the pilgrim hospital at the bridge by the third distance marker on the eastern highway?'

'No, sir, the hospital was not my work. It was the work of another family, the keepers of the King's cattle.'

He glanced my way, and I could see that he did not welcome this duty. Then he continued one question after the other, pausing when the scribe at his writing stand fell behind. Where was I born? Where was I raised? How had my family come to be in the royal household? Then: 'Have you ever, Lady Sray, been in the presence of an elephant said to be holy, known by the name Kumari?'

That question? I hadn't expected it.

'Yes.'

He led me through those initial encounters years earlier in the marketplace, the diamond on the beast's forehead, methods of divining the future and communicating it.

'Now tell me, who was the keeper of this elephant?'

'I cannot remember his name.'

His eyes met mine full-on for the first time. 'Lady Sray, you should try to remember.' But that was all. He did not press me again for the name. He turned to how Kumari had disappeared from the royal corral after the late King's death.

'It was my doing,' I replied. 'I went to the corral at night when the men there were sleeping. I led the elephant out, and took her away from the city.'

'You did this by yourself?'

'Yes. I set her free in the forest. She did not follow me back to the city.'

'That is a remarkable claim. The handling of elephants is a man's job.' Again, he did not attempt to bully me into changing my story.

I said a silent prayer to atone for the lie, then continued: 'I did it because Kumari was in danger with the change of reigns.'

'Was she?'

'She was. I did what I did to help a divine animal who had helped me and many other people in the city and harmed no one. She is gone now, but wherever she may be, I wish her the longest of lives.'

'Lady Sray,' said the Brahmin, 'on that account I can tell you a few things. Kumari is still living.'

'Oh! That is wonderful news.'

'Yes, but it is not so simple. Eight days ago, she was seen with a rebel force that appeared in the Upper Empire at the annual martial games at Chaiyapoom. This force was led by the King's son Darit. It attacked the King's party. The crown prince was killed, along with half the royal guard. The prince of the estate died as well. But His Majesty fought his way out and has succeeded in returning to the Capital. For this we all give thanks to Heaven. Our King is now mobilizing an army to go back and suppress the uprising.'

I took a moment considering it all. 'Brahmin, I can tell you that Kumari is a peaceable creature, with no interest in war or the taking of power. If she is with these rebels, it is as a captive. It is not by her choice.'

'That is plausible, Lady Sray. She did not take part in the combat. She was merely put on display, at the fringes of the battlefield, as a means of building fighting spirit in the rebel soldiers. She was held by a man who might have brought her there against her will.' The Brahmin waited a moment, then said:

'But there is more I must tell you, I'm afraid. Before the battle began, the rebel Darit gave a speech. He declared that...that you, Lady Sray, had blessed the rebellion.'

'*What?*' My hand came to my mouth. 'I did no such thing!'

The Brahmin's manner softened. 'I can see, Lady, that it's absurd to think that you did. But I must take your statement nonetheless. It is the King's order.' He proceeded to ask me many detailed questions, which I could barely answer, about Darit's visit to my retreat village and what passed between us there.

'Lady Sray,' he said at the end. 'This will all be recorded and presented to His Majesty. It is for the King to decide what to do, but I will make my recommendation.'

Alone again, I knelt at the shrine. I prayed and prayed but found no solace – not a word that I whispered registered with my own soul, nor, I believe, with whichever gods were listening. Heaven asks that prayers come from a settled heart, but my heart that day was a tangle of conflicting emotions, lies and half-truths. The guilt I had come here to confess to remained as concealed as ever; I had let the Brahmin leave the room without a word said about it. And yet somehow I felt indignant that new, false accusations were being laid on my shoulders. I found myself demanding that Heaven intervene to right this wrong. Through these claims of plots and rebellion, I was being denied the serenity that can come, so I believed, from placing oneself forward to receive a penalty deserved.

By the time I finally turned from the shrine, I had promised that when this arrest finally brought me face to face with His Majesty, I would spill out my confession promptly. There would be no more delay. And then I would do everything I could to convince him that whatever had happened those many years ago, I had never done anything in present times to try to harm him, nor could I even imagine doing such a thing.

57: Sovan's gambit

My son had not yet learned of the rebellion or my arrest, but that would quickly change.

The night lamps were burning when the watchman hurried to the footbridge of the water pavilion behind the house. Inside Sovan sat studying a slate-board message in which his supply master attempted to explain, without directly citing obstruction by lords of various estates, why there was a shortage of laterite blocks at the mountain-temple's staging yard.

'Pardon me, sir,' called the watchman. 'But a cart has arrived. It would be best if you came.'

Sovan followed him to the front of the house. There he understood immediately why he'd been summoned. In the light of a torch, a maid was helping a distressed young woman down from the cart. It was his sister, her hair matted, her clothing stained. She wore not a single piece of jewellery. Sovan hurried to her and took her by the hands. Her response was to stumble full against him. They stood together, he holding her up, she weeping into his shoulder.

The maid Yan spoke. 'I could think of nowhere to come but here, sir. We saw soldiers everywhere around the palace, even at your father's house. Some of them were drinking. It wasn't safe for my mistress, so we came here.'

'You did the right thing,' replied Sovan. Still, he had no idea what she was describing. He noticed now that the maid's hair was dishevelled too, and there was a bruise on her face.

Suriya came hurrying down the front steps. 'Goodness! What happened?' She took charge, leading Bopa around the house toward a bathing jar. 'Don't worry,' Suriya whispered to her, leaning close. 'You'll be safe here. We'll take you to get cleaned up, then you can lie down.'

Bopa mumbled: 'Please, please, I want to sleep.'

Husband and wife exchanged a glance – at least she could speak, then.

Inside the house, Suriya got her sister-in-law settled on a mat, and placed a linen covering over her. 'You have no fever, sister,' whispered Suriya. 'That's good. You'll feel better soon, I'm sure.'

Bopa's eyelids drooped and in a few moments she was breathing heavily in sleep. Suriya settled in to sit vigil; Sovan went outside to get more from the maid. When she had finished her own bath, she told the full story: the attack on His Majesty, the claim that I had blessed the rebellion, the soldiers at the fort by the river.

'After we left the fort, sir,' said Yan, 'we travelled for four days. But the King's soldiers were ahead of us and every village they passed learned from them of the rebellion. Some places were quite unfriendly by the time we came through. At one, we had to trade some of our jewellery just to eat. In the next one, men rushed the cart and stole the rest of what we had....' She seemed not to want to continue.

Sovan had to ask: 'Was there worse than that?'

'No, sir. But almost. Well, sir, they...they took hold of your sister. They pulled her right out of the cart. I fought them, sir, and I made them give her up just when they were about to take her into a house. I shamed them, really – I shouted at them that I am only a maid and she is a defenceless lady. Then we got going again, and didn't dare stop again until we arrived here.'

She began to cry, and Sovan put a hand to her shoulder. 'You need not worry anymore,' he said softly. 'We'll call in priests for her purification. We'll protect her. And we'll do those things for you as well. I have no doubt that she made it here safely only because of you. You have earned merit for the next life in a quantity most people will never achieve.'

That night, Sovan made no attempt to sleep. He paced, in the garden by the lotus pond, beneath a three-quarter moon. Through the window, he could see the lamp-lit outline of his wife, still watching over Bopa. All was strangely peaceful in this place, the members of his immediately family safe. But he knew that I must be in grave danger.

After a while, he called to his wife. 'I will go to the palace and see what I can do for my mother.'

Suriya came outside, put arms around him and held him for a moment. Then she told him to go. 'I will pray for you. Heaven will return you safely, with her.'

He went off alone in the darkness, riding a mare. When he passed through the city's south gate, he saw immediately why Yan had been so afraid. Two soldiers sat in a lamp-lilt wine stall, toying with a prostitute. On the ground outside, a comrade was sleeping off a drinking binge. Who could say if they were celebrating having survived the fighting in the north, or were merely Capital garrison men who sensed a breakdown coming? A male voice called. 'Come over here, what a nice horse that is.' Sovan dug in his heels to make the animal gallop. He went first to the house of Nol and me. I was not there, of course. Neither was Nol. A retainer explained fearfully at the gate that I had been taken by guardsmen, that the master was out of the city and a messenger had been sent urgently to fetch him.

At the bridge to the royal sector, Sovan saw more soldiers, but at least these were disciplined. They stood in a row, spears and shields ready, and refused to let him through. He tried three other ways in, but it was the same at each – hostile fighting men telling him to go away. He wasted several hours this way. Late in the morning, as he stood outside the north gate thinking out his next step, an aide to the Brahmin Subhadra happened to pass by. They spoke.

The aide declined to take a note to me, but he agreed to pass something to the Brahmin. Sovan quickly wrote out an urgent request for a meeting with him. Then he wandered away from the gate a bit – better than to have the soldiers order him to step away – and stood waiting. It was evening when the Brahmin finally appeared. Sovan rushed to him.

'My mother is all right?'

'Yes, no one has harmed her.'

'You must help me get in to see the King.'

'I'm afraid...I'm afraid he has already refused that,' the Brahmin replied. 'I asked. I knew it would be what you wanted.' He seemed reluctant to say more. But soon he did. 'I am deeply worried for her, Sovan. We have managed to safeguard her so far, but I don't know how long that can continue. She is accused of treason and insurrection. There are no crimes more serious.'

'Then I will have to do something, Brahmin, that will forcethe King to see me, and force him to listen when he does.'

Sovan was astonished he had spoken so boldly. In fact, this 'something' had come to him right as he stood there. So he told it to the Brahmin, ignoring the warnings that the priest immediately began to voice, and told him also to wait two hours before telling the King, so that no soldiers could overtake him and prevent it.

He hurried the horse back toward his house. He had suddenly realized the danger which his own family faced right now, and as he rode through darkness, passing night travellers and an oxcart coming in the other direction, he worried more and more that soldiers would come for them too. But when he reached the house, everything was as before. He gathered family and servants and told them that they would all leave immediately for the estate of a cousin of Suriya east of the Capital. It was just a precaution, he said, taken just in case. They would use a narrow track from the rear of the house through forest, so as to avoid anyone who might be coming out from the city on the road. Carts and oxen and horses were quickly assembled. He said a tearful good-bye to Suriya and to the children, but not to Bopa. She wasn't there.

'She's already left, in a cart,' Suriya explained.

Soon Sovan stood all alone, watching his family disappear down the track.

Now he went to the construction site. He told the watchman he found at the design pavilion to call the foremen at the various camps where the labourers lived. When they had assembled in front of him, puzzled by the night-time summons, he told them that work would stop on the mountain-temple. The twenty-two thousand pairs of hands on the project should all stay away from their jobs starting tomorrow. Those who wished to go to their home villages were free to do so. He thanked the foremen for their many efforts in recent years, adding how much he had valued the partnership. Then he dismissed them.

This is what he did next: He found one of the wooden handcarts that labourers used to move earth or stone, and brought it to the design pavilion. Inside, he opened the cabinets. He removed every copy of every building plan, every sketch of every future statue and bas relief. There were quite a few; the cart's bin was barely able to contain them all. He pushed the load to his house, past the pond and down the forest path to the kilns. Perhaps a dozen people were there, minding the fires. He told them they should leave, that this place would soon be very dangerous. They merely froze, worried for their master and what his pushing a cart might mean. Now he told them again to leave and they went.

One by one, he pushed the plans one by one through the holes in which the kiln fires burned. The heat strong on his face, he watched as each burst into flame and turned quickly to ash.

Then he sat down to wait.

Toward dawn, a group of soldiers strode in, carrying torches.

'Show us the plans, then!' the commander demanded.

Sovan pointed to the kilns. The man went close and peered into the fire holes, scrutinizing what remained, afraid to get too close, because His Majesty's authority was somehow invested in the plans, even if they were only ashes. Then he barked an order: 'Bind his hands!' When the cord was pulled tight, Sovan winced and wondered if he was really up to what would come.

At the palace, he was held in a guardhouse for an hour. Then two soldiers brought him toward the audience hall, pushing him rudely as he walked, his hands still tied. Inside, they pressed him to the floor, face down.

The King's voice boomed. 'Tell me this isn't true, what the Brahmin says, what the soldiers say! Tell me that you faked it.'

'Majesty, I cannot tell you that,' said Sovan, into the floor.

He heard the stamping of feet, and the sound of a blade being swished through the air above him. A very strong arm closed around his neck. The King had seized him from behind; the blade was cold at his throat.

'You will begin right now to draw everything again.'

Sovan swallowed. 'Majesty, I cannot. When I try to imagine the Temple of the Eighteenth Reign, I get only a blank.'

The King ran the blade across Sovan's skin. 'Do you feel that, Architect? I have killed quite a few men. You would be just another. I can find another builder. He will finish the job.'

'Majesty....' Sovan faltered – he had not slept in almost two days.

But then he found his tongue. 'He will not be able to...not in the way that the temple must be built. The vision came to me alone in a vision when I was young. It showed the precise form that Heaven expects this temple to assume. Heaven placed the vision there. And now...Heaven has removed it. If you kill me, the temple will never take its proper form...and that is the only form that will guarantee you your place alongside the gods in the next life.'

The knife made another short swipe.

'I have prayed, Majesty, and Heaven has told me that the inspiration will return, that I will be able to recreate everything precisely as it was, to continue with the construction as it must be done. I will be able to do this, Majesty, if...if the Lady Sray is allowed to go free.'

Sovan shut his eyes. He would say nothing more. The vision of the mountain-temple was the central religious experience of my son's life, perhaps the only real one. He did in fact believe that he was the sole vessel on earth for creating this glorious edifice. Now he could only hope that Heaven would accept his reasons for putting its construction at risk and would protect him and see him through.

58: Ransom

Nol wasn't present when the soldiers came for me because he was in Kralann, inspecting the tools and artisan teams that made the King's fans and parasols. A male servant, one with enough courage to deliver the news, was dispatched to run the distance from the Capital. He reached the village shortly before noon, exhausted, just as the headman was showing the master a new loom.

Nol gave off a bellow of horror and disbelief that terrified everyone who heard it. All went to their knees, headman included, but then Nol shouted at them, why are you wasting time? Get my palanquin ready! The headman scurried off to find the six young men who bore it. Nol hobbled as best as he could to the conveyance and as it left the village, bearers straining to hurry the load on their shoulders, he berated the men for being slow. Then he turned his attention to the still-winded servant, who trotted alongside: how many soldiers came to the house, who was their leader, what precisely did they say, what were the charges, how did the Lady react, why had the servants put up no fight? The man answered between breaths. He knew nothing about the reason for the arrest and didn't dare make up an answer. But one thing he did know – he'd seen it with his own eyes – and he told it to the master over and over, and I will repeat it to you now: that in being led away I had displayed a quiet dignity that left the soldiers ashamed and speechless.

I know that Nol found some comfort in that, but it did not last long. Though I was certain that the arrest was related to the young prince's killing those years ago, Nol was certain it wasn't. After such a long time, he reasoned, no one could connect the wealthy Lady Sray with a shy young girl who had disappeared from a far-away estate. It had been thirty-six years! To Nol, the only explanation was Rom. The woman had been jealous of him even in childhood, jealous of me, jealous of Bopa. He began to question how it was he had never dealt with that woman properly, why he had allowed a threat like hers to fester year after year.

As the palanquin passed the mountain-temple site, a plan

was taking form in his mind. He would go straight to the palace, never mind a bath first. He would step into His Majesty's presence and in a voice infused with outrage denounce whatever absurd charge Rom was making. No accusation against me could be anything but fabrication. He would reveal the sabotage of the crown prince's horsemanship, the sleeping drug fed to Bopa, the false accusation against the concubine Channary. He would recount all the things His Majesty had always refused to consider concerning Rom. This would be *her* ruin.

He reached the palace gate after sunset, just after my son had left to return to his house. A pair of sentries stood, lit by a torch. Only the King was allowed to ride onto the royal grounds, so Nol got down as nimbly as his joints allowed and began to walk through the entranceway. A guard stepped into his path.

Nol hissed: 'Out of the way! Don't you see who I am?'

'I do, sir. But King's orders, sir. If the parasol master comes, he is not to be admitted.'

'I don't believe it!' He pressed straight on, ignoring the guard's cajoling, but then two sets of hands took hold of him. He pulled at them, but the hands merely held tighter. He resisted again, with energy that surprised the soldiers, and in the struggle everyone fell to the ground.

'Parasol Master,' whispered one of the guards, hoping for a way out of the confrontation. 'If you give your word to go back, we will let you up.'

'All right.'

But the moment he was on his feet, he lunged forward. The hands grabbed at him again. This time the soldiers lifted him and placed him outside the twin gates and swung them closed.

He pounded on the wood, shouting threats and insults. All men harbour possessive feelings about their wives, do they not? I can imagine that at this moment he was having the worst kind of thoughts, that scenes were playing out in his mind, of me, eyes closed, beneath the King on a sleeping mat.

Nol's servant found words to get their master back to the palanquin. The bearers lifted the load and moved quickly from the gate, eager to get away from this place. They headed for the parasol pavilion, but half way there, Nol stopped them: Go to the house of the Brahmin Subhadra.

You can imagine how shocked the priest was on seeing my husband's beat-up condition. He called for water and wet cloths, then had servants help Nol inside to a mat. Finally resting, my husband breathed a bit more slowly.

He and the Brahmin had never entirely liked or trusted each other, but on this day their interests would surely be one.

The Brahmin had welcome news for Nol: I was safe in the chamber inside the palace. I had not been physically mistreated in any way. The King, he said significantly, had not seen me. The priest apologized for not stopping the arrest. It had come on the direct orders of the King, the first orders he issued on arriving from the field of rebellion. Nol stirred. Rebellion?

And so my husband heard the full story. When it was done, he swallowed and said: 'I was right, then. The concubine was behind this.' I suppose that saying this made him feel in control again.

'It does appear that way,' the priest replied. 'The soldiers are looking for her but so far she's missing. She's not at the concubine pavilion, not at the old orchid farm. She will be found, probably. But we will have to be careful even then. You know how His Majesty is swayed by her.'

'He'll see through her lies this time!'

'We can only hope so.' The Brahmin let that sit a moment, then said: 'Nol, there is another thing. A member of the Council of Brahmins has interviewed your wife. I'm afraid, I'm afraid that I must tell you she acknowledges having helped save the elephant from execution.'

'What? I can't believe it.'

'My friend,' said the priest, 'she explained in some detail. You told her the King had ordered the animal's death, so she used a piece of jewellery that you brought her from the campaign in the north to buy the animal's way out of the palace stable and take it to a place of safety. I venture to say it is in line with her character. She took great risks for the safekeeping of this holy beast. She gained nothing for herself.'

For a moment, Nol forgot his concern: 'But if she did that,

she endangered me, endangered the family! A woman cannot do such a thing without her husband's permission!'

'Parasol master, I have never been married. But I have learned that all wives have secrets from their husbands. And in the case of the Lady Sray, there was someone other than the husband who wanted to know those secrets. I mean the concubine, of course. She is still free, but her household staff is in custody. We have discovered that one of her men, the former bodyguard of her son, received a special assignment some years ago, to try to discover things about the background of the Lady. This man has confessed everything. He has told us that Rom believed that no one could have a character as pristine as the Lady's was claimed to be, that there must be something to learn about her. How sad – she cannot imagine true virtue.'

'Indeed she can't. Go on.'

'The man went to many places around the Empire that had some connection with the Lady. He looked around, he talked to people. Eventually he found something right here in the Capital, a man who was a foot soldier in the unit that provided the Lady's security when she travelled. The man had become quite ill, and was living without support of family in a Brahmin hospital, the one behind the central market. Rom's man took to visiting him, pretending to be from his home district and concerned for his health. He brought fruit and coconut milk. The man liked to talk, and he mentioned with pride the many trips his unit had taken with the Lady, and he recalled that on one the group visited an elephant corral outside the Capital, and the Lady had seemed quite interested in a particular animal there. Later Rom's man went and found that corral. He posed as a potential donor and friend, this time to one of the men who worked there. The two went drinking and after four or five cups of rice wine this assistant elephant keeper swore him to secrecy and told him all about his master, a man named Sovan, who had among the elephants a very special one. An elephant named Kumari. The whole thing came out, including the Lady Sray's role. Later, the concubine sent some other men to break into the corral at night and take the elephant away. She kept it for some time in a corral of her own. Then it was taken to Chaiyapoom to be cynically used in the rebellion.'

Nol kept silent. He was of course wondering now if next he would hear that the concubine's man had found evidence of the killing of a young nobleman. But the Brahmin said nothing about that.

They talked further, then it was agreed the Brahmin would go to court to take the measure of His Majesty's mood. Nol hardly noticed him leave. He was thinking through his next move. It involved property.

Forgive him, please – but my husband is a man who in his youth lost everything. He lived in poverty for more than a decade. The property he had now was near to his heart, as it would be to any man's.

He called for chalk and slate, then compiled a list. Two estates in the north, one in the west, which needed major work on its irrigation system, the honey farm that supported a traveller's rest place, sixteen hundred weight of silver, give or take a few dozen, held on account by various Chinese merchants in the market, four ferry boats, the horse-breeding stable, the hire-elephant business (twenty-eight animals at last count), the furniture factory, the forge that made bronze Naga heads for the handles of palanquins, the three teak forests with sawyers and elephants, the two quarries, also with men and animals. Then there was of course the full set of buildings and businesses outside the west gate of the mountain-temple site – how many? Nol would have counted them on his fingers. More than fifty, certainly. And the three villages further west, including the one where I had my retreat house. His house and grounds by the palace compound.

Beneath this list, Nol wrote out another, shorter one, the property that would be offered as blandishments to free me: one estate, the honey farm, one teak forest and two hundred weight of silver. Plus the elephant business – the King would be in particular need of elephants, to haul supplies for the campaign against the rebels. If His Majesty balked at this list, other things could be offered up one by one until his price was reached, and they were duly noted toward the bottom of the slate.

Again, please do forgive him! Such were his ways, placed in his heart by Heaven. When the Brahmin returned, Nol made an announcement: 'I am ready to go before His Majesty, with an offer.'

'I don't think you can for the present, parasol master. I wasn't able to see him myself. Your son has created an uproar in court and His Majesty is receiving no one at all.'

59: The magic amulet

And what of my daughter? She was by now again under the spell of the chief concubine Rom!

Bopa had fallen asleep on the mat of my son's house. We summoned an ancient Brahmin physician, who poked and prodded even as she slept, then proposed more sleep, more water, ground powders, and a small wooden support for the girl's neck when lying down. He chanted a prayer, then departed. Presently Bopa sat up. Suriya brightened at this and called for rice soup. Bopa slurped down a bit, then put it aside. She asked where her brother was. He's gone to the palace, Suriya replied. The family is doing everything possible for our mother. Bopa felt suddenly ashamed. She had forgotten about me. But don't forget that she had been through such a trauma of her own.

Then, with the rice soup going cold, a mysterious bit of news from a servant: Bopa was being asked for out front.

Suriya told her to stay. I'll go and see who it is. But Bopa rose and followed right behind.

Outside, in the flickering light of a torch held by the house's watchman – Rom. Standing by an oxcart, attended by three men with knives in their waists.

Bopa shrieked with joy, then raced past her sister-in-law. The two concubines embraced, tears flowing from the eyes of the younger one, who whimpered that she had missed the Elder Sister, missed her desperately, had thought about her all the time. The other declared that she felt that way too, more than could be known, that Heaven one day would punish the palace priests who'd kept them apart all these years.

Rom pulled back and took Bopa by the shoulders. 'Well, get your things! I'll take you back to the palace. Everything will be how it used to be.'

Bopa hurried inside. Her strength was restored – perhaps the Brahmin's prayers had worked. When she returned with her basket, she found Suriya in some kind of dispute with the Elder Sister.

'Perhaps Bopa should remain here for the time being,' Suriya was saying, in her composed way. 'Taking her would be quite an imposition on you.' The watchman, standing close with the torch, nodded to confirm that his mistress knew best.

'It would be no trouble at all,' countered Rom.

'You're kind, but surely it would. In any case, my husband, her brother, is due back soon. I think we should hear his opinion.'

Bopa was about to protest when one of the visitor's men stepped directly in front of Suriya. It was quite remarkable – he simply stood there, hand on the hilt of his knife, looking the woman in the eye, like he was daring her to keep it up. It had its intended effect; Suriya was shocked into silence, even her watchman seemed paralyzed. Bopa hurried past and got in the cart. I have no doubt that she never noticed that this man had threatened her sister in law.

Rom, looking amused, spoke. 'It's so kind of you, Architect's wife, to change your mind. She'll be fine with me.'

The cart rolled into the darkness, the two concubines aboard. Bopa gave a quick look back. Suriya was still standing still in the light of the torch – my daughter found the scene touching in an odd kind of way. The watchman had gone to his knees, as if he was apologizing for something. Bopa moved closer to Elder Sister, reaching for her hand, and the burdens of the past days seemed to lift.

'You must be thirsty,' whispered Rom. From somewhere she produced a small porcelain jar and filled two cups. It was honey wine. Bopa beamed and took hers. The cart lurched, spilling a bit on her sampot. The two women laughed. Bopa took a sip – well, why not a gulp? Down it went.

Rom turned suddenly serious. 'You have a sterling heart, you know, you always have. You've forgiven me even for how I behaved the day of the river rite.'

'We all make a bit of trouble from time to time, Elder Sister. Some mischievous spirit puts the feeling in us. In me as well.'

They laughed again, and the talk flowed easily on. Soon Bopa was recounting the attack on His Majesty. Rom listened carefully, appearing horrified, interjecting questions. You actually heard Darit's speech, did you? Did the King's men seem won over by it.

She seemed quite impressed that Bopa had been so close to such remarkable events.

Later the cart passed through a city gate, turned left, right, then right again, wheels splashing through puddles, then crunching across gravel. Presently it stopped. Bopa looked out. There was no palace gate, just a tiny, weathered house pressed close up to others like it. She was confused – this place was almost like the old childhood neighbourhood. She noticed too that the cart in which they had ridden was old, a farmer's thing.

Rom said: 'I was thinking that it's better that we wait until daylight to go to the palace. Don't you agree? Now let's go inside quickly.'

Bopa obeyed, as she always did. They climbed a set of rickety steps, Rom in the lead; the three men remained below. Inside, things were rather shabby too. The walls showed water stains; the matting was unswept and worn through in places. But Rom gave no sign of noticing. She sank to the floor, seeming suddenly tired. After a while, she spoke, in an intimate voice: 'I have to confess that I'm nervous about going to the palace. His Majesty will be focusing on organizing this war. You know how impatient he gets when there's something like that going on.' She lingered over that for a while. Then she began to weep. 'Oh, Bopa! I've got to tell you the truth! He may be very upset with me. Wicked people are saying that I told my son to do the awful thing he did!'

My girl was touched by her friend's distress. She took her hand. 'No one will believe it.'

'Yes, but it still troubles me. If only His Majesty knew what really happened. When Darit was about to leave for his banishment, I stayed up the whole night with him. I told him over and over that he had to accept the penalty. He had killed a man – it was only right that he be punished. But he wouldn't accept. He went off with his heart stirred up and now he's leading this terrible rebellion. His Majesty, his own father, was almost killed. And it's due to me! I'm Darit's mother and I failed to teach him Heaven's basic rule of respecting his father.'

Bopa put arms around the Elder Sister.

'Oh, thank you,' said Rom, relaxing. 'I'm so glad you're here.

When I heard you were at your brother's place, I knew that if I could just see you, then somehow things would be set right. Please forgive me – it was selfish of me to go fetch you that way. I'm sure you would have been more comfortable at your brother's house.'

She was quiet for a while, but then something roused her. 'I know, I know what we'll do! You'll go to him ahead of me and explain! You know, smooth the way. It's perfect. His Majesty trusts you, he listens to you. We've all been able to see that, always.'

Bopa felt flattered, but she confessed she was afraid at the thought of going alone with such an assignment.

'Come on, you can do it!' Rom replied, taking her arm. 'We'll work out what to say. You can tell the King you heard me arguing with Darit.'

'But I didn't.'

'Never mind. I can tell you exactly what we said. You wouldn't be lying. You'd just be telling him what happened. You've got to do it! I've done many things for you over the years, haven't I? I've even kept secrets for you, one's there could have been real trouble over. Think what would have happened if word had got out about you and the crown prince's riding instructor!'

Bopa laughed with her, though uncertain why the Elder Sister had said this, and whether it was in fact funny.

'And there's one other thing you must do, Bopa. You must speak up for your mother. She's in terrible trouble, you know.'

Bopa winced. She had forgotten again.

'Now, you mustn't argue that she didn't help my son. The King will never believe that, he's had suspicions for years that she was in touch with his enemies. We've all admired her holiness, her philanthropy, but His Majesty has always wondered if it was all meant to disguise something. Really, the only thing that will work with him is to admit her guilt. He'll like it if you confirm what he already believes. You can say you saw it with your own eyes. You know, put your face to the dust and beg him to forgive her. He will, I'm sure. It's in his heart to forgive when people admit transgressions.'

Bopa was afraid, but she did manage to get some rest that night, calmed by sleeping powder that Rom provided.

The next morning, Elder Sister helped her put on perfume, jewellery, headdress and a fresh green silk garment that had all somehow been summoned up at the bleak little house. She set off in the cart. There was no trouble with the sentries at the palace compound's north entry; concubines had rights to pass. She reached the main courtyard, but when she tried to continue to the audience hall, guards stopped her. So she did what Rom had directed in this event. She settled down onto a patch of grass. Sooner or later, His Majesty would come this way, Rom had said. You may have to wait him out.

An hour passed, then two. Soldiers, priests, couriers came and went, distracted, giving her odd glances. Bopa's eyes began to droop. But then came tense voices and the clattering of weapons loose in their sheaths. The King appeared.

Her face went down. 'Majesty!' she called into the grass. 'I deserve to address not even the dust beneath your feet!'

She dared peek upward. The King had stopped and was glaring at her, a hand on his hip. 'Another member of this family? Have you burned up something too? No, you don't have it in you for something like that.'

Bopa had no idea what he meant, but she proceeded with the words Rom had given her. 'Majesty! I beseech humbly that you not believe falsehoods that may have reached your ears. With the gods listening, I state...I state that the chief concubine has at all times been loyal to you in...'

'That's who you're here about?'

From her spot on the ground, she managed to keep going. 'Rom did not know what he planned, Majesty! She did not know! She went away the day before the rebellion began because she received a note that her father was gravely ill. I was there when it came. She went back to her village to be with her mother. She had no time to tell the palace she was leaving – that is how distraught she was. And through the prayers of Rom and many priests and everyone in the home village, Majesty, her father recovered and all made merit for the next life. But now Rom worries that her absence will cause misunderstanding....'

'Don't lie – she knew and maybe you did too!'

Here Bopa's resolve failed. The other points on which Rom had drilled her vanished from her memory. So she reached into her waist for the thing she'd been given as the final piece of evidence.

'Here, Majesty! I offer the magic amulet of the rebel Darit!' Keeping her face in the grass, she held it up.

'How did you get this?' He snatched it away.

'From the loyal Rom, Majesty. She took it from her son before he left Angkor for exile. Please, Majesty, please believe! The rebel was without it during the fighting at Chaiyapoom. Its absence enabled your force of soldiers to stand up to one so much larger.'

The King was studying it, squinting, holding it to the light. Bopa's memory returned. 'It was made by the gods in the time of the birth of the Khmer race. It was found inside a golden image at a temple by the Freshwater Sea five reigns ago and then it was blessed by a corps of one thousand priests and seers. Before Darit went into exile, I heard his mother arguing with him. "You must learn to respect His Majesty's law." She said it over and over. "You must show your loyalty to your King every day. You must accept your punishment." But he refused. So she waited until he went to sleep and she took the amulet from his neck and hid it. Now she presents it to you. She presents it to you as a testament of her loyalty and a guarantee of victory in the coming war.'

There was a long silence. Then: 'You swear this is the amulet?'

'I do, Majesty.'

'But it looks cheap, like something sold outside a temple at a night festival.'

Rom had prepared her for this. 'That is among its powers, Majesty. To protect itself, to avert covetousness, it takes on a very ordinary appearance.'

The King placed it around his neck, then glanced left and right, as if testing whether the world looked different with the charm's help.

He looked back down to her. 'So you have nothing to say for your mother? What kind of daughter are you, speaking up for the concubine but not for the woman who brought you into this life?'

Bopa opened her mouth to say what Rom had told her.

But...but those words wouldn't come. My dear girl could only stare dumbly at the King's feet, eyes blinking. And do you know, right there, with the King's anger so strong she could feel it like the heat from a fire, she found that in her mind had been placed a new realization. It was that lies could be told for Rom's sake, but not for mine. It was her duty now to speak from the heart and to place faith in Heaven's teaching that from truth justice will always flow.

'Majesty,' she said calmly, daring even to look up at him, 'anyone who knows my mother knows that to associate her with war and violence is impossible. Please accept this, which can only be true, regardless of what was heard on the battlefield in Chaiyapoom. Please let my mother go free.'

Then Bopa said something more: 'Majesty, if I am mistaken about this, I will give up my place in the palace and pass the rest of my life in a holy order.'

She put her head down again, amazed at her words. She waited, and waited more, growing anxious. From above her came a sigh of frustration. Then she heard the sound of feet on gravel, moving quickly away.

60: Heaven's eternal will

How could I deserve the sacrifices, the risks that were being taken for me that day? By so many people – son, husband, daughter. And, just a few minutes after my daughter's entreaties, by the Brahmin.

It occurred at the pavilion that was the King's military headquarters. There three generals, strong men with scars and war tattoos, were crouching before His Majesty, who sat on a dais. The King gulped from a bowl of water, then without any preliminaries at all began to lay out his plan. An increased tax of silver, men and elephants to be levied on every estate. Three new armies that would train outside the Capital until the rains ended. One to march to the Siamese border to hold off any attacks of opportunity there, another to go east to do the same with the Chams. The third, the main force, to move north and hunt down the rebel Darit. And then specific instructions on Darit's fate: His head would be brought back to the Capital, the rest of his body would be cut up and scattered in the forest as food for birds and animals. Special curses, written for him alone, would be applied. Darit's soul would roam the world in eternity, powerless, tormented, unable to achieve rebirth. The extremes of love the King had once felt for Darit were now extremes of hate.

With the plan laid out, the King paused for a moment to touch the amulet that hung around his neck. I think it made him feel a special confidence now, one that had stolen up on him, rather than appearing the instant that he placed the thing on his body.

He looked to the commanders, demanding comment on his plan. It of course generated praise from each one in turn, though likely each was thinking of something else, which of the three armies would be his.

It was then that the Brahmin arrived, uninvited.

'What is it?' The King was not open to an interruption.

'I have come, Majesty, to announce to you the Council of Brahmins' decision on how to honour King and commanders as they go off to war.'

'You can tell me later. When I've dismissed these men.'

'But Majesty, these honours will be made in ways not seen before in the history of the Empire.'

'I said later.'

'Majesty, I beg for your time now.'

The King put up hands in exasperation. 'Explain then.'

'The idea came upon me as I made sacrifices to Vishnu, Majesty, so it is my belief that the supreme consciousness of Vishnu is its origin. Two of my assistants will go back to the temple and will question the priests there to determine precisely the background of...'

'Brahmin, tell us the idea.'

'Of course, Majesty. It is this: When kings of future ages visit your mountain-temple, they will see not only images of Vishnu and his divine retinue, and scenes from the sacred texts, among them the Churning of the Sea of Milk and the battle between the Kaurava and Pandava clans. They will see images of, of – it is, ah, so extraordinary an idea, it could only come from a god. They will see – images of *Your Majesty in his earthly form.*'

The King's frown softened and the Brahmin felt emboldened to go on. 'It is an unorthodox concept, I concede. Until now, bas reliefs have depicted only beings from the Heavenly realm. The apsaras that are being carved are following that tradition – they are modelled on real women, of course, but in stone they take divine form. Heaven wishes now to progress art to a new level of perfection. Heaven signals that the images of the temple must reflect earthly as well as Heavenly reality. His Majesty does Heaven's work on this earth and so he must be shown doing that work, not in Heaven but here in the realm where we live. He must be shown as the font of justice and benevolent rule that he is, presiding at court on his dais, his parasols overhead. All this must be clearly depicted so that future kings, perhaps lacking the present one's wisdom, can see and learn from it.

'Now, just as a god in Heaven has loyal assistants, so does a King on earth. And just as we depict those Heavenly assistants on our temples, so we must depict the assistants on earth.' He turned toward the generals. 'Though in a smaller scale, of course.'

Their faces begged him to continue.

'I foresee a great scene of His Majesty at his most glorious as a warrior and to the side his senior commanders, some on elephants, some on horses, leading ranks of soldiers to war. Our best sculptors will create these images and they will last for eternity. Future commanders heading to the field of battle will first come to the mountain-temple to gaze upon these images and they will know that today's commanders are the men they must emulate.'

You will understand now why the Brahmin had risked the King's anger to insist on laying out the council's conclusions now. (Though I should say that at this point the council's other members knew nothing of any conclusions.) Subhadra wanted the military men to hear, and to begin thinking of their own immortality in stone.

Clearly they were doing that – a silence took hold. And then one of the commanders spoke up with a question, as if on cue from the priest. 'But construction of the temple has stopped. When will it resume?'

The King frowned, and the general chose to drop the subject. The talk returned to army preparations, but the Brahmin did not leave. He sat to the side until the generals were dismissed, then he kept on with a plan he had thought carefully through.

'The suspension of construction is a minor thing, Majesty.'

'How can you say that?' Suddenly the King pounded a fist on the dais; the priest felt it might explode into kindling. 'Twenty thousand people have put down their tools.'

'It is minor, Majesty, because it is so easily resolved. Your mercy in sparing the life of the Architect is commendable. You have sent him home, and through that action much merit will accrue for your next life. Heaven has the power to restore the inspiration to the Architect's mind. All that remains is...to free the Lady Sray.'

'I won't! She conspired against me, against the Empire.'

'Majesty, we have seen no evidence of that. We have only the self-serving words of a man who is leading a rebellion against you, who has lied many times before.'

'You say that, but what about those magistrates I sent to the parasol village? She is the patron of the village and yet even with that people can't deny to my officials that they saw her bless the traitor Darit. He knelt before her and she blessed him!'

'Were these people close enough to hear what was said, Majesty?'

'What does that matter?'

'The Lady is often asked to bless people, Majesty. They believe she can cure all sorts of illnesses. Perhaps Darit claimed to be sick.'

'I don't know – perhaps I'll go and ask her myself.'

He said that but he made no effort to go. Rather, he stepped to the edge of the pavilion and stood staring at the shrubs and gravels paths outside it, as if there might be some solution to this problem there.

Presently Subhadra spoke again. 'Majesty, may I suggest, may I suggest in the most humble, respectful terms that we must not allow any other considerations to be at work here. In the almost thirty years I have served you as Rajaguru, we have dealt with that of which I speak many times. The answer can never change – it is Heaven's eternal will. To each person on earth, whether King or slave, something is denied.'

'Why are so many people willing to risk their lives on behalf of this woman? Why do they side with her when I have made it clear what I want?'

Many men would have withdrawn at this point. But Subhadra did not.

'Majesty, I will always hope that in your court there will be no risk in speaking the truth.' And then he said words that I did not deserve. 'For me the reason I speak as I do is that I believe she is a soul that was born into this life on earth for reasons we cannot comprehend, that she belongs in Heaven, but that while she lives among us here, we must respect her presence, her life apart from us, and we must do what we can to help her in this life peacefully.'

The King said nothing to that.

'Majesty, I know there is great temptation that you have resisted so far. This woman is confined in a room just a few steps from here, and yet you have not gone to her. I commend you for that. But while you consider your final decision about her, let us at least move her to some other place, further away, where...'

The King spun around. 'Absolutely not! She will stay where she is, and I will go to her at any moment I choose. And you priests won't have any say about whatever I choose to do with her there.'

'Majesty, you must not...'

'I've had enough of you. You will leave now.'

The Brahmin did leave. He took a few unsteady steps away from the pavilion's door, then turned to assure himself that the King at least was not going to me right then. No, it seemed I was safe for a while longer: The King had resumed his stance at the edge of the pavilion, his mind searching for answers that refused to reveal themselves.

61: Abode of the gods

In the afternoons, I sat on my mat, reading texts for as long as my eyes would allow, or gazing westward down the great entrance causeway. In early evenings, as the sun made its departure, I ate the last rice of the day. Pristine darkness settled in, and I looked at the stars, or the moon, or the undersides of passing clouds, whatever Heaven chose to display that night.

My place now was a small sleeping pavilion that carpenters had hastily assembled at the top level of the unfinished mountain-temple. I was strangely calm and contented.

How did I come to be here? It was by Subhadra's doing. As he had walked away from the war council hall that past day, he had resolved that whatever His Majesty said, I would not remain so close at hand. He knew that moving me without permission would infuriate the King and make him want to go straight to me. So the priest chose a place where strictures against sacrilege and defilement would be at their strongest.

That night, he came to the door of the room where I was held. He showed the two soldiers standing guard outside it a palm leaf with writing on it. It was a list of silver ewers, but these two young men could not read and took his word that it was an order for my relocation. Soon I stepped through the door. The priest greeted me with warmth, an emotion I had never associated with him, and hurried me off. He gave no hint he was acting on his own or of where I was going. Perhaps he thought I would object to the destination, or become nervous and give away the plot. In any case, he put me in a closed oxcart. It began immediately to roll and travelled much longer than I expected. The sky was still black when it finally stopped. I stepped down and was astonished to find myself amidst rows of large stone blocks, placed as if waiting for something. Then I understood – it was a builder's staging yard. I looked up and saw outlines of the great temple looming in the darkness above.

A priest stepped forward to show me through a stone gateway and up a covered stairway. Two wordless assistants appeared to help me ascend the final steepest of steps. At the top I found my sleeping pavilion, laid out with texts, a mat and sleeping cover, a lamp and a day's supply of food and drink. And a small shrine, of course. Then I was again alone. I shuffled to the shrine and began prayers. But before long I stopped – my mind was too restless. I would try instead to settle in. I lay down, but I could not sleep. As dawn approached, my disquiet over King and rebellion gave way to concern I was offending Heaven by my presence here. Yes, this place was unconsecrated. Only two towers rose, and near me an arcade awaited its roof. Stone fragments and dust freed by masons' chisels littered the floor. But none of these signs of incompleteness reassured me. I felt certain that gods must live in this place already, or at least be watching over it.

The sun rose, morning commenced, hours became days, yet no gods revealed themselves. I encountered them only in the way I always had, as wraiths, silent listeners to my prayers, and their responses were whispered so softly that they were sometimes lost in the breeze. I had been certain that here stone must be smooth to the touch, that a lamp must burn with divine brightness. Yet one night I stumbled and scraped my knee – this stone was rough like any other. And my lamp burned just as a lamp did below. Its oil leaked. Gradually my concerns abated, but still I did not know what to make of this place and my presence in it, only perhaps that the gods had chosen to test me, to see if my faith endured when they declined to show themselves even here. Or perhaps the teaching to be drawn was that whether a prayer was said in this most holy of places or at a common streetside shrine, gods demanded purity of heart as the price of manifestation to the worshiper and I was coming up short.

Every morning, the two assistants climbed the steps to deliver food and incense and jars of water for drink and bath. I was allowed no contact. Rather, a voice would call out from below announcing their imminent ascent and that I would kindly keep away until they had stepped back down. Nor was I allowed any news of events below. I could see with my own eyes that construction of the mountain-temple had stopped but I could only guess the cause.

In this way my life continued for many days and nights. Then, one night I awoke with a start to see a figure over me.

I gasped and put hands together to begin a prayer of greeting. Then I saw it wasn't a god. It was Sergeant Sen.

'Lady!' he whispered, kneeling quickly at my side. 'You're all right, then! There are so many stories....'

'I'm well.' I managed to say that, sitting up. I looked to him, my sleeping cover falling away. I felt the strongest urge to steal into his arms and cry. But I did neither. 'Yes, I'm well, but...why did you come?' I was suddenly worried for him.

'To do my job, Lady. To take you away from here.'

'Sergeant, you have always worried about me, never yourself.'

'Heaven will see to me, and I will see to you. Now, Lady – what will you take with you? You have some things here? We must be ready. The King has placed guards below and they walk a circuit every fifteen minutes. We'll need to be ready to descend as soon as the next one passes. I'll take you to a hermitage far from here, and you'll be safe. It's all arranged. People all over the Empire know of you and they will protect you.'

'I can't go.' It took all I had to say that.

'But you must!'

'If Heaven wills it that I leave, the guards will withdraw and there will be no need to steal out. If Heaven wills it that I stay, I will stay. I can't be a fugitive, Sergeant. I once ran away from trouble and I never felt any peace again.'

'Whatever it was, I am sure...'

'Sergeant, I cannot leave. I must stay and face up to this. But you go away quickly. Please! You'll be found here.'

The old soldier blew out a breath. 'You are sometimes not of this world, Lady. While you are waiting for a signal from Heaven, many people below are doing their best to get you out. Did you know? Your son, your daughter, your husband, the Brahmin Subhadra.' He explained briefly the actions of each one. This was the first I had heard and how it did lift my spirits.

'How that lifts my heart, sergeant. But you know...you forget your own efforts.'

'A small thing, Lady.' He smiled in the darkness. 'One of the men walking the circuit below was in my squad some years ago. I had help. And before I came here I said prayers at a shrine, the one that you endowed outside the mountain-temple Pre Rup. Yes, I came, but I also guessed you would refuse to come down. You will face up to the charges rather than run from them and your virtue will carry you through.'

'I hope there will be enough virtue for that.'

'Of course there will be. We all know it. But anyway, I knew you would not come. So I brought you something to keep with you up here.'

I noticed now that he had a small woven bag. He took out something wrapped in straw and gave it carefully to me. I removed the straw. He watched so approvingly my every motion.

Inside was a set of Chinese tea cups and pot. 'You are so thoughtful, Sergeant.' I held up a cup in the starlight. How smooth it was, how like the ones from the set in the old little house, when life was simple.

We sat together in the darkness and for a while had no need to say anything. But then words stole into me. 'How I wish that those stars overhead were...Chinese stars.'

Then I made him come to my little shrine and I said prayers for his safe return to his barracks.

We passed back to the steps. There I had a final message for him. 'Sergeant, it is so hard to send you away. In your presence I have always felt safe and contented. I have always felt that I belonged. I hope that, that in the next life...'

'I hope for the same, Lady. I have said prayers for it ten thousand times. Most recently when I prayed before coming to you here.'

He took my hands in his and squeezed them gently. Then he disappeared down the steps. How nimble that aging body could be.

I lit a stick of incense and bent my head for another prayer, tears cascading from cheek to forearm.

Sometime afterward, troubling sounds carried in from out toward the western gate – shouts, the clank of metal on metal. I lay down and closed my eyes and said a plea to Heaven that there was some benign explanation.

When I awoke, I looked again at the tea set. In the light of day, I was astonished at what I saw. It was my set, the very one

Nol had sold the day that the Brahmin came to our house! The carefree people were still at play on the side of the pot. One of the cups had the very same chipped lip.

How long had Sen spent searching for these things, how many people had helped?

For so many years I had waited for a god to appear in front of me. And all the time, gods had been making themselves known through people, people like Sen, and I had stubbornly refused to notice.

62: The vigil

I remained ignorant of what those sounds meant, but by the next morning, people all over Angkor were trading whispered stories of the tragedy, the heroism of my dear Sergeant Sen. Without even a knife in his waist, he had set out to reach me, in defiance of the scores of guardsmen who walked their rounds at the unfinished mountain-temple. He returned without me. His body, bearing too many wounds to count, was found half way down the western causeway. To this day it is my deep regret that I did not keep him with me atop the great edifice. Had I, had it, he might well be with us today.

Subhadra quietly convened an inquiry. Watch commanders and guards were brought to the palace and interviewed under holy oath. Some of the men recounted taking part in the discovery and removal of the body. But all claimed, quite sincerely, it seemed, to have had nothing to do with the chase, other than to have heard it. Still, the man who had been on duty at the west gate offered some disturbing testimony. Shortly before the sergeant's death, he said, he had seen several figures in the darkness beyond the bridge and he had moved toward them, thinking they were members of his squad arriving to relieve him. But when he reached the place, there was no one. He was left thinking he had imagined them, or had seen a group of wandering ghosts and so said nothing to his commander.

The inquiry was broadened to include people outside the construction complex. Most had nothing to offer, but a girl who'd been walking by herself along a nearby road that evening recounted seeing a closed oxcart. A man was keeping pace alongside it. He carried no weapon, but looked so frightening that the girl stepped behind a bush to avoid his eyes. And fresh footprints were found on a trail that no worker was using. It had been closed pending an exorcism, after a load of laterite blocks being dragged by an elephant overturned, taking off the leg of a mason.

The Brahmin began to form a theory. A conspiracy had been born among certain individuals but in the end failed in its main objective. Somehow, word had been obtained by these people that the sergeant had a plan to enter the temple. An armed party had entered the outer temple grounds, away from the guards, to lie in wait. It let him pass inside undisturbed, in hopes that on his return there would be not one but two people to kill in the darkness. For now, there was insufficient evidence to bring a formal accusation. So the Brahmin continued the inquiry, interviewing more of the soldiers. When the King demanded to be brought up to date, he was told only that the dead man was a thief who had entered the site to steal whatever was lying about. The Brahmin did not like to soil the sergeant's memory in that way, but that was the only story he could concoct on the spot when the question was put to him.

Nol was given a full and truthful account, both because I was his wife and because the priests hoped his sharp mind would make connections they had missed and help identify who was behind this murder. But he had little to offer. I can only conclude that his concentration was dulled by fear for me. I was still safe and untouched atop the temple, but the fact remained that even there I was the King's prisoner. There is a village saying that a hungry man must never be allowed to guard rice. How long would this hungry man really stay away?

And there were new pains in Nol's back. And at the palace, daily humiliations. He began to feel that guards, scribes, priests, even common sweepers of floors – everyone in the royal household, it seemed – were casting judgmental glances his way, as if comparing him with the departed sergeant. It was all near intolerable. Pride prevented acknowledgment that their opinions meant anything to him, yet what pleasure it would have given to shout at them: I can hardly walk, my back exists only to generate pain! How could I climb the mountain-temple in the dark and carry my wife away?

But in his defence, I will say that he fought for my freedom in the only way he could, with offers of money and property. It is true that he did not immediately put up everything he had, but who would have done that? Even in the holy epics, captives are ransomed by just a portion of the wealth or magic bounty of the victim's loved ones. Was not the price of freedom for

Garuda's holy mother a single cup of the nectar of immortality? Garuda was not commanded to surrender everything he had. The challenge in these situations, on earth or in Heaven, is to determine which items the captor is really determined to have.

Nol's first effort in this regard came two days after his return to the Capital from the parasol village. He managed to gain admission to the throne room. He knelt before the royal dais, holding a list of offered property between joined palms, like incense at an altar. His Majesty snatched it, scanned it for a few seconds, then tossed it back. Is that really all she's worth to you? Those were his words as he strode from the room and how they would have stung, even though Nol knew that rejections of first offers are often accompanied by insults for effect. He would of course offer more, but he knew too that this could not happen until the King's anger had subsided.

That was what was happening inside the palace, but outside other events had begun, though they seemed at the time to be of little consequence. As the death of Sergeant Sen had spread from ear to ear, a few people of Angkor had taken it upon themselves to go to the mountain-temple site. They put down mats as close as they could to the western entrance. They prayed to Heaven to accept the sergeant's soul and to give me freedom. Some of them hoped too for a more immediate effect, that from my place atop the edifice I would see their gathering and take some small comfort. But I'm afraid that the dimensions of the temple my son was building were too big. I was able to see nothing at all of this.

After Nol made his appearance in court, word spread beyond the palace walls that ransom was being offered. Soon a woman arrived at the western entrance with a blackened cooking pot. She set it on a mat and announced that it too was being offered to His Majesty. This inspired others and by the end of that first day there were quite a few other things pledged for my freedom: an ox harness, an old bronze necklace, a spare woman's garment, a hoe, laid out with other humble things on the mat for all to see.

Later the afternoon of that first day, a squad of soldiers from the palace arrived. An officer, a spearman standing to either side, demanded that everyone leave. But this same cooking pot woman stepped right up to him and declared that regardless of what he and his men did, she would remain. The better thing, she said, was that he and his soldiers go. There was no honour or next-life reward, she told him, in applying force against people assembled in Heaven's service. Other people pressed closer, the same kind of resolve showing on their faces. The officer lost his nerve. On his order, the men stepped away. Many of them were more than grateful to do so.

As night fell, more people arrived. It was a grievous risk, but I am told that among them were a few of those same soldiers, who were now wearing the garb of ordinary folk and carrying possessions from the barracks to add to the mat. The stack of pledged property grew higher. More mats were unrolled and people lay down. No one had planned it, but a vigil was getting underway. A vigil in support of this lone woman who did not deserve such help and still was ignorant of it all.

The following morning, Nol sat on the veranda of our house, his mind doing sums again, thinking out new lists and sublists of property. He called for his scribe. He had made up his mind – he could not wait any more. He would dictate a new petition for presentation to His Majesty. He would offer much more than he had in the last time – two more villages, five hundred laks of silver.

But then a male servant approached, bowed, and said that the master should go and see a remarkable thing taking place in front of the new mountain-temple. What is it? The master demanded. A wonderful sight, the servant replied. An army come to free the Lady.

Anxious, Nol went quickly in his palanquin. But as he drew near, he saw that it was no army, just a mass of ordinary people milling about. He gave orders that he be taken home, but just then a boy at the edge of the crowd spotted him and spread the word. People turned to look. Some of the braver approached, crouching. Soon more than a hundred people were pressing all around the conveyance, jostling the shoulders of the slaves who held it aloft. 'Come this way!' they whispered to the slaves. 'Take your master straight ahead!' The palanquin began moving, though Nol had given no order; the crowd parted for it.

472

Ahead was the stack of ransom – people wanted him to see it. He squinted; his eyes weren't good enough to discern what the things were.

An aged priest stepped forward.

'Parasol master! We welcome you. We offer our support and our property. We hope that the things collected here will grow further in number and, when presented at the palace, will help win freedom for the Lady Sray.'

Now Nol was close enough to see how cheap and battered these things were. Common things from common farms and households.

'You are right, parasol master,' said the priest, reading his feelings. 'Most of these things are of little value.' He put his hand to the blackened cooking pot, which had been set aside to honour its status as the first donation. 'This would fetch hardly anything at the market. But it is the most valuable possession of the woman who gave it. She has used it for many years to cook sweets that she sells in the market. It was her family's only income. Now she has no way to make a living. But she accepts this result.'

'But why has she done it, then?' Nol demanded. 'Does she know the Lady?'

'Let her tell you herself, sir.'

Word was passed through the crowd that the woman's presence was wanted. Nol waited, aware that all eyes were on him. The gazes were all hopeful, sympathetic, as if his arrival were a signal that the goal was close to being achieved.

The woman was perhaps fifty, gap-toothed and wearing a torn sampot. She knelt before Nol's palanquin.

'Sir, it is like this. Some years ago I was traveling on my own to my home village when I fell sick with mosquito fever. I lay down in some shade by the road to rest, but the fever tightened its grip. I fell into a sleep that was filled with demons. Then I awoke to find a Brahmin physician at my side. Under that tree he gave me prayers, he gave me draughts, he placed a cover over me and helped me turn and stretch until I found a less painful position. He stayed with me until my husband arrived to tend to me and take me home.

'It was only then that I thought to ask how all of this had happened. I learned from my husband that a Lady had been passing by in a covered oxcart. She had seen me lying under that tree and taken pity. She judged me too ill to be moved, so she left a servant to tend to me and went ahead to a hospital that lay down the road. She brought back the physician, then gently questioned me, though I have no memory of this, to find out my home village. Next she went there to alert my husband that I had fallen ill and needed help. And then she went on her way. She asked for nothing in return and I felt dismayed that she had done so much for me and received not even a thanks or a prayer. Later I asked my husband, "Who was this Lady?" He replied: "Why, she was the Lady Sray, benefactor of many places across the Empire. The Brahmin told me of her good works."'

I do remember that woman, her form lying crumpled by the roadside. But it was a simple thing to alert the physician. A hospital lay directly down the road in the direction that I was going anyway.

Her story was done. The priest turned to Nol with a look that said, whatever you did not understand, sir, you now do. 'There are many people like her in this group. Not all have been honoured with the Lady's personal ministrations, but all know of her benevolence. We are doing our best to assemble ransom, though what we do cannot match the sacrifices that you are making to bring the Lady Sray home.'

That brought murmurs of agreement from the crowd. As one, people began to sink to their knees to praise my husband.

'No! No!' cried Nol, waving his hands. 'Stay on your feet!'

But people ignored the plea and put heads to the soil. A silence fell over them. Nol remained suspended in the litter, at a loss. Then he let out a deep breath and told the slaves: 'Take me home.'

Those slaves shouldered a burden that day, but not as heavy, I think, as a different kind that my husband had carried for so many years. By the time he reached home, it had lifted entirely. He called for his scribe.

63: The King's decision

Early the following morning, court runners sought out Nol, Sovan and Bopa at their separate places and delivered an order to attend to the King in three hours' time. But not at the palace. They were to await His Majesty at the mountain-temple's entrance bridge. So they bathed and dressed and made themselves as presentable as they could, given that in previous days they'd hardly slept. Little communication had been allowed between them. Now, at the bridge, each was buoyed to see the other two alive and free, for at least another day. Tears flowed from the eyes of Bopa and Sovan, and I believe that even Nol let down his guard in this way. But overall their mood was of course quite grim. Not one of them had any idea what this summons meant.

Soon the King arrived in full procession, parasols fluttering overhead. Prepared for the worst, my family knelt and made obeisance as they had a thousand times before. The King gave no acknowledgment. His train simply continued across the bridge and through the western gate. The Brahmin Subhadra was with it, and he nodded in my family's direction, but it was unclear if he was conveying regret or reassurance about what was to come. All they could do was fall in behind. Sovan extended an arm to help his father keep up.

In the temple, the King led the way up to the second level, still giving no sign of the purpose at hand. At the Heaven-steep steps to the summit, Subhadra chanted an invocation. His Majesty moved toward the steps, alone, to climb to the summit. Nol and Sovan pressed forward to put up some kind of challenge – I doubt they knew what. But Subhadra whispered to them that it was all right. You will follow, right now, he said. Slaves with boards stepped forward to lift them.

What of me, then? From my place atop the temple, I had watched the procession advance down the western causeway. All I knew, from the sight of the royal parasols, was that His Majesty was coming. Whatever the purpose of this visit, it would also be the time for my confession.

Soon the priest's invocation carried up. I went to my mat, put head down with eyes closed, and tried to prepare myself.

Presently I sensed a pair of feet before me. I found courage to peer up.

'Majesty, at this time I must...'

But the King put out a palm to silence me. He had always been gentle in those few times we came together. I sensed the same quality in him now – his hand almost floated on the air as it bade me be silent. But there was some unfamiliar property in him too, an indefinable sadness in his eyes. What was its cause? Perhaps resignation over conclusions and actions that could not be avoided.

Before I could think further, there came a surprise – my family members, all of them, joining me one after the other on the mat. Each greeted me silently.

Then came the priest. Whatever was to come would now begin. My confession would again wait.

'Lady Sray,' said the King, 'we have come to inform you that you will be freed. You will pass down from here, then...then you will leave the Capital, for a place very far away, a place that you will choose. You will be free in all respects, except that you will never return to the city in this life.'

'Your Majesty is merciful.' I was trembling.

'It is not to do with mercy. We know now that you had no role in the rebellion. Prayer helped me reach that conclusion. But also the number of people who turned out in your favour. Villagers, priests, even children. And, of course, these three members of your family. We believe that only innocence and virtue in my... my Heavenly Sister could prompt such actions. And we are sorry to say it was necessary, this taking of grave personal risk by so many people.'

The Brahmin looked on proudly. These were not words he had composed. His Majesty was on his own, speaking his heart.

'Parasol master, you have served me more than thirty years. Last night you came to court with deeds to all your property. You also submitted a petition requesting release from royal service and permission to take your wife to some distant place. We grant your petition. Your service will end as of today and you will depart with your wife. Your property will serve a noble cause. It will help finance the war that we must pursue to restore tranquillity and order for the Empire's people. But the palace will provide a stipend so that you and she may live in comfort, but away from the Capital, for the rest of your days.'

I could not, but how I would have liked just then to lean into Nol, to feel his protective arm around me. How had I ever questioned that he valued his property more than he valued me?

Now it was Sovan's turn. 'Architect, you will now recreate the temple plans precisely as you saw them in your vision. You will recall all the labourers and work will resume as quickly as possible. Sculptors will proceed with the bas reliefs, including sections that will depict the current reign and its major personalities.'

'It will be done, Majesty.'

'Bopa, you will become chief concubine.'

'Majesty!' There was nothing more to say to that.

Now the Brahmin took a step forward. 'I will say a prayer to seal this accord in Heaven's eyes.'

But the King raised a hand to signal 'not yet.'

'We have one more thing to say. It is a small thing, and we trust that the Council of Brahmins will find it theologically acceptable.'

I noticed now that the chief sculptor had joined the group.

'The Lady Sray,' the King said, 'has performed admirable works for more than a generation, building shrines and hospitals, repairing hostels, caring for the sick and needy. It is fitting that her image will be found here, in this place that will endure for eternity. Her daughter, the new chief concubine, will be at her side. Sculptor, come forward. You will sketch these two, right now, precisely as they are. Then you will carve them on the temple's wall.'

The King fixed his gaze on me. I dared look back to him, and again I saw sadness and resignation in his eyes.

With a charcoal stylus and drawing board, the sculptor began to sketch.

And just then I broke down, fully, in tears and frightful shudders. What a mix of emotions suddenly battered at me, with all the strength of a monsoon lightning storm – love for my husband and children, the pain of a still-concealed secret, gratitude for my freedom, and, I will admit it, regret that I would never again be in the presence of His Majesty. The sculptor paused, to give me time to collect myself, and I did, but only partly, and his sketch surely reflected that. Presently my first feelings were overtaken by shame at allowing the display of such unseemly emotions in so holy a place. I stood with my left arm folded tightly over my breasts, my right pressed against my side. I was trying to hide myself, I think. My eyes settled on the stone at my feet. But my daughter's stance was a pleasure to the eye. She beamed, she faced the sculptor full-on, displaying body and spirit with the most striking kind of confidence. She whispered to me. 'It's all right now, mother.' She laid a hand on my shoulder, and held it there.

The sketch was done. The Brahmin chanted his closing prayer, then announced: 'His Majesty will now say prayers of his own.' That was it. We were free to go in peace, to climb down and leave this place for good.

Nol took me by the hand. I leaned into him, trembling again. Son and daughter pressed close from either side; we walked as a family toward the steps.

'*Majesty!*'

We froze. It was a female shriek, coming from below.

'*Majesty!*'

Nol's grip on my hand tightened.

'*She killed your brother!*'

It was Rom.

From behind us, I heard the Brahmin saying, as calmly as he could: 'Majesty, it is best to pay no attention. This woman creates discord in everything she does.'

From below, the same words: 'She killed your brother!' Then, after a catching of breath: 'I have a witness here who will tell you!'

How long we all stood, paralyzed, I don't know. But then His Majesty was almost flying past us. From the top of the steps, he peered down. How could it happen so quickly, but his serenity had completely vanished. His stance was now like something from a battlefield, his face contorted.

'Send her up! And the witness too.'

'Majesty, I don't think we ought to allow...' That was the Brahmin, who had now caught up.

Never mind – Rom was already springing up those steep steps, sashes of her sampot fluttering behind her. She reached the top, then turned to watch two men raise on a board the witness, a very aged man.

At the top, he collapsed to the stones.

'Don't die on me, old man!' Rom shouted, a finger slicing the air. 'Tell your King!'

He said nothing. The King stepped close. 'Tell me what? Who are you?'

'There is no reason Your Majesty would remember.'

'Say your name.'

'I am...I am Sao, the cart driver, old and withered. From the estate where Your Majesty was born.'

The King peered down on him, trying to remember. 'What do you have to say?'

'Nothing, Majesty. I wish only to stop offending you with my presence.'

'Tell your King! Tell him that the girl who came to the estate that day – that girl was this woman right here!'

'Old man, what does this mean?'

His eyes turned sorrowfully in my direction. 'I cannot deny it, Majesty. This Lady here, many years ago, when Your Majesty was a small boy, is the girl who came to marry the apprentice blacksmith.'

'You mean the girl who disappeared the day my brother was killed...'

'Please, Majesty! She was pure-hearted, not someone to be involved in murder. All of us could see that! I drove her in my cart to the estate. I can vouch for her.'

'I can too, Majesty.' It was Nol speaking now. He stood calmly, an arm enclosing me.

The King's eyes clouded for a moment. Then he bellowed to the guards: 'I will be alone with these two! Move everyone else below!'

Sovan sprang toward me, but guards' hands were quickly on him, pressing him hard to the stones.

Subhadra said: 'Majesty, I don't think...'

The King put the heel of his hand to the old priest's chest and shoved him back! The Brahmin staggered, gasping for breath.

'Keep quiet, will you? You've made trouble for me for too many years!'

The guards, frightened now as well, quickly removed all but Nol and me.

We knelt, waiting while His Majesty paced up and down, now seeming almost disoriented. How could this end? But I knew Nol would not abandon me. On that mat, our folded legs touched.

Finally the pacing stopped. He stood over us. 'So the Lady Sray is the girl who came to my family's estate?'

'It is true, Majesty. I was that girl.'

Nol broke in: 'Whatever was done, Majesty, was done by me alone.'

'*By you?*'

'Yes, Majesty. I was there, and it was I who killed your brother. My wife is not capable of violence. She is a person who is rare on this earth, a person who proceeds through life with a full purse of merit, without sin. I have known this from the moment I first saw her.'

A dagger was in the King's hand, its point at my husband's face.

'You ate my rice for thirty years, you accepted land, wealth and authority from me. You did all these things and yet you killed my brother?'

'I did not know it was your brother, Majesty. I did not know until just now.'

The King shuddered. 'Give me the truth! Are you ready to give me the truth?'

'What I have said is the truth, Majesty,' replied Nol, his voice steady. 'I was passing along a road and I heard sounds of trouble from behind some trees. I went to look and came upon a girl, my wife today. She was being assaulted by a man whose garment was off. I saved her in the only way I could.'

'My brother, committing rape? You're making that charge against someone from a family that Heaven has chartered to rule!'

'I make the charge, Majesty,' replied Nol. 'I make it on the witness of Heaven and my missing ear. It was your brother who cut it off.'

'Was it?'

'Yes, Majesty.'

'He did it like this?'

The blade flashed; my husband's remaining ear leapt to the floor. Oh, how I screamed on seeing that. The King seized Nol and threw him down hard. His head stuck the stone floor in an awful way.

I reached to him, horrified; he lay still. My touch lasted just an instant – the King seized me by the upper arm to break the contact.

'Despicable,' he declared, with a glance at the body. 'I can't stand to look at him anymore. You'll come with me.' He pulled me along a corridor, like a leopard dragging prey. I strained to look back to Nol, who remained still on the stone, eyes vacant.

We rounded a corner, and the King forced me to the floor by a window. He began to shout. 'All these years, posing as something sent from Heaven! Sita reborn, they said, so pure that even the King must stay away. And all the time a murderer! For so many years I've wanted to touch you. And now I find there's never been a reason not to. You've been living with a monstrous lie every day of the year.'

'I...confess to the falsehood, Majesty.'

He knelt at my side and ran a finger down my neck, examining, me shrinking from this violent touch, which continued over my shoulder and breast, down to the waist of my garment. His hand went to its knot. 'This is the body of a woman, not a god. She has a flawed character, but not a flawed body, even with the passage of years.'

Suddenly his hand left the knot. It seized my throat between thumb and forefinger.

'Please, Majesty...*I can't breathe.*'

That appeal had effect; he released me. I fell back gasping.

Now he was staring at my mouth. 'What's that?'

'I don't know what you mean, Majesty.'

'Your body has a flaw. A missing tooth in the back of your mouth. I saw just now.'

'I have never claimed flawless beauty, Majesty.'

'I know – you've let others do it for you. How did you lose the tooth? Is there a story of deception behind that too?'

I waited for my breathing to calm. 'It came out at the place of your brother's death, Majesty.'

'How?'

'Your brother, Majesty. He struck me and knocked it out.'

'He was resisting the attack that you and your husband organized!'

'No, Majesty. At the time, I was alone with your brother. He was trying to subdue me.'

The King raised the back of his hand to strike me, but I stopped it with words that I suddenly found. Perhaps my husband was dead already, and his newly freed soul had come to me in this corridor to continue the many years of protection.

'Majesty, it was not the way you say. Truly.' I began the story of coming by oxcart to be married and how at the estate everything had unfolded with such promise, save for the powerlessness of my new friends to protect me from the attentions of the master's elder son.

'You enticed him! Like you did me!'

'Never, Majesty. I tried only to stay away from him. As I have tried to stay away from you.'

Then the wedding, the sounds of movement in the brush outside the nuptial house, Koy's death on the road, the last encounter with the elder son in the forest clearing, the force with which he tore my garment away.

I was about to say that I was the cause of everything, that I had allowed a confrontation to take shape, that I should have declared myself undeserving of the wedding and never gone to the estate. But I did not say any of that. I found I no longer believed it.

'Majesty, my future second husband happened to pass by. There was a fight. A prince, trained in war and wielding a knife, went against a small man with a shovel. Heaven chose that the small man should win.'

The King stood abruptly up and turned his back. Silence followed. He began to pace, then stopped again, agitated, staring out the window by which I sat. My eyes closed as I mouthed a prayer. Then came a loud metallic clang that caused them to fly open. The King had thrown his dagger hard against a wall and was pressing his hands to his eyes.

'Majesty, for almost forty years, for reasons I cannot explain, Heaven has chosen to test character by instilling a desire that is wrong. First in your brother, then in you. And I acknowledge it, in me as well.

'Your brother chose not to resist. But you and I were different, Majesty. We held faithfully to Heaven's conjugal teachings. You allowed me to continue as wife to my husband and mother to my children. I did my best never to cross your path. Majesty, I can only say that this desire can only still be against Heaven's will. I belong only with my husband. So, let that spirit of resistance take hold again. Let us part. Let me go to my husband. He is a decent man, and he needs me. He is badly hurt, if he is not already dead.'

I waited. Then he bent toward me and whispered. 'Go, then, Lady Sray. I must not harm you, I must not touch you. We will remain apart, I promise. But go quickly, please.'

Those were the last words our King ever spoke. Just then I heard scurrying feet. Nol came sprinting wildly down the corridor, clutching a melon-sized stone fragment. I think I managed to shout 'don't,' but I can't be sure. The King made to stand up straight and face him and Heaven chose that instant of incomplete balance for a collision of two unequal bodies. Nol collapsed to the floor, dropping the stone; the King was propelled backward, stumbling. The sill of the window met his calves. He began to fall, backward again, hands grasping at thin air. He made no sound at all. His head and torso passed through the window, then his legs, and with that our King was gone altogether. After the briefest of intervals came the sound of a horrible impact below.

I crawled to Nol and held him.

After a bit, we dared peer down from the window. The King's body lay still in the second-level courtyard below. Guards and courtiers were rushing toward it.

I went for a cloth and water and cleaned my husband's wound. He fainted against me. I whispered a prayer and kept the cloth pressed to him, determined to stop the bleeding.

64: A pop barely discernible

Two days later, Subhadra drafted a rescript announcing to the Khmer people that His Majesty Suryavarman had been called to the lofty realm of Vishnu. The passage to the next life was quick and painless, coming in a fall from a scaffold during an inspection of the unfinished monument. From what more holy place could His Majesty have departed! Sixty days of mourning began. A grand funeral was staged. It was overseen by the new King, a white-haired cousin whom the Brahmins selected in the belief they would control him in the same way they had the orchid-loving man of an earlier reign.

And what of our family? The priests spent a long time mulling over that. To this day I give thanks that from these tragic circumstances we all emerged with lives intact and futures before us.

My son was the first to go free. He was of course the only person who could complete the great monument. But he was told that the rate of building would slow, the flow of workmen and stone from the Empire's estates would decline. The priests presented these facts to him in terms that seemed meant to fend off protest, but in fact the change was to his liking. I have told you how he worried over the project's strain on the lives of the Empire's ordinary folk. Sovan is still at work at the monument today. His vision of Heaven on earth is almost complete. It is called Angkor Wat and it is the largest place of worship in the world. I am convinced it always will be.

Bopa was released shortly after her brother, though of course she no longer had a place as a concubine. The new King would select his own. My girl became a pensioner, living in a small house beyond the royal quarter, free to come and go, having no duties. The faithful maid Yan remained in her service and I am sure has kept my daughter on the right path in life. No man will dare come near Bopa for now, but perhaps when a few more years have passed, Heaven will find a way for her to marry a good man and have children. Whatever happens, I am happy to say that she finally recognized the true character of the Elder Sister. She never saw her again, but no one else did either – the Elder Sister disappeared as completely as if she had never walked this earth.

My husband and I were of course the thorniest problem for the priests. We were held in custody in the palace compound for many weeks, in fact in the same room where I had been initially confined. Soldiers were at the door again, and it was all very frightening, but with Nol there with me, I did feel protected. We were questioned over and over as to what precisely had happened at the King's birth estate thirty years earlier, and on the temple's third level on the day of the King's death. We made no effort at subterfuge. Time and again, we gave our accounts, never wavering. In each of these sessions, I expressed sorrow for the death of the monarch. It was a genuine emotion, though I don't think that the priests recognized what kind of sorrow it was or how deep it went. This I had to keep from my husband as well. Somehow I did, and as time progressed the weight of grieving began to lift.

Nol and I were gradually given rights to leave the chamber and move around the compound. We began to think we might eventually go free altogether. Subhadra was our ally in this extended interim. In the end we were saved by an official determination from the Council of Brahmins: Heaven had deemed it time for a change of reign; Nol and I were mere tools in this turning of the cosmic wheel. The priests found support for this ruling in the texts, but also in the good things that were already happening in the new reign. As I have said, the construction levies on the estates were reduced. Soon after, the rebellion collapsed of its own weight. In some far-away market town, Darit was put in a cage by former collaborators and turned over to authorities. The holy elephant Kumari was returned to proper hands, with full respect being displayed to her. Many people believe that she was still the vessel of the soul of the orchid-loving King, but I am convinced that regardless of what Darit had claimed at the martial games, the King's spirit had long since departed her to continue its journey toward rebirth, wanting no part in the fomenting of violence.

Peace returned to our border regions as well. The Chams

and Siamese called off their attacks, seeing there was no longer disarray and weakness inside the Empire. Countless young men who had been taken into armies put aside spears and war garb to return to their home villages. They planted rice and saw to repairs that had gone unattended for too long due to the pressures of building the great temple. Families again lived together. In short, Heaven and earth came back into balance.

I have also been told that the Brahmins had taken notice of the vigil for my freedom at the temple's west gate, and of smaller gatherings in villages in many parts of the Empire. How grateful I am that so many people stood up for me, though I was never worthy of such support.

So one day, we were told we were freed, but on condition that we immediately leave the Capital. An ox cart and driver awaited us outside the palace gates, with a second cart loaded with clothing and other possessions packed up from our house. We were not allowed even to stop there, however. It is no longer yours, we were told. Your property, your holdings have all reverted to the crown. I suppose the Brahmins told themselves that in this they were only honouring the late King's order. Certainly I felt no objection – Nol and I were well rid of this burden.

The priests did, however, grant permission for me to pray one more time before Bronze Uncle. I placed a lotus blossom in his lap. He smiled down upon it as I gave thanks for his years of help to my family – I am sure he was with us atop the mountain-temple that day. In a way, this final visit was like the very first one. Nol stood behind me, watching, protecting against whatever danger might still face me.

And so it was that we left Angkor. One week later we arrived here in Chaiyapoom.

I remember that day well. I was first to get down from the cart. A small crowd of the estate's people had gathered. No doubt they wanted to welcome us, but no doubt some of them, children in particular, wanted to learn, what is it to look on a man who has no ears? I helped my husband down from the vehicle. Together, we made our way toward the river bank, slowly, because his limbs were all the more stiff and uncooperative from the long ride. But it was he who was directing the way – I had never been here. When he pointed out the house, I closed my eyes and voiced silent thanks. Small, peaceful, at water's edge. And with ducks quacking beneath it!

More men than were needed helped carry our baskets to the house. Too many women entered the house to help unpack those baskets. There were so many ducks below that I asked my new neighbours, might you be willing to take in a few? And so much charcoal that I declared that anyone who ran short should come and help themselves.

Later that day came something for which I was entirely unprepared. Kumari arrived at the estate, led by the aged Sadong. She is yours now, Lady Sray, he said. I am now only Sray, I responded. We released the elephant to live in the forest; the estate's farmers would place feed in a clearing for her.

My husband and I settled into a routine. Before dawn, I cooked rice to be given in offering to the priests who tended the stone temple by the little waterfall, and for our own needs. Later I fed scraps to the ducks and led them off to paddy land where they foraged. If the females among them were productive, I made gifts of eggs to neighbours. At midday, I went for prayers at the temple. Afternoons we passed at the house. Sometimes Nol would sit at the doorway, engaging passing people in conversation. If there was disappointment for me in this new life of ours, it was that he was not always content in it. Any neighbour who happened to have returned from the Capital recently, or even just some market town a short distance away, was questioned by Nol very closely about what had been seen and heard there, so closely that I could sense the neighbour making a mental note to pay better attention next time.

When day turned to dusk, we walked together on a trail that followed the river downstream, Nol using a walking stick, me supporting him by the arm. We rarely made it further than the waterfall. Farmers returning from the fields through the failing light would come across us there, sitting on one of the boulders at river's edge. I brought sugar cane; sometimes the holy elephant approached and ate from my hand.

It was as quiet and peaceful an existence as I could have hoped for, and it was only rarely that I thought of the two other men whom Heaven had placed in my life path.

When I opened a jewellery box and touched a pair of old golden bangles, I saw a King standing by a temple's window, freeing me to go, disarmed by virtue that was shown to have resided within him. In my mind's eye I studied him, for just a few instants before I made myself stop. And yet I never felt that he could see me. I believe that his spirit was staying somewhere far removed, keeping to the promise. I believe also that it prevailed on the brother ghost to finally leave me be, for I never again felt that presence.

When I poured tea from my Chinese set, I recalled an old soldier climbing nimbly down steep temple steps, having risked everything to come to me. His spirit I did sometimes now sense alongside me, but only at those times when Nol was elsewhere and therefore unavailable to protect me.

Years passed, and then this real man of my life was taken from me. One morning I awoke to find him lying still and spiritless on the mat beside me. I wept as I wrapped him in a white shroud. A pyre was built and lit. I wept again. His ashes were collected and placed in a small brick shrine built for the purpose. It bore no inscription, yet everyone knew who was the man whose ashes lay inside, born of this estate, yet achiever of astonishing things in the Empire at large.

Soon the elephant died too, in a forest clearing where she had lain down.

Twice a year now, my children and grandchildren come to visit me, and for a week the house is merry, but then they say their farewells, climb aboard their carts and begin the long journey back to the Capital. The neighbour women come to help me with daily tasks, washing my garments, sometimes cooking my rice. We banter about this or that. Ducks quack beneath the house; I hear the song of paddle on water as boats pass along the river. I close my eyes and wonder, why did not Heaven allow me to live my whole life in a place like this? I have no right to pose such a question, of course. But I will say that at night it is only when I imagine the life not lived that I feel contented and fall asleep.

I will follow Nol before long. My body will be wrapped in the same kind of white shroud that his was. I have asked that a clay lamp be placed by my head to burn its way through a supply of oil in the same way that a person uses up the years of a life. Let anyone who will come pour holy water on my right hand, which will be left uncovered to receive final blessings. But let there be no further mourning. I will have exhausted my allotted portion of life, according to Heaven's plan.

I have a vision of what will follow. When the lamp has burned itself out, when the sun has sunk to near the horizon, my remains will be brought to a pyre built of fallen teak gathered in the forest. A priest will kneel and with tongs will set a hot coal in kindling straw, then bring his lips near and gently blow. With a pop barely discernible, a tiny flame will be born, and in that flame will my soul be found. The wind will take over, creating a roaring fire through which my soul will rise, unbothered by the heat, and be delivered to the darkening sky. It – I – will gaze down for a moment and see that what was flesh on the pyre has become ashes, the final remnant of the vessel that for an ample span of years contained my essence.

And may it be true that my spirit will not roam for long, but will quickly enter a new body, as easily, as inevitably, as a woman trades one garment for another.

Afterword

Angkor is a very real place, located just outside the town of Siem Reap in northwestern Cambodia. For more than six centuries, it was capital of the Khmer Empire, one of the world's great lost civilisations. Visit today and you'll see the old glory at every turn. Angkor Wat is the best known and largest of the temples (in fact, it's the largest religious structure anywhere in the world) but it's just the start. A short walk away you'll find a city gate topped by the serenely smiling faces of stone deities. Pass through and you'll come to a palace compound with bathing pools, shrines and a grand reviewing terrace. Elsewhere there are moats, canals, bridges and paved avenues. Two sacred reservoirs measuring close to eight kilometres east to west have island temples at their precise centre points.

If Angkor disappoints, it's in how little of its human history it reveals. It was once a city of perhaps a million people, but today even its most important personalities are phantoms known only in the barest outline. The names and personal stories of countless men and women lower down in society have been lost entirely. Sometimes when I find myself in a solitary spot in Angkor, I take a moment and try to picture a few of the vanished. They can seem so close – they climbed this same temple stairway, walked this same stone parapet. What would it be to spend an hour with just one of them? I'll never know, so I settled for spending quite a

Angkor Wat

few hours with a computer and keyboard to conjure up Sray and her life that might have been.

The empire in which she was born was founded around 800 A.D. by a conqueror prince who unified a string of Hindu mini-states that had emerged in Southeast Asia early in the Common Era's first millennium. The art of building in stone and brick was already well advanced in this part of the world; the new political order and the proud ethnic identity that gelled within its borders took this form of expression to heights rarely seen in human existence. The labours continued unbroken generation after generation. Religious faith seems to have been the engine; most everything you can see at Angkor today is in some way a representation of the Hindu pantheon and cosmos.

The Twelfth Century was the civilisation's golden age. One of its pivotal figures was King Suryavarman, who ruled from roughly 1113 to 1150 AD. He appears to have been born in an outlying province, the grandnephew of a monarch whose reign had brought a weakening of central controls. Suryavarman believed he had royal rights and likely took power by force. Over the course of his reign, he revitalized the empire. He built Angkor Wat and other large temples. Trade flourished; he sent envoys to China. He fought multiple wars on multiple fronts.

Late in the century, the Khmers repelled a foreign invasion and then embarked on yet another epic round of building in stone. The glory seemed set to endure forever. Yet then came decline. In the Thirteenth Century, construction largely stopped. Rancour erupted between adherents of Hinduism and the rising religion Buddhism. The empire shrank in the face of attacks from neighbouring states. Sometime in the Fifteenth Century, the Khmers largely abandoned Angkor. The court moved eastward to the region of Cambodia's current capital, Phnom Penh. The reasons are still debated. Perhaps it was a strategic withdrawal to a more defensible site. Perhaps priests had determined that the city had lost heaven's favour. Or perhaps the society had exhausted itself and the region's environment (there is evidence of long-term drought). Whatever the reason, tropical trees and grasses moved in aggressively. Stones came tumbling down.

Angkor lay hidden from the outside world until 1863, when the diary of the French naturalist Henri Mouhot was posthumously published in Europe. He had spent three weeks among the ruins and dared write that Angkor Wat was grander than anything left behind by ancient Greece or Rome. The French took colonial control of Cambodia and a century of restoration work began. But the war that reached Cambodia in 1970 put a stop to it. For the next quarter century, Angkor shared in the suffering of the country's people at large. Bullets scarred its stones, roots split them, bats roosted unmolested. Most damaging of all were looters who took advantage of lawlessness to carry off thousands of pieces of sculpture.

Today, Cambodia is at peace again, impoverished and struggling to make a go at democratic government. Guards stand watch at the temples. With extensive international aid, restoration is again underway. Angkor has quickly become a heavily trafficked tourist destination. Today the biggest threat to the monuments may be the millions of pairs of shoes, mine included, that tramp over stones that were intended for just the barefoot tread of kings and their attendants.

Those are the essentials of Angkor's history, but what was daily life in the ancient times? The Khmers left hints in inscriptions that they carved into stone at many of their buildings. Most announce epic deeds and virtues of gods, kings and other worthies, but reading between the lines you can pick up an idea of popular existence. The most illuminating of these messages, found at the Eleventh Century temple Sdok Kok Thom, inspired an earlier book of mine, *Stories in Stone*. The purpose of the temple's three hundred forty lines of Sanskrit and ancient Cambodian is to document a Brahmin family's long service in the Khmer court. But in telling that story, the great chronicle touches on religious practice, land purchases, the transfer of slaves, the settlement of wilderness, even the labour schedules for the upkeep of the temple.

If the inscriptions let you hear the Khmers, bas reliefs let you see them. King Suryavarman has been holding court in the south gallery of Angkor Wat for the past eight and a half centuries. He sits cross-legged atop a carved dais, looking fully at ease with power and adulation. Fourteen parasols float overhead. The entire Khmer court, it seems, has come together for a group portrait in stone, their jewellery, headdresses and respectful posturings on display. Mostly it's men who are close to the king – generals, Brahmins, courtiers. But a few steps away a princess rides a canopied palanquin in his direction, the sash of her garment spilling over its side. A woman of lower rank glances backward as she walks in procession, holding a blossom aloft. And there are in fact close to eighteen hundred *apsara* scattered about the whole expanse of Angkor Wat.

Other reliefs at later temples show the rest of society – fortune tellers, sweetheart couples, cooks, thieves stealing fruit from a dozing market vendor. Further hints of common life come from a Chinese envoy named Zhou Daguan. He arrived in Angkor in August 1296 and wrote a detailed account of a year-long stay. It's almost as if he walked around with a reporter's notebook in hand. Curious and perceptive, he reports that the temple towers were gilded, that people got up during hot dry-season nights to cool off with baths, that fireworks brightened night-time festivals.

In imagining the old life, there's also help to be had in looking at today's. The fact is that a lot of things haven't changed much. Markets that you see in bas reliefs look not much different from ones you can find in any Cambodian town today. Ox carts that roll across the reliefs are barely distinguishable from ones you can now see traveling country roads. The lotus blossom remains ubiquitous. Spirits are held to inhabit everything and guide human destiny. Brahmins serve in the royal court in Phnom Penh. And every so often, the Cambodian public becomes enamoured with a particular elephant said to have spiritual powers.

Yet the old times also present countless imponderables. For instance, why was Suryavarman the first king to be depicted in a bas relief? Why does Angkor Wat defy the tradition that a king's state temple is dedicated to Shiva and faces east? Scholarly exegeses stress the theological. Suryavarman identified with Vishnu, lord of the west, it is said, and therefore the temple faces

The Tonle Sap in rainy season, viewed from Phnom Krom.

that direction. But why did he choose that god? The explanations that Sray offers are entirely speculative, but grow in part from my belief that practical concerns and human conniving have their influence even in a society firmly rooted in the supernatural.

As for the temple's apsara, anyone looking at them today can sense that they are individuals, modelled after real women of the times. For photos of quite a few of the close to 1,800 of them at Angkor Wat, see the website Devata.org. But how did they come to be present in such numbers? Which women got the privilege of lending their likenesses to eternity? And why is there one apsara on the temple's second tier who looks so different from the others – a bit older, lacking in jewellery and headdress, seeming not to want to pose at all? The answers offered in the story again combine the temporal and spiritual.

Sray's account of how Angkor Wat was designed and constructed likewise draws on supposition. No building plan survives. But generally we can conclude that basic architectural forms came from India, that draft designs were sketched on palm leaf (the loose-leaf paper of the times), that boats and elephants moved stones from far-away places where sandstone formations jut to the surface. Quarries from the times have been found, with half-cut blocks still waiting patiently to be finished and transported. Many thousands of people, likely a mixture of merit-seeking volunteers and slaves, flocked to Angkor to build the temple.

Other temples that show up in Sray's story are real as well. Pre Rup, built around 960, is still sprouting shrubs up its towers, its red bricks putting on a light show in the hour before dusk. The Trinity Temple, dating from about 900, is known today as Phnom Krom. A thirty-minute climb up a rocky hill will reward you with the charms of a smaller Hindu monument – you may even get the place to yourself – and a dazzling view onto land and water in all directions. (Other prominent temples of Angkor such as the Bayon and Preah Khan make no appearance in the story because they were built after Sray's time.)

The Freshwater Sea is known on modern maps by the Cambodian language name Tonle Sap, and the Great Dual Vector River is the Tonle Sap River. In another link with the glories of the past, modern Cambodian kings each year preside at a three-day Water Festival that marks the river's reversal of course. Geologists attribute the switch to topographical conditions found nowhere else in the world. For most of the year, the Tonle Sap River drains the lake, taking water in a southeast direction to the Mekong River. But in the late spring, the Mekong swells with the meltings of Himalayan ice and snow far to the north. Its waters rise and back up into the lesser river, causing its flow to reverse direction and feed the lake, which then expands and renews surrounding lands.

Other places in the story are imaginary. These include the temple and estate house at Chaiyapoom, though Khmer ruins can be found in the modern-day Thai province of that name. Bronze Uncle's shrine is an invention, though all evidence is that there were countless such places around the empire. And all residences in the story, whether palace or hut, are by necessity imaginary, because none have survived into present times. All were made of wood or bamboo and fell victim to the region's humid air. As far as I know, no kilns have been found near the spot where I placed the architect's house. But kilns have been found in many spots around Angkor and are being excavated as scholars try to expand understanding of life outside aristocratic circles.

Finally, the four members of the story's central family in the story are entirely fictional. There is no record of a pious woman named Sray endowing monasteries or deflecting royal attentions, nor of a one-eared man named Nol being recalled to service as a parasol master. No diffident young woman named Bopa is known to have become a favourite concubine. And no headstrong young man named Sovan can be shown to have created Angkor Wat. But as Henri Mouhot wrote in his diary: 'Was this incomparable edifice the work of a single genius, who conceived the idea, and watched over the execution of it? One is tempted to think so; for no part of it is deficient, faulty, or inconsistent.'

– John Burgess
Washington, D.C.
September 2012

Acknowledgments

This book took shape over the course of many years, with quite a few people lending a hand along the way. Ambassador Um Sim educated me on (among many other things) Cambodia's all-purpose length of fabric, the *krama*. Beatrice Camp and David Summers took me to a village in northern Thailand where people make parasols the old way with knives and bamboo. Sos Kem advised on Cambodian language and lore. Angkor guides Saron Soeun and Koy Vy showed me many of the places that appear in the story and shared their deep knowledge of the region's history, culture and nature. Other help came from people whose names I neglected to write down. A monk in Luang Prabang brought out for my inspection his temple's best ceremonial parasol. A curator at the National Museum in Bangkok shared knowledge of royal court regalia. All of these people helped me, but any flaws in the resulting depiction of Twelfth Century Khmer society and history are my responsibility alone.

As writing progressed, I imposed on a generous group of volunteer manuscript readers. They included Cheryl Buck, Heather Cass, Peter Eisner, Sos Kem, Patrick Keown, Tim Patterson, Vornida Seng, Ambassador Um Sim, and Sharon Zackula. I feel special gratitude to Barry Hillenbrand, who did a meticulous read and scrub of the final draft, and to Ivy Broder, who read not once, but twice, three years apart. Other help in the long slog toward completion came from Steve Kroll, Mollie Ruskin, Tomasina Galiza and Somboon Sornduang.

My thanks go to M.R. Narisa Chakrabongse of River Books for taking an interest in a piece of historical fiction with an unusual period and setting. Managing Director Paisarn Piemmattawat and the River Books staff saw to their usual job of elegant design and production.

My family played a big role too. It was my parents who first introduced me to Khmer antiquity. My late father David Burgess visited Angkor in the mid-1960s and brought back an entrancing set of temple rubbings that were hung in our home. A year or two later, my mother Alice Burgess took me to see the place for myself. My daughters Katharine and Sarah, who came along on a family trip to Angkor in 2002, read drafts and helped me fine tune. Finally, thanks go to my wife Karen, who from the start encouraged me to run with the story. She read, she helped on tone, characters and structure, publication and promotion. The book exists as much through her efforts as mine.

– John Burgess
Washington, D.C.
September 2012

Further Reading

Michael D. Coe, 2003. *Angkor and the Khmer Civilization,* New York, Thames & Hudson

Ian Mabbett and David Chandler, 1995. *The Khmers,* Oxford, UK and Cambridge, Mass. Blackwell Publishers

Claude Jacques and Philippe Lafond, 2007. *The Khmer Empire: Cities and Sanctuaries from the 5th to the 13th Century,* Bangkok, River Books

Charles Higham, 2001. *The Civilization of Angkor,* Los Angeles and Berkeley, University of California Press

All of the above books offer solid introductions to Khmer history and culture.

John Burgess, 2010. *Stories in Stone: The Sdok Kok Thom Inscription & the Enigma of Khmer History,* Bangkok, River Books. This book recounts French linguists' recovery of Angkor's lost history by cracking the code of stone inscriptions, notably one great text found at Sdok Kok Thom temple.

Zhou Daguan, translated by Peter Harris, 2007. *A Record of Cambodia: The Land and its People,* Chiang Mai, Silkworm Books. This is the full text of the writings of Zhou, the Chinese envoy who visited Angkor in 1296 and is quoted in almost every book about the Khmer Empire.

Henri Mouhot, 1966. *Henri Mouhot's Diary: Travels in Central Parts of Siam, Cambodia and Laos during the Years 1858-61,* Oxford, Oxford University Press. This classic of Khmer history literature, translated into English and reissued, recounts Mouhot's travels in his own words.

Vittorio Roveda, with photographs by Jaro Poncar, 2003. *Sacred Angkor: The Carved Reliefs of Angkor Wat*, Bangkok, River Books. Using scenes from the great bas reliefs at Angkor Wat, this book delves deep into Khmer mythology.